Memoir
from
Antproof
Case

15. V. 95

M — 1 l. l L

Mark Helprin

Memoir from Antproof Case

a novel

Harcourt Brace & Company

New York   San Diego   London

Requests for permission to make copies of any part of
the work should be mailed to: Permissions Department,
Harcourt Brace & Company, 6277 Sea Harbor Drive,
Orlando, Florida 32887-6777.

Library of Congress Cataloging-in-Publication Data
Helprin, Mark.
Memoir from antproof case: a novel/Mark Helprin.
p.   cm.
ISBN 0-15-100097-2
I. Title.
PS3558.E4775M46   1995
813'.54—dc20   94-43626

Designed by Lori J. McThomas
Printed in the United States of America
First edition
A B C D E

FOR JUAN VALDEZ

Contents

By indirections find directions out.

— H A M L E T, I I. i

Memoir
from
Antproof
Case

I Protest the Sexuality
of the Brazilians

CALL ME OSCAR Progresso. Or, for that matter, call me anything you want, as Oscar Progresso is not my name. Nor are Baby Supine, Euclid Cherry, Franklyn Nuts, or any of the other aliases that, now and then over the years, I have been forced to adopt. No one knows my real name anymore: it's been too long. And all the things that I myself once knew are like a ship glittering in the dark, moving away from me as I am left in homely silence. My time is drawing to a close, so I thought I would take one last shot.

And here you have it, the chronicle of my failure and my isolation, which are told through victory, and of my victories, which are told through failure and isolation: loneliness, really. My life has not been simple, but I am sure of my story.

Though you may not be half as peculiar as I am, if you separate out your vanities and illusions, the petty titles to which you hold fast and by which you are defined, the abstract and insensible money in your accounts, your bogus theories, and your inane triumphs, what have you other than a body that, even if you are now as healthy as a roebuck, will eventually war against you until you are left with nothing but memory and regret?

You may run quadruple marathons and do one-arm handstands, but only blink, look up, and see yourself hobbling about like a bent insect half-crushed under a heavy heel. That's me, who can hardly walk, struggling each day to the highest points of the Parque da Cidade, a thousand feet up in the quiet and the clouds, to green platforms overlooking the sea.

People in Niterói know me as an old man who walks up the mountain, and they are right. I come here to feel the breeze and imagine for a moment that I stand on the cold hills of my childhood, where arctic wind brought tears to eyes that could see for two hundred crystalline miles. This was the Hudson, north of New York; rugged country, and snow. Since the beginning, my mental equilibrium, such as it has been, has depended upon hard walks in which I can forget myself and look at the landscape. I also climb this hill so that I may look back at Rio, a stately hive across the bay, and remember my life there, too.

My lives of North and South, hot and cold, seem perfectly balanced and entirely inadequate. I often wonder why I struggled so hard if it has been merely to get to this place, but struggle, I suppose, is automatic, and it has its own rewards. Even now, after I struggle up the hill, I feel peace like a gentle hand stroking my brow.

Did you know that an ejaculated sperm travels over eight thousand body lengths a second, which is as if you or I were flushed through a water closet at 34,000 miles an hour? This original shock may be the origin of the admonition, "Do not go gently . . . ," for according to the principles of physics, a fluid passing through a conduit will do so at differing rates, the material at the center traveling faster than the material at the sides. The resulting shear forces tend to tear the cells apart. Meanwhile the rotund egg sits enthroned like a bowerbird, waiting with closed eyes for a speed-crazed sperm to knock at the door.

Struggle starts at the beginning and before, and at rest the life in a man is like the cocked spring of a lizard's tongue, waiting unsprung for a fly to come. Even as you are still, the tanks fill up, detonations accumulate, schemes pile on, and dance halls are opened within the brain. Even priests, who attempt to be tame, are propelled by the very same force into rarified precincts no less ecstatic than those they forswear.

Which is part of the reason I moved to Niterói, though only part, the other part that they are less likely to find me here and kill me. I have turned this over and over in my mind for many years, and I concluded long ago, or ventured upon the chance, anyway, that my life may end at any moment, perhaps on a flight of very steep steps in Santa Teresa, after I am shot in the shoulder with a pistol of exceedingly small calibre.

No one comes. The gun, a miniature, sounds like a firecracker or a backfiring motorbike.

"You won't hurt Marlise, will you?" I ask.

The assassins have been tracking me. They know. "She's the one who . . ."

"The young one, with the reddish hair."

"Not real red hair, like those Irish bitches," one of them comments.

"No. She's a Carioca. Her hair is more the color of clay."

"What's a Carioca?" he asks, being himself from Jersey City.

"Someone who lives here, who comes from here."

"I wouldn't shoot a woman."

"She's pregnant."

"Your kid?"

"Someone else's."

"That's too bad," he says, "I'm sorry."

I shrug my unwounded shoulder. Then they hear a police siren, and though it is very far away they run like hell.

Professional killers favor tiny pistols that shoot .12-calibre slugs, the kind used in hamster hunting. But who knows? They might be equipped with locking-barrel .44-magnum automatics. I saw one like this in the gun store in São Paulo when I bought my pistol, a Walther P-88. It's very heavy. Carrying it actually throws my back out, as my muscles make just enough damaging adjustment to keep me balanced as I walk. I had to bribe half a dozen people to get it, and, with ordinary crime rising explosively, I carry it. I'm too old to be wounded yet again, even with a hamster gun, and when they appear, if I haven't died already, I'll kill them.

Part of the reason I moved to Niterói is that if they don't find me, they won't shoot me, and if they don't shoot me, I won't have to shoot them. I've paid twenty people—the newspaper boy, my former barber, the landlord, even the police— to say that I died. The only problem is the naval academy, where I go three times a week. Though now I cross the bay and come from an unexpected direction, some risk remains. I've been there so long that anyone who wants to find me will.

I might have moved into the interior, or up or down the coast. By bribes and solitude I could have lost myself in one of the quiet cities of Uruguay, but then I would have been separated from many of the things that keep me alive. They are, in ascending order, the city itself, the naval academy, Marlise, bittersweet recollections, and Funio.

The naval academy sits on a peninsula that used to be an

island and was at one time the capital of *La France Antarctique.* That the French thought Rio de Janeiro *antarctique* is because the whole world here is upside-down. If you are not born under the equator you can never quite get your bearings.

The naval academy is filled with young cadets in the ill-fitting naval costume of northern civilizations. Torn from their upside-down roots, they have been made to study tactics, ballistics, naval history, electronics, and, of course, English, which is what I teach them.

Unless you are the daughter of a Brazilian admiral, and perhaps not even then, you may not have realized that Brazil has a navy. And, after being informed that it does, you may wonder why it does.

Picture a map. Consider Brazil's immensely long coastline, upon which its cities, some great even in the eyes of the uncaring and faraway world, are strung like light bulbs over the terrace of a seaside restaurant. Then look at Brazil's connection with the rest of the continent. It is cut off from the major cities of South America—Buenos Aires, Santiago, Caracas—by rivers, jungles, the Andes, and vast distances over lands that lead nowhere. Brazil is, in effect, an island, and an island needs a navy.

Why? To reduce a complicated answer to its blurry X ray, it is because the economy of an island can quickly be ruined by a naval blockade. Thus, you might expect the Brazilian navy to be devoted to antisubmarine warfare, and it is. Its single aircraft carrier (Brazil is one of only a few countries that have aircraft carriers), the *Minas Gerais,* is configured mainly for hunting submarines. Its seven submarines are, similarly, hunter-killer types assigned primarily to the tracking and destruction of other submarines. Don't tell anybody, but the navy is planning to build three nuclear submarines to give it greater range and endurance in the South Atlantic, and has started on a test reactor in São Paulo. This is a military secret I overheard in the cafeteria, and the truth of it is supported by other evidence, such as the fact that many of my former students are now physicists and power plant engineers who send me occasional postcards from decidedly non-oceanic locations.

I might have sold this secret to Argentina, but I feel grateful to Brazil and loyal to the navy, and, besides, I have in my life more assassins than anyone might need, and I don't fancy the Brazilian secret service hunting me down in Niterói, because Niterói is one of the few places in the world where they might find me.

The rest of the navy consists of fifteen antisubmarine frigates and various amphibious and patrol craft. The patrol craft are for use against submarine and other incursions, the amphibious arm, I think, for counter-attacking enemy bases established on Brazilian territory, and for putting down rebellion. There are lots of survey craft, for mapping the horrendously complex undersea environment, which, because of thermal strata and currents, must be represented not as a clear crystal but as a constantly mutating three-dimensional relief. And submarine tenders, tankers, barges, etc.

My students live in fear of being sent to the Mato Grosso to serve on the *Parnaíba*. Ninety unfortunates of the Brazilian navy labor unceasingly upon this "river monitor" built in 1937, a year that for the young cadets is so ancient that they recoil in fright at the very mention of it. Though I fail to tell them, I was that year the same age as Jesus when he was crucified.

But the *Parnaíba* pales in comparison to the *Capitan Cabral*, a Paraguayan patrol boat that was built in 1907 and now cruises the upper Paraná River. This, however, is not the queen of the Paraguayan navy, for that honor goes to the *Presidente Stroess-*

ner, a river transport laid down in 1900, even before I was born. Unlike me, it has lost all its teeth, and now goes unarmed.

The cadets wanted to make a float for Carnival, the *Presidente Stroessner,* a ship in a wheelchair, but were instantly overruled because of the diplomatic incident it undoubtedly would have provoked. And besides, who knows or cares about the Paraguayan navy? Paraguay isn't even on the ocean. They argued that it was this that made the scheme perfect for Carnival, which honors irony and absurdity.

I hate Carnival, but at least I know that it is a pageant of humility in which a huge mass of mortals parades before God in shame and sadness, declaring the corruption of the flesh. Being a northerner and uninterested in public humiliation and self-flagellation, I detest its rituals, but, unlike the idiots who fly down here in search of sex, I know that the celebrants are not seeking sexual pleasure but crying out in their weakness. This is too humble for me, I suppose, so I don't do it.

The cadets, who are like puppy dogs, think they love Carnival. They see the whole thing as nothing more than sex and dancing, because they have not had the time to meditate upon the meaning of sex and dancing, two items that, at my age, I find it difficult to approach by any other means.

What a shock it is to their ignorant systems to arise at five in the morning when half of Rio has yet to go to bed. What a shock to find themselves subject to military discipline; learning Teutonic languages; exercising, jumping, and boxing until they're as sore as snails. They start the morning with coffee, a cracker, and a bit of cheese. Then, as I make my way through the darkness, breasting waves of revelers returning from Rio to Niterói, they do their calisthenics. When I arrive, I turn on the air-conditioning and I crack the whip.

That each and every one of them stinks of coffee never fails to enrage me. They don't understand the evil of coffee, the horror, and what will become of them if they drink it. Their mouths drop open in astonishment and fear as my eyes narrow, my face tenses, and I run them through mental exercises that make their stomach-burning rope-climbs seem like relaxing on a couch.

Marlise says never to talk about coffee. She says that I must simply not mention it, that I can't change the world. Indeed, the former commandante took me aside years ago and told me that if I ever brought up the subject again or threatened instructors or cadets who drink coffee, I would be dismissed. *I* wouldn't have to drink coffee, he said, but I hadn't the right to prevent others from doing so. After all, this was Brazil, and who was I to prohibit the entire Brazilian návy from partaking of so innocent a pleasure as coffee drinking?

"It isn't a pleasure," I snapped. "It's a sin. It's the devil's nectar. It's filthy and unhealthy and it enslaves half the world."

I didn't go on, as I might have. I restrained myself because I knew it was hopeless, but my eyes narrowed with rage and I had the fey look of psychosis that I get when I smell brewing coffee, so he said, "Look. The guns of the Brazilian navy will be turned against you if you persist in overthrowing coffee urns and thrashing stewards. We're serious. Leave us alone."

Another reason I moved to Niterói is that here one finds less coffee than in Rio proper. It's ubiquitous even here, of course, but Niterói has less of everything. In addition, with more open spaces and far less urban density than in, say, Ipanema, I don't have to adhere to my formerly elaborate pathways, crossing and recrossing streets like a hyperthyroidic shuttlecock and shunning certain routes altogether, to avoid expresso bars with good streetward ventilation, roasting emporiums, and other dens of coffee sympathizers, apologists, hacks, flacks, and geeks. In Niterói it is possible to smell a sea breeze that carries neither suntan lotion nor the stench of caffeine. Are you thinking that caffeine is odorless? Ask a dog. Be warned, however, that the dogs here speak only Portuguese.

Portuguese is a magnificent language—intimate, sensual, and fun. The great poets make it sound like a musical incantation of slurred elisions and rhythmic dissolves, and day-to-day, corrupted, vital, and undisciplined, it is ideal for the dissolute life of a modern city, though what it gains in humor and intimacy it loses in precision and resolution. In fact, it is, when compared to English, almost like baby language.

Do not misinterpret me. I love baby language, for babies, but among adults it can be rather annoying, especially if you have been here thirty years with not a day of relief, having arrived fully formed and mature, and having come, as I did, from a place where language is not a perfumed cushion but a tightly strung bow that sends sharp arrows to the heart of everything.

The language of my boyhood was the language of ice and steel. It had the strong and lovely cadence of engines in a trance. The song of the world in snow, it was woefully inadequate for conveying material ecstasy, but more than enough for the expression of spiritual triumph.

In my classes we never get to that kind of distinction, for the cadets are neither sufficiently advanced nor interested enough to go beyond their requirements. They must be able to converse on board ship and to read the naval and scientific literature that pertains to their specialty. This covers a wide range, and I merely introduce them to the possibilities, hoping that by dint of their effort or as a gift of natural talent they will become fluent in and appreciative of English

But it does come as a shock to them. They shiver through

my class and find no comfort in their ancient wooden chairs. As the sun streams in through the window or a tropical rain falls outside, I bring them to an altitude of 1500 feet in the Hudson Highlands in the winds of March, which pops their ears, dries them out, and shuts them up.

I tell them, "You, you idiots! You are trapped in the last outpost of Antarctic France, and I, I am the polar bear!" Long before I brought it up, they began to call me the polar bear. I have white hair, a white mustache, a white suit, and blue eyes. In Rio something like me belongs in the air-conditioned part of the zoo. My friends are the penguins. Penguins don't drink coffee, no animals do, except for some domesticated types addicted by their degenerate owners either as a joke or as an effect of the addict's need to propagate addiction. I would rather kiss a dog on the lips than the most beautiful woman in the world if she is a coffee drinker, and I have. This sacrifice was to demonstrate the strength of my convictions, and thereby enlighten a group of addicts, but it didn't work. I kissed the dog, they kissed the woman, they all went away, and the dog ran after them.

I am not the only English instructor. No. The other one is an Egyptian Copt, in appearance the black Albert Einstein, who goes by the name of Nestor B. Watoon. Nestor B. Watoon learned English from a Pakistani in the Berlitz school in Addis Ababa.

I know this because Watoon has to tell me everything, because he is my slave. No way in the world exists for him to keep his job without my continual intervention. He is known among his students for going to the bathroom ten times an hour. They expect it whenever he stands up.

"I be right back, a big promise," he says, and hops away. Of course, he doesn't go to the bathroom, he runs to my office to find out how to say something in English. Then he darts back, after asking, for example, "How you say the plural of goose?"

He has become my slave in return for my constant availability, on account of which I must stagger my class and office hours to accommodate his schedule. Watoon survives by doing what I tell him. He stopped drinking coffee years ago. He runs errands. He supplied my lightweight bulletproof vest. If he dies, life will be very difficult for me. If I die first, he goes to the poor house.

Without Nestor B. Watoon, the cadets of the Brazilian naval academy would not think that popcorn is a fruit. They would not have the opportunity of following in the footsteps of a young lieutenant who, attending an official funeral, approached the official widow, made a sad bow, and said, *"Bon appétit."* They would not think that the opposite of cool was "worm," or that "turban" engines come in several "virgins."

The defining moment of Nestor's life came when he accompanied an American carrier group for several days' patrol in the South Atlantic—I stayed behind, fearing arrest on the high seas. It broke my heart not to be able to sail with my compatriots, and to its everlasting mortification the Brazilian navy had to send Nestor Watoon in my place.

The Americans seem to have enjoyed his company. I don't know what he did, though I can imagine. The cruise lasted only a short time, but the damage is to posterity, for Nestor took a notebook, and no matter what I say he will not correct or vary the usages he picked up. This book has become his bible, and its phrases will reverberate in joint exercises and in the careers of various naval attachés, tarring the Brazilian navy perhaps for centuries.

In the Watoon holy book it is written, for example, that the English for *Russian admirals* is "shit eating wussies." He was cordially received by all hands, as attested to by his entry,

"Expression of general approval—yaw mutha." And since it is not unknown in this country for military men to rise to high political position, I can imagine a future exchange, long after I am dead, in which the American secretary of state requests Brazil to lower a tariff, and his Brazilian counterpart politely replies, "Suck my ass." His students slavishly imitate him, believing it is true when he tells them that he speaks the King's English. What king?

I cannot pretend to be unmoved by the purity and innocence of the youthful naval cadets. They are the sons I never had, as is Funio. In observing them I often feel that I am watching a film in a darkened theater. There before me, as in a dream, the characters move silently, laughing, or their eyes sparkling with anger and animation. Sometimes in films you see the characters without hearing what they say, with music the only commentary. This I find most touching, for in my detachment I am sometimes closer to them than I would be in life. The audience watches from the darkness as if it has died and is revisiting all that it knew of life from a perspective even more benevolent than that of the disinterestedness of age. When your chances have run out and your prospects disappeared, and you are alone in the dark, looking back, you live life to the fullest and the clearest, and this is when, belatedly, you really know love.

My cadets are far from this now, but the years will quiet them. They will be lost in making love, like Paolo and Francesca, for what seems like eternity. They will ride waves, stage coups or fight them, and raise children. They will struggle for fortune like salmon struggling against a snow-swollen river. They will know failure and triumph intertwining, locked in a braid of life and death. But eventually they will sit in a quiet room and understand that the bright days and fiercely contested struggles have been solely for the purpose of bringing them to this poignant and tender silence.

What astonishes me more and more is that even after such moments, when the human soul is brought to its utmost purity, the play starts up again, the fight resumes, the illusions flood back. Even in an old man like me.

I cross the bay before sunrise to confront several classes of strong-hearted boys who know virtually nothing but have the energy of saber-toothed tigers. I am fully engaged but I am also watching as if from a darkened room. I am angry, and I am touched. I laugh, and I am deeply moved.

An image I see again and again lies at the heart of my artless confession if only because it is, somehow, the unadorned truth. I'm not quite sure what it means, but I cannot stop seeing it. A family is walking in the Jardim Botânico, in the depths of the trees, slowly making their way down a long sandy road that runs between ranks of impossibly high royal palms. They are alone, half in shade and half in weakening sunlight. It is not a dream, for I have seen it. Some distance behind his father and mother is a boy of three or four, walking with bare feet and wearing nothing but a pair of shorts. He pulls a plastic wagon on a white string, and all he knows is what is before him. Perhaps he is Funio and I am the father, although I think not, for the father is young, and my heart is broken because I will die when Funio is still a child.

When I came here I was already a grown man. I had long finished with being a soldier, and was just finished with being a thief. I had a mustache that was blond, not white, and I was as strong as an ape in the Bronx Zoo. The ape is an animal that you hope, as you watch it accomplishing its isometrics against the iron bars restraining it, will break through even if it means that it may turn its attention to you, because you have enough idealistic principle left, planted by nuns, priests, or rabbis, to wish for his freedom. He does deserve freedom. That we put him in a cage is beneficial to us but a rather obvious transgression of the golden rule.

I went free. I escaped. I contradicted laws, disappointed expectations, and defied balances. I was fifty years old. Marlise was twenty, but I hadn't met her yet. I met her when she was twenty-three. She didn't know a goddamned thing, and she was so beautiful she didn't have to. Our simple appreciation of one another created a spark that in its white brilliance and its breathlessness answered riddles, settled questions, made us happy. We surrendered, one to the other, but in private, according to the rhythm of a hundred million years rather than to satisfy a semipolitical requirement, as is so often the case today with men and women.

When I arrived here I felt as if I had burst into another dimension. For years I did not long for home, because I thought I had suddenly popped into heaven. Rather than lose myself in the illusory treasures of the flesh, I fell in love with a girl thirty years my junior, and treated her with extraordinary tenderness. In those days I spent a lot of time upon the outcroppings that lead to São Conrado, watching the waves strike the base of the gray glacier of rock, feeling the wind, and eyeing the beach beyond.

Whatever brought me here may be the same thing that enables a man to look death in the face. That I was allowed to live the rest of my life was not my good fortune but rather my customary burden, something I never feared would leave me, if only because I wanted it to. Let me, however, return to specifics: I hate to look too deeply into myself, because looking too deeply into yourself makes you into a myopus.

I met Marlise when she was working as a teller of the Banco

do Brazil in a branch at the bottom of the hill in Santa Teresa, where I lived, in 1957. I wanted to deposit some money and was directed to the window behind which Marlise had been imprisoned for a year. When I saw her, I dropped my deposit slip. I didn't know what to say, so I blurted out the truth. I told her that I loved her.

She thought I was crazy, and spoke to me in the effective and insulting language that banks supply to lovely female tellers for use in such circumstances.

"Marlise," I said, for her name was engraved on a block that pivoted in front of her window, "Marlise, I love you. I say so directly, because I have twenty-five or thirty years left, after fifty in which I have been a soldier, and a prisoner of war, and God knows what else, in which, like everyone, I have lost and I have loved, and I understand now that I have no time to waste, Marlise, and that, though you are young, neither do you."

It may have been the *in which* construction, it may have been a church bell that was ringing and calling to the depth of everyone's heart, even as they were standing, as I was, in a bank line. It may have been the hour, or the day, or her fervent desire, or the simple fact that I was telling the truth, but she believed me, she accepted what I said, the bell rang, she kissed me through the bars, the manager popped up like a pheasant, and we were married, quite impractically, that afternoon.

Can you imagine a bank teller, a beautiful girl of twenty-three, kissing a customer through the bars? This is what the countries of the north have grown great in imagining and lacking—but I had it. We kissed, and we had a moment of truth, as in the chiming of a bell, or maybe a bull fight, that has kept us together through all the subsequent and difficult years.

I don't approve of liaisons, much less marriages, between people of vastly different ages, but I couldn't resist her, and I pledged myself to her as few young men could, not knowing themselves well, or having been deeply wounded. If she had married a younger man other than a Jesuit or some other kind of priest, who knows what might have become of her?

I was fifty-three and as lean and solid as a weight lifter. I had fifteen sound years left during which I ate mainly endive, tuna, shrimp, and fruit. I didn't smoke, drink, or use drugs, and in spitting in the devil's eye I get strength.

Until she was thirty she didn't even know the difference. In frequency perhaps, but not in hallucinatory intensity. I made up in gratitude what I lacked in vigor, and I could tell her stories. When we finished, I would embrace her as if my life depended upon it, which it did.

When Marlise entered middle age and I became old we looked at one another askance. This red-haired bank teller with huge tremendous bosoms and teeth, who still fit trimly in a bikini, was like a steadily burning coal, while I was like the ash at the end of a cigar. She began to have affairs. I forgave her, I forgive her, for she brought me Funio, and Funio, though of another man, is like a son to me.

About eight years ago, we went looking for Marlise's father, who was a priest and who, rather than leave the priesthood, gave her up. I have always said that he made one wrong decision after another. The first was to take his vows, the second to break them, and the third, not to shatter them completely.

For Christ's sake, what are angels? Here was a man whose heart rose, it is safe to assume, in contemplation of saints and angels, and when an angel was actually delivered to him—even if by his indiscretion—he should have taken that angel in. I took Funio that way, though he was not mine. After one tear, literally, one single tear that I shed because of Marlise's betrayal and my old age, I allowed his raw cry to fill me full of life. But I'm pulling ahead of myself.

We went to the North, which is like a country in Africa—vast, dry, hot, and poor. The air smells of mangoes, carrion, and the sea. We had heard that Marlise's father was resident in a parish somewhere near Natal, and for two days we traveled by bus, boat, and on foot to a forgotten strip of coast where the Atlantic drives upon the shore in great white bales of brine that have been propelled across the vacant ocean from the Bight of Benin. The beach was thirty miles long and backed along its entire length by a mile of pristinely white marching dunes as soft and dry as talcum.

We drank bottled water and ate fruit that we washed in the waves. Church and parish house were twenty miles up the beach and just behind the dunes, where a river made a wide bend before it breached the walls of sand to pour into the sea.

"How do we get there?" we asked at a little town north and west of Natal.

And they said, "You walk."

"On the road?"

"There is no road."

"No road?"

"No."

People from country places sometimes honor me with a reply, perhaps because I look like one of them who has survived into old age. And, if you call the fields in the midst of which I was born country, which they were then but are no longer, I suppose I am. I closed one eye and skeptically cleared my throat.

"No road at all," was the response.

"How do they get their produce to market? How do they get mail and supplies?" I asked.

"By boat."

"Then we'll go on the boat."

"If you want to wait six weeks."

"What about a fishing boat?"

"You can walk twice as fast, and walking costs nothing."

"A jeep?"

"No way to get across the river."

"A raft."

"Two and a half days to build it."

"How *do* we get across the river?" I asked.

"You swim."

"Why not go in a canoe?" By this time the whole village had gathered around us, more toothless mouths than I had seen in years, and the people were enjoying our ignorance immensely.

"If you want, grandfather, you can cross in a canoe, but you will have to swim in the ocean a hundred times to keep cool, so why waste effort by not swimming?"

We sensed that this might be an elaborate joke, that just beyond the dunes was a superhighway with air-conditioned bus service, or a Swiss-made monorail with complimentary chocolates on the seats. But we did like the idea of walking twenty miles on a deserted beach and we entered the river with the whole village watching, our fruit and bottled water in plastic net bags floating beside us.

When we emerged, our clothes were fresh and clinging, our hearts beating. After a few minutes of walking by the edge of thundering surf as high as a house we were alone in a place where we would not see a single soul or the work of man for the rest of the day.

Nothing stopped us and no one could hear, so we sang. I have a strong voice even now, but it is Marlise who sings precisely, sweetly, and well. And we did swim a hundred times.

Ever since I was a boy I have loved the idea of swimming in my clothes, so that I could cross a river or a lake and keep moving after I had emerged from the water. I like the way a wet shirt feels on a hot and windy day, and khakis crisp with sun and salt, as stiff as a starched army uniform.

When my plane went down in the Mediterranean in 1943 I swam at least ten miles to shore, and here, with no mirrors in which to see myself, and a heart buoyed by bright sun and the surf, I felt almost as free, almost as triumphant.

The difference was that now I was old, and the death I had escaped had become, once again, not always so unpleasant to contemplate, except that I had Marlise, who at forty-two was at the peak of her glory. I will never forget her as she walked in the wind, barefoot, disheveled, and perfect. I will never forget the streaks of salt that curved down her back and whitened upon her shoulders. Nor her dancelike movements as she strode through those magnificent hours. When the wind changed, and blew her hair in front of her face, she tied it in a thick rope that was as red as her lips, and I thought to myself that I had done the right thing, that had I stayed in the office and risen high in the esteem of others I would not have had a hundredth of what I had here—the clean sea air forced into my lungs as if I were drowning in it, and midday as bright and hot as a lamp.

After we came to the river, beyond which the beach continued to stretch as if to infinity, we turned inland and walked a mile or two through irrigated fields that were so still we could hear the ocean singing in our ears long after we had left the sound behind.

We found the priest in the wooden rectory of a wooden church. He was drinking coffee and reading the Bible. I grasped my stomach, pivoted, and sought the outside.

He rose immediately, assuming that I had come to him, as

undoubtedly some did, to seek last rites, but Marlise took him aside and whispered, gesturing with her hands. Then she gave him one of the strong mints that she carries for the purpose of . . . well, I think you know by now. I have heard only the beginning of her practiced monologue, because I always absent myself after the words, "Forgive me, but my husband is a crazy person."

It's mortifying, especially in light of the fact that I am right and they are wrong. And I'm hardly the one who's crazy. Catherine the Great, who looked no more like Ingrid Bergman than I do, but was in fact a dead ringer for Edward Everett Horton, used to make her own coffee when she arose—as I arise—very early in the morning. Her customary recipe called for one pound of ground coffee to four cups of water. She was known to be a jitterbug, and now you know why.

I knew immediately that the priest was not Marlise's father. He was a midget and she is statuesque. He was many shades darker than she, though she had been in the sun and he had not. He had deeply socketed pop-eyes and caterpillar eyebrows, whereas her eyes are wide and almost oriental, and her brows ride above them as high and delicately arched as single willow branches.

Either his lack of physical resemblance to her or her diplomacy in getting him to pour his coffee down the drain had temporarily driven from her the question we had come to ask. But when I returned and the three of us stood in the cool shade of the rectory front room, it returned, probably because of her strong sense of mission but possibly because we had come such a long way.

"Father," she cried, sinking to her knees, in tears.

"Yes my child," he answered, in requisite but puzzled compassion.

"Are you my father?" she asked.

"Yes, of course."

"Literally?"

"Why do you ask?"

"We heard a rumor."

"Where?" he asked indignantly.

"In Rio."

"Rio! I've never been to Rio. From whom did you hear this rumor?"

"From my mother."

"I don't know your mother, I never broke my vows, not even once, and if I had it is unlikely that the child of such a union would have been like you, unless the mother was . . ."

"How about a giraffe?" I asked, cruelly, but the smell of coffee does make me cruel. Marlise hit me in the stomach, with many times the impact of an assassin's .12-calibre bullet (but sans penetration), and I went down. She's sensitive about her height.

Then came the first inkling I had of Funio, because, out of nowhere, Marlise announced, "I'm a *pregnant* giraffe."

Constance had been too busy to have a child, and Marlise had had such a miserable upbringing herself that she could not bear the thought of bringing a baby into the world, until, evidently, just before the wire—for she was of an age when these things cease to be matters of concern except in retrospection. I had reconciled myself to dying without an heir.

Now, in my doubled-up position on the cool stone floor, I was overcome with the other prospect. I think I knew for half a second the ineffable presence a father feels when his child is born. I have heard that you cannot sense the Divinity any more clearly than at that moment.

The priest was justifiably confused, but did what came

naturally. He congratulated me and began to offer a prayer, until Marlise screamed, "No, no, no! It's not his."

For a second time within seconds I had the breath kicked out of me. The little priest dealt with illegitimate children every day, but I never had, not in the painful way that you must when you learn that your young and beautiful wife is carrying the child of another man.

Marlise was inconsolable, too. The priest knelt down and tried to comfort us. "You must come from somewhere very far away from here," he said in amazement. "We don't see strangers often. I tell you, would you like some fried bananas?"

That is how I was introduced to the idea of Funio, although not to Funio himself, not knowing whether the baby would be a boy, a girl, or a giraffe. After a while I was too stunned to do or feel anything, and I sat in the darkness, eating fried bananas, which I detest, wondering why I wasn't angry.

Had I been younger I might have razed the village, for ever since the age of ten I had been on intimate terms with rage. Once, I smashed a donkey cart in Brooklyn Heights, leaving the donkey and the rest of the world unharmed, after I peered into the kitchen of a brownstone on Joralemon Street. There I saw two young schoolchildren—a boy and a girl of about six and eight—sitting at a breakfast table, in school uniforms, two-strap briefcases beside them, the girl in blond pigtails. I could hardly believe my eyes. They were reading the newspapers and drinking from two huge cups of coffee. Nothing in the world angers me more than the abuse of children, and to see innocence so casually and systematically destroyed was more than I could bear. I would have attacked the parents but for the fact that the children would not have understood, and the windows were protected by heavy iron bars that, though I was sore for a week thereafter, I could not bend.

Never will I forget the expression of those poor children, their huge, toilet-bowl-shaped, globular vessels of coffee held an inch above the saucers, their jaws hanging down. They looked a bit like the priest who fed me fried bananas. And the donkey cart was the first cartlike object I had ever destroyed, though I have made restitution for my delay at least a hundred times over in smashing expresso wagons and coffee urns.

Now that I am eighty and Marlise is fifty I understand her affairs. Had I been fifty, with an eighty-year-old wife, I too might have been tempted to go outside the marriage. At the time she became pregnant with Funio, I was still able, though I suppose that she, in her greatest glory, wanted not a smoldering stick but a blazing torch.

When I had an inkling of what she was doing, I tried to retaliate. I met a nightclub dancer, a woman even younger than Marlise, whose job was to arouse men (somehow) by gyrating in a costume of silver bands, a plumed headdress, and purple-tinted mirrors. She did not look particularly human, and even her breasts were heavily covered with powder and rouge. I began to see her, and then I began to see my doctor. Nothing is as chilling as sex in reprisal, except perhaps that this sad and abandoned woman had offered herself to me because she pitied my age.

You cannot abrogate the passage of time, so I returned to the quiet benches in the parks where old people are supposed to sit, and I returned to walking up the mountain, and there, in the dim asexual beauty of reddening dawns and skies that firmed to blue, I discovered my real and appropriate strengths.

Funio is going to rise above his difficult origins. I have been a father to him, and my greatest sorrow is that I will die when he is young. But though he will cry I don't think it will break his stride, or, at least, I hope it does not. I can think of nothing

I would rather do than live another forty or fifty years and watch him move through the world. He wallops you with his brilliance. I don't like the idea of child prodigies, and we are trying to ignore that part of him, for a brilliant child can be ruined if he is made to do tricks like a circus animal.

When Funio was four years old he thought that license plates were price tags, and he was amazed that they seemed to vary nonsensically. I was taken aback one day when we were driving to São Conrado and he asked why the Volkswagen ahead of us was more than three times as expensive as a Rolls Royce. "It isn't," I said.

"But look at the price tags!" he chirped.

When it hit me that he could do long division both instantly and accurately, I began to ask him questions. Just before we walked onto the beach I asked him one that I'll never forget. "Funio," I said, "let us say that the number of letters in your name is X, the number of letters in Mama's first name is Y, and that X plus Y minus Z equals ten."

"*Z equals two*," he said, as if to say, "What else, stupid?"

When he was five he wanted to run the checkbook, so we taught him double-entry accounting, which he mastered without a hitch. Last year he began to correct some of the papers and exams from the naval academy—as he is perfectly bilingual.

What is to become of such a child? We have made him promise not to accelerate his progress in school, to hold himself in check at least until he goes to university, so he can be a child. He is socially and emotionally a child, and one grows not only according to the pace of one's intellect but in the cultivation of one's heart and soul. Not that they have been too far outdistanced by his mind—they haven't, but the lessons of the spirit take longer, and because they are often received like blows, they tempt the weak and cowardly into imagining that they can be manipulated like an algebraic quantity, or rushed, or controlled, when they can only be endured.

He does merely perfectly at school, and when they try to accelerate him he clams up. In class he daydreams and does problems in his head. At home he reads history, novels, the encyclopedia, and of late he has become interested in economics, to which he was led by his interest in statistics.

And he is a little thing, as dark as a Sicilian, with enormous eyes and his mother's Chiclet-sized glacially white teeth, but his are configured differently, the two upper front teeth being inappropriately massive, except perhaps for a chipmunk.

His school uniform seems like part of him. Except when he was a baby, he has never appeared in anything but blue shorts and a white shirt. He swims in the shorts, I suppose, because he sees that I swim in my khaki shorts, and he knows the story of how I went down in the sea.

Perhaps it is justice, or a miracle, that he can absorb anything I tell him, for I love him above all, and I cannot last long. When he was a baby, I took him on my walks, I carried him up the mountain, and at the top we went to the place where I always go, where I held him on my lap and we watched the sea below, the tiny whitecaps moving just above the power of light to resolve them, at least to my worn eyes. I have told him much that I assumed he could not understand, but I think that, somehow, he did.

One thing, however, that he cannot know, because he cannot feel it, is the fleetingness of the moment. When we go to the beach, I have an open heart for the ocean, as I always have, but now, even as we are thrown by the waves and tossed forward in the sun, I rise from the scene and look upon it with affection, as if I am gone or hearing the story of others. And I remember how my own father held me, in the ocean, in an age that now belongs mainly to history, and will, with the passing of my generation, revert to it entirely. I would be lost and entranced with that recollection did not the ocean insist on slapping me in the face with its endlessly rocking foam and if the wind did not roar above the water. Funio is tossed on the waves even more easily than I, and after he goes under, he pops up like a cork.

I would not have lasted a minute in this place were it not for the Atlantic. It is the same ocean in which I learned to ride the waves at Amagansett, in 1910, when I was six years old. Well before I fled the United States, that area had become a fashionable extension of Southampton, but when I was a boy it was still a whaling village, and the most fashionable thing for many miles around was an encampment of United States Marines who had yet to hear the words *Belleau Wood*.

The waves are a difficult place in which to feel pride or distraction, for they speak intimately and are buoyant with the promise of eternity. I still swim four times a week. Each day after my Alaskan immersion in the naval academy's powerful air-conditioning, I go briefly to Flamengo, and on Saturdays Marlise, Funio, and I go to a more splendid beach—to São Conrado, or to a cove on the coast, where the waves are clear and the distant water is green.

Rio would be intolerable without the surf, and not just for me. The *favelas* would explode were it not for the beach, where rich and poor alike can bathe in the same ocean and receive the same blessing.

Foreigners—I'm a foreigner, but I've been here a long time —often fail to understand that the beach is Rio's cathedral and the sea its most holy sacrament. The tourists come for titillation, not realizing that the great sexual power that pervades this city is downshifted at the beach in the same way that cowboys used to check their guns at the doors of a saloon.

Until Marlise stopped me, I would correct this misconception by persuading many of the northern European women who had removed the tops of their bathing suits to replace them. To stem this barbaric practice I would approach a group of recreants (among whom were usually half a dozen young men who could have broken me like a match-stick) tap my cane on the sand, and point it at the parts that required modesty.

Sometimes they laughed, but then they would observe my wiry frame, my scars, and my narrowed, determined eyes. I think the butt of my automatic and the way my still strong hand curled around the bamboo stick may have influenced them too. And when I barked enraged commands in my raw and mysterious German, their amusement would turn to the sudden whiteness of fear. Then I would clinch it in English, because they all speak English. Taking a leaf from Watoon, I would say, "Beware, shit-eating wussies! Visigoth scum! You are as dung and vomit to your fathers, who were brave and fearsome soldiers but who were beaten to paste by the English-speaking world, by me. The power of the West is clear, and the New World will crush the recreants of the Old. Unless you want me to unleash upon your soft and decadent flesh the accumulated ferocity of the North American continent, *cover up*."

It worked again and again, until Marlise snuck up behind me as I was confronting what turned out to have been a group of speechless Canadians. How was I to know? Perhaps they were of Teutonic stock. She marched me to a deserted section of beach, and as Funio built a castle, we had what she refers to as the definitive argument, or the earthquake, and what I refer to as nothing more than a change in the balance of power between a poor and dignified old man with only a few sad years left to him, and a huge—though still beautiful—middle-aged harpy who just happens to be, now that the old man has lost some height, a foot taller than he. The conversation was in English, because whenever something serious comes up I can no longer speak Portuguese. It went something—no, exactly—like this.

"Look, bitch," she said, narrowing her eyes and pointing her index finger like Uncle Sam, which is what I do.

"No, no," I told her. "*Bitch* is a vulgar expression for a woman. Don't use it. It's as stupid as it is ugly."

"What I say for man?"

"Woodpecker."

"Look, woodpecker," she said, "it all finish. This your invoice."

Then she lapsed into Portuguese, which I truly did not understand, and she had to return to English. After all, I taught her English.

"What you think I am, antelope?" she asked indignantly.

"No," I said. She was, at that moment, just a few shades of red beyond the color of antelope, but her flesh was almost as sleek and her expression very close, which is why I, on occasion, had told her that she looked like an antelope.

"Why you scare peoples on beach? How crazy you are? You shoot them because they naked?"

"Of course I wouldn't shoot them because they're naked. What's your point?"

"From now on everything change or I go, take Funio. You never see us again. Next time you walk in door, house quiet. You like farmer who chicken hit by lightnings."

"I think I understand."

"Number one, you leave peoples alone on beach. Number two, you never talk about coffee."

"I don't."

"No. You slipping."

"All right."

"You never tell Funio you stupid ideas."

"Why? He's got to know, because someday he'll wonder where he came from. He may want to be immensely wealthy."

"He happy, okay?"

"But, Marlise, happiness. . . ."

"He already like you. He like to see girls on a bikini."

"No he doesn't. Look at him." He was surrounded by in-credible pulchritude, and entirely intent on his sand castle. "Marlise, his passion is trains. He's memorized the railroad timetables for half a dozen European cities, hardly trying. What goes in, stays in. For him it's effortless. Can you imagine what he might do with. . . ." And here I stopped for a minute, counting on my fingers, mumbling, looking up at the sky like a blind beggar.

Marlise never understood this, because she didn't know. She didn't know because I never told her. I never told her, because I knew she did not understand immense wealth. Whenever I counted on my fingers and looked skyward like a Sufi she thought I was having an attack of shell shock. She moved for-ward, embraced me, and cried.

"Marlise, Marlise," I told her, "I've put all my hopes in Funio. I myself will die with a wink."

Still, she had made up her mind, and she never retreats.

"You tell him nothing. You promise."

"Marlise!"

"No, no. You promise. No counting. No mumbly. No nothing."

Even a rhinoceros retreats, but not Marlise. I promised her. I think the way she is may be related to the general character of the Brazilians. They seem always to be enough out of sync to hit the bumps rather hard. The first Brazilian woman I ever encountered was married to a senior vice president at Stillman and Chase. They were a magnificent family, with three or four children, far too genuine to be associated with Stillman and Chase, the largest and most pompous private bank in the world, and her husband, Jack, like me, had been to Harvard, had been a pilot, and had been wounded.

Until he married Maria-Bethunia he had had a shot at becoming executive vice president. His downfall came quickly, when the wives of the leading Stillman and Chase officers held an exhibition of formal portraits they had commissioned of their husbands. Their intention was to replicate the era of John Singer Sargent, and they made a very beautiful show.

Thinking to upstage everyone, as indeed she did, Maria-Bethunia flew to Vallauris to persuade Pablo Picasso to do a life-size portrait of Jack. She was a crazy Brazilian, Picasso liked her, he agreed, and he painted from a photograph. The curator of the show was electrified, and, naturally, gave the Picasso the place of honor. I suppose he was astounded that Picasso had reverted to a realistic style, but for Maria-Bethunia anything was possible. The problem was that it was a life-sized nude, and that Picasso, who was always a little funny, painted everything to the proper proportions except the genitals, which were enlarged to five or six times their normal size and totally erect.

When the exhibition opened, Jack was in Boston. He flew home after the gallery had closed, and went directly to a reception for the finance minister of the Belgian Congo. Everyone was there, with all the women stealing long glances at Jack. "Jack, was that really you?" one of them asked. Unaware of the nature of Maria-Bethunia's surprise, and assuming that he had been portrayed as in the photograph submitted to Picasso

—fully dressed, smiling, with an expression of distinguished amazement and exaggerated respect—he answered, "I must have been thinking of you." He had to leave Stillman and Chase even before I did.

Like Maria-Bethunia, Marlise is so entrancing as to make the wreckage of a career or a vast change in plans seem like nothing. I promised her. Again, we embraced. The sea and the wind were all around us. And I was happy, for nothing is as beautiful as a promise right after it is made.

But many a way exists in which to go around a rhinoceros, which leads me to the far more practical subject of why I have written this, for whom, and where it is to be kept.

The most important reason will come clear to you as you read, but I have also written in protest of the sudden shock I received when I was born, a shock that would be repeated many times during my life—as I was hurled thrice from my physical position in heaven, made to discover that my first wife drank coffee, and far worse. All that I have seen broke my heart so long ago that I think of myself as a kind of museum that no one ever visits. Who would visit? The Brazilians would not quite understand my brand of broken heart. Nor would I expect them to.

For my part, I do not quite understand their disgusting public dancing and their thoughtless copulation, though I receive an occasional flash or two of the pleasure and the logic, as if I were a gunner in a pillbox who sees through his narrow firing slits the sun glinting on the sea below.

This country is not for old men, this place of green gems standing in a sapphire necklace of the sea, where flesh crowds upon flesh exactly like mackerel compressed within a net. If only Scotland had not had an extradition treaty, my life would not be perpetually assaulted by bared breasts and rum-injected coconuts (unless, of course, Scotland has changed). I was not constructed to celebrate the senses. I have never been able to celebrate anything. Nor have I wanted to, as celebration has always seemed to me to be the merely mechanical replication of a vital moment that has fled. When the war ended, for example, people danced in the streets and drank coffee. I didn't. I wept for those who had died and the families they left behind, and then I went to sleep. Only the next day did I allow myself to be enlivened by hope.

You can imagine what it is like for me, then, in a country where, if a fly alights successfully upon a mango, ten thousand dancers take to the streets in delirium and euphoria, a country where a man who wins the lottery spends twice what he has won on a party to celebrate his winnings. They're not Scotsmen, these Brazilians. They know quiet observation only when they're sick, and they cannot ever leave anything unmolested. They stand in groups to watch the sunset, and gossip about the growth of plants. Even the wind isn't allowed to curl the waves in peace; they sing about it.

And yet, they have no consciousness. It's as if they lack the part of the brain that rigs time into the geometrical construction in which one is trapped. Life for them is like floating in a warm river. They do not have the northern gifts of apprehension and perception, our bright sense of fire, our sharp dread of ice, but they live their lives as if they are riding on rainbows.

Though they cannot see it, even the dissolute life they live is still a part of the truth—a ripple upon the sea, a diamond-flash in the stream. That I know and that I have known. What sometimes escapes me as I detest them for their licentiousness, their repulsive addiction to coffee, and their bulbous, floppity nakedness, is that their existence is not merely a part of the truth but also a means of seeking it out, a methodology, if you will, like the dance of the bee, or an orchid swaying on a warm breeze, all without pain, all vigorous, lovely, and full of grace.

I have always thought of the year 1900 as the nozzle of a big pastry bag that unfurls icing when you squeeze it, and that for almost a hundred years the curl of civilization has been unraveling in discord. Though the rest of the world has left the antipodes behind, we are stuck in a better time. In Montevideo, everything is so old that it could be 1910, and, oh, if only it were so. I wish the world would stop hurtling ahead at such great speed. I wish that tranquility would, by action, cease to be overawed. In a sense, the century itself explains what I have done, although my purpose is not to make excuses.

In the early 1950's—the month was June—I went to Rome for Stillman and Chase. The cities of Europe still had the feel of war. Many buildings were in ruins, many more pocked and damaged, and concrete fortifications littered the fields and beaches like remnants of a receding glacier. I remember the sound of the sea at Ardea on the Tyrrhenian, which had not been broken from its insistent rhythms by or since the years of war. The immutable brine washed through the stones like a heartbeat, just as it had when, almost ten years before, I climbed out upon a beach of the same sea in North Africa, still alive after having gone down in my plane.

In those ten years I had put on a little weight—I was in my late forties—and had lost the grace I once had for running free and sailing over obstructions like a deer. And, except in the early hours of the morning or late at night, when I dressed in my habitual khaki shorts, polo shirt, and mountain boots, I was imprisoned in expensive suits.

I had to be in Rome for a few days, including a weekend, and did not have enough time to visit the airfields from which I had flown against Germany, vaulting the Alps in a roll of voluminous air that lifted the wings of the P-51 so buoyantly that they bent with the strain. Nor was I able to arrange a trip to Venice as I had wanted, so I stayed in the city, and on Saturday night I went to an opera recital in the Villa Doria. I was very lucky in that the gentlemen who sang were at a high point. These were the greatest singers in the world, and they knew it. Despite the fact that they were singularly unhealthy champions of pallor and girth, they were angels of song. Perhaps they had trucked with the devil, or perhaps in their operations in such elevated realms they had simply needed their bodies less and less.

I was ecstatic, and, like a young boy, I imagined myself in their place. Then I returned to the Hassler, where I stopped at the bar to get a bottle of mineral water before I went up to my suite. In the corner, almost hidden in darkness, were the four greatest male singers in the world. While I had walked through the night among robbers and bicycle thieves, these four huge blimps had taken a taxi. Suddenly, at the end of the long green tunnel of cool night air filled with my memory of their singing, there they were.

With the bottle in my hand, held at the neck the way you'd carry a fishing pole, I stared at them. The glasses on the black lacquered table around which they were sitting were beaded on the outside and sparkling like ice. At the center of the table was a bowl of celery and olives.

When the singers saw me, they looked at one another, shrugged, and motioned for me to approach. It was not as if circus stars had invited an awed child into their midst—we were roughly the same age, I had a very vivid and emotional sense of Europe, having recently played my small part in the greatest opera in all of history, and, to my profound discomfort, I was dressed like a minister of finance. Still, my heart jumped, and

I was anxious not to be lost in their august consideration of music and art.

But, of course, being artists, they wanted to talk only about money, and they displayed an exaggerated respect for me, as my business was money at its most arcane. People love that. I asked question after question about the structure of an aria and the ineffable beauties of harmony, timing, and tone. They asked question after question about exchange rates, tax treaties, and arbitrage. And then, as the night deepened, we began to talk of our childhoods, and that is how I got to know them, and they to know me.

They are all dead now. I watched from afar as they dropped, one by one, and though they were very rich, when they passed away they were not remembered for their money.

I knew then, at the bar in the Hassler, that my questions were better and more important than theirs, because their work was far better and more important than mine. I remembered the line of silver trumpets (in Italy, the brass sections are often silvered) echoing off the garden walls of the Villa Doria, and as we spoke—they of growing up in villages and cities in Spain and northern Italy, and I of the Hudson and the private sanitarium at Château Parfilage (it was a lunatic asylum, actually)—I decided that I would quit the firm.

When I told them this, with great conviction, they thought I was drunk, but I pointed out that I had been drinking only mineral water. At first, as a gesture of elegance and courtesy, they were opposed, as you must be if someone tells you he is about to throw over his career to join the circus. And, I suppose, being familiar with their own magnetic effect, they were always cautioning romantics who wanted to follow in their perilous and glorious footsteps.

But, then, inexplicably, they warmed to the idea. The Spaniard asked if I were independently wealthy. I shook my head from side to side like a ventriloquist's dummy.

"To know," he asked. "How you live?"

The two Italians chimed in simultaneously (these people could time a note the way Robin Hood could shoot an arrow). "When you leave," they said, in C major, "you should be very meticulous. Make sure to turn off the lights, and take all the money with you."

"Now, you may have a point there," I said. "You have really hit upon something, you know?" They could sing for a million years and they would not have a hundredth of what passed through Stillman and Chase in a day. And I, I could have a heart attack in Greenwich after several more decades of asphyxiation, and die in a private room in a teaching hospital, or I could spend a few magnificent and tense years planning, coming alive with illicit electricity—and then abscond with enough to buy five hundred houses in Greenwich and die in as many teaching hospitals as I wanted.

"What a good idea!" I said. "I hadn't thought of it!"

"Bankers, after all," said the Austrian, who—what else—was more serious than the others, "are the worst kind of dogs." I hadn't really seen myself that way, but I was not offended.

We made a plan. They were as animated as if they were singing, but I was fooling them, for as we went through the elements I was thinking in parallel and in secret. In the end, I seemed to have lost my enthusiasm, for, among other things, the scheme was as implausible as one would expect of a plot hatched in a bar of the Hotel Hassler by four opera singers and an investment banker who had spent part of his boyhood in a mental institution. But, though I concealed it well, I was burning with excitement.

I'm getting ahead of myself, which is strange to say when one is speaking of events of almost half a century gone, as the only real way to get ahead of oneself is to tell the future and report from death. Is approaching death what has driven me to write this memoir? Certainly not.

If things work out well, then you will come to understand exactly why I have written it, although I use the words *written* and *said* almost interchangeably—not because I am unaware of the difference, but because I have found, even at the start, that the power of a memoir is to turn voice to word and word to voice until they are fused together as smoothly as a sheet of oil upon a slab of ice.

My motive, as you will come to know if you are who I hope you are, is very plain. Perhaps my words will have some other effect, but my purpose is as simple as a machine designer's urge to diagram his engine, or the explorer's desire to draw a map. I have a homely task to fulfill, and this is my method of fulfilling it.

Should you be someone entirely unknown to me, well then, the arrow has been lost, the seed driven by its sad and diaphanous parachute to a vastly different realm, where it will sparkle in barren silence for an infinity. The decision is not mine. It belongs, as does everything, to the wind.

Let us assume for a moment that I missed the target, and that I will never know who you are. Still, I will address you as *you*. If you are a man, then perhaps we could have flown together, or robbed a bank, two activities that are always absorbing and enjoyable if done properly. In the case of flying, the great thing is to be carried where you could not have imagined you would ever be, and to come back alive. In the case of robbing a bank, the requisite is that no one be hurt, which is actually as difficult as or more difficult than extracting the money. Ideally, the reallocation of funds should not come at the expense of honest citizens, banking organizations, the government, or the polity, but, rather, purely by a swift attack upon what is corrupt, illegitimate, and untenable.

And, if you are a woman, perhaps I would have loved you. That is not to say that you would have loved me. I don't assume that. In fact, I assume the opposite. I have been difficult and objectionable, some would say absolutely impossible, since I was born, well, since I was ten—and yet I had in me far more than my expected share of love. Perhaps this was because, in a life that was a paradigm of unrequitedness, with so much investment and so little expenditure, love grew upon itself and was many times multiplied.

If you doubt the veracity of my story, remember that in the compression of eighty years into so short a span as this memoir the time between events is lost, and it is only the grace of time slowly unfurling that gives to the shocks of one's life the illusion of expectedness.

I had planned to write chronologically, but then realized that, of course, I don't think chronologically. Writing a memoir is like fishing. You cast your line and you pull on it when a fish strikes, but you never know what will be on the other end, for the ocean is deep and is filled with marvelous creatures that do not break the surface in expected order. Nor do they swim under the waves with the whales leading and the minnows at the end of long straight lines. A memoir, like a fish, will not thrive under every discipline. Another way of putting this is that if you alphabetize the Iliad you will have approximately the Athens telephone book. When I think back, things don't line up, they stand out, so I will take them as they come, as once I took them as they came.

One copy of the manuscript exists, and one copy alone, be-

cause at the reproduction store in Niterói the self-service machine is next to a coffee urn. I begged them, almost on my knees,
with a clothespin on my nose, but they would not move it.
Therefore, to protect this story from that which would destroy
it, I have taken great pains to secure a totally antproof case, to
which, I trust, you will return these pages one by one as you
finish reading them.

Miss Mayevska

*(If you have not done so already,
please return the previous pages to the antproof case.)*

HOW CAN YOU know history? You can only imagine it. Anchored though you may be in fact and document, to write a history is to write a novel with checkpoints, for you must subject the real and absolute truth, too wide and varied for any but God to comprehend, to the idiosyncratic constraints of your own understanding. A "definitive" history is only one in which someone has succeeded not in recreating the past but in casting it according to his own lights, in *defining* it. Even the most vivid portrayal must be full of sorrow, for it illuminates the darkness of memory with mere flashes and sparks, and what the past begs for is not a few bright pictures but complete reconstruction. Short of that, you can only follow the golden threads, and they are always magnificently tangled.

The dominant images of the year 1919 are those of a world awakening from the nightmare of war—troops returning, families reunited or shattered by grief, the armistice, the peace. For Americans, it was a time of recrossing the Atlantic, east to west, of the return to a world as quiet and full of hope as Childe Hassam portrayed in paintings that even now have not lost the least part of their lustre. For me, however, little was tranquil as I followed the crooked and contradictory threads that illumine not only the times themselves, like bones that glow within the gelatinous plate of an X ray, but which point to where the times are headed.

In the spring the Atlantic was crowded with busy steamships terribly overloaded on the western passage and nearly empty upon return. I was one of the American boys on the sea, but I was not returning to the New World, a hero. *Au contraire.* I was a passenger on the east-bound *Jeanne d'Arc,* I was fourteen years old, I was fair-haired, smooth-cheeked, as lean as a ballet dancer, and I was in a straitjacket.

I had no need whatsoever to have been so constrained. At that age, especially, I was as tender and innocent as a milk-fed veal. But you know very well what happens to innocent and tender milk-fed veals, and where they end up. The judge whose bitter imagination had contrived my sentence actually had brought a cup of cheap nauseating coffee into the courtroom where I was being tried. What justice could exist when mine own judge was himself one of the many fiends I was compelled to eradicate?

With no coffee nearby, I was very gentle. I was easily moved, always in love, and most willing to sacrifice. I worked hard, and because I lived more or less alone and had no entertainment, and was totally serious, totally nervous, I was far and away the most accomplished student in my school, though my record was minued. This was only because I was never able to force myself

to engage those subjects that did not excite, confound, or in-
vigorate my imagination, and also because I was always immediately willing to defy authority.

Even as a schoolboy I made mortal enemies among adults—
my Latin teacher, for example, a cruel, balding young man of
twenty-seven with a canine tooth that hung out over his lower
lip even when his mouth was tightly closed. The first day in
class, we took a look at him and we knew that God had put us
on earth to carry forth the victories of the angels, which were
achieved not only on the pale blue terraces of heaven but in the
most unlikely corners of hell. Though I received consistent zeros
in Latin, by the time I exited his jurisdiction I had scarred my
teacher, scalded him, lamed him, and punched out his pointed
and drooping tooth.

Others were worse. When I was not yet ten, an art teacher
whose name was Sanco Demirel ordered me to have my hair
clipped. I threw back at him a simple flat *no*. He immediately
charged through the rows of desks, lifted me into the air, and
transported me to the book-storage room. Rage often builds
upon itself, and his was no exception. As I flew, painfully
gripped, high above my accustomed altitude, I feared for my
life.

He slammed the door of the book room and took a cane from
the top shelf. "Bend over!" he commanded.

For me, this was a defining moment. I decided then and in
an instant that defiance and death are preferable to subjugation,
and I narrowed my eyes, signaling for a fight. Irritated beyond
measure, he began to chase me around the room, flailing with
the cane. Books flew about like chickens, but I was able to
escape. It did not take long to make him apoplectic, and I knew
that if he caught me he was going to kill me. I rattled the door.

It was locked, the latch frozen, and I hadn't the strength to move it, but he thought I was about to escape.

He was at the other end of the room. So much lay littered between us that he despaired of catching me, and threw the cane in frustration. It missed, it clattered, and it was soon in my hands.

He remained unfazed, for I was only half his size. The straight end of the cane was quite narrow. As soon as I realized this, and that my possession of the cane gave him an excuse to beat me to smithereens, I put it in the pencil sharpener.

As I began to turn the crank, his jaw dropped. Had he moved quickly he would have had me, but he hesitated. When I removed the bamboo shaft from the gray sharpening machine, I was no longer a fourth-grader about to be turned the color of blotched jam, I was *Achilles*.

The shaft was three feet long, with a six-inch tapered point of razor-sharp, hard, blond bamboo—and I was as agile as a gnat. I could jump and twist unlike any grown man, and my reflexes were so fresh that I was able to toss five pennies from the back of my hand and catch them one at a time before they hit the floor. I will never forget the light and uplifting moment when the power fled from him to me. A beam of sunlight came through the windows above the highest shelves and enveloped me in a bright golden disc.

The first thing he said, shrinking back, was, "I didn't intend to hurt you."

My answer to that lie was, "Sanco Demirel, you are going to die."

I have always been fiercely protective of children, especially myself, as the task was almost exclusively mine from a rather early age. I had not then the moderating experience that later years would fail to bring, and I fully intended to kill him, right then, in the book-storage room. I jumped the piles of overturned primers, fragrant pine drawers that had flown from cabinet carcasses like extracted elephant teeth, and chairs turned helplessly on their sides. And, by God, the ray of sun followed me, shining upon the golden sword that I was ready to thrust into any one of a hundred terrible places in Sanco Demirel's cruel bullying body.

He threw a textbook of physiology at me, and as it flew through the air—easily dodged, I might add—a red and blue diagram of the circulatory system flashed from the flipping pages. Thus, I decided to stab him in his Psoas Quadratus Anastimositum. The sadness, loneliness, and determination of my eyes half-closed against the roaring sunlight convinced him that I was going to reach him and that I really was going to kill him, and he climbed the bookshelves in an attempt to escape through the narrow windows above. This exposed his Psoas and I felt the surge of grace and rage that is the mark of a warrior. As I closed for the kill, the door was smashed open by our rotund headmaster, whose expression I shall never forget.

As I grew older I grew subtler, recognizing the need to balance decisive action with the possibility of escape. In the eighth grade, just before we entered the war, I was molested by a pederast, the so-called dean of men, who pushed me down and grabbed for my private parts. Though we were alone in a deserted hallway, we were not quite alone, for the school dog, an old Labrador named Cabot, lay in the corner like a shadow.

In our biology class we had been studying muscle power, and as an illustration the instructor had used Cabot to bite upon a compression-meter. Evolution, he explained, had favored those dogs who could crack the bone and get the marrow. The compression-meter had been the handle of Lewis Teschner's tennis racquet, sliced in half, with a stiff spring between the two parts. To hold the apparatus together, the biology instructor had used the tape that we wrapped around our wrists in boxing class. Cabot was a sweet-tempered and unassuming dog who had never bitten anyone in his life, but for several years he had been rewarded with kisses, pats, and dog biscuits for sinking his teeth deeper and deeper into the compression-meter. As the object was to increase the force and tighten the hold, he had been trained to bite, to bear down, and never to give up.

I thought I had had it. The dean of men was 6′5″ tall, 250 pounds, a natural-born fighter, and the boxing coach. As he pummeled and grappled me in unspeakable combinations, I saw, through the fog of rape, that his wrists were taped. He had either just taught a boxing class or was about to teach one.

Another second and I had made the connection. "Bless you, Cabot!" I screamed. This, somehow, excited the dean of men, but it also got Cabot to his graying feet, tail swinging back and forth. I looked at his smiling dog's face, and, hardly able to speak, I said, "Test, Cabot, test!"

Cabot lifted his head in readiness, as dogs will, and looked about for the compression-meter. He found it—he thought— and approached, just as he had been taught to do in class. He wagged his tail. "Bite, Cabot, bite!" I commanded. And he did.

This dean of men immediately disengaged from me, the object of his affection, and rolled onto the floor. "Bite, bite, bite!" I chanted, just as we had done in class. "Bite, bite, and never give in!" And that dear dog cracked the bone, got to the marrow, and did not ever have to pay for it, because, to my never-ending satisfaction, the dean of men implicated a phantom bulldog that he claimed, to universal astonishment, had been lying in ambush near the urinals.

On the way from the Tombs to Château Parfilage I was

accompanied by a New York City homicide detective, a nine-teenth-century Irishman by the name of Grays Spinney. The judge knew that a straitjacket and certain requirements of nature do not go well together, and, mindful of the cruel and unusual punishment clause in the Constitution, had provided both himself and me with a way out. As soon as we were beyond the three-mile limit, Spinney sized me up and took off the restraints, though he replaced them for transit through Paris, Geneva, and the other cities of my eternal humiliation.

On the Hudson and in the valley of the Shenandoah, spring was rising. The angle of the sun was perfect, the light not over-bearing, the young grass short and uniformly green, the night euphoric with blooms and warm breezes. And the beautiful sights of spring were punctuated by banks of red and yellow flowers that looked like distant strokes of oil paint laid upon forest and field.

But on the North Atlantic the waves were combat gray, the sky a miasma of spray and fog. Tiny icebergs the size of polar bears blew across the sea like marshmallows, and Spinney, who had spent his life dipping into the Tenderloin in pursuit of der-bied gunmen, got me to the porthole a hundred times with sudden exclamations such as, "Jaysus Christ! A neked Iskimo woman ant a blooody fookin' kangaroo!"

Though he was a detective of exalted rank, he was not literate enough to read the *Police Gazette* without assistance and, after hundreds of inquiries—"Does L-I-V-E-R spell Lady Gau-doyva?"—I became his private secretary and amanuensis. In a process that confirmed the genius of Isaac Newton, my every effort was repaid as he recounted to me in equal measure his years, begun in "Eteen-hundert ant soventy-soven," as a cop.

He was near retirement and full of regrets. "Murther is en-

toyerly uninthirestin," he said. "The raysult is alwess the sim
—a did boody. If Oy ware you, a tinder farteen-yar-olt buy,
Oy'd be inthirested in the bonks."

"The bonks?"

"The bonks. Killin is amurl, but ayven assa paylease afficer,
Oy don't see anythin amurl about robin bonks. Ya know, we
hod a fellah who wint boy the name of 'Robin Bonks,' ant he
would git himself al dresst oop ant walk into a bonk. 'Gut
marnin,' he'd say, 'Oy'm inthirested in oopinin an accoont.'
'Whot's yir nim?' they'd osk. 'Robin Bonks,' he't reploy, ant
see how lang he coot tayke it befar he hot to tayke oot his gon."

Spinney leaned over the top bunk rail as if to confide in me
the secret of the universe. "The bonks," he said, "iss whar payple
kip thir minny. Ya dawn't haf ta goo lookin far it. It's al in one
playce. If Oy ware you, gooin oover ta larn Frinch ant Chairman
ant al thot, Oy'd figger oot how ta git meself inta Harberd or
Yell, and thin grotchulee warm me woy inta sum infistmint bonk
or sumthin. Ya folla?"

I did, but I tabled it.

I cannot remember anything worse than being confined within
a straitjacket—even going down into the sea, my windshield
covered with oil and blood, the engines dying and the wind
whistling death—except perhaps for shock "therapy," something to which I was subjected before I was sent abroad, a thing
more terrible than I can describe, inflicted upon me by that
coffee-drinking bastard who called himself a judge.

With great economy of means, a straitjacket inflicts semiper-
fect paralysis upon someone whose most pressing need is to
thrash. Without exit through despairing limbs, the pain of the
interior is the greatest torturer. Of the two types of straitjacket,
the worse is the kind that pins your arms in front of you.

Supposedly this is more humane, and better for the circulation, but it leads to a feeling of suffocation and powerlessness that is hard to convey.

Electroshock is somewhat more apprehensible to the general public, for most people have learned to dread the electric chair merely through its description. Can you imagine an instrument that, while offering every pain and terror of death by electrocution, denies the holy rest that one earns in suffering through the experience, so that one is preserved to be electrocuted again and again? I believe "electrotherapy" is still debated. Those who, quite insanely, advocate it, claim that the patient benefits. I'll tell you how you benefit. When you finish you're half dead (something that could be accomplished with a severe beating or by a simple toss off a low cliff) and therefore quite tranquil. One is grateful to be alive, that the torture has passed, that the pain is gone. Lesser details appear almost insignificant. After my electrocutions I was even able to sit next to a coffee pot.

For a fourteen-year-old boy who grew up within the shadow of Sing Sing, straitjackets and, particularly, electroshock were difficult to bear. Picture going to the top of the Eiffel Tower, visiting the Louvre, and strolling down the Champs Élysées— in a straitjacket. I did this. I sat with Spinney at the Café de l'Opéra, he with his mustache and watch-chain and nickel-plated pistol, and I in my white encumbrance. He was charitable enough to place me as far from the expresso machine as possible, and when the wind was right I was relatively untortured. With winks, glances, and devil-may-care expressions, I tried to meet women. And when they all looked away, I assumed that it was because my skin was bad or they thought I was too boyish. It never occurred to me that most women might not be interested in getting to know a boy in a straitjacket who sat at a table at the Café de l'Opéra winking, blinking, and raising his eyebrows at them.

Many soldiers were still in uniform, no longer burdened with the immediate fear of death, well rested, sunburned, some not too much older than I—all heroes and victors. The streets sang with wonderful green buses and trolleys that had yellow tops, and open-air platforms at the back. I would have loved to have jumped on and off them as they were moving. I would have loved to have held a French girl in my arms and kissed her. It would have been the first time I had kissed a girl.

Something was very beautiful as Paris awakened from war. Life from every quarter had begun to flood in. The trees were the softest green I had ever seen, greener than in the valleys of the Shenandoah or the Hudson, an ancient and delicate color that I will never forget.

Château Parfilage maintained a small office in Montreux purely for prestige. For the English-speaking world and the French, a lakeside address, with red tulips in well tended beds by the water, was ideal for a mental institution. The Germans preferred the mountains, the Italians the sea, and famous and rich people a place where noxious gasses bubble up through the mud.

Château Parfilage was very much in the mountains, but the Germans had become disenchanted with its methods, so, to attract the English and the French, who, after the war, were extraordinarily crazed, the directors rented office space in Montreux. "Oy nivir seen a newt hotch ass shmal ant affice-like ass this," Spinney said, looking around. "Oy've bratcha anuther newt, Sisther, boot whar iss he supposed ta sleep?"

A tiny nun, no less than my age now, unbuckled my jacket and set me free forever, explaining that it was a sin to put anyone, much less a child, in such a thing.

"Sisther, whot if the divil's in 'im, ant he's throshin like to kill himsolf ar soomeone alse?"

"You put him in the middle of a wide meadow," she said, "where he will be alone with God and the ants."

Within twenty minutes she and I were on a small train winding through the hills above the lake. It was a bright, blue day. We opened the window, and I leaned out to feel the wind and smell the sun-warmed vegetation. What could be better than to be on a train crawling steadily through sunlit uplands, with open windows, and mountain air gusting in, pulsing with the rhythm of the rails? On the climb to Château Parfilage we were lifted into a world of brilliant white—the white of snowfields, ice, and clouds.

When Sister Jacob de Meunière saw that I was content with the Alpine sun that glinted across high prairies of clean ice, she said, "If once you were insane, you are probably insane no longer, but you must stay with us for time enough to convince those who cannot believe, or see, or know, that you have achieved by long and painful labor what God has just given you in a burst and in a flash."

After the train, we went by pony cart. When the pony wanted to eat, he stopped to graze, and Sister Jacob knitted. I jumped out of the cart at these times and often as it was moving (during most of my life, and certainly in my boyhood, I thought it better to be able to jump on and off a moving conveyance than to be the richest man in the world). I ran to the edge of steep defiles, to see the view. As I remember it, my stepping on and off and circling the slow-moving pony was something close to the movements of a foal or a kid. Funio does this, and he breaks into spontaneous dances. A child moving freely is one of the most beautiful things one can behold. When my father took me surfcasting at Amagansett I would go ahead on the beach road, stooping to grind the heather between my fingers for the scent, rising to run on soft sandy stretches that led to the cold blue sea.

So high that you could see France straight to the west and the Black Forest to the north, the château sat on a small rise in the middle of a great meadow walled in at its edges by palisades of evergreens as dense as the teeth of a fine-toothed comb and cooler and more fragrant than I can convey from a garden in the hot sun.

The building itself was a graceful construction of monastic stone, with a courtyard in which were fifty thousand geraniums and a round fountain filled to the brim with frigid water newly liberated from the not-so-distant glaciers.

I had never seen a field so wide. I had never been in air so clear. I had never seen snow so pure and white, for as white as is the snow on the Hudson, it is always tinted by the blue of Canada. I had never seen so many wildflowers jealously and proudly guarding their high posts in colors both bright and apoplectic. France was so distant and purple as it fled to the Atlantic that looking at the world was like gazing through a prism. And I had never been as high as I stood at 3,000 meters, nor so close to the sun, nor so unprotected from its benevolent glory.

I alighted from the cart and went up near the plodding pony so as to walk the rest of the way, to feel every inch of the road that led to a mental institution that I now believe may have been one of the few refuges of sanity in a world everywhere insane.

Though the rector of this institution was no bigger than a Saint Bernard dog, he had about him the aura of power that attaches to people who are gigantic. I immediately felt protective of him, and yet in awe, thinking that not only had he long before finished high school—which I had yet to enter, and never would—and, indeed, college, and then medical school, but the various layers of medical apprenticeship that give one a place on the links for the rest of one's life. It seemed that in Switzerland physicians were more monastic and scholarly, their social standing lower, their intellects better exercised, and their sense of humility sharper than that of their well tailored American brethren.

I took a seat opposite him, hardly able to look away from the snowfields of the Jungfrau, which, though distant, managed to throw their fiery light through his narrow windows and directly into my eye.

"American?" he asked in what I did not then know was a Danish accent.

I nodded.

"Then the first thing I must tell you is that nothing is expected of you."

"Nothing?" I asked.

"Only hard work, study, arising at five, and service in the fields. Nothing more than would be required of a monk, a Roman galley slave, or a virtuous king. In my experience, Americans have always felt the need to amaze everyone. Perhaps that is because the New World is less tired than the Old."

"What about the psychological stuff?" I asked.

"What psychological stuff?"

"You know—jackets, shocks, expensive interviews."

"We don't go for that sort of thing."

"You don't?"

"No, not at all. Ten years of that isn't worth a month of bringing in the hay."

"You mean this is a 'keep-busy' sort of a place? We have one at the tip of Long Island. It's called the Butterworth sanitarium, and it doesn't work. They go in as walnuts, they exit as coconuts, and they die as pistachios."

"I beg your pardon?" he said, failing to understand my schoolboy slang. I'm not sure I understood it either.

"This isn't a 'keep-busy' place," he continued. "Here you work only five days a week. On weekends, if you wish, you can be overcome with terror, lethargy, and regret. The idea is not to keep all your plates spinning, but to let them fall."

"Is coffee here?"

"No. Neither coffee, nor tea, nor alcohol, nor tobacco. No drugs of any kind. No excessively fatty or sugared foods. No motor vehicles. No chocolate. No electric lights, no Victrolas, no telephones, no telegraphs, no magazines."

"No coffee?" My lungs felt as if each one had been freed of the intrusion of a cinder block. My neurasthenia began to clear.

"Coffee is the work of the devil," he said. "I am a physician, and I know whereof I speak. That people actually drink this substance is one of the world's continuing tragedies, a pitiable opera of madness and self-immolation."

I was astonished, and pleased of course. He went on. "A careful consideration of its chemical components shows why. Have you taken organic chemistry?"

"I don't know what it is. I haven't even started high school."

"Regardless of your academic progress, coffee, when steeped for more than a minute at or above ninety-five degrees centigrade, leaches tri-oxitan methyl parasorcinate, loxiphenyl-metasolicitous, oxipalmate dendrabucephalous chloride, indo-crapitus paraben, sulfuro-hydrogelous-exipon, moxibobulous-3 toxitol, and benzene esters of noquitol-soxitan.

"Studies have shown that any of the de-ionized loxiphenyls is highly carcinogenic in the presence of a saturated oxitan. Even minimal exposure to the sulfuro-hydrogelous-exipons almost invariably causes cardiac atomatoxsis and aggravated renal palagromia."

"Are you mocking me?" I asked.

"Perhaps a little," he answered, "but certainly we have no coffee here. I detest coffee. I understand fully what drove you to do what you did, and will make no attempt to rid you of your anger and disgust. You *don't* have to live in the world. What they say when they want to drive the truth from the soul of an honest man is, *You have to live in the world.* Well, you don't. You can live in a place like this, you can live alone in nature, you can rise so high that nobody will dare make or drink a cup of coffee in your presence, you can kill yourself, or you can sleep. . . . One thing is sure. You simply do not have to adjust to that filthy, horrendous, addictive bean that has created a population of slaves spread throughout every part of the globe.

"Not, anyway, for the next four years. These will be your anchor years. You'll remember them as years of freedom, responsibility, agonizingly hard work, love, and revelation."

"You mean I won't be going to school?"

"Your education will be entrusted to God, your own curiosity, and Father Bromeus."

"Who's that?"

"He takes care of the cows, and is the drillmaster."

"What do you mean, 'the drillmaster'?"

"Most people here are adults. We can't afford to train the adolescents in all the academic subjects they require, and yet by cantonal law you must present yourself every now and then for examinations in French, German, and Italian, in history, physics, mathematics, chemistry, botany, the history of the destructiveness of coffee, and other things."

"How do you go about that," I interrupted, "without a system of education? I don't speak those languages. I'm terrible at mathematics. How is one supposed to learn chemistry without a laboratory?"

"Don't worry a bit. We have designed our own educational system, and it works. I thought of it myself after I visited the United States in 1910 and watched a game of baseball.

"What you call the *pitchers* were practicing along the sidelines. Well, being a man of science, I leaned over the rail and asked, 'Do you always practice with the same-sized ball?' In fact, they did, or at least they said they did. 'Why?' I inquired. 'Why not?' they inquired back.

"I then told them that it was obvious in regard to physics and physiology that they would enormously improve their performance if they practiced with balls of radically different sizes—a pea-sized pebble on the one hand, and a soccer ball on the other. The difficulties and exertions of doing so would make them champions with a ball tailored for the fist and of the proper weight and density for throwing.

"I don't know if they followed my system, but we do, as you shall see. By the way, do you play an instrument?"

"No."

"She does."

"Who is *she*?" I asked.

"She is here because of her abhorrence of grasshoppers."

"Aren't there grasshoppers in the fields?"

"Not at this altitude."

"Where did she come from that she abhors grasshoppers?"

"Paris. They have lots of grasshoppers in Paris."

"I didn't see any."

"How long were you there?"

"Two days."

"*Voilà.* Anyway, the infestation doesn't start until the latter part of May and early June. Miss Mayevska lived there all year 'round, and every year at the beginning of summer she suffered great emotional distress."

"Should you be telling me this?"

"Everyone here knows about it. In August, she and her family used to go to the South of France, and when she was fourteen it was the year of the locusts, which is why she is here. All Provence erupted with a plague that, to her, was absolutely overwhelming."

"Is she French? What kind of name is Mayevska?"

"She is a Polish Jewess, but yes, she is French, although if one listens hard one can detect the traces of an accent."

"I see."

"Not yet you don't."

Although I continued the practice in the Second World War, I learned at Château Parfilage (and associate most strongly with the years of my confinement and freedom there) the nomadic technique of using a blanket. Marlise hardly knows what a blanket is, but up there where the air was thin and blizzards could strike close upon the heels of a brilliant summer sun, you needed to wear your blanket.

One blanket of thick virgin wool in a tight weave, long enough to be doubled or even quadrupled and hung from the shoulders as a wrap, was enough for winter or summer. We had no fires in our rooms, and of course no modern heating system, but it was a delight to sit within the folds of the blanket, studying or, as in the case of Miss Mayevska, playing the piano.

I did not see Miss Mayevska, but was almost always able to hear her at the piano, even if at times just faintly. I had thought that I would encounter her during the first meal, but because we were in an insane asylum we took our meals on the monastic pattern, savoring them in our rooms, in the cold, as we obsessed.

My first task, dictated by Father Bromeus for reasons that he would not disclose but that later appeared quite obvious, was to memorize the telephone directory of Zurich. To this day I can recall names and numbers that are no longer associated and that are forever lost, but that once made the hearts of boys and girls race as they saw on the page a code that would bring them, by voice and ear, to the houses of their beloveds.

The object of Father Bromeus was to train my mind to take in information. This was the French half of the education I received at Château Parfilage. I can still tell you that the atomic weight of cobalt is 58.93, that the altitude of the railroad station at Neuchâtel is 482 meters, that Shakespeare used the word *glory* 94 times, that the Italian word for *diphthong* is *dittongo*, that (though I cannot tell you who invented the pickle) Johann Georg Pickel invented the gas lamp in 1786, and that Roberts captured Bloemfontein on March 13, 1900, though Bloemfontein was never able to capture Roberts.

Father Bromeus presented me with so many tables, lists, texts, photographs, paintings, and musical compositions to memorize that I spent hours and hours a day at it. Soon I had mastered rapid apprehension and assimilation of virtually any material, never to be forgotten unless I deliberately banished it. Only later would the next test come, which was just as shocking as suddenly being presented with the Zurich telephone book. This was the task of analysis, which, with Jesuitical discipline, Father Bromeus divided up into interpolation, extrapolation, induction, reduction, and deduction.

When I had started upon these things, I was examined. "I have learned from Father Bromeus," the rector said, "that you have at your command the information necessary to tell me how you would, from this location, kill all the grasshoppers in Paris."

"I beg your pardon, sir?" I asked, never having been forced to this kind of thought.

Because I was not allowed to employ anyone in Paris or use the railroads to ship tens of thousands of birds and bats to the City of Light, I had to design and manufacture a huge cannon. This involved everything I had learned about physics, metallurgy, chemistry, geometry, and geology (I had to mine my own metals, make my own tools, build my own buildings). Unfortunately, to get the grasshoppers, I had to destroy the whole city. My answer was only hypothetical. How was I to know that it would become the underlying logic of the rest of the twentieth century?

Every day, the rector would present such a problem—sometimes purely scientific, sometimes technological, poetic, historical, political, or aesthetic, and often a combination of several of these. His queries were always interesting and often ingenious. Even when they were fruitless, the many frustrating approaches that we followed toward their unobtainable solution made such problems immensely entertaining. He might say, "You are to write a sonnet after Shakespeare, in French, using the rules of Italian prosody," or he might drop me into the forests of northern Canada and instruct me (all in theory, of course) to survive the winter and construct a coliseum of snow and walrus bones.

Where I erred, he corrected; when I was lost, he showed me the beginning of the way. My favorite problems were the short imperatives: "Solve the problems of Revolutionary France." (First I had to figure out what they were.) "Design an electrical machine for the flawless generation of music." This I did, in theory, and many years later in Brazil I encountered what are called synthesizers, and I smiled. "Develop the economy of

Egypt." I had a good plan: they didn't follow it. "Tell me what this is," he would say, handing me a flask of goo. Having committed to memory many of the techniques of qualitative and quantitative analysis, I would return in a few days with a list of components in their absolute and proportionate quantities.

All this while doing hard labor in the fields, rising at five, climbing ice-clad peaks, and cutting and hauling firewood. As if to confirm that life is the academy of fate, the only question he asked more than once was, as usual, in the form of a command. In fact, he presented me with the same challenge four or five times, and each time I took a few days to make an intricate plan. His exhortation was, "Rob the Bank of England."

In Paris at the several cafés in which I had lingered in my straitjacket, with Spinney, I had seen women dressed according to the fashions of the times. Their hair was carefully coifed, their faces made up, their fingers lasciviously adorned with rings, their necks with necklaces, their wrists with bracelets. I assumed—from what the rector had told me about her beauty, and because she was a Parisienne—that Miss Mayevska would be an exemplar of such seductive arts. I assumed that she would be able to afford the silk, perfume, and gold that can so magnify a woman's natural beauty, for after all, Château Parfilage was one of the most expensive mental institutions in western Switzerland. But though I had heard her gorgeous transcriptions, often in my dreams, for several months before I actually met her, I hadn't had the slightest idea of Miss Mayevska until I saw her face. Never have I loved anyone more, and never will I.

This does not prejudice my affection for Marlise, but I have loved Marlise solely according to the tropical paradigm, which means that in our sweat-filled, screaming, gasping, semihallucinatory dalliance we have achieved a certain intimacy. Our flesh and fluids have been pressed, mixed, or imbibed with such vigor that at times we have been unsure which one of us was or was not the other.

But I never slept with Miss Mayevska, though I must have kissed her for a thousand hours, and it is with Miss Mayevska, though I have not seen her since August of 1923, that I will always be most the intimate.

At first I fell in love with her merely because of the rector's suggestion. It is easy to fall in love that way, but it is also easy to fall out. Then it was after I heard her own transcription of Bruch's Opus 46. Father Bromeus, always a literalist, made me compare the two scores. To adapt the work for the piano she had added a great deal, subtracted much, and varied the tempo quite often, but the soul of the piece was still in it, and it was just as beautiful, or more.

I still had not seen her, but it hardly mattered, for the way she played went straight to my heart, as if we could communicate only through the high messengers of the spirit that, one hopes, remain after death.

But as precisely attuned as she was to the most refined apprehension of the world and to questions of purpose and ultimate disposition, she was also a girl of sixteen, and therefore, mischievous, ambitious, and charming, although I did not quite understand her youthful charm, thinking of her as an older woman.

The first time I saw her . . . and if I close my eyes I can remember the day, the hour, and the feel of Alpine sun against my face . . . was in the highest meadow we had, as we were bringing in the hay, in August of nineteen hundred and nineteen.

It was a sight to see: patients and staff, men, women, boys, and girls, two dozen nationalities and as many neuroses and psychoses, some in odd ethnic costumes, some barely able to move at the high altitude, others laboring like spiders in a windstorm. Brueghel would not have been surprised by the colors —an otherworldly blue sky, and golden sheaves thrown down all around us like the muted but sparkling armor of Achilles, shining calmly in the light of a twirling and levitated sun. Nor would he have been surprised by the expressions of the laborers, which ranged from the cockeyed to the stunned to the intensely fearful. But they were all nice people: I knew them quite well.

At about eight in the morning a second group had joined us. I had not even noticed them, so busy was I at the work. I stepped to the back of a hay wagon, burdened with four sheaves, to show to anyone in the world who might be watching that I was strong, but I dropped three on the way. Intending to toss into the wagon the one I still held and quickly run back for the others, I threw it so high that it lingered above me for an instant that seemed to empty the air of time.

And then I turned, because another sheaf had been thrown, and although it did not glide like mine it made a graceful arc and it, too, seemed to hesitate at the top for an unusually long moment.

Miss Mayevska and I stood not a foot apart, our faces flushed from the early morning sun, the bracing air, and our labor. I had never seen such fine, buoyant, black hair, nor eyes so deeply blue, clearly magnified through gold-rimmed spectacles with whitened edges of ground glass. She was breathing through her mouth, which gave her an expression of expectation and surprise.

We stood frozen in place for some time, and then she smiled. It was the most exquisite smile I have ever seen, with tiny crescents between mouth and cheek, as in nearly all beautiful women.

I had no more control of myself than a hart struck deeply by an arrow, and I felt so much like embracing her that I had to do something to prevent my arms from seeking her by themselves, so I spoke, but without knowing what I was saying, and I said, "Oh! Moose Mishevsky. Miss Mishoovsky," and then (she told me much later) my lips moved without making a sound, as if I were a lunatic in an insane asylum.

I worked near her for the rest of the morning, stealing glances so often that I repeatedly bumped into the hay wagon. I was ravished by the tentative, apprehensive way she moved through the hay, and I could not help but love her for her nonsensical affliction. The only thing wrong with her, the one thing in the world, was that she feared grasshoppers. I had always liked grasshoppers, and loved crickets, but I renounced them forever. Tell me why it is that they put her in an insane asylum because she grew hysterical at the sight of a grasshopper? (She could not even shell peas, because of what a wide pea pod, viewed from the side, resembles.) Tell me why it is that, later, as I flew patrols over the Mediterranean and returned to a base in Tunisia, she, her husband, and her two girls were put in a cattle car and sent to their slaughter in a death camp on the plains of Poland not far from the place where she had spent her infant childhood?

That is, I suppose, part of the reason that my love for her has grown, and keeps on growing, and why I love her as a believing Catholic loves a saint. But even before the war, when we could not imagine her fate, I loved her with a seriousness and melancholy that was unusual in a boy.

And then I was seventeen, which is not to say that I skipped fifteen and sixteen but that those years passed very fast and in a near-continuum of falling snow, terrible storms, and brilliant Alpine days (the very opposite of the climate here), and that I passed these strenuous days and nights in the company of monks, nuns, and the inmates of an insane asylum. I myself was not insane. What I had done was entirely justifiable and in self-defense. The problem, it seemed, was that the result was so horrific it called for some sort of reaction from the system of justice.

You hear a lot about the reasons for crime, how it comes from unrelieved suffering, and is in its greatest part a tragedy. But that is not so. Crime—and I should know—is first and foremost a phenomenon of opportunity. One commits a crime not to avenge oneself upon a world that has treated one cruelly, but, rather, for a sense of accomplishment, for the joy of getting something for nothing, for the thrill and the risk, for the freedom of exiting the social structure, and, most of all, I think, for the unparalleled and incomparable elation of *escape*.

If your crime involves great skill and meticulous planning, so much the better, but, as I believe I have said, crime is unpardonable and inexcusable if it wounds. The only decent crime is that which strikes against evil. Otherwise it is detestable. For example, robbing banks in Kansas hurts innocent people, whereas robbing banks in New York does not.

I have always thought that the theft of immensely expensive jewelry, as long as it involves no physical harm, is no more immoral than a good game of Capture the Flag. With apologies to the various dukes, duchesses, and movie stars who have connected with some of my very agile colleagues, million-dollar stickpins are easily insolent enough to make them fair game. Oh, yes, I know . . . the economics of it is that the fool with the million-dollar stickpin has freed his money to work for someone else, who might buy an asparagus farm and provide real pleasure for ten thousand Belgians, or invest in a mine from which will come the metal that will form the arm that holds the massive silvered light by which a team of surgeons saves the life of a child. But, even if the thief takes the diamond, the money is still free to work.

Most people like me are the way they are because they find themselves warring against the social system from the outside. Pity them not, however, for in the vast majority of cases it has been their choice and they have committed some despicable and harmful act.

I, however, was set apart by a series of entirely coincidental events that elicited from me an entirely justifiable response. In those days we had the electric chair and it was used. I ought to know: for a few months I thought I was going to sit in it, and the most notable of these contraptions was in the town where I grew up (so to speak). Nonetheless, my ultimate disposition, despite a physical attack (before the sentencing) upon the judge who sentenced me, was to be sent to what turned out to have been perhaps the finest prep school in the world. It certainly had the best view and the most favorable student-teacher ratio of any academy on earth. What it lacked, I suppose, was what *I* have always lacked—the society of fellows.

In some ways, I prefer the company of women. Miss Mayevska, Constance, Marlise, and other women, I grant you, have either left me or died, though I'm hoping that Marlise will be the first to break the pattern. Perhaps after I'm dead she'll see the kind of pictures that float before my eyes as I sit in this garden.

It's very early in the morning in the park in Niterói, and a red bird just darted across my line of sight, from right to left. It was one of those tropical things, with a long yellow and blue tail, that the boys in the *favelas* try to trap because they can sell it, for five years of ordinary income, to bird smugglers who come on yachts from New York. I hope he is never captured, even if his plumage forces me to recall the fate of the Walloon on the train. After almost seventy years, I am beginning to feel regret—not because I had any choice in what I did, but because he may have had redeeming qualities that I unwittingly canceled along with the rest.

Though now I am in the garden, watching the newly risen sun pave the sea with yellow gold, and tangled in the blurred red ribbons of birds that streak by and set the mild morning air on fire, my memory insistently places before me the image of Miss Mayevska, at nineteen years of age, exquisitely wrapped in black sable, standing at midnight in the blinding Arctic sun.

It isn't a dream, it happened, though it was so long ago and so far away that now it has made of time the most beautiful adagio. The memory would have become only theory were it not for the continuing strength and presence of Miss Mayevska, who, despite her death, exists in some invisible chamber of fact and truth, as if forever.

When I was seventeen, in my last year at Château Parfilage, she had already left and gone to study music in some grasshopper-free suburb of Berlin, a city that had been impoverished but had not yet gone mad. Little did I know then that I would someday fly over Berlin, businesslike and deathly afraid, numbed and sick, angry, determined, and ashamed, escorting bombers that dropped bombs that undoubtedly broke to smithereens the piano at which Miss Mayevska had studied in the years when I had loved and touched her. How wonderful was the time when neither she nor I knew of the destruction that lay ahead, when she was just a girl, when she was alive, and I had not been broken.

She arrived at the gate in June of 1922 (she had been released the previous autumn), and of course they let her in. Very gracefully, she greeted all those she had known, but she was making her way to me, and she found me as I was building a fence in one of the pastures high on a hill that overlooked half the world. I ran to her, dropping a hammer and a handful of carefully wrought pegs, but even as she drew closer, framed by an apron of snow that covered the Berner Oberland, my heart ached, because I knew I would soon be parting from her again.

Not for a while though: she had come to spring me. Because I was confined to that place by law, the rector reported my absence to the Swiss police. Had we remained in Switzerland I suppose they might have found me, but we didn't and they didn't.

We arrived at the local railway station at exactly the moment the train pulled in. This we could do because we all knew, to the step and the second, how long it took to get down there by foot or by pony cart, as the younger among us had the job of picking up the mail. The trains ran on time then, not that they don't now (although I wouldn't know, and Brazilian trains are not much of an example, as the populace has yet to discover whether one rides inside or on top). Apart from lake steamers and pony carts, railroads were the only means of transportation. No network of highways, no airplanes to speak of, and, naturally, no ocean liners were present to distract the Swiss from their single-minded devotion to keeping the trains on time. Actually, it was triple-minded: the French part of the Swiss mind loved the trains themselves, the marvelous *linearity* of the railroad; the German part insisted on punctuality as if each and every German were a ticking time bomb that required periodic and exact disarming; and the Italian part, which liked very much the food on the trains, deferred to the other two parts even though it thought they were crazy.

Before anyone missed us we were in Bern. Not more than three minutes after we exited the portals of the Bern station we were seated in the private office of the director of the Bern branch of Switzerland's leading bank. With no wavering or hesitation, without even the blink of an eye, Miss Mayevska withdrew a hundred thousand Swiss francs, which was, then, a fortune.

She did it by giving a numbered code and answering a few questions. I asked how she had access to such wealth and what she planned to do with the money.

"We're going to the North Pole," she said.

"Oh."

"I know that someday I'll be gone, so even if my temptation is to be thrifty I insist upon using the money now, in a flash, for something memorable."

Each member of the family had several accounts in several Swiss banks, and safe-deposit boxes scattered here and there, with money for emergency or escape. "For Jews," she told me, "money is, most importantly, a life preserver. We amass it, when we can and if we do, not from greed but out of fear."

"How can you enjoy it?" I asked.

"We don't," she said. "But we try."

I begged her to return it, feeling some of the age-old anxiety that had led her father to provide secret stores all over the continent in case his children should be hunted like rats. She told me not to worry. He owned a shipping line and many buildings in Paris, on or near the Champs Élysées, and her withdrawal would trouble neither him, nor her, nor their chances in the fearsome future. She gave me fifty thousand francs to carry, and we took a walk through town before we boarded a sleeping car that carried us, lying in one another's arms, to Hamburg.

Our ship was the *Meteor*. We had to wait ten days for it to depart, and during that time we rented two rooms in a small garden hotel, pretending to use them both. This was when I discovered that people who encounter one another while sneaking through hotel corridors in the middle of the night pretend against all odds that they and the people they see are invisible, and at breakfast the next morning turn a hot red color that is reminiscent of a velvet curtain in a Danish opera house.

And even if the next morning it is a double world, it is all the sweeter because one is moved by love—sweeter, in fact, than the cup of tea into which one absentmindedly dumps sixteen teaspoons of sugar.

Hamburg, being a sea port, was the site where German sailors brought from the tropics those fragrant, yellow, and acerbic things they called *Zitronen*, a word that to me suggested an electric bicycle or a granular disease of the cells. We had lots of *Zitronen* in our hotel, enough to cut the sugar and make the scene sunny even in the fog.

Each day we walked many miles. We shopped for clothes to wear at the North Pole. We went to music halls and the theater. And Miss Mayevska played the piano in the hotel salon, astonishing the other guests, for in those times great musicianship was recognizable even to the common man, was a badge of honor, something appreciable and respected. I suppose we could have stayed there forever, Miss Mayevska and I, but then the *Meteor* came, gliding down from the Norwegian fjords.

Though we were to stop in Edinburgh and Iceland, where one might conceivably meet a grasshopper, most of the voyage was to be in northern places where the grasshopper potential was nearly zero. We were going to the edge of the permanent pack ice of the Arctic Ocean, at about 82 degrees latitude. The cruise promotions said that if conditions permitted, we would actually reach the North Magnetic Pole, but that was just a lie. They lied as well about the aurora, but, still, we saw it half a dozen times arising with startling precision in the exact middle of the few minutes of darkness we experienced each night as the ship navigated carefully between Spitzbergen and the polar cap, in seas remarkably free of ice.

No one would look for us in the Greenland Sea, for, after all, very few people had even heard of it, and it was the kind of place that led to instant dismissal as the destination of an adolescent who has fled a mental institution. And Miss Mayevska had heard that the light was like the light of purgatory, that, as far as the human imagination could tell, this was the light in the timeless chambers after death—a sad gray certainty behind which waited an uncertain brightness greater than that of the sun, a leonine roar of white and silver, something that, like the aurora, danced in buckling walls, fans, rays, curtains, and arcs, and did so in every bright and pastel color known and in others yet to be seen. She wanted to sense this brightness through the gray that masked it from mortal view, and she wanted, as well, several weeks of the absence of what she called "my great fear."

The *Meteor* was old but fast, and between Hamburg and Edinburgh I had just enough time to injure my back on a mechanical horse. I have neither seen nor heard of mechanical horses since then, and no one may ever want to describe them again, in which case you would never know them, which would be a pity, for they were ridiculous and sad, and they foretold all that would go so terribly wrong with the rest of the century.

In Rio, where ever since I can remember the bodily ideal has been founded in roundness, smoothness, and softness (round breasts and buttocks, shoulders that curve as smoothly and uninterruptedly as the descent of swallows) of flesh the consistency not of a leather saddle or even a sausage but of a balloon half-filled with warm water . . . even in Rio the fulcrum of desire has become firmness, strength, capacity, and solidity. Which is to say that now women, no less men, exercise for strength.

I regret that it was not so when I was not an old man. Perhaps if Constance could have run ten kilometers and levitated on a high bar she would not have felt the need to leave me. On the other hand she probably *could* have run ten kilometers and levitated on a high bar: she was very athletic. Perhaps had Marlise had the dolphinlike breasts and strong lithe arms of a swimmer, we would not have so many arguments. Who knows? I do know that even in the Botanical Garden women run past as if tormented by devils, as if breathing their last: but when they are beautiful and move gracefully, they look like goddesses.

Not long ago I saw a girl running against the blue sky in the gardens of Niterói. She wore a peach-colored tank top. Her face was mottled red with the blood coursing through it. And she glistened with sweat. Wisps of displaced blond hair rode softly on the heated air, and her green eyes seemed impossibly alight and deep, with so many flecks of blue and gray that I jumped to attention, my heart pounding, and I thought, 'She must have been born in a jewelry store.'

In my day, exercise was equated with work, because most work involved exercise. As only aristocrats had to devise ways of straining themselves so as not to atrophy, the health establishments, such as they were, reflected an aristocratic bias. For example, the scales in the *Meteor*'s gymnastic salon had tasseled chairs mounted upon them, lest the weighee demean himself by standing. Every position on the exercise equipment was reserved as if it were a box at the opera, and attendants cleaned and polished each apparatus between occupants. The Indian clubs were varnished like the paneling of the elevators at Brooks Brothers, their necks rewrapped daily in Irish linen, the knobs at the end of the handles plated in gold.

But everything in that place was as nothing compared to the row of fifteen mechanical horses, each facing a carefully executed oil of the hunt, each a perfectly rounded rosewood half barrel

surmounted by a London saddle and attached to pistonlike de-
vices projecting from heavy plates on the floor. Massive wheels
and reciprocators, painted red and green, moved them. The smell
of leather and the creak of stirrup straps led the eye to look for
horses tossing their heads, for sharp hooves embossing the dirt,
and sweat-strained chestnut-colored flanks. But the horses had
been replaced and machines ground on under the aristocrats in
tweeds and long boots, their crops weaving perilously through
the air like fly swatters with Saint Vitus' Dance, although some
seemed just to float, chest-high, as if on a current of tropical
air.

I suppose that one of the things that qualified Miss Mayevska
and me for the mental institution was the characteristic we shared
that moved us, together, to the kind of dismay that caused us
both, without plan, to enter the salon and ask accusingly,
"Where are the horses? This is madness. What have you done
with the horses?"

We were immediately ostracized, but the low nobility with
whom we traveled began to think that we were the high nobility.
We were either that or revolutionaries, to have the nerve to
challenge fifteen mounted Prussian landowners, all former army
men. As lunatics, we knew that you cannot do without the living
horse under the saddle, that to ride on reciprocators and wheels
that have neither life nor breath is a sin against God.

I have always been decisive. Indeed, part of the reason my
life has been as it has been is that I have looked to God rather
than to man for the limits of action. When the war came I did
not dither, I simply joined. And I volunteered at each stage,
like a madman, until I found myself, by my own writ, riding the gusts of high pressure that fled in spheres from the
unprodictable stars of white phosphorus cracking in the air
around us. We flew through valleys made in the sky by lighted

trajectories streaming up from the ground in lines that were as delicate as the traces of luminous sea creatures lapping in the waves. I trembled with emotion as I hurtled through this, thinking that I was going to die, but I didn't, and she did.

Action, not for its own sake, but without regret, was the river I rode in my early life, and there was something that I almost did, which, if I had done it. . . . My God, if we had done it, we might be living now together, and she might have borne my children. My course was set, my entire life decided, not by war or the sweep of history, but by the breaking of a biscuit.

The *Meteor* was not a large ship. It was about the size of the royal yacht *Britannia*, its stern raked and rounded in the fashion of a later day. It had many yachtlike characteristics, and was so unlike the boxy Las Vegas–style cruise ships of today that it is as if the sixty years between the two were six hundred. Many of the so-called ships that I see in the harbor at Rio are nothing more than the thoughtless fusion of a jukebox, a cafeteria, and a whorehouse set afloat and asquare by naval architects not worthy of the name, computer-sucking apes whose lives are spent scattering giant slot machines upon the sea.

But the *Meteor*—swift, silent, fitted with grand pianos, a string quartet, and nothing more sinful than a mechanical horse—was shallow of draft and nimble of maneuver enough to take us into the Scottish firths so deeply that you could lean from the deck and pick an apple. The *Meteor*'s library (Tolstoy, Shakespeare, Goethe, and new and exciting authors like Yeats, Bunin, and Rilke) was inserted deeply into the creases of Scotland—including even the German newspapers (hung on cane racks), which had then, as they have now, nary a space as big as a beetle unfilled by language as dense as a diamond.

We disembarked over still water and were taken in huge carriages—they must have been huge, each one held twenty-five

Germans—to the lakes, castles, and hotels of the interior. The sight of that country drew me in as if I had been born for it.

Miss Mayevska could not begin to understand the brogue. Indeed, not a soul on the ship had the faintest idea of what the local people were talking about, but not only did I understand, I quickly picked up the patterns of speech and could talk as if I had lived there all my life. I was proud of this, for, as I had no family left, my home was in the language and I loved it as if it were as warm and alive as the beautiful young girl by my side.

We were taken in our tremendous carriages to a hotel in the countryside, chosen undoubtedly because it was beautiful, isolated, and luxurious, and because its name, *Trossachs*, was a word the Germans could pronounce as well as the Scots. The hotel was surrounded by hills and glens, and it was in the glens that we felt most strongly the inimitable peace of early June. I have heard it said that Scotland is so beautiful it is banal.

From my position in the garden, in a fume of early light, I cannot understand the notion of banality. So many people spend so much time protecting themselves from the ordinary and the worn that it seems as if half the world runs on a defensive principle that robs it of the tested and the true. But if the truth is common, must it be rejected? If the ordinary is beautiful, must it be scorned? They needn't be, and are not, by those who are free enough to see anew. The human soul itself is quite ordinary, existing by the billion, and on a crowded street you pass souls a thousand times a minute. And yet within the soul is a graceful shining song more wonderful than the stunning cathedrals that stand over the countryside unique and alone. The simple songs are the best. They last into time as inviolably as the light.

I could not speculate like this were I not sitting in a garden on top of a mountain in Brazil, alone, in daylight that is quickly becoming as hot as the bees require.

I had been in love with Miss Mayevska from the beginning, when I first met her—indeed, by suggestion and description, even before I met her—but in the few years that passed since that time I had grown just old enough to love her deeply. This means, among other things, that I would have immediately sacrificed myself to protect her—and I would have—but it didn't work out that way. I was lucky, and she was very unlucky, and there was nothing I could do about it.

One of the most endearing things about her was that although she was naturally beautiful—of the blackest, softest hair, the clearest widest eye, and the most noble and delicate face I have ever seen—she did not dress well. She could afford any item of clothing in the world, but (except for the magnificent sable parka she bought for the trip) she wore the awkward clothes of a suffering clerk.

The countryside around the hotel reminded us of the fields above the Parfilage, where we had labored together in the years when our courtship was sustained by perhaps one hidden glance every day or two, and no more. And we knew simultaneously and suddenly that we might be happy, for the rest of our lives, on a farm in Scotland. Even with just the money we had with us we could have bought good land, a good house, and the machinery that would make our production efficient enough so that we could pay the people who helped us a wage that would enable them to prosper. That, I understood even as an adolescent who had escaped from a mental institution, was one of the benefits of capital that a certain person who worked in the British Museum had entirely glossed over, and indeed the very phenomenon freely applied has transformed the industrialized world, changing peasants into yeomen.

Still, I didn't really care about economics, not then. I begged Miss Mayevska to marry me. We would stay in Scotland. We would lose ourselves there, for Scotland is as good a place as any to be lost. We would have sons and daughters.

She almost agreed. I assaulted her with the tenderest, most imaginative, and most implausible representations about farming. I told her my very specific plans. I told her that I would be faithful to her for the rest of my life, and I would have been. I told her that I loved her, and I did.

She was as apprehensive as any young girl might be. Young boys are mercurial, and they are supposed to be. I imagine that she feared being left on a farm in Scotland, with a child or two, after I had gotten on to something new and changed my mind.

In the middle of June we went with all our heavy Germans to Edinburgh. We made an obligatory stop at the bridge over the Firth of Forth, admiring the ironwork floating perilously high above us, and in Edinburgh we stayed at the Royal Hotel Macgreggor, overlooking the river and the park.

On a blazing but cool afternoon, we stood in a street nearby, about to make the fateful decision I had been urging. We were supposed to go back to the ship after an early dinner in the hotel, and if we were to break from the tour we would have to do it that afternoon, within the hour.

We were standing in front of a bookstore window half full of new books in the process of being set out for display. The woman whose job it was to put them out was having tea. She was middle-aged, a classically beautiful Scotswoman who, nonetheless, because of the way her hair was done, vaguely resembled a water buffalo.

As we spoke, she was watching us and we were watching her. She drank her tea from a china cup with a gold rim, and she had three delicate shortbread biscuits on a matching plate. She had eaten two already, very slowly, as if defying some law or principle. Just before Miss Mayevska was going to give me her consent, and I am sure she was, the woman picked up the last biscuit and pulled it across that vast and dangerous space between the plate and her mouth.

With a non-euclidian hold at its end, and no Firth of Forth bridge to support it as it sailed across the gap, its structure collapsed, it crumbled, and it fell to the floor. "Oh dear," said the woman, noiselessly lip-read through the glass, and put down the tea. She swept up the biscuit, placed it aside, and returned early to her work.

The word *yes* was just about to come from Miss Mayevska's lips when the woman lifted a heavy book up and over the wood panel that separated the display window from the interior of the shop. It was a French book, with a painting on the cover. It was what today—and I hate to say it—would be called a *coffee table book*. The title was *L'Aurore*. The painting we saw was so compelling that it was as if the aurora had removed itself from the sky onto that small square behind the glass. As soon as Miss Mayevska saw it, her heart skipped north.

Within two weeks we found ourselves by a rushing stream of immense power on the Nord Cap of Spitzbergen, as close to the pole as one can get in Europe. The water was achingly cold and entirely pure, born of a white glacier that had never felt a footfall. We remained there alone for the few hours it took the world to dim and darken and the aurora to arise. The sky looked like wheat fields in all their beauty, but it was dancing in celestial splendor as if in a dream of death.

Miss Mayevska's face was framed in dark sable, and her eyes were filled with the otherworldly color of the aurora.

The First Man I Killed

(If you have not done so already,
please return the previous pages to the antproof case.)

SIX MONTHS HAVE passed since I last sat in the garden, surrounded, as I am now, by inchoate insects just hatched from little eggs, who fly in lines as tight as the singing electric wires of a tram line shining with the sun. I know nothing about the lives of insects, but it occurs to me that when I was seized at this very bench and I collapsed upon the ground, the great-great-great-great grandfathers and grandmothers of these little things were yet to be born.

And when they are born, they are nothing like our rounded and needful human babies that teach you, finally, what love is, and why you are here. No, the insects require no training, no care, no tenderness. They step right into the world, looking like a cross between an expresso machine and a 1928 Packard, and then they begin flying arcs and circles, tracing lines of red and gold in the rising sun in the gardens of Niterói. I suppose the parents don't even stay around to watch the eggs open.

It is a great privilege not to be hatched and then loosed upon the frightening speedways of the air to hunt a few bouncing gnats, lay an egg, and expire. In relative terms, these little buzz bombs can fly at 4,000 miles an hour. And they have no emotions, no regret, no deep unfulfilled desires . . . I think. If, in fact, they do, they're in trouble.

I almost died on this very bench. I had come here at my usual time, before the streets and alleys fill with the sickening smell of brewing coffee, and spent my usual half hour catching my breath and watching the sunrise. I then uncapped my pen and took these papers from the antproof case. At that moment, a ship's whistle sounded far below.

I am unable to ignore such a summons, and I rise, always, to see what great creature has sidled in from the sea and how the wind washes the smoke over its smooth decks. As soon as I stood I perceived the source of the sound—a red ship laden with silver and blue containers, backing into a berth on the other side of the bay.

When I sat down I saw that my pen was rolling away from me. The bench is not quite level, and the pen was rolling like one of the logs upon which the Egyptians moved giant blocks of sandstone.

I reached to my left to grab it, but it escaped me by a micron. I extended myself. It escaped once more. And so on, until I found one part of me at one end of the bench and the other part at the other end. The bench is about five feet long, and my torso, from coccyx to glabella, about three feet long. This momentary extension, I believe, temporarily disconnected my arteries from my heart, which then stopped.

As luck would have it, gravity seized me and threw me upon the ground, snapping the arteries back into their accustomed ruts, and I survived. But the shock and pain of the temporary disconnection were such that I could not arise, and I lay by the bench for half an hour until a gardener discovered me and called an ambulance.

To my astonishment, the ambulance arrived at the hospital without killing anyone or turning over, and I was raced through the halls on a gurney as if I were in danger of death. I tried to explain, in Portuguese that had begun to fail me and turn into the plain idiom of my youth, that luck and gravity had reconnected my heart to the rivers of my blood, but no one understood. They were agitated, and I was tranquil. They worked about me as if in war, and I watched. I kept telling them not to rush, but they had probably seen too many American movies in which emergency rooms run at the pace of hand-to-hand combat.

"Look," I said, "the body is like a guitar. It has a certain music. Find the tempo of the music. Put on the music. I'm not a machine. Treat me with the rhythm of my own heart, and I'll be fine."

And those fools, they tied me to the table and gave me an injection of atropine. I needed rest, not twenty cups of purified cappuccino. It nearly killed me. Then they pounded on my chest like monkeys trying to open a coconut. They broke my sternum. Blood began to pour from my mouth.

I thought, this is it, I'm going to die even before I finish my memoir.

"Funio," I said, as they beat me relentlessly. "Funio, Funio," I cried, because I missed him. But then, as I jangled down the violent laundry chute that I thought would be my last, the music started. It came from within (they were too serious, those idiots, to have a radio), and it stabilized me in the surf that was tossing me about—until I felt that I rose above it, suspended in the sun, like Botticelli's Venus.

All was quiet, and I saw what seemed to be a great spiral shell of dawn-colored blue and glistening gold, braided and braiding, the one color twisting about the other, and I heard one note, a single call, a pure sound that gave me the strength to break the bonds with which they had tied me down.

They jumped back. Wouldn't you? I'm eighty years old, and the straps were thick. "I'm all right," I said. "All I need is an ice-cold glass of papaya juice."

This they understood, not because they're doctors but because they're Brazilians, and they turned off the timer that had been timing my death, let down their masks, and put away their stupid needles.

Then began six months of what was supposed to have been rest. The first two weeks of my recuperation were spent in the hospital itself. They took me to a room on a high floor overlooking the bay. I shared this room with a voodoo priest.

He had the same ailment I had: his blood vessels had been temporarily detached from his heart. It has happened to me now a few times, and now I know just to wait it out as you would a cramp or a headache. You see, the vessels are attached by means of some highly elastic material, and when they slip out they are under enormous pressure to resume their normal positions.

Of course, my physicians lampooned my understanding of cardiology, but I countered simply that as I had passed the age where they could make any claim to be effective, whatever kept me going was good medicine.

"You lose people at all stages of their lives," I said, "even adolescents as strong as wildebeests. And eighty-year-olds? All you can do with us is mimic the roles of drug pusher, jailer, and extortionist."

"We can't prolong life beyond its natural cycle," my physician replied. "We're not gods."

"Then let me go."

"We can't. You'll die."

"If I stay I'll die too, and I would much rather die in the rose garden in Niterói than here in this hideous hospital, next to *him*."

"What's wrong with him?"

"Oh, nothing," I said. "He's just a voodoo priest who watches television continually. He's a robot, a slave, a zombie. He spends many gleeful hours with soap operas, and watching cleavaged women spin game wheels. He shrieks when they give away toasters or wind-sailing boards, and the only time he rests is when it's time for the news. Then he switches off the apparatus and paws through the chicken hearts and lizard tails that are brought to him by a steady stream of women whose heads are wrapped in bandannas."

"Would you like to be moved?"

"You *can't* move me. I've asked and been told that it's impossible."

"You insult me as if I'm in a trance," the priest said, turning away from a scene of a man and a woman arguing next to a waterfall. "I hear you."

"You are in a trance. You watch that thing all day."

"It has good programs."

"Even if it did, and it doesn't, you would be wrong to watch it. It's a usurper, like a catbird, or carbon monoxide, or Claudius."

"You," the priest said, pointing his finger at me, "are a crazy person. *You* attacked *me*," he stated indignantly, "because I was drinking a cup of coffee."

"It wouldn't be the first time," I said under my breath, and then, because the doctor had left and the voodoo priest had turned away from me—not because he lacked the strength for argument but because a new program was starting—I fell back upon my pillows in weakness and defeat, but I remembered.

I had lost my battle with the world. No longer could I set foot in my own country, or speak my own language other than to a mischievous child prodigy or to oversexed Brazilian naval cadets who were required to take my course. I had long before alienated all my friends, or they had alienated me. I came to dislike most of them rather severely after a period of twenty or thirty years, when I would discover that I hadn't known them at all, and that they were capable of such things as abandoning their children, converting their faith, or attacking me because I do not drink coffee.

And coffee, of course, a drug, a filthy, malodorous poison and entirely destructive addiction, has vanquished the human soul, spoiled innocence, and destroyed childhood. It is virtually omnipotent: I have never convinced anyone, not even one person, not to drink it.

Miss Mayevska happened not to drink it, which was pure luck. But maybe, had she drunk it, she would have stopped—she, of all the people in the world—for she really loved me.

Constance drank, at first in secret. And Marlise. . . . Although of course Marlise would not drink at home, she drinks every day, several times—expresso, cappuccino, mocha, and God knows what else. She thinks it's perfectly normal and innocent, and has been drinking coffee since she was four. She does it as easily as breathing. That gorgeous body, that I have never been able to resist, has coffee flowing through its interior channels in total hideous corruption, and you would never know it. By the time we kiss, I can't even taste it. But it's there, it's working, it's horrible.

All over the world, people drink it, blindly, by the million, by the hundreds of millions, by the *billion*. And they must have it, they think they cannot do without it, and yet it is not a food, or water, or oxygen. No one would ever give it up for me, or for anyone else. It is more powerful than love.

The voodoo priest and all his powders were as nothing compared to expresso, cappuccino, and mocha, which are stronger than all the religions of the world combined, and perhaps stronger than the human soul itself. Even the voodoo priest consumed his many cups of coffee each day after I had been ignominiously wheeled into the hall.

At mealtimes the stench was appalling. People cannot even eat without it. They cannot wake without it. Many cannot sleep without it. They refer to it as *my*. "*My* coffee." On at least one occasion I have assaulted a waitress who approached me, asking, "Would you like your coffee now?"

"Madam!" I say, "it's not automatic! You assume too much! Just because you and most other people in the world are fiends and addicts does not mean that *I* am!"

Though I have made a thousand attempts at resistance and though I have as my model the French Underground, which ultimately was successful, I have not a single ally, not a single friend, and am doomed to fail. The gentle world has been enslaved by the drug and lubricant of the synchronous, the conforming, the coordinated, the collective, and the congruent.

My one strength, my one victory, is memory, for in memory I purify, in memory I am alone, in memory I appear before the highest judge, far above the static and the clouds, as if in the sunlit clearings of the garden in Niterói, where all is tranquil and the world below is cool, windy, and blue.

I sank back on my pillows in defeat, remembering my first mortal combat, which in many ways set the tone of my life. It was a melancholy thing brought to me so suddenly and unexpectedly that I have always equated it with an electric shock, something I came to know well soon after the defense of my existence was deemed to have been a sin.

Perhaps I should begin by telling you, if you don't already know, that cities—and the city of New York is the city I know best, the city of my birth—have a voice. I am not furthering some useless metaphor invented as the engine of a crackpot academic paper that stretches for pages and pages without ever coming to rest upon a concrete noun, or a color, or the story of something that really happened (or might have).

No. The city has a voice, and a song, that change over its history and can actually be heard. In 1950, when Manhattan had virtually no air conditioners, when office windows opened, and there were elevated trains, the white sound that lifted off the streets was very different from that of a quarter of a century later, when, as in São Paulo, the buildings no longer baffled sound, and millions of air conditioners were humming at a high pitch.

The presence or absence of automobiles, and then the variations in their number, the marked changes in engines and exhaust systems, horns, radios, the way doors sound when they are shut, etc., etc., all determine the symphony of the city. By 1950 most of the animals had disappeared from the street: no longer could you hear a hundred thousand horseshoes clomping on the macadam. I remember the sounds of crowds walking on leather soles, muffled and shuffling, that then turned into a billion dancing crickets with the advent of metal heel taps for men and high heeled shoes for women, and then these great choruses quietly stood down as if in awe of synthetic rubber.

I could probably write a book about these sounds—the ferry whistles; the changing jackhammers; the bus engines and pneumatic bus doors that over the years were as complicated as a piece by Debussy; the evolving howl as the dampening spiderwork of fire escapes disappeared and tall buildings became colossal whistles in the winter wind; the coming and going of hurdy-gurdies, sound systems, and trees—for, once, even in Manhattan, you could hear the trees. In winter they clicked against the windows with their skeletal twigs. In spring the soft new leaves hushed the city's other sounds to an adagio. In summer they received sudden rainstorms, as if to mimic the heavy surf or a waterfall. In autumn they rattled and jangled, as if to prepare for Christmas. And in three seasons they held the birds. Even if you see a bird in Manhattan now, I've been told you can hardly hear it. You wonder about your hearing, or if you have fallen into a silent movie, or if the bird is a deaf-mute who is going to walk up to you and hand you a little printed card.

As the million sounds of the city change over the years they do so with such slowness that the only way to hear them is in memory. In 1918, when I was fourteen years of age, the music of the city was played by horse's hooves, ferry whistles, steam trains, open windows, the wind in grilles and ladders, leather shoes upon the pavement, tapping canes, the cry of the junk men and food sellers, an occasional sputtering engine, and hundreds of thousands of trees that knit the streets back into the fabric of forest and field.

I lived with my uncle and my aunt, thirty-three miles to the north of Grand Central Station, in the town of Ossining. I stayed in the carriage house so as to escape the twice-daily stench of brewing coffee. Both my uncle and aunt were users, and had been so for many years, at times trying to prepare and drink coffee in my very presence.

Though I lived at a healthy remove, sometimes the wind would blow injudiciously and I would end up on the floor, convulsed, retching, struggling to breathe. Sometimes I would pass garbage cans and catch the smell of coffee grounds, which led to my first encounter with ambulances, which in those days were drawn by horses. Now I make wide diversions around garbage cans.

The summer of 1918 was the summer of Château-Thierry, Belleau Wood, Cantigny, and the Second Battle of the Marne. Although the American victories that marked the turning point of the war were attributed to a commander in chief we called "Pinchy-face," everyone knew that they were really the distant thunder of Theodore Roosevelt, whose presidency and character had shaped the American fighting man forever. For four years the Europeans had been doing a bloody isometric exercise, and then we came in, and as soon as we got going, everything started to move.

Some older boys that I knew had already enlisted, and some were actually serving. I was waiting my turn, hoping that America would drive to Berlin by autumn, and that the war would last three more years so I could do my part. (Perhaps I thought the investiture of the enemy capital might be very time-consuming.)

Whenever I could I ranged through the fields and woods with my Springfield rifle. As I had been doing this since the age of six, I was a keen shot, and I could move about noiselessly, always aware of everything around me. My preparation for war was not just childish fantasy. I had some idea, at least, of the reality. For reasons that I cannot easily relate, I understood that this was not a game. On the other hand, I was a boy of fourteen.

When school ended that year, as it did, almost always, on the 12th of June, I began, as I had from a very early age, to work. Only this time, as would befit a world changed by war, I milked no cows, picked no beans, spread no manure, and gutted no fish. Through the good offices of my uncle, I had obtained the job of runner and clerk for Stillman and Chase, the premier financial house of the world.

It was a nightmare job, and I would have done far better laboring in the fields. As I was supposed to arrive at offices on Broadway and 100th Street at eight A.M., I had to arise at five. This has become a lifelong habit, but I had never done it even on the farm and at first it was rather difficult. By the time I dressed, made breakfast, and set out for the station, it was six. I made the 6:40 train, reading the war news until Marble Hill, and switched to the Broadway IRT, a local all the way down.

If the train was late, so was I, and at Stillman and Chase if you didn't punch the clock by eight you were docked a day's pay. I was supposed to serve coffee to the account brokers, but of course that was impossible. I traded with a Negro boy, and he served the coffee while for an hour I shined shoes. From nine to ten he and I polished brass, wood, and marble, and then, at the market's opening bell, he kept polishing and I started running.

I made four round-trips each day between 100th Street and Wall Street, although the last return left me at Grand Central, where I boarded the train home. I carried a big canvas-and-leather bag sealed with a two-pound padlock and identified with a green leather patch that bore the inscription, *S&C—1409.* In this bag were orders, confirmations, stock certificates, and money.

We never carried more than a thousand dollars' worth of anything in the bag, but a thousand dollars then was enough to buy two automobiles, and runners were always being held up. Some disappeared, perhaps to start a new and richer life in a little town like Los Angeles, or perhaps to float face down in the East River. It was a dangerous job: you couldn't read on the subway, because you had to keep your eyes peeled.

That summer they tried to rob me about a dozen times—grown men, often in groups. Because the bag was locked around my waist they had either to kidnap me, cut the bag open, or cut it away from me.

When they tried to cut the bag away, it was with huge bolt cutters, and in the struggle they were never very accurate. I have bolt-cutter scars at my waist now, though they have faded. Over the years, the women with whom I have been intimate have always been intensely curious about these marks. The first time she saw them, Marlise said, "Oh, you old enough to be bite by dinosaur."

Cutting the bag open was no picnic either. We called that a "Mayor Gainor," after the mayor who was assassinated by a series of mechanically precise knife strokes in the gut. From my unfortunate perspective, the knives looked like windmill blades in the nickelodeon. I have their scars, too.

The kidnappers were the worst, because they would put a pistol up against you and threaten to shoot if you didn't go with them. If you *did* go with them, they would almost certainly kill you, so we refused to go, and some of us got shot. "Nothing's in the bag but orders!" I would shout, on the downtown run, or "Confirmations!" on the uptown. "The old man in the next car has a diamond stickpin, a cop is coming, I've got to go to the bathroom, I'm going to throw up." Then, in the moment of truth, I would break away. Breaking away has never failed me.

Not all was terror. I met a girl named Maggie, a cashier in a sheet-music store in Times Square. Maggie is not much of a name, but to me it was the most beautiful sound in the world.

She was fifteen, a superiority that I found totally oppressive, and she treated me with disdain that turned to amazement after I began passing to her the twenty-page love letters I would compose on weekends.

In her actual presence I was paralyzed and would turn the color of freshly butchered meat. I think she must have wondered why it was that I never seemed to breathe. Mostly I couldn't speak, but sometimes I would grunt like an ape. And once when she accidentally touched my hand I got an instant and unstoppable erection that required me to walk from the store doubled over with my forearms pressed against my thighs. With the Stillman and Chase bag strapped to my back, I looked like the Hunchback of Notre Dame all the way to Wall Street.

She had a blood-and-milk complexion, slightly carroty because she was Irish, strawberry-blond hair, green eyes, broad shoulders, and beautiful hands. If I had not been so awkward perhaps she might have understood how much I loved her. Even though I was an insane fourteen-year-old boy, I would have loved her as she may never have been loved in her life.

Once, my uncle looked at me askance and said, "Why is it that every two days you bring home a fresh copy of 'I'm a Yankee Doodle Dandy'? You don't even read music."

"I like it," I said.

"But having two copies doesn't change it, does it?"

"Yes," I said, floundering. "Yes, it does."

"How?"

Here, God threw me half a life preserver. I didn't hold it against Him, for when it has really been necessary, He has thrown me whole rafts of them. "It's like money," I said. "Every dollar bill is the same, isn't it? But you want as many as you can get."

Then God threw the other half of the life preserver to my

uncle. "They're not the same," he said, somewhat embarrassed. "Each one is different: *the serial numbers.*"

"That's idiotic," I replied, and so it went, as it always did in my affectionate struggle with my uncle, whose only fault was that he was not my father.

I was taken from him the summer that I worked for Stillman and Chase. And then, in another summer, when I had begun to work for Stillman and Chase in a more elevated capacity, he was taken from me. No one at Stillman and Chase even blinked. I walked around in a daze for two weeks, but for them it was business as usual. I didn't like that. Institutions, you see, can wear down the soul with relentless and uncompromising force. They expect mothers to leave their children, fathers to work themselves to death, and fourteen-year-old boys to get stabbed and cut and have cheap pearl-handled pistols shoved up their nostrils.

No one ever complains as one would if just a man were to require the same. As an apprentice, you learn not to harbor a grudge against the abstraction that loots your days, breaks your health, or demands your life. But I was taught something different. For whatever reason, I see corporate bodies, entities, even principles, the way primitive people saw the stars. I group their million unaccountable points into one bear, or one archer, or one Perseus holding the head of one Medusa, and I hold them accountable as if they were the man sitting next to me on the trolley.

Perhaps the people who staff the institution, by reason of their human frailty, cannot always be held accountable, but the institution itself need not ever be let off the hook. It lives by the myth of its singularity, and by the myth of its singularity it can be taken by the throat.

All of which has nothing to do with the first man I killed, except that it makes clear why, in the summer of 1918, my thoughts were martial and I was continually armed. I was not going to lay down my life before highwaymen, or, better, subwaymen, without a struggle. I carried a Colt .45 automatic of the type issued to our soldiers in France, and which had been developed to stop the fanatics of Samar.

I practiced in the woods, and at twenty-five feet I could blow out the glass eye of a stuffed owl. What is more, with my lightning reflexes, strong hands, and youthful freshness, I could withdraw the pistol, release the safety catch, pull back the slide, express a round into the chamber, aim, and fire, all in less than a second.

When my uncle gave me the pistol he impressed upon me the need for restraint, and I was determined not to use it unless I thought I was about to be killed. I was meticulous about justification, and in my mind's eye I see a boy surrounded by flailing blades and fists, fighting like a dervish, cut, bruised, and bleeding, but never making use of the powerful weapon he carried, never giving death too much the benefit of the doubt. And although the pistol was by my side when I killed the first man I killed, I didn't use it. But the fact that I was possessed of such a deadly weapon when I was apprehended near the scene of the struggle was not a point in my favor. My 'attorney' tried to make it so, maintaining that I did not resort to it even while brutally attacked, but his arguments were always very badly bungled by his everpresent co-counsel, Jack Daniels.

Because I was out of the country and in an insane asylum, I never had the chance to appeal. When you write to the authorities from such a place you are at a disadvantage in regard to your credibility. And I was in an insane asylum because the judge gave me a choice of attending the world's finest private school, in the most beautiful region of the Swiss Alps, or sitting in the electric chair.

Before you consider what happened to me on the beautiful, hot evening of August 20th, 1918, please understand that, apart from my persecution by coffee—every child in the Western World is pressured to accept this drug—my other difficulty in adjustment has been that from the earliest age I have been congenitally unable to know my place.

When I listened to idealistic ministers and politicians taken up in flights of rhetoric about the American ideal, I believed them. I still do. I believe that all the children of God stand before Him as exact equals. I believe that temporal power is an illusion and an irrelevancy. I believe that, because the president of the United States and, let us say, an illiterate sharecropper, occupy God's affections solely according to God's criteria, neither is owed either more or less respect than the other. Though these are the things that I believe, there are some things that I *know*. They are that upon these ideals American democracy was founded and that every citizen may, by right, and in any circumstance, properly demand them, and that I and everyone else serve only one master.

As you can imagine, I have had problems. Given that my place in various hierarchies has been an illusion accepted only by others, I have suffered continual charges of insubordination. And yet, on the several occasions that I have met, for example, presidents of the United States, we have gotten along very well even though I cannot speak to them in the language that everyone else seems to use, even though I cannot bend my knee.

Apart from presidents, prime ministers, and popes, all of whom in my experience have been easy going and delightfully egalitarian, I have had immense struggles with teachers, conductors, police, professors, and people from all walks of life who believe that their rank as they see it requires me, for example, to jump out of their way when they walk down the street. Some people think that if they dress in a certain fashion they are entitled to deference from other people in different attire. Is this not madness?

My irritation with this kind of thing may sometimes cause me to be rather blunt. When, for Stillman and Chase, I used to fly back and forth between the United States and various countries in Europe, I noticed that the pilots would always make what appeared to have been inspection tours in the cabins of the planes.

Because the passengers knew that their lives depended upon the mental and biological vagaries of these aeronauts, they would make submissive gestures, which the captains and copilots lapped up as they strode royally down the aisles.

But what were they inspecting? Seating position and weight distribution? Cracks in the fuselage? The quality of the engine exhaust? Of course not. They had nothing to inspect. They were on their way to the bathroom. After I realized this, I would sometimes drop my reading glasses a notch and, without looking up, say rather dryly but so that all could hear, "Ladies and gentlemen, the captain is triumphantly proceeding to the toilet." You can imagine how cordially I was treated after that. A certain kind of person grew very angry at me for mocking the authority upon which we depended, and, man or woman, would berate me with a finger wagging, afraid that the captain would punish me by crashing the plane into the sea. As I had actually crashed a plane into the sea, I was confident that the pilots would not consider this option.

Given my difficulties with rank and hierarchy, I sometimes wonder why I had such a good time with the Pope.

I was by then a full partner at Stillman and Chase, which means that had I been someone else I would have thought that I was higher than the Pope, for the partners of Stillman and Chase were a Cromwellian bunch who considered the Pope to be a kind of jungle medicine man.

I was the right person to send, as I believed that the Pope and I, and anyone else for that matter, were of the same rank, and therefore I was less likely to offend him. Which may have been why they sent me, although they didn't care whether they offended the Pope or not, and it was more likely that they sent me because I had spent so much time in Italy during the war, and knew the language.

The United States, the only undamaged major industrialized country, was for the Vatican a source of immense concern in regard to the investment and stability of Church funds. After several days of meeting with various accounting cardinals in what amounted to a dissertation defense of our foreign investment strategies, I was granted an audience with the Holy Father. I think the accounting cardinals assumed I would turn to jelly and count every second as if it were a gold bar, but as fate would have it we bumped into the Pope in a corridor rather than in a reception room, and I, buoyant after passing my orals, ran up to him and said, "Oh hi! We were just on our way to see you."

The cardinals didn't like this, and didn't like that shortly after we began to walk I went to an open window in the corridor and stuck my head out into the evening sun. It was May, the time in Rome when perfection takes its name amid the balances of light and dark, blazing sun and blinding moon, the Tiber flowing, still cool and powerful, the birds surfing upon the rollers and breakers of green that have newly crowned the avenues and hills.

All day long I had been inside a magnificent frescoed chamber, listening to the warm wind as it coursed through the trees. I could not resist the open window, and, as soon as I felt the sun on my face, my expression became, I suppose, beatific. The next thing I knew, the Pope, who had dismissed everyone else, was standing next to me, his head thrust out the window too, his little white hat in his hand.

"How often do you get outside?" I asked.

"I have a garden, where I go every day."

"Is that enough? Do you ever swim in the sea, or spend weeks in the mountains?"

"Not really, not since I was a boy."

"Why not?"

He shrugged his shoulders.

"Look," I said, "tomorrow's Sunday. Why don't you put on some regular clothes, and we'll take the train to Ostia."

"I can't do that," he said. "I'm the Pope."

"Oh come on. It won't be crowded. The Italians think the sea is too cold for swimming now, but the Tyrrhenian is warmer than the sea off Southampton will ever be, and I swim there in May. I swim off Mount Desert Island in *June*."

"Mount Desert Island?" the Pope asked. "In Purgatory?"

We began to talk—about places we knew, childhood, the music in natural sounds such as the surf, the wind, and the songs of the birds, and we touched upon many things, from politics to beekeeping.

I left about nine, after some nuns had served dinner in the Pope's little garden and we played bocce. I remember what we ate: a mixed salad with tomatoes, arugula, lettuces, and a few thin slices of mozzarella; beef broth with gnocchi; a piece of broiled fish; bread; and mineral water. It was served on a small wooden table that must have been five hundred years old, and the china and cutlery were as simple as if we had been in a *pensione* near the station that catered mainly to soldiers, Sicilian migrants, and African exchange students.

He was very surprised, indeed, astonished, when I asked him about his parents. He was moved, and he said, "In all these years, no one has ever asked me about my father and my mother, and yet I think of them every day. Why *did* you ask?"

"It seemed to me," I told him, "that you must think back all the time, and that your memories must be very vivid."

"Yes, yes," he said, "but how do you know that?"

"Well," I continued, putting down my fork, "God puts more of Himself in the love of parent and child than in anything else, including all the wonders of nature. It is the prime analogy, the foremost revelation, the shield of His presence upon earth. As you don't have your own children, you must refer to that holy relation in memories dredged deep and with great love."

He half-closed his eyes, and nodded as I spoke, as if, as I spoke, he were remembering.

"*I* do," I said. "I love children, and I don't have any yet, so I often think back, using my memory not as self-indulgence but as holy instruction."

"*Yes*," he said. "I frequently visit orphanages. The children . . . they. . . ."

"They break your heart," I said, "for in them, too, the arc is broken, and God's warmth must ride over an abyss."

Now, you may wonder how I can jump so quickly from the holy to the profane in this, my narrative, but in life it happens all the time. The one alternates with the other continually. In fact, they seem to be locked in dependency, and my memoir takes me, as if in some sort of planned traverse, from a quiet garden in the Vatican, where I was the sole dinner companion of the Pope, to the great hall of Grand Central Station, at 5:06 in the evening of the 20th of August, 1918.

It was a Tuesday. It was so hot that men loosened their ties as they descended the stairs to the immense room, and you could see pigeons on the high ledges fanning their wings as if they had just been in a bird bath. The whistles were blowing in the caverns below, the sun streaming in the windows, and I was fourteen years of age.

I knew virtually nothing. I was consumed with passion for young Maggie in the sheet-music store, whom I never kissed, never held. I wonder if she's still alive, and I wonder if she wonders if I'm still alive. Maybe she does.

My great thought at that pregnant hour was that I might have a chance in the evening to swim in the Hudson before I got home, for we were having a cold dinner of smoked chicken and salad, which could wait without prejudice. I bought the evening newspaper, took a drink from a fountain, and walked to my train. The surface of the concrete ramp leading down to the trains was salted with ground glass, and as is often the case in New York the pavement sparkled as if in a fairy tale.

Although I could not, without looking, tell you what clothes I am wearing now, and have never been able to remember what I had for dinner five minutes after I finish, or whether I locked the front door, or closed my safe-deposit box, I can tell you exactly what I was wearing then.

A straw boater. Everyone wore a straw boater in the summer. Everyone. Not women, of course, but women did not commute. A few could be seen on the morning trains, going down to shop or visit, but they usually returned in the middle of the afternoon, so that they could go to the market and then prepare dinner.

By evening, the trains were men's clubs. Liquor was served by the gallon. Cards were played on tables and knee boards, and conversation was usually confined to the seven great topics: fishing, money, war, politics, automobiles, women, and woodworking. Had it not been for the fact that we were speeding along at forty miles an hour and no hair was being cut, it could have been a very crowded barbershop.

A blue whipcord suit. It was my first suit. I had been in knickers up to that point, but Stillman and Chase runners wore suits. They weren't supposed to have been boys, although I certainly was, but I could pass for a young man because I was tall for my age. On the train I always took a window seat on the river side, and spent the hour transfixed either by the scenery or by my evening newspaper. That way, I didn't have to talk, my voice didn't have to crack, and I could pretend to be older.

In July the sun was too strong and the shades were down on the river side, but by August you could look out the window. That evening, the window was open and the breeze came in as the train moved north. It was a warm breeze, but it was a lot better than the hot pressurized air of Manhattan.

The man on my right had gulped down two Scotch-and-sodas, tried to read the war news, and fallen dead asleep. The conductor woke him just before Tarrytown, and he got off there, leaving me the prize of an empty seat. I put my right hand on the wicker and my left foot on the sill, and as the train wound toward Ossining, began to whistle softly to myself. Although I was the owner of at least two dozen copies of 'I'm a Yankee Doodle Dandy,' as I looked over miles of open water, the blue-green hills beyond, and herons wheeling on the hot afternoon wind or stalking daintily through the marsh, I whistled the Third Brandenburg.

And then the Walloon sat in the empty seat next to me. "Be quiet," he ordered. "Put your foot down, and shut up."

His commands were tense and inexplicably full of hate. I was used to being suddenly wrestled to the ground, or to having a knife put to my throat. I knew how to deal with something like that, but not with gratuitous hatred.

I learned that he was a Walloon only after it was all over, although I understood immediately from his accent and dress that he was foreign. He was about six feet four inches tall. Well, he was exactly that, and he weighed 196 pounds on autopsy. Twenty-seven years old, he had close-cropped silver-blond hair and, though he looked pale and unhealthy, he was an accomplished athlete. Not pertinent, but for me unforgettable, was the fact that his intensely blue eyes were magnified by pewter-rimmed spectacles.

I weighed 117 pounds and was fully one foot shorter than he. I was used to being bullied. All boys are bullied by older boys. I would have swallowed my pride, taken my foot from the sill, and stopped my whistling, but for one thing.

He had in his hands a cup of steaming hot coffee. No one ever drank hot coffee in the summer on the trains. To this day, I don't know where he got it. The police and the trial lawyers couldn't figure that out either. The rather odd supposition of the detectives was that someone had handed it to him from the platform at Tarrytown.

I tried to be polite. I even downplayed my movements of avoidance. But after five minutes I couldn't help myself. The stench stimulated in me a reaction of utter revulsion and disgust. I stood, reeled, retched, and bolted into the aisle. In doing so, I spilled the coffee, all of it. Some fouled my suit, causing me to retch even more and stagger away in horror, as if a tarantula were clinging to the small of my back, but most of it went directly into the Walloon's lap.

It was boiling hot. Summer suits were then, as now, of very light and, more importantly, very porous material. He screamed at a volume that you would not, could not, believe unless you have had a boiling hot liquid poured on your lap, and he ripped open his fly—I suppose to let the cool air in—and fanned the area with both hands, desperately, all the while screaming "Ahh! Ahhh! Ahhhhh!"

This provoked amusement among the other passengers. In fact, it created hysteria. And when the Walloon, still screaming and fanning himself, got up to chase after me, someone, and then everyone, began to sing, "It's a long way to Tipperary, it's a long long way."

"It's a long way to Tipperary, it's a *long long* way!" they sang as I made my way down the aisle, half in uncontrollable laughter, half in unspeakable terror. And when I reached the vestibule, I heard someone say, "Go get him!"

My God! I thought to myself, he's going to beat me to a pulp. He might kill me by accident, or on purpose. There was hardly any difference—not for me, anyway. Should I use the gun? "No no no!" I told myself. "If I kill him, I'll be executed!"

I had to find a conductor. But the conductors had taken all the tickets. I knew they were at the rear of the train, in hot black suits like missionaries on their way to the Congo, huddled over books, papers, and money as they tallied the fares and bundled up tickets.

The cars seemed more and more empty the farther forward I was driven. I had developed a lead when the Walloon stopped to button his fly even though by that time no one else was around. As I would leave the car I had just dashed through, I would hear the door open at the other end.

He could run faster than I could. He could throw open heavy doors far more easily. He was gaining very rapidly, and he was almost on me. The train rushed past Scarborough. I knew that if I could last until Ossining, I might escape. But if the train made an unscheduled stop at Sing Sing, as it often did, the Walloon was going to kill me.

Naturally, the train began to slow for the stop at Sing Sing. This was where, winter or summer, condemned prisoners left cars full of prosperous commuters for a gray valley of stone that rose in steep walls on either side of the tracks.

If you didn't know how it went, you might think that I was safe. Even though no one met the party exiting at Sing Sing, the passenger there descending would, by definition, be accompanied by agents of the law. All I had to do was get off and run to them.

But the trains were fourteen, sixteen, eighteen cars long. If the prison party were in the rear, I would be almost at Ossining, too far away to be noticed. My only salvation lay with the engineers, or with disappearing into the warrens of the town I knew as well as a rat knows his tunnel.

I was confounded, however, when I discovered that the car I was just about to enter was locked. Three cars back from the engine, I could no longer go forward. Turning to look behind me, I saw the Walloon opening the door of the coach I had just been through.

I opened the door that faced him, and stepped through. He halted. Even in the midst of his anger, caution got the better of him, and what seemed to be my bold and inexplicable move stopped him dead. Perhaps I shouldn't use that word, yet.

I had had no urge to heroism, and this he discovered as he saw me desperately yanking at the handle of the bathroom door. They were steel, they had locks. In this, my first mortal combat, I sought a toilet compartment as a citadel. And in this, my first mortal combat, I was uncontrollably singing to myself, and the song—I could not help myself—was: "I'm a Yankee Doodle *dandy*, I'm a Yankee Doodle *boy*!"

The bathroom was locked solid. A spirit exists throughout the land that locks the bathroom doors on trains and in city parks, and it existed even then. I went back into the vestibule and tried to pull open the door to the outside, but in my desperation I jammed it into the hinged platform that covered the steps leading down, and the two fused into an angular barrier.

As I was trying to disengage them, the Walloon appeared. I jumped back. Even had I time to explain, I would not have bothered: he had murder in his eyes. "You spilled coffee on me!" I shouted with fading indignation.

At this apparent taunt, his eyes widened and he bared his teeth. I thought of taking out the .45 and shooting him, but it was too horrible to imagine, even more horrible, I discovered, than the anticipation of my own disfigurement. By that late moment I had revised my estimates and was hoping that he meant to punish rather than kill me.

I shrank into a corner and covered my face with my hands. The train was beginning to move again. The Walloon grabbed me by the lapels and the neck, and started to beat my head against the steel partition. This was when I knew, even in the fume of combat, that my latest estimate had been a futile hope. The more he banged my head against the metal, the purpler he grew, the tighter he clenched his fists, and the more he cursed in Walloon.

I tried to get to the gun. I might just as well have tried to sing a Walloon lullaby. It didn't work. The gun was in the Stillman and Chase bag, banging nobly against the partition half a second after my head. My gun, I thought, is mocking me as I die.

I wondered if I were sustaining multiple concussions to my brain, and I had the nauseating thought that, eventually, the skull would be smashed and the brain would be crushed. I felt guilty for not having shot him. I tried to say something. Nothing came out.

Then, one of the many small gifts of God that shower upon the earth like a misty rain. The train went over a bump, the kind of obstruction or unevenness that leaps through the dragonlike segments in the rail like a whiplash. Drinks must have been spilled, and hands of gin and poker tossed into the air like roosters.

It is likely that a juvenile delinquent in Ossining had put either a spike or a metamorphic rock on the rail. The door and the hinged platform disengaged explosively, and the air rushed in.

The Walloon hesitated for an instant, turning to see what he had just heard. In this long, long moment, which passed before my eyes as if life had stopped and I was viewing it from afar, I actually felt that I was the recipient of a question slowly voiced by a miraculous higher presence.

Do you want to live, or do you want to die?

My fear vanished. In the fog and the roar, I was no longer aware of fear, but only of this simple question. I cried, or at least I felt what you feel when you cry, for I hadn't the time for a tear to roll from my eye, and then I smiled.

"Live!" I said from deep in my chest, as strongly as I've ever uttered any single word. And the word was not merely beautiful, it was electric, it was full of sound and light, it had history, it smiled, it was like the greatest blast of the greatest organ in the greatest cathedral, and, on second thought, it made even that seem undramatic.

Your eyes narrow when you take blows, and widen when you deliver them, and just the opening of my eyes served to call forth strength that then called forth other strengths and then exploded into one single movement. With a roar like that of a beast on the savannah, I rose with the Walloon, lifted him in

the air, and pushed him with ineluctable force through the opening to the outside.

As a body in motion tends to remain in motion, and nothing
was in his way, he sailed out of the train like an astronaut blown
from an airlock. As he flew backward, his expression was that
of amazement. He had not quite synthesized the thought, or at
least it had not yet made its way to the muscles of his face. What
he might have wanted to think, had he the time, was, "How
did he do that?" For, indeed, I had made him airborne.

He was one of those people who are forever wan, pale, tense,
and unlucky (law firms have had worse names). I have encountered them all my life. Something gray about their souls drives
off all the sweet and colorful things that they might otherwise
pick from the air like fruit. If they travel to Hawaii, it will snow.
If they cut hay, it will rain. If they have to fight a battle, it will
be at the juncture of four map sections.

Ah, but he was unlucky, unlucky supreme. The platform in
Ossining was in the midst of revision. Part of it had been torn
up, and the debris piled just south of the station, toward Sing
Sing. Perhaps the blessed delinquent had obtained the magic
steel or holy rock from this pile: I don't know.

I do know, purely from hindsight, although the prosecutor
went so far as to suggest that I had arranged it, that a section
of iron fence had been torn up and cast upon this pile. It was
a row of iron spears sunk into concrete, now pointing at a
perfectly martial 45-degree angle. At some point in history,
fences must actually have been made of spears.

The unlucky gray Walloon flew backward through space,
puzzled in his last moments, until he was perfectly impaled upon
the row of spear points that were exactly perpendicular to the
plane of his body during its final trajectory.

For more than three years, the Belgians had been held up to

the world as its greatest martyrs. Witnessing the impalement, even I suddenly felt a spur of guilt, and reached into the air to check for a sharp Hun-like spike growing from the helmet that was my head. It did not help that the judge was himself a Walloon-American. Throughout the trial he made many not-so-subtle inquiries, the obvious objective of which was to determine if my forebears were Huguenots. At each one, my uncle had to kick Jack Daniels from behind, and operate him like a puppet, so he would object. We very badly wanted to change counsel, but were advised that doing so would somehow imply that we were guiltier even than charged, and, besides, Jack Daniels was the dean of the Ossining criminal bar, and any lawyer not a native of Ossining was, of course, doomed.

The case for self-defense was so clear-cut, however, that I probably would have gotten off despite all the irregularities and despite Jack Daniels's brilliant summation, which began with the words, "Sir Honor! Surely, this was a clorse of surf de-florse!" and went on for an hour or two like that, with the jury at the edge of its seats, straining forward, trying to understand what he was saying.

My outburst and attack at the end of the proceedings was what did me in. I suppose I should have known, I suppose I should have been expecting the provocation, because at the end of trials in Ossining it was customary to serve coffee to the judge in an effort to sober him up for his soliloquy.

Thus, I was launched from childhood in the New World into the beginning of manhood in the Old. This was a great and salutary shock to my system. For despite the fact that I was wrenched early from my home, which I loved, and shamed in the streets of Paris on my way to confinement in an asylum high in the mountains, I was blessed by the great light of civilization.

Granted, it was then, as the smoke of war began to clear, a

muted light, but its weakness allowed me to look straight at it without being overwhelmed. And as it grew in strength, I followed, so that my education, though idiosyncratic, was nonetheless perfectly timed.

Though taken from my home, I was given Miss Mayevska, the emblem of my heart. Though removed from the Hudson, I was given the Alps. Though separated from my native idiom, I was presented with the languages of Europe. Though summoned for punishment at an early age, I was given, perhaps by the shock of events, a most wonderful gift. The great loves of my youth—for my parents; my home; Miss Mayevska; for God Himself, undoubted, untarnished, immediate—remain.

Constance

*(If you have not done so already,
please return the previous pages to the antproof case.)*

IT MAY BE silly, but when I remember Constance I often think of a little red plastic hat, no larger than my hand, bobbing up and down in front of me on a clear and frigid night in the White Mountains of New Hampshire. The hat rode upon the massive head of curly hair atop an economist walking in front of me over a log bridge that led to a conference room.

He held it in place by clasping the tiny brim between thumb and forefinger. The hat would block out some stars and then let their light through to my eyes, and before he went in, he rested it on a bank of powdery snow.

Amidst the conversation once we were inside, the bluff, too-deep, artificially jovial speech that conceals men maneuvering for position like warships at the Battle of Trafalgar, no one gave a thought to the hat. We had filed into a room overlooking a snow-covered field, there to discuss monetary policy and the rebuilding of Europe. Who cared about a tiny plastic hat that was made in Japan?

I did. I looked at it sitting in the snow drift, and I thought to myself (or, rather, I felt) that it was time to father the child for whom such a thing might have value and to whom it could bring amusement. So I went back out, took it from the snow, and put it in my pocket. After I had taken off my coat and assumed a place at the table, I briefly experienced the beatific feeling, the contentment, and the love, that one feels when cradling an infant in one's arms.

Perhaps it showed on my face. Certainly, of the people who were in the room, all eager to promote their causes and show themselves off, I was the least competitive and the least in the mood for combat. At that moment I could think of nothing but babies, and a great wave of tenderness swept through me.

This was in the winter of 1947, and the conference on monetary policy was one of many that took place in the wake of Bretton Woods. The White Mountains were to economists then what Paris had once been to artists. And it didn't hurt that in the off hours you could ski.

I had had no desire to attend this meeting. I was neither an economist nor an academic, nor well acquainted with monetary theory. My job at Stillman and Chase was to assess the condition of a particular country and make predictions about its future, its political stability, military capacity, and social peace. With this, the financial gnomes would tailor their own recommendations, which would then be transmitted to me and to the other partners, and I would comment on them as far as I could in terms of my original judgments.

For example, if we wanted to finance a railroad somewhere, I might insist that it be routed away from a secessionist area with a history of disrupting lines of supply. Or I might say, don't advance a nickel to country C, because country B will swallow it within two years.

My sense of economics was derived from nothing more sophisticated than an understanding of ten or twenty basic economic relations and a thorough and intuitive sympathy with the Swiss. I measured a country's economic prospects against the Swiss model, mixing in decidedly noneconomic phenomena, but my appraisals never failed, if only because, finally, the study of economics is dependent upon an understanding of politics, character, and art.

Switzerland's economy can be understood in sixteen words: freedom, democracy, discipline, savings, investment, risk, responsibility, secrecy, pride, preparation, perfectionism, asceticism, peace, foresight, determination, and honor. The Swiss have a million excellent incentives to do well, but their original spur was that they had absolutely nothing and were too isolated on high to hope that anyone would listen to them complain.

I could fill this entire antproof case with an essay on Switzerland. I grew up there, and the foundation of my sympathy is that I spent years in the mountains. The mountains, shrouded in fog or shining in the sun, are the heart of the country, and perhaps the heart of the world.

The directors of Stillman and Chase wanted to expose me to monetary theory and get me out of the office. I never accommodated to the office. My forte was investigation. I would go to a country, put a knapsack on my back, and walk for weeks: talking to everyone I met; going into the factories, workshops, and stores; interviewing the editors of as many newspapers as I could in the medium-sized cities; studying all available statistics; poring over maps; and checking the workmanship and design of indigenous products. I would walk along the rail lines and see how well they were maintained, and at what speed the trains traveled and how full they were. In a few weeks, hardened, sunburned, with a portrait of the country's economy fully formed in my mind, I would visit the leaders of its government and business community, and listen to them skirt around the many flaws that might have been hidden from someone who had not covered five hundred miles on foot.

I was to Stillman and Chase what T. E. Lawrence had been to the English generals: they could not do without me, but they wished desperately that they could. I made or saved them immense amounts of money—in current dollars, literally billions.

Because of this, they tolerated my idiosyncrasies. In most investment banks, however, I wouldn't have lasted five seconds, but I started at Stillman and Chase in 1917 and was so senior at the firm that they tried to view my peculiarities as tradition.

To wit: I arise at five in the morning, a habit I learned during my first stint at Stillman and Chase, as I have mentioned. So I was always at my desk at 5:45. They loved this. To them, I was the ideal Protestant, except that . . . I insist upon an afternoon nap. No matter where I am, I must sleep for an hour or two after lunch.

I have a favorite blanket, of Pendleton virgin wool, rust-colored on one side and gun-metal-colored on the reverse. If anyone other than me touches it, he's a dead man. When I roll up in my blanket on the floor, I'm asleep instantaneously. In '29, they thought I had committed suicide. No one could get in my office because I locked the door, and I used to take my telephone off the hook. It isn't my fault that the American business world considers taking a brief rest to be a form of vicious moral degeneracy. Why should they? In Europe, everyone takes naps.

And I must exercise, every day, for about three hours. I can't now, but I used to run five miles, cycle ten, row two, and devote a full hour to calisthenics, gymnastics, boxing, and weight lifting. This tended to make a rather large hole in my morning schedule, especially because, after exercising for three hours, my custom—indeed, my requirement—was to practice the piano for two hours. I can't play the piano well, but I struggle along even now on my antproof zinc-plated Brazilian Schrobenhausen, which sounds like forty crates of silverware falling down the stairwells of the Empire State Building. Two hours a day, every day, and you can stay limber enough to play all your favorite pieces. Stillman and Chase had a magnificent concert grand that was my main reason for going to the office. It was the best Mozart piano I've ever played, and as I played mainly Mozart, what further can I say?

They also were not fond of the fact that I cannot wear a tie. I mean, I wear it, but loosened. If it's tight I feel that a hangman's noose is closing around my neck. The longest I can go with a properly knotted tie is about half an hour. Even when I was walking around with the Pope, the tie was loosened. The Pope didn't even notice. After all, he doesn't wear a tie.

My other idiosyncrasies? I can't wear shoes. My feet are highly unstable on account of the huge curvature of my legs. I was born several months ahead of schedule, with a lot of bones not exactly the way they should be. My leg bows give me almost supernatural strength—the Roman arch—but I need very stable shoes, so I wear only climbing boots. At formal functions, they tend to stand out.

And, finally, I need oxygen. Perhaps it is my history at Château Parfilage, or the constant pertaflexions of my brain, but I need huge amounts of oxygen. Though I get it mainly by being in the open, when inside I must have a fan blowing in my face.

Shortly after the White Mountains incident, Stillman and Chase remodeled the executive floors in such a way that the windows would no longer open. I was astonished. Fresh air is elemental. If you doubt me, try holding your breath for two minutes. How could anyone deliberately shut out the air? Buildings with windows that don't open may be economical but they are also insane.

The engineers told me that if they were to cut a window for me all the air would exit at that point, and the resulting lift would suck out everything not bolted to the floor—papers, books, lamps, my blanket, even me. I was in despair, and then I thought of scuba.

Only my secretary knew, and she would warn me so I could put the scuba tanks in a closet before I received a visitor. Once, however, I forgot that I was wearing them, and rushed to meet the Italian minister of finance at a partners' lunch. The directors were mortified, but the minister of finance, whom I knew, said, "Do you have those things, what do they call them, flippers, too? You must come next summer to my house in Portofino. There you can see many colorful fishes."

For whatever reason, the firm sent me to the winter conference, and I was eager to go because I love the mountains and in winter they are flooded with light and oxygen. There I was, at a huge square table seating thirty, rocking an imaginary baby in my arms like a nursing mother, as the conference began a discussion of certain economic theories of which I have always been highly skeptical.

Strategically located between the participants were silver trays upon which were a bottle of Glenlivet, ice, water, glasses, and peanuts. Soon everyone was drinking Scotch and eating peanuts. It smelled like the zoo in Edinburgh. When grown men eat peanuts they toss them into their mouths in a motion that makes them look as if they're challenging themselves to a duel. The fact that they were academic economists and rather inebriated made it all the stranger. I waited for music, perhaps *The Nut-cracker*.

Then I caught a glimpse of the only woman in the group. She was sitting three professors to my right, mainly obscured. Those in between us were rather bulky, and she had taken a nervously diminutive position, not knowing what to do or what to say. No one spoke to her, as, I noticed, no one was speaking to me, and she, like me, was not insulting herself with liquor and peanuts.

How could they not have spoken to her! She was such that even now, thirty-seven years later, upside-down and half a world away, I burn with my recollection of her. So many women make their mark or carry their beauty in their body, or their hair, or their coloring. All this she had, but with Constance it was her face, that basic and elemental portal and expression of the soul, that made her so absolutely arresting. The coalition of features that other women try to alter, enhance, or hide, drew my eye to it immediately and was the source of a thousand strong emotions.

I shall not name them: the list would be too long. The moment I saw her, I felt a rush of vitality that I recalled having experienced before only as I bailed out of an airplane that was on fire. For an instant, I stopped breathing. I tried not to look at her.

To look at her meant leaning either forward or backward and turning obviously to the right. My position would have been betrayed. And, then, her effect on me was one of paralysis and reevaluation. Every time I meet a woman like Constance (only three times, and the first time I was too young, the third time too old), I want to change my profession, move to a mountain cabin or a weather station on an atoll, and spend the rest of my life embracing her. And whenever it happens, I behave rashly.

I sat there, heart pounding, face flushed, gales of pleasure sweeping through my body like a strong summer rain sweeping over the sea. I prayed that she was not married, and that she would marry me. I suppose I knew she would, but I was deathly afraid that she wouldn't.

When at last I was face to face with her—and I'm getting ahead of myself—I was stunned by her name tag. It read: Constance Olivia Phoebe Ann Nicola Devereaux Jamison Buckley Andrews Smith Faber Lloyd.

"Which one are you?" I asked, archly.

"All of us," she answered in precisely the same tone.

"Your name suggests," I told her, "the merger of England and Venezuela."

What was I doing? I loved this woman with every atom of my body and each ether of my soul.

"The next thing I expect from *you*," she said, "is that you'll ask if I'm Italian."

"No. I was just wondering if you were a platoon, and I wanted to tell you that your name tag is not in compliance with the housing code. You'll have to build an annex."

I sat back as if I had inhaled half a blimp of nitrous oxide. A buffet dinner was arrayed along a table under windows that looked over a snowfield. A fire was burning in the fireplace, and, of course, once I had caught a glimpse of Constance, in me.

To get from the train to the conference site one had to summon a horse-drawn sleigh, which would come, bells ringing, in the moonlight. It is hard to imagine that for the sake of automobiles that rush around like cockroaches we have forsaken the inimitable beauty of horses drawing sleighs over the snow.

Because I had had to make a stop at an affiliate in Boston I had arrived on the last train. My secretary was told that at the time of my arrival the sleighs would be engaged in a hayride, and that I would have to walk from the station. As it was a distance of five miles or so, I had changed into my cold-weather parka and pants, and I carried whatever else I had with me in a pack.

How delightful it was to walk in the light of the full moon and in the ten-degree air, from which every hint of corruption had been precipitated. I was forty-two years of age, I had survived the war, and I was ready once again to fall in love. Miss Mayevska, her husband, and children, were gone. I felt that I owed her my own happiness, and that in my children I would see hers. My feelings were conflicted, but I decided that at every opportunity I would seek the vital, the holy, and the beautiful; that for her sake, as well as for the sake of others, I was obliged to make the best of whatever came my way. And I did, I suppose, never allowing calculation to dim sadness or joy.

Arriving at the conference just in time, I carried my pack inside and laid it in a corner. Even before I saw Constance my face was burning from the cold, and I may have looked far younger than my years because I was relaxed and happy after the walk.

Circumstances beyond my control had spared me many of the signs of middle age. I had been demobilized only for a year and a half, and had kept the habit of air-crew fitness, even enlarging upon it with my three hours of exercise, my afternoon naps, and my ten miles of walking each day to and from Wall Street (Broad Street, actually). And, as you know, I don't drink coffee (subtract twenty years).

All of which is to say that they thought I was a student. When I came in I was handed a name tag, and as I didn't have my reading glasses I pinned it on without noticing that it said

STUDENT OBSERVER, WABASH COLLEGE. I was entirely unaware
of this until the next day, after much had transpired, when
Constance proposed that she visit Wabash College.

"Why?" I asked.

"So I can be near you," she answered.

"That's very sweet of you," I answered, thinking that perhaps
Wabash College was near Wall Street, "but I live uptown."

"You don't live on campus?"

I laughed.

"Most people do."

"Most people do what?" I asked.

"Live on campus. Don't they?"

"What campus?"

"Wabash College."

I was puzzled. "What exactly are you saying, Constance?"

"Most students of Wabash College live on the campus of
Wabash College, is that not so?"

"It sounds reasonable," I said.

"But you live someplace else?"

"Of course I do," I protested.

"Why?"

"Why *what*?"

"Why do you live someplace else? Why don't you live on
campus?"

"On the campus of Wabash College?"

"Yes."

"Why should I live there?"

"Where is it, anyway?" she asked, somewhat irritated.

"I don't know."

"You don't know?"

"No."

"I'll bet you're not on the honor roll," she said.

She had thought I was a student on the GI Bill. And so had they, the professors from Harvard, Yale, Columbia, and Wharton. That was why they ignored me—or tried to—whenever I spoke. That was why I had been so irritatingly invisible.

That I did not realize this was soon to become the cause of acute conflict. The man on my left was having problems. He was clearly unhappy with just about everything, and angry with what remained. Early in the discussion he made a statement that, in my view, had no grounding whatsoever. He was pushing an academic supposition that entirely avoided the reality of nations acting within the international system (my specialty, which had put me right on the mark enough times at least to allow me to offer an opinion). I contradicted him—directly, but in the polite, hypothetical way that prevails at graduate seminars or in the court of a shogun.

And when I did he looked at me and, evidently, read my name tag. "That's nonsense," he said. "You don't know what you're talking about."

I was shocked. Not two months before, I had had a conversation with Harry Truman, and although we spoke frankly and did not always agree, the president was completely untouched by arrogance of any kind. I left the Oval Office with admiration for him that has only increased with the appearance of each of his successors.

Who was this professor who dismissed me as if he were the Queen of Hearts and I his obsequious supplicant? I read his name tag. Igor Jaguar. Professor of Economics, Harvard University. Igor Jaguar? Well, he did have an unusual accent.

When he finished a little dissertation on the beauty and all-around predictive ability of the Jaguar Theorem, I once again contradicted him, marshalling my arguments as carefully and forcefully as I could, for, after all, I had been affronted.

Smiling at me patronizingly, he said, "All right, dunce, you've said your nonsense, and we've had enough of it. We've finished with your comments for the rest of the session."

Instead of puffing up and saying, "I *beg* your pardon," or some other thing like that, I laughed. I was a fully grown man who had seen some of the world, and even as an undergraduate—at Harvard, when Professor Jaguar had not yet made the scene—no one had ever spoken to me that way. I glanced at the assembled economists for confirmation that Mr. Jaguar had exceeded his mandate, but I found no sympathy. Their expressions suggested that they would hold me at fault for bringing out Jaguar's lunacy, and, unfortunately, they had interpreted my laugh as nervous acquiescence.

Someone else spoke up, changing the subject. And then someone else, and someone else. Although I was stung, I was ready to forget the incident and proceed diplomatically. At the end of a discussion of the implications of the decisions agreed upon at Bretton Woods, so very nearby, I asked a question. I said something like, "I'm not aware of the means by which this resolution was adopted. What is the background of the decision, its legislative history, so-to-speak?"

Jaguar kept silent, but someone else said, in a manner that, for no reason I could discern, suggested grim hatred, "If you are advanced enough to attend this seminar, we shouldn't have to explain such things to you. It was your responsibility to keep yourself informed about Bretton Woods."

I thought I was dreaming, or that I had gone crazy, and my combativeness began to rise. I felt the kind of upwelling rage that visited me one terrible day in Brooklyn—the second man I killed, for which I was not tried but more or less commended.

Sometimes the fury arises within me and I think I was born to fight with a mace. Still, I stifled it. I decided that to explode would be unseemly. I did, however, give a very firm response.

"It was not possible for me to follow the conference," I said, "and if you are unable or unwilling to answer me, it isn't because my question is in any way unreasonable. The question is perfectly reasonable."

A mumble. And then a hush. And then, in a tone that dripped with contempt, someone *else* said, "We expect a certain level of competence. Bretton Woods was only two years ago. Where were *you* that you were ignorant of it?"

That was it. I had had it. I shed my one tear. I don't know what they thought it was, but when I'm backed up against a wall I remember all I love and am always moved. I shed only one tear because I cut off my deepest emotions with the resolve that recalling them has summoned in their defense, and then I am ready.

I narrowed my eyes. I said, not so much in anger as with an inhuman growl of fact and truth, "I was in a fucking airplane, over fucking Berlin."

This silenced everyone except Jaguar, who ignored his cue to turn from the blast. "All I can say, GI Bill turd, is that 'Wabash College' would have been less of a lesser place had you been shot down," he said, smiling as if in some sort of triumph and as if he were not in grave danger.

I did not detonate at that moment. I have always reserved the right to time my own detonations. "I was shot down," I told him, "twice."

"Too bad you weren't killed, then, you little *idiot*," he shouted.

I was so enraged that I became motionless. Moments passed, then, perhaps, a minute. Someone started to say something, as if the seminar would continue, but in a fog of red I rose from my chair and my gaze fixed upon Jaguar. As the seconds ticked,

I heard the voice of the speaker trail off. And then, as I stared at Jaguar, silence descended.

My eye fastened upon the buffet. Spurred by the memory of those I knew who had given their lives, I said to Jaguar, so quietly that it could hardly be heard, in a kind of hoarse whisper, "Are you hungry? You look hungry. It's time for dinner, but don't get up, I'll serve you."

Things such as I did next are rarely done, because human inhibitions are so powerful. But coffee and its evil manifestations are justification for primal rage, as is defense of the innocent, and I include as innocent those who cannot speak, cannot move, cannot make their wishes known, those for whom love is only pure and forever unrequited, for they are gone and will never come back.

Among them is my cousin Robert. I hardly knew him. When we were little we would play at family gatherings, and during religious ceremonies we shared the same chafe and oscillation rate. We were too young to understand how we were related, or that it had meaning, or that we had a physical resemblance to one another.

Once, at an interminable family gathering where the girls wore patent-leather shoes and the rooms were too hot, we fled to the basement and tried to take apart a refrigerator. And once, at Thanksgiving, when it was unusually cold, we escaped onto a reed-bordered lake and skated for hours in the chill wind.

He died in his B-25. The B-25 was a weapon with which Americans slaughtered Americans, one of the worst and most dangerous planes ever produced, a coffin. A third of them were lost in training, so you can imagine how they performed in combat.

Do you think the crews didn't know? They knew very well. And their families knew. I remember exactly an eight-by-ten black-and-white photograph of my uncle, my aunt, Robert, and his younger sister. My grandmother is there, too, and another woman, probably the sister of Robert's mother.

They stand in front of Robert's parked B-25 on a field in southern California, looking into the camera as if they are looking at death. He is the only one who is smiling, though he knew as well as or better than they exactly what his chances were. How brave he was to face a pointless death each time he went up, and he kept on going up.

I made one step forward and thrust my left hand into Jaguar's lapels, clamping them like a vise. Stupidly, he grabbed my left forearm with both his hands. I then jerked him toward me about half a foot, brought my right hand, swordlike, even with my left ear, and struck him across the face.

Because he had probably never been hit in his life, he acted as if I had killed him. But this blow was merely to turn him around, after which he did exactly what I wanted him to do. He threw himself facedown across the table, with his waist bent at the edge. I used my left hand like a mechanical grasper once again, and in a sudden and irresistible movement seized the back of his belt and pants.

I have always been very strong, and I was in superb shape at the time. Thus it was possible for me to take him by belt and neck, lift him into the air, and carry him as if he were on a gurney. No one in the room moved a muscle, as physical confrontation was not their métier. Their mouths hung open and I think some of them must have stopped breathing, for the silence had a curious quality about it that suggested the sudden absence of oxygen.

We started at the head of the buffet table. "Here's some roast beef," I said. The roast was only partially carved, and under red heat lamps it looked like something from a painting by

Hieronymus Bosch. "You like roast beef. Have some," I commanded as I pounded his head against it. The impact was cushioned but substantial. He was still breathing and making sounds, so I knew he hadn't had a heart attack.

"Which does this remind you of more," I asked, ferociously swinging him through the air until his head slammed against the uncut roast and sent it flying across the room, "golf or baseball?"

His howlings of protest showed that his pride was hurt far more than his body, so I said, "What was that? Baseball? Right. So you get to eat all the potato salad you want." When his head emerged from the bowl of potato salad, he looked like Santa Claus.

"Robert was my cousin," I shouted. "Just another jerk who went down in his B-25. Just another turd who never even got to go on the GI Bill. For you, not even a number. You don't even have to think about him."

I was in the same state in which petite mothers find themselves when they are able to lift six-hundred-pound gates off their trapped children, and I could have clasped him to a quick death.

"But now you are going to think about him. You're going to think of him every time you come into a gathering of people. You're going to think of him every time you see food. You're going to think of him every time you see or hear an airplane. *Swear it!*" I screamed, shaking him as a terrier shakes a rat, "Swear it!"

Had he not made some incomprehensible sounds that had the unmistakable quality of acquiescence, I would have killed him. I said, "Say, 'Robert, thank you for dying for me in your lousy B-25.' *Say it!*" And he did.

I let him go. As he stared ahead in shock, I picked up my knapsack and walked out into the arctic air, quivering and distraught that it had been Robert who went down instead of me, because in family gatherings, and on the pond, and during the few times that we had been together, I had known. I had known even then, although I didn't know how, that I was a survivor and that he was not. I had had the wit. I had had the fury. And I had had the luck.

I had been made that way, and he had been made gentler, somewhat awkward, and never as sure. But he was by far the better man, the quieter man, and he died in my place. The truth of it is that it should have been me, but there was never anything I could do about the truth.

I often think of him. You see, the colors up there were different, and the air . . . was different. Half the time you felt as if you were dreaming, and the forces that played upon you—the blinding light, the gravity in turning or diving, the great cold, the air too thin to breathe—were such that you were always near the gates of death, and it was easy, far too easy, to be taken. I have fallen through the sky, my arms pulled away from me by centrifugal force as I tumbled, a ball of orange fire and the crack of thunder following, the straps and buckles on my clothing whistling in the wind.

Though my actions at the conference would not affect my career (my reputation was already compromised), I felt vaguely unsettled about what I had done. Nonetheless, my indiscretion had served me well, for as I exited a dark stand of spruce onto the moonlit frozen road, I heard footsteps.

Constance emerged from the darkness, moving so beautifully that I was comforted, and when she reached me, I felt infatuation. Still, those were different times. I recall then a delicacy, a reticence that held her away from me for longer than we wished, and although I wanted at that moment to take her in my arms, this was something that would come later on. In the meantime, love was well forged in the discipline that kept us apart.

Though I was middle aged, our affair had the kind of otherworldly traction into which adolescents and young people slip so often, though my ability to maintain otherworldly traction had lessened markedly. As compensation, I found myself better able to appreciate the factual.

The process has continued until, at eighty, I am well content with the little things that I used to think were of little import. I can see more deeply now, and my satisfaction with less and less grows alarmingly, so that I fear it will not be so long until I reach the end of life, where I will have to be satisfied perfectly by absolutely nothing.

I remember Constance as if I were looking at photographs. I see her dancing, turning gracefully, and each progressive moment is frozen, with a click, as if with a camera. As she comes into the light it shines on her hair and in her eyes and in her smile. She is turning toward me, open, trusting, full of love. She is wearing a sequined top that reflects spears of light like a magical thistle. So it was.

The train upon which I had arrived had turned around and been the last train out, the station was dark, and the only hotel held Igor Jaguar and his colleagues. We walked all night. We did not encounter a single car on the whitened road, or a single light in the few towns through which we passed in silence out of respect for the sleeping.

As long as we kept moving, we were perfectly comfortable: we could have run the whole distance. Our pace was rapid, and we covered thirty miles by the time the sun came over the mountains the next morning. When we boarded the train, we took separate compartments, had the beds turned down, and slept all the way to New York, where we were disgorged into Grand Central Station at the height of the evening rush hour.

Perfectly rested, windburned, and smelling of the bay rum

that both of us had splashed on our faces after washing in cold water and looking up at the standard Pullman shelf loaded with standard Pullman toiletries, we seized upon the frantic motions of New York in early evening, but without the customary filter of fatigue, and we had dinner at the Oyster Bar.

Constance was twenty-eight, and did not at first believe me when I told her that I had gone with my father to the Oyster Bar the first week that it opened, in 1912. She pretended, at least, to be shocked at my age. Naturally, I was flattered.

She had assumed that I was, indeed, a Wabash student on the GI Bill. I royally let slip that, actually, I had been an undergraduate at Harvard, and taken an M.Phil. at Magdalen College, Oxford.

Thus began a series of surprises and double shifts that, in my time with her, were never to end. "Harvard!" she said. I was used to the delicious squeal of feudal self-abnegation that you hear when you mention that name (how disgusting it seems now), and I assumed that she was, well, you know . . . impressed.

She wasn't impressed, she was merely pleased, for she had been to Radcliffe, and this meant that, though far apart in years, we shared certain things in common. I was more or less delighted. After all, that she went to Radcliffe meant that she would be able to understand me when I spoke, which is what we at Harvard thought the purpose of Radcliffe was. Though it was true that Cliffies got better grades, it was because they were more passive and therefore able to mold themselves to the wishes of their instructors, they did not find themselves in competition with the professors, they did not exhaust themselves in sports or debauchery—as we did, or said we did—and they gave their undergraduate years their full shot, because they were not going to have careers.

But Constance, I quickly understood, was never passive, and did not have the habit of molding herself to anyone's wishes. And, she rowed.

"You rowed?" I asked.

She nodded.

No wonder her upper body, her shoulders, her arms, and her breasts were so beautiful, so perfectly formed, so well defined.

"And what did you take up after college?" I asked, thinking of, perhaps, quoits.

"I still row—in Long Island Sound."

No wonder her upper body, her shoulders. . . .

"I myself rowed singles," I told her, amazed. "We can go out together. I rowed for six years, four at Harvard and two at Oxford."

"I rowed for eight," she said.

"You mean, you've been rowing for four years since you were graduated? You should count only those years when you were in college or affiliated with a competing club."

"No," she told me, ever so cheerfully. "Four years in college, and four years in graduate school."

"Graduate school?" I asked, quite surprised.

"Yes."

"Where?"

"Harvard."

"Oh. In what . . . in what did you. . . ."

"Economics."

"You went for a doctorate?"

"I took it last year," she said. "My thesis was about the effects of political philosophy on economic theory. It's going to be published," she said, with more than a twinkle, "in a month."

"By whom?" I asked.

"Oxford University Press. What do *you* do?"

I didn't want to tell her. "I was demobilized fairly recently," I said. "I was a pilot."

"I know," she said. "Over Berlin."

"Yes. Many times."

"Shot down twice."

"Yes," I said, "twice, though only once over Berlin, and once over the Mediterranean."

"But what do you do now?"

"I haven't settled in yet," I said.

I didn't want her to know that I was a partner at Stillman and Chase. I didn't want to impress her that much. I didn't want to suggest, merely by announcing what I did, that her knowledge, while admirable, was merely speculative and theoretical, while mine was, well, the real stuff. And I didn't want to overawe her with the aspect of money, at least not yet.

My salary and my year-end apportionment were awesome. I lived on an entire high floor in a building on Fifth Avenue, overlooking Central Park. I had a cottage in East Hampton. I wanted to surprise her with all this to make her happy, but first I wanted her to love me for myself, so I decided to do things as in a fairy tale.

The next day, I rented a small apartment in a brownstone on the Upper West Side. When we met subsequently, under the clock at the Biltmore, I told her that I lived in this apartment. I just mentioned it casually. In a few days, I would have it furnished after the fashion of a demobilized pilot still smarting from the effects of war, still casting about for a peacetime profession. I moved some of my books, some war memorabilia— swagger stick, cap, framed commissions, cannon shells, etc.—

and a few pieces of furniture to the new place. I told Constance, quite truthfully, that I did not yet have a telephone there, but that I was expecting to have one installed within a week.

"I never asked where you live, Constance. I don't know what I would have done had we not been able to meet here and had I not been able to reach you."

"I live at the Barbizon," she said nervously, and then she exhibited a magnificent rose blush, from tip to toe. She looked as if she had been on the beach at Krakatoa just before it blew up. Her color ebbed and it flowed for three or four minutes.

It was, I would learn not that long after, the color she turned when she made love, and the color she had probably been on the moonlit road when she ran up to me, though in the moonlight I had not been able to see it. And when her complexion burned, the heat vaporized the expensive and understated perfume she wore so well, which, for me, was bliss.

But why had she blushed when she told me she lived at the Barbizon? Because she didn't live there. I knew it was a lie, but I couldn't prove it. Every time I called her, they said she was out, or sleeping. When I went to pick her up, she would come down to the front desk as if she actually lived in the place, and she paid rent, but she never stayed there.

Who was I to complain? I had set up my own subterfuge on the West Side, and there I entertained her as if I were a moneyless former pilot whose troubled memory kept his heart and soul in the sky over Europe.

Though crowned with deception, our courtship was sweet. Because I was never to know Constance when she was older, our love did not proceed beyond the initial all-consuming passion of, say, Romeo and Juliet, the kind of love that blinds. You see it all the time in restaurants, when a man and a woman sit at a table and face one another, unable to turn their heads, locked together like cats in intercourse. At my age I tend to regard such display with something akin to fatigue and contempt, but I remember it at times with pleasure. It is the state to which sexual love is the handmaiden, and without which sexual love is like a dance without music.

Soon, which according to the old calendar meant six or eight months, our thousands of hours of kissing and embracing and fondling led to the irresistible, full, wet, prolonged . . . oh my . . . that custom had led us to avoid. Such a thing was not, as it is so often these days, an activity upon which to embark after ten minutes' acquaintance, or a gymnastic rite, a social prerequisite, or a form of orgasmic arm wrestling.

It was the climax of many months' testing, resolution, and moral struggle. It was the signal of true love and lifelong commitment. It was a mutual capitulation to the most elemental commandment, but only after a prolonged battle had proved us to ourselves, and, perhaps, elsewhere.

The greatest blizzards start with the finest snow. I must have been insane to start such a demanding regime in my early forties and well past my physical prime. We would lie together for days on end. I believe insects do this. Two crane flies were once locked in perfect symmetry on the upper part of my bathroom door. I blew a puff of air at them, and they flew away, linked as one. Their flight was graceful and quick. What miracle allowed them to know, suddenly, without study or reflection, how to be a biplane?

I see promiscuous young people on the beach, whose flesh is contained by their bathing suits in the manner of a melon resting in a slingshot. What do they know other than the most obvious? What could a voluptuary with a tattoo upon her tan overspilling breast know of Constance, with her lean strong shoulders, her unvarying modesty, and the great sensual explosiveness when finally she allowed herself complete abandon?

I hear the filthy, devilish strains of the lambada, and they mock the North. They mock what we have learned from the cold sea and the high wind. They mock the seduction and the Fall.

You do not know the reason for her deception, but you know the purpose of mine. I did not want her to love me for my money, and I did not want her to feel that what she did was, compared to what I did in the real world, with real people, and the whole economies of actual nations, a fruitless academic exercise.

Many love stories, I suppose, end with a flourish even more pompous and more destructive, in which heart-breaking passion is exhausted in the service of mere vanity. I suppose we could have moved to Connecticut and bought some ponies and sent our children to a school that called itself a hall. It could have ended with me in the saddle, the master of a dead horse. It didn't, because every time I turned around I encountered a double switch.

The first inkling that not everything was as I assumed came to me the next summer: that is, the summer of '47, in August, which in New York is when heat settles over the city like a sparkling, blinding veil. I remember the city then as a colossal essay in black and white, with more shades of gray than the world now knows. The city was quieter and more subdued than it is at present, perhaps because all the old forms had risen to their greatest height and this was the pause before the fall. The death of the old kingdom and the birth of the new seemed to have come during the Blizzard of '47, when the city was covered as never before and never since by a great white shroud. It stopped every man, woman, and child, stopped the streetcars, stopped the theaters, stopped the stocks, stopped the buses, and stopped the clocks.

It brought families together in complete quiet, and when everyone had been assembled in a city as tight as a bowstring, they suddenly felt a great shock. The snow was thrown from cornices and ledges the way it would have been had someone picked up Manhattan and banged it against the ground, and the streets were buried in a white fume, as if a child had turned over a snow glass, righted it, and watched the last of an old age float down and away.

My great regard for the period that led up to this arises because it is where those I can no longer reach reside. I want more than anything to go back to them, so I see in memory everything that surrounds them with what is perhaps a mistaken tenderness, but it is tenderness nonetheless.

Had I not gone into exile, I would have remained in New York, and it would have changed, and I would have been overwhelmed. As it is, I have it as it was, although it is always just beyond my reach, but I see it, and I will see it clearly until I die. Who knows? Perhaps with infinite dissolution comes infinite velocity, and I will be tossed back into the heart of the time I love.

I see it as if it were real. Constance and I are on the Bear Mountain boat. Like all the people against that gray background, she is a study in vivid color. She is so sunburnt that her white sundress is tinted rose. As we move north on the Hudson in a slight breeze the roar of the West Side Highway comes to us over the water like the sound of faraway surf.

I put my left arm around her and gently pull her to me. Through my suit and her dress I feel her body as if there were no such thing as cloth. My fingers curl lightly around the top of her arm at the end of her shoulder, and she has taken me just as lightly by the waist. Beyond us lies the city, its old glory shining through but about to change forever. The ferries will no longer pull trails of steam and smoke across its golden bays, and horses will disappear from the streets. Wood and stone have had their day, and flowing coats, and windows that open in trains, and the irrational manners that protect the delicacy and charm of the human soul.

Though a young woman, far younger than am I, Constance is of my time, and she too understands all that will soon be lost. As I stand on deck in the August heat, I cannot take my eyes from her. I am amazed at how much I love her.

But she was not who I thought she was. I began to suspect this after we had sailed across the Tappan Zee, in a haze of blue and white. Long after we had passed Ossining and I had strained unsuccessfully to see my old house through the trees—it was impossible to see the house from the river, although you could always see the river from the house—we rounded a bend in the upper Hudson.

In perfect majesty, symmetry, and order, a great estate appeared on a hillside. In our smooth motion across the water we could see ranks of maneuvering apple trees, by the thousand; neatly trimmed fields; roads without ruts; stone walls both straight and plumb; brightly and uniformly painted gates and wood fencing; and huge barns that were neither weathered nor tilting.

Everyone on deck looked out at this well ordered wealth, and was impressed by the labor and the beauty of the design. Whereas the expressions of the passengers were those of admiration, longing, and envy, and even I calculated swiftly that never in a million years would I be able to afford such a vast and peaceful domain, Constance went partially vermillion and her expression was that of a burglar with a flashlight in his face.

As the boat came close to shore it sent a wave of white foam through basalt-black water to embrace the scattered boulders on the bank. A white house appeared far above us, perfectly framed in the trees, each of its smooth pilasters and columns rising as if from the crux of a massive oak.

I turned and looked to the mountains on the other side of the river, to see what one would see from the house, and when I did I saw Constance with a tear sparkling just under her right eye. But as soon as I looked at her carefully, it was gone.

My profession, my calling for many years, had trained me to seize upon the small signs and transient evidences of invisible powers, to tease from an unwavering landscape proof of thundering rivers below.

"What is it about this house that affects you so much?" I asked. She seemed to have been seized by emotion, and to be fighting it off.

"Nothing," she said, her voice cracking.

"Nothing?" I asked.

Then, as I watched, she slowly went to pieces. I embraced her, and she hid her face by pressing it against my neck. She cried until we passed the estate, and then, after she regained her composure, she explained to me that her parents, whom I had never heard her mention, had worked on this estate, and had died there.

"Both of them?"

"They're buried on the hill."

It seemed unlikely that she would be the child of the near-feudal servants of a great estate and then gone to Radcliffe. . . .

"The proprietor," she told me, "was a Harvard alumnus and a great benefactor. The children of his servants and staff were given the best secondary education, and not a single one failed to go to the Ivy League."

"What about his own children?"

"They went to the same school."

"Wasn't it difficult?"

"No," she said. "When they were very young all the children were innocent and equal. As they grew, they became aware of their parents' standing, but they had known each other from too early an age to be affected by it."

"It must have been a wonderful school," I said.

"Four tutors, seven children," was her answer. "One of the barns that you saw was a laboratory, another a library."

"Noblesse oblige."

"I suppose so."

"Didn't it make you angry?"

"No. I loved my parents very much. They weren't perfect, and at times I was embarrassed by their situation, but I suppose that made me love them even more. At first you love them because they seem all-powerful, and then you love them when you discover that they are so terribly vulnerable, but you love them nonetheless, more and more, though at times, as you labor through your own travails, you hardly know it."

Except for a slight feathering of the prop in one instance, and a good deal of omission that changed the sense of everything she said, what she told me was entirely true. Though she was at times mysterious and inaccessible, her character was such that she could not lie, and she never did lie to me. She did, however, dissemble.

That was hardly a sin. After all, I myself was pretending to be someone I wasn't, all in service of the surprise I was preparing for her, though with every day that passed in her presence I realized that the Cinderella stuff was totally unnecessary. I was in love with her: that was all that mattered.

Soon after our river trip, on a Saturday in August, I had

crossed the park and was walking down Fifth Avenue on my
way to pick her up at the Barbizon. I was a little more than half
my present age, and could jump over benches that now I seek
as a drowning man lunges for a life preserver.

Just as I was passing one of the great Fifth Avenue mansions,
the kind that sits in its own little park behind an immense stone
and iron fence, Constance flew from the front door, which was
closed behind her as if by a servant. Frozen in my tracks, I
watched her snap her fingers and turn around. She had forgotten
something. She bounded up the steps, took out a key, and was
in and out in less time than I required to suspect that it was
perhaps someone else, but to realize that, in fact, it wasn't. She
shot through the gate like an acrobat, went to the curb, and
seized a floating taxi with the authority of General MacArthur.

Then she was gone, and I was left to survey the house. At
the time, it simply took my breath away. Later, I would learn
the details. It had five stories and a basement, and totaled 48,000
square feet, not including garages, greenhouse, swimming pa-
vilion, and squash court. On the first floor was a ballroom of
immense size with an eighteen-foot ceiling. The library was of
double height, with a wrap balcony and six rolling ladders, and
its French doors gave out onto the great oaks in the garden.

The kitchens were studies in copper and stainless steel, with
two chefs in starched white bonnets who played chess most of
the day at a table by a big window. A man was employed solely
to polish wood, another to polish metals and marble, another
to clean glass. Though half the glory of a house is how it shines,
the other half is flowers, which were everywhere, as if you were
in the gardens of Niterói. Well, not quite: nothing can match
a carefully tended garden in the tropical sun. It is as beautiful
as the youths who tend it—young girls in straw hats and dark
purple-and-blue blouses, whose faces are flushed and perfect,

and strong energetic boys who cannot take their eyes from their lovely co-workers. Something there is that really makes the heart skip, about a beautiful girl, in the hot sun, with a watering can.

I stood on Fifth Avenue looking at the house and gardens where Constance had seemed so much at home. What, I asked myself, is going on? But it was clear: this was her house. When, later, she could no longer keep up appearances, she invited me in, and soon after, when I married her, it became my house, too.

Through no fault of her own, Constance Olivia Phoebe Ann Nicola Devereaux Jamison Buckley Andrews Smith Faber Lloyd was a billionairess. It had never occurred to me that the geometric dispersion of family fortunes could, in fact, run the other way to become geometric concentration, either by some form of primogeniture or by strategic marriage. Her ancestors had been so prudent, thrifty, and calculating that they had melded several dozen immense fortunes into a great snowball of wealth to which more wealth never failed to adhere. Part of her faith and passion was that she would never under any circumstances have more than one child. And that child, by God, would not marry a pauper.

"But what about me?" I asked, given that she had married me, and I, full partner at Stillman and Chase or not, was by any standard of comparison with her not only a pauper but a piker, a pipkin, and a pumpkin.

"You're an exception," she said. "Besides, the line is descended from the mother."

There is no question that she loved me as I loved her, but from the moment I saw her inserting the key in the lock of that great door, I was attacked by the octopus of anxiety as I wrestled with the worm of doubt, so to speak.

Here in the gardens I can tell the truth, though it still brings waves of seasickness. Yes, I was a fighter pilot with the Distinguished Flying Cross, an ace. I was shot down twice, and the first time I survived in the sea and made my way through the desert to take to the air again within a week, with tanks full and guns loaded.

All right, I didn't have a Harvard doctorate, but I had a Harvard A.B. and an Oxford M.Phil.. I was a full partner at Stillman and Chase, and senior at the firm by what appeared to have been a freak of circumstance but which was actually my uncle's careful calculation. In my early forties, I was an athlete in excellent health. I was becoming comfortable with presidents and kings, and I was already completely comfortable with popes. But when Constance took me home to her magnificent house —and there were others, that is, other houses—something dreadful happened to me.

From that evening on—Christ, her father was a Nobel laureate and dead to boot—I could not look in the mirror without seeing a hamster: a round-shouldered, pointy-faced, dirt-brown chicken croquette with legs and white whiskers. Her billions diminutized me. I was a kept man. A gigolo. A rodent. I tried to deny it, but when I attempted to give myself encouragement in front of the mirror, never once did I fail to turn into a gerbil before my very eyes, though sometimes I thought I might have been a guinea pig.

Even though I would not admit to this affliction, Constance made every effort to counter it. Her inborn grace led her to assure me by fact and deed. She made me co-beneficiary of the many trusts that watered her well, protesting that she had gained them by accident of birth, and I by accident of love. She had her lawyers put everything in both our names.

"There it is," she told me when it was done. "It's irrevocable. It's mine, it's yours, it doesn't matter. Perhaps we should give it away and live in a cabin on the beach."

"What beach?"

"Southampton."

"What about the piano?"

"We could build a music studio next to the cabin—sort of a Williamsburg-like arrangement, with a formal garden flanked by dependencies, and the stables, swimming pool, tennis courts, and greenhouses on the other side of a great lawn."

"How would we eat?" I asked, somewhat sarcastically.

"We'd fish and gather berries, and both Fortnum and Mason and Petrossian deliver by air mail."

As brilliant as she was, her sense of reality was unique. For example, one day I came home to find Constance pacing the library and in a foul mood. I asked her why she was upset. She told me that she had stopped in a hardware store on Lexington Avenue to buy one of those tiny little things for pulling the stems off strawberries. (I would call them tweezers except that they are to tweezers what a hippopotamus is to a praying mantis.)

The proprietor had been so nasty that she had confronted him, explaining that she, as a customer and a human being, deserved simple courtesy—at which point he erupted in obscene curses, foam, and spittle.

"So what, it's New York," I said, as I prepared to run to the store and tear him limb from limb.

"I'll get him," she said, "in my own way."

"You mean you'll buy the block and evict him."

She denied it.

"Start fifty hardware stores on either side of him?"

"No."

"What?"

"I'm going to make him believe in a pagan god," she said, "and then I'll take his god away from him."

"Of course," I answered. "I knew it, but I just didn't say it."

She then revealed a rather astonishing plan. I hardly breathed, for I understood that she had the means of actually carrying it out.

"Look," she went on, in a way that was simultaneously sweet and terrifying, "I'm entitled to retaliation, am I not?"

"Let me do it for you."

"He has a baseball bat."

"Did he threaten you with it?"

"He had it in his hand."

"I'll make him eat a tea strainer."

"You can't do that," she said. "You can't do things like that, not anymore. The newspapers would seize upon it as a case of persecution."

"You mean that possession of great wealth makes you into a doormat?"

"No, but you're forced to take roundabout routes."

"Such as making someone believe in a pagan god. . . ."

"Yes."

"And then taking that god away from him."

"Exactly."

"But, Constance," I protested, "isn't that too *obvious?*"

"It's not obvious at all," she told me, "though it will take four or five years. The end result will be that he closes his store and retires a bitter and puzzled man."

"No wonder you're afraid of the newspapers. For what this man did to you with a few words, you're going to ruin him."

"Yes, and I'll make him wealthy in the process."

"How wealthy?"

"Millions, if he's thrifty, and if, in the end, he resists temptation."

"That's good revenge," I said brightly.

"It is."

Her plan could have come only from the unfettered imagination of someone whose entire life had been spent trying to understand the value of money because it seemed to her to have no inherent worth, in that her supply had been unlimited.

First, she was going to hire a corps of managers and set them up in an office building. They would arrange for an actor with an unfailing resemblance to Father Time to go into the hardware store in July and ask for a sled. Constance had noticed that her tormentor had a dozen Flexible Flyers piled in a corner. The actor would be made up in such a way that he seemed to glow. Constance had designed, in theory, a system of tiny battery-powered ultraviolet lights for illuminating phosphorescent powders that were to be sprinkled on the actor's shrouds and scythe.

Making his appearance during a summer lightning storm, he would ask for a sled, purchase it, and leave. The next day, two shills would come in and ask for sleds. The following day, three, the following day, four, ad almost infinitum.

In just short of three years' time—ninety-five days short, to be exact, without a leap year—a thousand people a day would arrive at this man's store, fall, winter, and summer (New York has no spring), to buy a sled, and only between the hours of nine and five.

Which would mean that at average intervals of slightly less than thirty seconds he would sell one kind of sled—all other models and accessories would be rejected—for one price only. The buyers would walk out if he tried to raise the price or even to lower it.

At the end, after overhead and taxes, he would be clearing about five million a year in current dollars. Were he himself not at the store, the legions of Constance's shills would not buy. He would be very busy, his life a blizzard of sleds.

On the hottest day of summer, when no accidental buyers were likely to appear, all the shills would be called off. The previous day, when it had been only 119 degrees Fahrenheit, he would have sold a thousand sleds. For a week he would be bereft. The neighboring merchants, who had tried to sell sleds too, and who, though they dressed as Santa Claus, advertised, and cut prices to the bone, had not succeeded, would think his luck had finally run out.

Just as the merchant was ready to retire, Father Time would come into the store and ask momentously for a baking pan. Then the cycle would begin again, only to be ended and restarted once more, as Father Time requested various other items.

When the merchant prince of sleds, baking pans, and apple peelers had been irrevocably conditioned, Father Time would ask for a black horsehair pillow embroidered with a picture of a purple spider. Naturally, you aren't going to have such things made up one at a time if you plan to sell hundreds of thousands of them.

In the wholesale directories, for several years running, Constance would have placed a listing for a factory in New Bedford that specialized in embroidered horsehair pillows. The factory she created would be 'failing,' and would require a major capital infusion: coincidentally, the exact amount the merchant prince had managed to save. He would be highly reluctant to gamble his new wealth, but Father Time would appear again, demanding the pillow and offering an outrageous price. And then a thousand shills would leave immense sums to reserve these pillows, and call anxiously all day long.

When the pillows were completed, giving the declining economy of New Bedford a charitable boost (though not exactly preparing it for a future of high technology), and the merchant prince had warehouses packed full of them, Constance would dissolve her operations and command battalions of public relations flacks to fill the newspapers and magazines with stories about the Lexington Avenue storekeeper who was stuck with half a million black horsehair pillows with a picture of a spider embroidered upon them in purple thread.

Then, and only then, would she appear to this broken man, to ask for a strawberry tweezers. If he made the connection, she said, fine. If he didn't, he didn't.

"Do you think he will?" I asked.

"I have no idea," was her answer.

She could have done this. She might have done it. But she didn't. Instead, she donated $25 million to Albert Schweitzer's hospital in Lambaréné.

I tried to make the fact that I suddenly had several billion dollars immaterial. I didn't feel justified in using it, and I never did. I accompanied Constance to our houses in Paris, Rome, London, and Palm Beach, but as far as I was concerned these were nothing more than very lonely luxury hotels. With my salary from Stillman and Chase, indeed, on my swindle sheet alone, I could have afforded to stay at such places, and they would have been more cheerful because other people would have been there.

But the vast amount of money, like a looming cliff, was always present. Everything echoed off it. It blocked the light of the sun. Its great presence was inescapable. We were its curators, and it possessed us, not vice versa. I will never forget how, when I was a child, my father and I went to Virginia to tour the battlefields where his father had fought in the War of the Rebellion. It was 1913. We walked all day in some areas, and hired horses in others.

Near one of the more beautiful battlefields, in sight of the Blue Ridge, was a dilapidated estate through the woods and pastures of which we rode to get from the scene of one skirmish to another. We encountered the mistress of the house riding through a hollow, and she invited us for tea—I did not drink the tea itself—in a vast garden of boxwood.

The house was falling apart and the fields were insufficiently tended. The boxwood, however, was perfect. She put all her energy and resources into taking care of it. She had to do this, she explained, because it was 250 years old, and listed in the historical registers.

A chill went down my spine. There we were, surrounded by billions of leaves and an ancient, incorrigible tangle of roots that reached deep into the dark ground, and this grotesque maze that had been seated in the Virginia soil for a quarter of a millennium, and might live for a millennium more, had enslaved the woman who was sitting across from us. How many others had it appropriated to itself, and how many more would it in the future?

My father, who was directly spoken, shared my revulsion and took it upon himself to offend—and perhaps save—that woman, and as we left he said, "Madam, this disgusting root has made you its slave. You must kill it if only for the sake of the children not-yet-born who will be otherwise captured by it. Cut it down, sever the roots, burn them out, and salt the ground."

So it was with Constance and her fortune, and she was far too intelligent not to know it, but she did not have the courage to leave it. And I, though I had the courage to leave it—I ached to separate myself from its smothering weight—did not want to leave her.

We had no option but to lead the wasted lives of the very

rich. The magic of money and capital rests in magnification. If you look at the George Washington Bridge, for example, only a little of what you see is technology. The rest is capital. The hundreds of thousands of tons of steel were strained and boiled from rocks in the ground, formed, transported, and erected by armies of men who never would have been so concentrated or coordinated were it not that dollars can be collected by the billion and brought together to one abstract point that even Euclid would not be able to find, there to be a power like some science-fiction death ray or a sorcerer's magic wand.

I have found that large concentrations of capital either make their owners into monsters of vanity and petulance or sadden them beyond redemption. Constance was saddened, which is what happens when you have everything you want.

She wanted me to be president. "Of what?" I inquired.

"The United States."

"Me?" I asked silently, my lips moving and my thumb pointing at my solar plexus.

"Yes," she said, and went on in one of her semirhythmic fusillades. "You're a good speaker. You're totally honest. You're an experienced analyst of international politics. You have a fairly good knowledge of economics. You're a war hero. You're handsome. You were born in the United States, and now you count your dollars by the billion. Why not?"

"But Constance. . . ."

"You went to Harvard, like the Roosevelts and the Adamses, and Wall Street would back you, even though you would be a hypnotic populist."

"But Constance. . . ."

"You could start with the Senate. I'll buy a few strategic newspapers and back you editorially. You have such a will to fight! What a marvelous idea! I hadn't thought of it!"

"Constance."

"What?"

"I could never be president, even if I wanted to be."

"Of course you can, if you want to be."

"No."

"Why?"

"Because I'm a convicted murderer who grew up in an insane asylum, that's why."

As she thought about this, I could see that she was sifting through encyclopedias of history. "I don't think it would be an impediment, dear, do you?"

Despite her historical analysis, I did. Besides, deep in my heart I really did not want to be president of the United States. If you pay a certain amount that varies according to his political fortunes, you get to stand next to the president and have your picture taken, and he has to smile. The only other being that I have known who is paid to stand next to you as your picture is taken was a chimpanzee on the Boardwalk at Coney Island. His name was Tony, and he smiled only if he liked you. Unfortunately, he liked me. I was twelve years old, and he must have thought I was a girl, because he kissed me on the lips. It was my first kiss. . . .

It was, perhaps, a just punishment, for I and my friends had journeyed three hours to Coney Island for the express purpose of standing underneath the Boardwalk to peer upward, necks bent, into women's dresses. As our field of vision was narrowed to about one degree, and the average woman walked by at two or three miles an hour, what we saw we could seize upon for only about a fiftieth of a second. If you combine this with the odd perspective and the fact that we didn't know what we were looking for, we didn't see a thing—for which my punishment was being kissed on the lips by a chimpanzee (I brushed my teeth for an hour and a half). And yet we went back again and again, so potent is the power of continuing the species (granted, Tony was another species).

My real and abiding dilemma was brought home to me not on a boardwalk but on a dock. Constance's Grandfather Devereaux had constructed a retreat in the Adirondacks. Though they called it a camp, the main lodge encompassed eight thousand square feet, with a seaplane hangar, boat house, music room, hotel kitchen, heated towel racks, and wireless station.

One day up there in the summer, we went canoeing. The water was pure, the lake vast and blue, the forest empty and quiet. It had rained the night before and the dock was wet and steaming in the early morning sun. Constance was in the bow of the canoe and I was untying the stern painter when she remembered that she had left the suntan lotion in the house.

I ran to get it. Though I was forty-five, I had a fully equipped gymnasium and the time to use it. So I bounded up the hill, took the steps four at a time, burst into the house, rocketed up the stairs and around the landings, seized the plastic bottle that smelled like a piña colada, and decided to break all speed records in returning to my seat in the stern.

It was a dash worthy of Jesse Owens. I flew. The faster I went, the faster I went. Unfortunately, or perhaps fortunately, the dock was divided into two sections, the far section about five feet below the part that was closer to the shore. A ladder led from one level to another. Constance was in the canoe at the end of the dock, her hand shielding her eyes from the sun as she watched me burn up the track.

I sped down the first part, intending to jump the five feet at the drop, but I never got the chance. I had forgotten that the surface was slick, and when I tried to stop I was launched feetfirst into the air.

First I went up, and then I went down, about seven feet worth of down, and I landed, banana-peel-style, absolutely flat on my back. The force was such that we never saw where the ripples stopped. A little more, and the planks would have been broken as if by a karate chop. I felt the blow in every muscle of my body, including my head. Constance said the noise was like a bomb blast. She thought I might have broken my back, that I would die, or spend the rest of my life in a coma.

But the joy of falling through the air and then the shocking, sobering collision with the dock revived me in more ways than one. I was less hurt than tingling. My old self was awakened, and I knew that it was still alive, that what I had had once I still had—in muscle, and bone, and in the spark inside that is always alight, and that flares in fright and struggle.

My impact against the dock, and then the knowledge that I was unhurt, freed me from the yoke of my billions. No more runabouts, motorboats, yachts, and swimming pools. No more household staff, hospital wings to dedicate, or tables to buy at benefits for the library. No more sitting in vast, beautifully furnished rooms wondering if I were dead. No more yearning for childhood, when, because I had nothing, I had everything. No more appeals from escaped Polish harpsichordists to fund institutes of musical mechanics. No more Belgian chocolates and Dunhill leather. No more nothing.

I had decided to throw over the money, somehow, without leaving Constance—to start again, to be my own billionaire. I had to do this even though I knew in advance that I would throw that over too.

This may seem contrary to human nature, but my most glorious moments have been when I was close to the abyss, and the greatest power I have felt has been when I was at the mercy of the elements, for then I merged with them and every atom in my body became pure, painless, infinite lightning.

I think that when I was blown backward from my plane and my eyes were filled with the fireball of its explosion, as many opposites met in the same place—speed and stillness, sound and silence, wind and the vacuum of the upper atmosphere, consciousness and dreaming—I may have become, for just an instant, an angel.

What is an angel? An angel is a being that has seen God. An angel has passed through the veil of death to the infinite light on the other side, to the weightless and silvery brightness, to the end of gravity, the perpetual velocity, the lightness. Just for an instant, of course. I was astonished at first, totally motionless, and then, as I pulled my ripcord, I smiled.

How can I explain this when, even at the end of my life, I don't understand it myself?

I used to marvel at the recollections of old people. How is it, I wondered, that they so often combine the qualities of elegy, fluidity, and economy? And it hardly matters who they are. A diplomat faking his memoir, an Eskimo lost in the story of a whale hunt half a century past, an old woman in quiet reconstruction of a family lost to time. . . . They speak in elegies because they remember the dead, they are fluid because they have forgotten the static that slows a narrative, and they must be economical simply for lack of energy.

I myself make no claims in this regard. You already know me. Despite my age and my sometimes tender reflection, I'm bursting inside like the fuse in a rose, as barbaric as a seven-year-old, and now and then as impatient and sexed as a fourteen-year-old boy in heat. Why?

I can't say. I no longer heed the great things that are the

guides of youth: I have no illusions of justice; and for me love is a cross between memory and dreaming.

Whence comes my energy, my appetite, my defiance, and my desire? There seems to be something stuck in the brain, not a branch or a clog, but something like a pulsing coal, a tiny furnace of beating blood, a hot diamond or emerald, something crazy, beautiful, and sweet. It drives me forward as if in my old age I am a young man on a horse, jumping walls and streams, my heart racing. It is as intoxicating as those beautiful women who seemed most of the time to have been just out of reach, as demanding as battle, as dear to me now as a religious vision. But what is it that I cling to, what abstract energy, what magic, what life?

The Sky Over Europe

(If you have not done so already,
please return the previous pages to the antproof case.)

WHAT KIND OF security clearance do you think is required
for an instructor of English at the Brazilian Naval Academy,
given that Brazil has no enemies other than sloth and coconut
oil? And the navy is not very security conscious, though it and
the other branches of the armed forces are far more methodical
than the rest of the country.

I imagine that they never looked into my case other than to
pass upon my original application, and that if they had, they
would have found very little, as most of my existence has had
the privilege of having played itself out prior to the advent of
computers. And, besides, I am unsure of what charges were
filed, if any. Some things are kept quiet to avoid political em-
barrassment. It is possible that I need never have sought out a
country with no extradition treaty, that I might simply have
hidden myself in London or Madrid.

Not long ago, the commandante became interested in my origins, and he has embarked upon a languid investigation that I hope he will abandon as soon as he encounters frustration, which is what he does with everything else.

The Brazilian air force has decided to acquire some better planes and form the best older ones into a counterinsurgency group. This makes sense, as the propeller-driven AT-26's are no match for modern fighters or air defenses, while their slow speed makes them ideal for jungle air support.

The new pilots of this group are being trained on the T-27, the *Tucano*, a lesser vehicle but not that much different from the AT-26. As the object is counterinsurgency, many of these men are being shipped to the United States to learn the subject from us. I myself would send them to query the North Vietnamese.

All the pilots speak English, but were given to me for some polish—not Polish, polish. Rather than teach them the diplomatic niceties they wanted for their sojourn in the North—*I fuck your sister?*—I strengthened their aeronautical vocabulary, and in doing so I found that I could not restrain myself from offering them a few pointers about flying.

What could I know about flying? They knew just by looking that I was born before the era of flight, and that to get me into the cockpit of one of their planes they would have had to use a crane. What would I know about a metal-shelled monoplane with machine guns at the wings and streamlined bomb racks? What would I know, indeed.

Over the course of three weeks, I taught them not only the language of flight, but enough hard-learned lessons about guiding planes and using weapons to give them an edge in combat relative not to the Paraguayan air force or the aces of Surinam

but to the Luftwaffe, which, admittedly, they were not likely
to fight, although their Argentine cousins had recently and foolishly set themselves against the RAF.

I introduced them to maneuvers their instructors had never
dreamed of, half of which they refused to believe were possible,
except that I was forced into them many times and I always
burst out on the other side.

"How do you know about this?" they would ask, dumb-
founded.

"I just know," I would reply.

"But how?"

"When you get older, your brain chemistry changes," I told
them, "and you become wise. One thing you will discover is
that life is based less than you think on what you've learned and
much more than you think on what you have inside you from
the beginning."

Their mouths were still hanging open when one of them said,
"You mean, you know about how to deal with a loss of hydraulic
fluid in a dogfight, and the tricks of feathering a propeller in a
dive, from heredity?"

I was trapped, but so what? I nodded with absolute certainty.

A week before that batch of students left, the commandante
called me in. After reflexively asking if I wanted a cup of coffee,
he winced and held his breath. I let it pass.

You see how powerful this wretched substance is? People
need it to make a connection with another person, to wake up,
to keep awake, to go to sleep, to work, to play, to eat, to embark
upon a journey, to disembark from a conveyance.

How many times have I entered a room and been asked, from
completely out of the blue, "Would you like some coffee?"

Of course I wouldn't like some coffee. What makes them

think I want coffee? And the waitresses! They say, "Would you like your coffee now?"

It *isn't* my coffee, and how dare they assume that the only question is *when* I will drink it? Even after I told them no, they would come around again and ask, "Have you changed your mind about coffee?" "Of course I haven't changed my mind about coffee," I would say. "I'll never change my mind about coffee. I'd rather die."

I had to stop going to restaurants. The sight of people enjoying coffee was so offensive that I stormed out half the time anyway. They drink it with zombie-like expressions that suggest the union of sexual pleasure, religious fervor, and state ceremony.

The users and apologists look at me with wonder, and say, "Ah, but I enjoy it!" Yes, you enjoy it! Heroin addicts enjoy heroin, perverts enjoy their perversions, and Hitler enjoyed invading France. You enjoy it, furthermore, mainly because without it you suffer. The mechanics are similar to those of blackmail and extortion, and the gangster in the piece is a tiny bean that has seized control of half the world.

"How are you?" the commandante asked.

"I'm fine."

Never had he asked me such a tender question. As far as I can remember, from the beginning of time, no one in uniform had ever asked me this. Given that you might be vaporized at any moment or ripped in three by a cannon shell, queries such as "How are you feeling?" seem ridiculous. I believe it has always been this way, the world 'round, even in armies at peace.

"I was fascinated to hear," the commandante said, continuing his formal tone, "that you have a knowledge of aeronautics."

I said nothing.

"And it occurred to me that we have never spoken about your background."

I said nothing, but my expression hardened.

"What did you do before you came to us?"

I rose to my feet and turned toward the door. As I was beginning to move, he said, "No! Wait. Sit down. I didn't mean to offend you. I'm just curious."

"I worked for a bank," I said, having decided on the instant to answer him. I was not afraid of offending the commandante—they needed me more than I needed them—but I knew that if I made myself a total mystery he would become far more interested than if I threw him some shrimp.

"What kind of a bank?"

"A very small bank," I said, thinking of its physical size, "in New York."

"Not Manufacturing Handover Truss?" he asked, trying to impress me with the fact that he could (sort of) name a New York Bank.

"Oh no, nothing like that. Manufacturing Handover Truss has many, many branches, and we had only one." I excluded foreign cities and domestic affiliates, of course.

"What you did there?" the commandante asked in his smoothest English.

"I was a clerk-messenger," I replied, going back to 1918.

"And why you come here?" he asked.

"It hot here," I said, adapting to his syntax. "No snow. Good for body. Very relaxing."

"No treaty of extradition?" he asked.

"What that?"

"Why you leave little bank?"

"A discrepancy."

"A discrepancy?"

"Yes. I myself decided to leave, entirely of my own volition, after I became responsible for a discrepancy. It was the kind of thing that could easily have been rectified by a simple journal entry, and probably was."

The commandante, who was no fool, closed one eye, lifted one eyebrow higher than the other, and asked, "How many zeros?"

Deciding that he was asking me about my war record, and wanting to avoid tooting my own horn, I took advantage of the fact that I had shot down only Messerschmitts and Heinkels. "Absolutely none," I averred. "Zero Zeros."

"Then your leaving the bank was strictly a matter of honor?" he said, returning to his own language.

"A matter of honor and entirely my decision."

He seemed much relieved, though I cannot imagine why he might have been anxious.

"The air force guy whose name is Popcorn, you know him?"

"He's in my class."

"He says you have to have been a fighter pilot, but he can't figure out which war."

"Of course he can't," I said. "I was born in nineteen-hundred and four. I was fourteen when we signed the Armistice at the end of the First World War, and thirty-seven when we entered the Second, well beyond draft age." I did not volunteer that I had volunteered.

"So you were not a fighter pilot."

"All my life I have been interested in aeronautics and the principles of flight," I continued, truthfully. "I read books. I imagine. I believe that I could fly a 747 purely by logic, and I often dream of being the passenger who is called to land the plane after the three pilots have had heart attacks."

"That's a strange dream."

"Yes. The only thing I don't like about it is that I would be very uncomfortable dressed as a nun. But I *love* to fly! In fact, let me take you up in a small plane, and I'll show you how well theoretical knowledge can be translated into practice."

"No!" he said, holding both hands in front of him with his fingers spread. "That won't be necessary. Obviously, Popcorn is crazy."

"Very."

"You won't go up with him, will you?"

"No no," I said. "I'm too old to fly."

I'm too old to fly. With these words, I was magically thrown back to the war. I felt as if I were in a fog on a moor, and I could hardly see the commandante or feel the heat of Rio in summer, for suddenly I was a much younger man, in the sky, over Europe.

I must have made my way from the commandante's office blindly, for I remember neither how I exited nor if I departed politely, mesmerized as I was by the roar of the Merlin engine in my P-51. I used to think of the Merlin as if it were fifteen-hundred and twenty horses that could work continuously for twelve hours. Although my father bought an automobile when I was six years old, until then we traveled about on horseback or in a wagon, and even after that we used the automobile only on special occasions, because it was hard to start and you had to change the tires all the time.

I had thought that people would always have horses, and was amazed that before I was twenty the streets of New York were crowded with automobiles, and that people used them, for example, to go from Albany to Syracuse.

Horses were my first language. I knew the power of one good horse, and it was impressive, for one good horse could pull a wagon that, fully loaded, weighed a ton. It would have to be on fairly level ground; if you wanted to pull a wagon like that up a gradual incline you'd hitch up another animal. With a four-horse team you could run the steepest hills of Ossining all day long, even when winter had captured the town, icicles hung from the gutters, and escaped slabs of packed snow slid down Main Street at fifty miles an hour.

A good horse can carry a 150-pound man as if he didn't exist. Many times I have rocketed along blind and dangerous trails because my mount has forgotten that he carries me. If 150 pounds is to one horse an almost inconsequential burden, what of 1,520 horses that carry the five tons of a fully loaded P-51 —including armament, ammunition, bombs, fuel, and fuel in drop tanks? And when you were over the target, you were much lighter and leaner, having burned two thousand pounds of fuel and shed your drop tanks. And as you expended ammunition, you grew lighter still.

Simple division says that each horse is carrying six and a half pounds, about the weight of four horseshoes. What we are talking about then is a naked horse that could fly, that never got tired, that had no friction from the ground, less friction in the thin air than near the surface, and the help of gravity in half its maneuvers. A P-51 could really fly. And so could I.

Although in 1941 I was working in the department that advised the bank on political risk, and although I believed the United States would eventually enter the war, I knew very little about the Orient and had estimated that our participation would be delayed until 1943 or 1944, by which time I would have been forty. Forty was then far more significant an indication of diminished physical prowess than it is now, and I believed that, having been too young for the first war, I would as well be too old for the second.

Then came Pearl Harbor. Though thirty-seven, I volunteered.

They would have me, however, only as a desk soldier in Washington. As I circulated among the various combat commands, trying to gain entry, I learned that someone who could fly was worth a great many points to the recruiters, who would bend almost any rule to take him in.

I announced that I was taking leave from Stillman and Chase, went to an ordinary bank, withdrew $5,000 in cash, and got on the train to Poughkeepsie. Then I walked fifteen miles to Alford Field, found the director of the flying school, and asked him to teach me to fly like an acrobat.

"I can't," he said. "In three weeks I'm going to San Antonio to teach army pilots."

"That's great," I replied. "We've got three whole weeks."

"Not much we can do in that time," he said. "Not safely."

"Did I say safely?"

"No, but I did."

"It's war," I announced. "The whole thing is unsafe. I'll give you five thousand dollars."

"Five thousand for three weeks' work?" It was an immense sum.

"Look, don't get carried away," I said. "I want you to work me fourteen hours a day. That means a lot of flying time, gasoline, extra pay for your mechanic, spare parts, room, board, and the chance that I may crash your plane or even kill you."

"That sounds attractive," he said.

"Hey," I said, "I'm a fast learner. You put me through my paces and I'll wear you out. I can drive just about anything."

He was a few years younger than I, much taller, unsophisticated, and a great pilot. "All right," he said. "For the time remaining to me, which I'm pretty sure is the last three weeks of May, and may be the last three weeks of my life, I'll do it. We're going to be drinking a lot of coffee!"

"The hell we are," I said. "We're not going to drink even one cup."

We started with theory. Sitting down right where we were, I grabbed a pad of paper and he talked for the rest of the day. I was jamming it in like a window-smasher at Tiffany or (as I would later) when I stuffed chocolate-covered cherries into my mouth as I heard Constance coming down the stairs so I could swallow them before she got to the kitchen. I would then pretend to be washing dishes in one of the deep stainless steel sinks, whereas I would actually be drinking a gallon of ice-cold water, because I knew that she wanted to have sex on the steam table, and when I kissed her I didn't want to be found out.

"Why is it," she would ask, "that whenever I find you in the kitchen you're bent into that sink like an ostrich, and when you straighten up you're dripping with ice-cold water as if you've just gone down with the Titanic?"

"I don't know," I'd say, and then all would be lost as she opened her silk robe.

But the only reason I could spend three hours on the steam table with Constance was that I was alive. If I had been dead I wouldn't have been able to do it, although she had a way of showing me her body, which (while I'd been sneaking chocolate cherries) had already been primed and would be just slightly engorged, rosy, and relaxed, a condition that could, perhaps, have awakened the dead. But I couldn't have met her had I been killed in the war, and that I wasn't was partly the result of my three-week ordeal at the hands of Larry Brown, my flying instructor.

Everything he knew, he copied onto me. Even as we ate— no coffee, no coffee ice cream—he went over theory or criticized my technique. I logged more than 150 hours of flying time, of which the last fifty hours were solo and the final twenty-five spent in dogfights. I nearly crashed at least a dozen times, I cut a couple of telephone lines, and I got to love flying not only for what it was, but for the way I learned it.

In May of 1942 the weather was perfect. I would skim the Hudson at 150 miles an hour within two feet of the water to fly beneath the bridges, and then rise into a full roll by launching myself over the banks and their high treetops as if I were the stone from a slingshot. He taught me how to appear from nowhere and disappear almost as fast. He showed me that every shape on the land is cushioned with beds of moving air, that the mountains and hedgerows and hills have along them invisible rivers that flow like water over a weir, and that you can use them to tighten your turns, cushion your dips, and bounce yourself to high altitude faster than you ever thought you could go.

He never came back from San Antonio, this Larry Brown. It happened like that all the time. Too many planes had to be built too fast. Even the P-51, a majestic fighter, was designed in a hundred days. Now it takes a hundred days to put together a seat-belt buckle.

It had taken Larry Brown a lifetime of flying to see the rivers of air. Perhaps he felt that he was never coming home, and did not want those beautiful, silvery waves to flow unrecognized over the Hudson and its green hills. Perhaps it was the great intensity of my course. Perhaps it was the perfect weather. I don't know. I do know that, before the three weeks were over, I could see them too.

No matter what I did, and despite my special preliminary, my reflexes were not as fast as those of pilots fifteen years my junior. Nor could I shed a lifetime's inhibition in regard to g-force, being upside down, and doing barrel rolls. These things were not incorporated into my nervous system with the same accommodation afforded by my younger colleagues.

It was obvious as we flew that I had neither their agility nor their daring. I was the old man, even though I had dropped ten years from my age and joined at "twenty-seven." And as the war continued, I reached my fortieth year and then my fortieth birthday, and I was dogfighting ME-109's over Germany.

When we were based in Italy doing the transalpine run, a flight surgeon who was examining me figured out that I had been basting the goose.

"How old are you?" he asked.

"Thirty, sir," I answered.

"Like hell," he said. "You're older than I am."

"How old are you, Colonel?"

"Fifty-five."

"Actually, I'm eighty-nine," I told him.

"Fifty?"

"No."

"Forty-five?"

"Of course not."

"Forty. You're forty, and you shouldn't be flying combat missions. I tell you, you're not in shape for that anymore."

"I'm in excellent shape for my age, considering what I'm doing."

"I could ground you either because you're overage or because, for someone who's supposed to be thirty, you're a wreck. I think I will. You'll get someone killed."

"No. I won't. I've put down eleven ME-109's, and although they're getting harder and harder to find, I know I'll put down more. I'm forty years old, that's correct. I don't have such great reflexes, but I compensate with tactics and technical modifications. And I don't drink coffee."

"I want to talk to your wing man."

"I don't have a wing man. My group has flown dispersal and convergence since Tunisia. My favorite situation, sir, is when I meet an enemy fighter element and it's one against three."

"Why?"

"Because then I use the flaming peacock. I use it when outnumbered or if I'm desperate. It works."

"The what?"

"Flaming peacock."

"And what is that, exactly?"

"It's a secret."

He sent me back up even though he thought I was crazy, or perhaps because he did think I was crazy, but I did have a flaming peacock. I invented it in Tunisia, and it saved my life on more than one occasion.

From the beginning, my group was assigned to individual patrol. Even later, when escorting bombers from England, we'd rendezvous with them on their way in, picking up a flight individually, like guerrillas appearing one by one from the forest to join a column on the march, our transit over Germany having been accomplished always alone.

In Tunisia we were based at a field near Monastir, and our patrol area ran deep into the Tyrrhenian, although there we did not often find the enemy, and if we did want to find him all we had to do was approach Sicily. The Licata-Malta-Pantelleria triangle was like an arena. If you entered it, you had a fight. North of Sicily, you could patrol for a week and see nothing, unless of course you increased your radius and approached the Italian coast. As we didn't use drop tanks, we seldom got that close to the mainland, but after Anzio we flew from Sicily and could refuel in Calabria.

For some, the question of fuel was fatal. You didn't want to get into a fight carrying a lot of fuel. First, the weight was paralyzing. Messerschmitts were lighter and smaller. They could climb faster and were more agile, although not by much. They carried far less fuel, and when we were fully loaded we tried to avoid them for reasons of maneuverability alone.

If you could fly out your wing tanks, you were in better shape, because they were more exposed, and without armor. When they were empty the aircraft could roll faster and change direction better, as the center of gravity migrated to a more advantageous position in the fuselage. You felt cleaner, lighter, less encumbered.

On the other hand, everything in the air is a trade-off, and the less fuel you had, the less likely you were to get back. For a while I believed that the Luftwaffe was doomed not because we were better in combat, but because of Germany's position as a compact land power with short central lines of communication. They never had the range. We and the British had always designed for vast distances. The Messerschmitt carried 160 gallons of fuel, and I carried 269. When they used drop tanks, which they didn't like to do because then they had to forgo their wing cannons, they could add another 140 gallons. We could carry that and an additional twenty-five gallons, without sacrificing armament. Even if the ME-109's bested us in combat, they often did not make it home. This, anyway, was my theory, which arose as a corollary to the desire to be light in combat.

We were better in combat anyway and I'm not entirely sure why. The Luftwaffe had an enormous array of planes, most of which were very capable, complicated, and imaginative. Maybe that was it. They looked menacing and cruel, whereas our aircraft seemed mild and unpretentious. They were smooth and not very warlike to behold. But the gentlemanly, graceful Spitfires and P-51's, with no armament showing, engaged the

terrifying and barbaric German planes that bristled with weapons and aerials and experimental protuberances, and we slid
through the air like lightning to strike them down and husband
the sky for ourselves, and ourselves alone.

Though I patrolled almost every day, and often fought for
my existence, the months at Monastir were for reasons that I
still cannot discern the most peaceful and tranquil of all my life.

I lived alone in an airy tent with open sides. Rising before
dawn, I washed, dressed, and attended a ten-minute briefing
that consisted of a dissertation on the perfect weather and the
winds aloft, and the assignment of patrol sectors: which sector
never made much of a difference. On rare days, we escorted a
flight of bombers over Sicily, but mostly our job was air superiority, which meant hours of lonely flying that sometimes
led to mortal combat.

I returned to the field by noon. After my debriefing and then
talking to the mechanics, I had a lunch of soup and salad. Then
I went back to the tent and lay on my cot, immobile, exhausted,
and subdued. When I was rested, I exercised, which was what
kept me young and able to fly.

I ran six miles by circling the field. I did calisthenics, lifted
weights, and swam a mile in the sea. In laps accomplished in
the surf, the body must continually adjust for the absence of
water or its sudden swell from beneath. You are always rolling
off the back of one slick whale onto the back of another, but
the hard going gives you grace and makes you part of the sea.
Undisturbed by waves or foam or sudden deep immersions, you
learn to move and breathe like a dolphin.

After exercise, I made a fire and boiled water for shaving,
something for which I had no time in the morning. At first I
used the dinner fire to heat the water, but the bottom of the

pot got fouled with drippings. Then I discovered that doing all this in the late afternoon, after an hour in the sea, was refreshing. The water always seemed astonishingly sweet, and that it was hot was a miracle.

By the time I returned from a tranquil walk in a grove of immensely tall date palms, where I would pace quietly between the rows, listening to the evening breeze in the jalousie-like fronds and spikes above, I would be called to dinner, my only social hour.

Our air wing was grouped in three bases, and at Monastir we had four squadrons, each with twenty-four fighters. There were also bombers, reconnaissance elements, and transport planes. It was a large base, with empty corners.

In one of these we had our tents. Each squadron was divided into four flights, and in each flight were two elements of three aircraft. Little settlements of tents dotted the ground over a huge area. At dusk, fires sparkled across the plain as they undoubtedly had in all the wars there since the beginning of time.

The two other pilots of my element were skinny post-adolescents, Malcolm Gray and Eddy Pond. Malcolm was an ass from Yale who never got the chance to grow out of being an ass, because he was blown out of the air over Darmstadt, and only his parents grieved. Having loved him since he was a baby, they knew that time would probably have made him less of an ass, and besides, you love your child perhaps even the more if he is an ass, because you suffer for him. Who knows, maybe his father was an ass, too, and thought that Malcolm was a prince.

Malcolm's problem as far as I could see was that, because he had gone to Yale, he really thought he was better than everyone else.

"Yale is for preppy shitbirds," I would say to him.

"Oh really?" he would answer. "Where did *you* go?"

"I went to the University of California at Zarazuela," I might say.

"Is that," he would then ask in his full Connecticut, with teeth bolted together inseparably, "a dancing school for Mexican rabbis?" This he found rather funny, and, to be honest, given his way of speaking, so did I.

The Germans hit him when he was on a daylight raid. I was told that he didn't bale out, that his plane broke in two at the cockpit and he went with the rear section, windmilling down.

Eddy Pond, on the other hand, lived through the war so that after it he could sell insurance. I ran into him in Grand Central on a November day in about 1951. He had come to see a Holy Cross football game being played against, I guess, St. John's, and he was walking through the lower level of the station, with a glass of beer in his hand. He was ashamed of the beer, I think, but he had no place to put it, so he held it without drinking as we stood by the information booth for five minutes and talked about Tunisia. Then he went to the football game, and I went home, and I never saw him again.

The three of us would meet for dinner every night in a little sandy place near our tents. We had a Tunisian cook, who found fish, lamb, goat's meat, fowl, and safe vegetables and fruits for us. Tunisia had been a French colony, and after Rommel took it the sanitation did not suffer.

Dessert was always the same: dates. And in the morning our breakfast was always the same: tea, fresh baguettes, cheese, and jam. You couldn't drink more than one cup of tea (or, in my case, hot water), because you would try to avoid peeing into a bottle as you flew. I often brought a chocolate bar and bread with me into the cockpit. If I opened the slide panel and flew upside down, all the crumbs would be vacuumed out.

Perhaps it was because I thought I was going to die, or perhaps it was the otherworldliness and isolation of the place, my laps across the waves, the wind that always blew from ancient lands along the coast, or the sea's great swaths of green, white, and blue. I don't know. But I do know that, somehow, my days there were contented.

All placidity vanished, however, as soon as I started the engine of my plane. Everyone knows that young fighter pilots are arrogant, but few understand that this arrogance is merely a misguided effort to achieve the requisite state for flying an airplane in combat. To do that and survive, you must indeed have something that might seem—to a boy—to be arrogance.

But what you need is not arrogance. It is, rather, enthrallment, and surrender to speed. I used to sing to the accompaniment of my engine. As this is a confession of sorts and will be read (if it does not fall prey to the ants) by only one person, I confess that I would not only sing, but dance.

Up there you are very busy, and you can check your gauges and instruments 'til kingdom come, and you must watch the whole sky, even behind you and, as far as you can, into the sun—especially into the sun—but meticulousness, skill, and care sometimes must be abridged, sometimes must be abandoned in favor of the life in things like engines and air and sudden climbs to great altitudes.

Alone over the Mediterranean, lost in skies of cloudless blue, as free as an angel, I could hear deep notes rising from fifteen hundred horses running, and I would sing in time and in counterpoint.

I danced, after a fashion—strapped into a parachute, strapped into my seat, burdened with all kinds of things strapped onto me. I moved the plane in wasteful, unauthorized, dangerous, beautiful maneuvers—in banks that lifted the load to the point of almost breaking us apart, in dives that sought the hypnotic blue of the sea, and in climbs in which I thought that if I kept the throttle out I might come near the precincts of God.

I found that, as I listened to the silver sound of the engine, fears that had been ferocious and unbearable suddenly were tame, and I could take what I did to the limit, dancing on a knife edge, absolutely certain, rising powerfully on voluminous waves of grace that would vanish neither in combat nor in limping home nor in touching down, but only after my time in the sea, returning the music whence it had come.

The first Messerschmitt I ever saw broke my rhythm. I was in one of the huge empty Mediterranean quadrants from which I could see neither the coast of Africa nor the coast of Sicily, and he appeared several miles away at 10:30, already climbing, having seen me first.

I was heading south, with the morning sun on my left, as he was gathering altitude to come at me in a shallow dive from out of the glare. I found myself saying, "What am I going to do?" There wasn't much I *could* do, because he was already far above me and beginning his turn. The safe thing would have been to dive under him and loop up in a back flip, to equal his altitude or at least decrease his advantage. But the great rhythms of the engine, beating through my chest and cradling my heart, dictated other tactics.

I said, "Fuck it," and turned into the sun, climbing at full throttle with superchargers. I held my left hand in front of my face and peered through a little hole I made by holding my thumb almost flush with my index finger. It is not impossible to see a plane coming out of the sun, just very difficult and painful. Because your eyes must continually seek their rest, you are not so much looking as looking away. What you see becomes a series of stills from which you must calculate the movement of your target from one frame to the next, something I would not have been able to do absent the rhythmic counterpoint of the engine and my sense of being outside the aircraft and watching it move through the clouds. With these, I could calculate. I could indeed. I picked up the Schmitt and I stuck to him even though he was framed in a painful white halo.

Had it not been for the elevation of my spirits that morning I would not have been able to put a black dot coming out of the sun in my sights. We had only seconds before colliding, and we both were firing, knowing that if either of us got a hit we both would die. The paths of my wing cannons converged at three hundred yards, and our combined speed was close to a thousand miles an hour, which meant that if I had put my fire on him properly we would have collided in another two thirds of a second.

Although I didn't know his fire convergence distance and I assumed he didn't know mine, I knew that he knew what I knew. And it was he who broke off, because he wanted to live, whereas it was I who held and fired, because I cared not so much about living, and I was angry and happy and most probably half mad.

We rolled and looped without knowing precisely where we would come out relative to one another. That was the throw of the dice, but now, at least, we were starting on an equal basis. When I completed my loop and came out level, I saw him. The cannons in his nose were firing. Before I knew it, they scattered past me, knocking a few holes in my tail section. I had no shot, but he had no more position. He dived to my left because to get his shot he had had to pull ahead of me. He was giving away his life for a sweep shot, and what good is a sweep shot against an armored fighter like a P-51? You have to be very lucky, and he wasn't.

I dived after him: he knew it. He snaked: it hardly mattered. I snaked too, and soon I was locked on. I fired, but to no effect. I was waiting for him to pull up and give me the broadside of a barn. He had to, or he would go into the sea, and when he came out of his dive I fired my six cannons in a very long burst, and I got him.

He leveled out, smoking. His canopy opened, long seconds passed, and then a minute, and then another minute. I followed above, waiting for him to bale out. "Come on! Come on!" I screamed. "Get out!" He was steadily losing altitude, and the white smoke had turned to black. As the seconds passed and fire leapt from his engine cowling, I thought my heart would burst.

Then I saw him pop up from the cockpit and put his foot on the bulkhead the way you would if you were going to jump out. I felt tremendous relief, because I thought that, though I had taken a Messerschmitt from the Luftwaffe's order of battle, I had not killed a man. The British would pick him up in the Malta Channel, and he would spend the rest of the war weaving baskets.

I was happy when I saw him topple out. But he had hesitated too long at the edge. He hadn't jumped, he had fallen. I banked to circle him, and watched him descend, arms and legs flailing but somehow still, chute unopened, until he disappeared into the sea.

Then I turned for home, with neither music nor dancing but,

still, with the determination that when I went up again (the next morning) I would have the music and dancing as much as I might need.

In my first contact with the enemy I had been working with a very narrow margin, and following thereafter were a number of margins narrower still. Though I knew how to go into a fight, and could exploit the union of euphoria and the power that comes from smiling at death, I did not want to die there, so I began to build.

The boys with whom I flew were coming into their strengths, whereas mine were flowing away with age. The heart of their lives was being formed in the battles they fought in the air, and they had begun to forget whatever else they hardly knew anyway. Never would there be anything they would do better, and nothing they would remember would hold half the light of their great days in the air. But as I was at the brink of middle age I had to trick my way out of death. I conspired with the mechanics to modify my plane.

War in the air was still quite chivalrous. Even now, it remains more so than war at sea or on land, perhaps because of the openness of the battlefield, the purity of the forces required for advantage, the bias toward individualism. Forty years ago, deception in air combat did not go beyond camouflaged planes, radio silence, and surprise attack. Other than that, you were expected to triumph because of the superiority of your technology and your greater skill and bravery in flight.

I thought that this might not be enough, so, first, I ran thicker cable from the cockpit to the control surfaces. We got the cable from light bombers, and it hardly added any weight, although we were sufficiently cautious to keep a running tally of the increase, making up for it in operations by loading slightly less fuel.

Then I reinforced—and, in some cases doubled—the hinges, flanges, bolts, and other attachments, the pivots, divots, davits, and rabbits that in a maneuver were the points of strain. At first the mechanics were skeptical. They said, "The airframe won't take the strain you want to be able to inflict on the aircraft."

I answered with a question: "They don't build these without a margin of safety, do they?"

"No."

"What is it?"

They threw up their shoulders. They didn't know.

"Let's say it's ten percent," I said. "Drop it to two."

"If we drop it to two," one of them said, "and if your hand shakes a bit, you might collapse a few spars. Or the wings will come off. It's happened."

It was easy to convince them that my new operational limits were only for use when there was no hope, when, boxed in with nothing to draw upon and nowhere to turn, I would be shot down anyway. The ME-109 pilots knew what we could do, and choreographed their movements accordingly. I was going to surprise them.

Then I had the mechanics build the flaming peacock, which was a steel box cut into the fuselage aft of the cockpit. Instead of the plane's aluminum skin, the surface over the box was a metal plate held in place by a cotter pin. Inside, under a screen to keep it from blowing away, was a magnesium flare surrounded by four condoms full of the worst Tunisian olive oil, and two big paper bags of ground pepper. This was sprinkled with three 50-caliber shells' worth of gunpowder and packed with excelsior.

We tested it on the ground, where it made a disgusting mess, and then in the air, where the great volumes of oxygen and the pressure of the wind helped to create exactly the effect we wanted. First you pulled a line that yanked the cotter pin, and then you pulled another line that set off the flare. The flare exploded the gunpowder, which exploded the olive oil and the pepper, and blew away the plate. A great burst of flame, sparks, burning crap of all kinds, and huge masses of white smoke issued from the peacock, and, as any chef knows, the olive oil just kept on smoking.

I had noticed in my very first engagement that when my opponent fell away from me, wounded, I leveled out and held my fire. It was instinctive, as well as the knightly thing to do. And it was practical: you didn't want to lose altitude and open yourself to attack. Also, you felt constrained to stay within the arena of action. The same impulse that leads a dog to stay within his territory or a bull to stamp the ground led pilots to break off when their opponent was falling toward the sea. The more methodical the pilot, the more likely he would stick to this paradigm, and the pilots of the ME-109's were, thank God, Germans.

The first time I used the peacock I didn't really think it would work. I was coming off Licata, fifty miles out at sea and still in sight of land, with half my fuel and half my ammunition left after strafing an olive grove that concealed a truck park.

Three ME-109's appeared at 9:30 high, two thousand feet above. The one in the center came straight at me in a shallow dive, and his two wingmen broke off to complicate my life. The one in the north rose and then banked to get behind me, and the one in the south dived and began to come up in anticipation of my evasion.

If I looped back to get the plane behind me, I would show my belly to the plane in the center. If I dived to the east, the plane behind me would have his chance—to the west, the plane in front. Meanwhile, the one in the middle was going to get off a good long shot.

The only thing to do was what I did, turn at the center plane and fire a long burst in the hope of diverting him. It worked; he was easily diverted because he knew his wingmen were on me, and he rolled off to his left.

He almost certainly did not think that I would follow, because, if I did, I would have the wingmen on me in a fatal rear lock. But I did follow, and locked in on the center plane, now fleeing from me to no avail. I hit him, and he dropped away, smoking.

In normal usage, I was dead. I had two ME-109's hard on my tail, converging, at different altitudes, firing like mad. They were vengeful and sure, as they should have been. I pulled the cable to the flaming peacock. The door was blown out into the blue, followed by what appeared to be the burning viscera of the plane. I dropped with the distinctive forward jerk of a bird taken on the wing, and let myself fall languidly toward the sea.

They broke off, still tracking me, but from far above. A few feet over the waves, I began an all-out forward run. By the time the peacock went out, I was invisible against the sea and they had turned back. I banked to the left and started to climb. Then I put on the superchargers. By the time I reached altitude, I could hardly see the Messerschmitts. They were nothing more than specks that appeared and disappeared. Had they gone back to their field, I would have missed them, but they continued their patrol, turning west. That would give me a broadside, out of the sun.

I took it. I hit one so hard that he broke up in the air, and the other simply fled. At this point I was very low on fuel and ammunition and I back-rolled for home hoping that the remaining Schmitt would not come back. He didn't.

Just enough fuel was left to skim the beach before landing. We were not supposed to do that, but it was often too enticing not to. It was like shouting out that you were still alive, and your voice was not your voice but the voice of your swift and powerful plane, with an engine that shook the ground, with six cannons, and light wings that rocketed through the clouds. The planes returned as if from nowhere, propellers churning in golden light, avenging angels descending from unimaginable wars in the ether. After my first kill I understood that we were singing a terribly sad song. But I'm not ashamed of having sung that song, for, no matter what you may suspect, it was the most beautiful thing I had ever heard.

Months of daily patrol made me confident that, despite the narrow margins of my kills, I had been born to shoot down ME-109's. I suppose I thought I had stumbled upon the slight and perpetual edge that is the hallmark of a great athlete. A bicyclist who repeatedly wins the Tour de France by nine or ten seconds after coming from behind and overtaking a customary rival will endorse hot cocoa and stretch pants until the sun burns out. The human race is intoxicated with narrow victories, for life itself is a string of them, like pearls that hit the floor when the rope breaks, and roll away in perfection and anarchy.

I was on a SLOC patrol north of Benghazi, I had dropped my wing tanks, and was using the last of my loiter time before heading across the top of the Gulf of Sirte back to Monastir.

The sea below was empty and dead, the Libyan Desert still covered with corpses and armor, and the road from Egypt seldom traveled. By that time, German and Italian aircraft hardly ever appeared over the territory from which their armies had been driven, though they had the capacity to do so. They flew from aerodromes in Sicily, particularly one beneath the hill town of Erice, a huge hornets' nest on a checkered and hospitable plain.

As we were used to flying straight at their greatest strengths, the Benghazi SLOC was considered merely a formality, an opportunity to rest, and I wasn't paying attention, as I should have been, to the sky around me. Not only did enemy planes never show up in the Gulf of Sirte, having no longer any reason to be there, but I was lost in memories of a woman I had once known in Boston. Had it not been for the war, I might have married her. To the accompaniment of very gentle and happy semi-indigenous music that my radio brought me dimly from French West Africa across thousands of miles of silent desert and cobalt-blue skies, I was looking into her eyes, my arms resting on her shoulders, as I moved back and forth, to and from her face, kissing her in adoration each time I came in. This had lasted for a long time, and was totally hypnotic both when it happened and when I recalled it.

I had neglected my instruments and gauges, had glanced at the compass only unconsciously, and my one thought of the sky was that it was the color of her blue eyes. I had kissed her for so long that we were both delirious. It was on a cold winter day, in a parlor room in the Back Bay, as the radiator hissed and the wind blew. I had kissed her like this because it was such a joy to see her face.

Had she known that I was still kissing her, twenty thousand feet above the Gulf of Sirte, she might have been as numb with pleasure as was I. That was the problem. My mouth hung half open and my eyes focused on infinity. And as I sank deeper and deeper into the kiss, a spray of cannon shells tap-danced up my fuselage and across my wings, all in a second. I woke with a terrible start.

I never saw the plane that had passed over me. He undoubt-

edly rolled back to get behind me again, but I was too busy to
search for him. My first instinct was to bank left, but the aircraft
did not respond.

In the movies, when planes are shot up, they catch fire and
dive smoothly until they can "explode" behind a hill. Naturally,
pilots just simulating a crash can fly smoothly: their aircraft are
intact. I was flying anything but smoothly: the cannon shells
had severed enough spars and ribs to make the plane shake like
a renegade washing machine. The more it shook, the more things
popped and broke, and to keep myself from breaking into pieces
I cut the throttle until I was almost gliding. I had only half my
controls, and was doing everything I could just to stay in level
flight.

Where was he? I didn't know. I guessed. He was several
thousand feet above, watching to see if he had to come in for
the kill or if I was going to be a hole-in-one. I kept on saying,
"Fuck you! Fuck you! Fuck you!," as if he could hear me as I
was knocked around in my own cockpit like a bug who had
gone to sleep in a jackhammer.

I was spitting like someone at the end of an hour of rough
dentistry. You don't spit in your cockpit, because then you have
to live with it. "Why am I spitting?" I asked myself. Then I
looked, and I realized that I was spitting blood. But I felt no
pain. I must be wounded somewhere, I thought, but I have a
lot of strength, and I feel no pain. My flight suit was binding
me like a pressure bandage.

Then the engine caught fire. Why, I wondered, had it burst
into flame after such a long delay? The answer that I was able
to give only much later was that everything had happened in a
few seconds that were greatly hollowed out in time.

"The goddamned windshield," I told myself, "is covered with
blood." I couldn't see. But it wasn't blood, the engine was

spraying oil, which was then applied to the glass by the atmosphere acting as a 300 mph airbrush. Still, if I could get home, I could land with only side visibility. I looked to check my instruments. They were shattered and covered with blood. The glass had been broken in the frames, and shards of it covered my legs. The panel was dripping wet.

Whose blood is that? I thought.

The shaking had not subsided, and when the engine cut out, the ride got a little smoother but a lot less controlled. I decided to bale out.

The engine was dead, the plane was buffeting and on fire, I was blind in front and spitting blood. I unlocked the canopy and pulled on it, but it refused to slide. The frame had been bent and would not move even an inch. I had to ditch.

Looking down, I saw that the sea was now fairly close. Though ten or fifteen miles from the coast, I was unable to head in closer, because I couldn't steer. I remembered a trick for crash-landing in the sea that a British Hurricane pilot had told me in the officers club in Algiers. Just before you go down, you fire all your guns simultaneously. Due solely to the fact that for every action there is a reaction, thirty seconds of sustained firing through six cannons could slow you perhaps enough to save you.

I put my flaps down and pulled hard to keep the nose high. This seemed to tame one frequency of vibration and liberate another. Even though the engine was dead and the prop feathered, we were making a lot of noise, in wind that shrieked through broken glass, in the roar of oxygen-pumped flame, and as the wings and fuselage vibrated like a metal roof in a July downpour.

My speed was high and the waves unfortunately vigorous. Because I had to slide in on my belly, I hadn't been able to drop the wheels to increase drag, for I assumed that I would not have been able to get them up again. As the sea rose to meet the plane I fired the cannons and felt them slow the forward momentum. They were deafeningly loud.

The plane banged down, bounced, and flipped over. The next thing I knew, I was hanging upside down in the cockpit, underwater, slowly sinking.

I undid my harness and fell onto the canopy. I thought I had broken my neck. How was I going to get out? I was already sitting in water up to my thighs, and the canopy wouldn't slide open. The water was silent, blue, and clear, with nothing in it but dissolved azure and rows of streaming sun.

After I kicked and punched the parachute out of my way, I half ripped off and half slithered out of my flight suit. It, too, was bulky, and covered with attachments, projections, and accoutrements that might have caught on the metal and drowned me.

The knife I carried had a heavy bolt at the butt, and I used it to attack the glass canopy as if I were in mortal combat with a wolf. Seawater came flooding in, colder now because the plane had sunk deeper. I took the last of the air and put my head through the opening. As I passed through, the plane began a graceful cartwheel, the tail turning in an arc that reached up and failed to break the silver surface. I was free. I rose toward the bottom of the waves, bubbles of air preceding me on the way up.

When I burst into clear air and felt the spray on my face, I was choking with brine, bleeding in the water, whooping, laughing, and crying for joy. I had hours of swimming ahead, and despite the fact that I was wounded I did the first mile or so like a porpoise, leaping into the troughs of the waves with an explosion of foam and the spray stinging my face. I was alone in windblown reaches of water. The Mediterranean is an old and gentle sea, shallow and warm, blue and green—the color of sapphires and sea turtles.

I will never know exactly how many miles I swam—whether it was ten, or fifteen, or less, or more—but when I reached shore I was exhausted as never before.

In the sea I had felt a pain in my left side, and when I crawled onto the sand beyond the breakers I discovered a little hole there the size of a small-caliber bullet. Although I didn't know it, a rivet had been propelled into me. Had it reached my heart, I would have been slain in battle not by a German bullet but by an American metal fastener.

Because I was now only occasionally coughing up blood, I didn't worry. And yet I was sufficiently anxious that I didn't fall asleep on the beach, which was the most beautiful, empty beach I had ever seen, and I had seen some very lovely beaches (after all, I was an investment banker).

It was several hundred yards wide, and sloped so that the waves rolled in and broke with a semi-Southampton thud, and the sand was the soft white color of a good broadcloth shirt— which is to say that it was slightly yellow and gold, just enough to make it a cousin of the sun that beat upon it from dawn to dusk.

Unfortunately, I was already thirsty, and it seemed ironic that my only choice was to walk into the interior, for I am sure that someone downed in the desert almost certainly would have made for the sea. But as I saw no hotels, seaside restaurants, or mahogany launches, I headed in the direction of the road.

I had studied the map. Along the entire length of the Libyan coast, the road paralleled the beach. In some places they ran close together, but at other points the road was almost forty miles inland. Having no idea of my location, I imagined that I might have exhausted my luck and come ashore at the forty-mile section. I had.

Weak, bleeding, and dehydrated, I did not relish the prospect of walking forty miles in the hot sun, but I hoped I would not have to. At least I'd kept my shoes, even diving for one when it slipped off as I swam. Before setting out, I cut my pants into shorts and bandaged my wound with one of the dismembered legs.

Soon, the land fell into a huge rock-littered depression. I passed the hours hoping to come across a plant, but I was in the world of minerals. As I walked, I chanted, "Animal, vegetable . . . mineral. Animal, vegetable . . . mineral." I tried to hum Beethoven, Mozart, Haydn, and Schubert—not Bach, who does not lend himself so much to humming—but I could not make the transition.

After five or six hours, and, presumably, fifteen to twenty miles, I could hardly stand, and had ceased to chant. I rested my eyelids by closing them most of the time and blinking every few seconds, long enough to take a still photograph of what lay in front of me, which I then altered in the remembered image as I walked. I was good at this, having practiced when I was a child, initially to see what it was like to be blind and cheating as I did so, and then to see whether with memory alone I could do justice to time, space, and distance.

Why did I cheat when I pretended to be blind, why does every child? For the same reason that our sympathy and love for those who have died is not strong enough to make us follow. Knowing that our turn will come, we cheat our love and hold on to life. I had opened my eyes simply because, knowing that someday I would be blind, I was not able to resist the light.

I was so drained as I stumbled across the desert that all I wanted was sleep, and in the early morning I surrendered, falling against a convex dome of perfectly white smooth sand. It was cooler than I thought it would be, and as soft as cornstarch. In this magnificent bed, sleep was heavier than ever before or since, and as I began to lose consciousness and dream I hoped I would not die, though I knew that if dying were the price of rest I could not resist payment. My limbs relaxed and I was immediately pulled under.

I awoke at night, in cold primitive air that smelled of ageless sand and rock. When I opened my eyes I was blinded by a rash of stars in the sky, and I had to blink to adjust to the light.

This was the only time in my life when for as far as I could see I saw nothing that lived and nothing made by man. The sky stretched for 360 degrees in a bowl undisturbed by spires or hills or ranks of trees. And yet the air moved in columns of heat, refracting the starlight, making the pins of phosphorus jump and dance, and it did so as if I were looking over the prospect of a city on a frigid winter night ribboned with air rising from active chimneys. Though the sky was broken by translucent wavy columns they rose not from fires but from large rocks or dark patches of sand.

I always feel enormously revived by the sight of stars, and as I walked west-southwest, guided by the North Star in a line perpendicular to the coast, I was very happy to be in Africa, at night, alone (as far as I knew) for hundreds of miles. Had I struck southward I might have wandered through a thousand miles of desert, seeing no one, not even a lizard or a palm, until the wastes of French Equatorial Africa turned green.

Africa, it seemed to me, and still does, is the last bastion of dreams. Its perimeters have been clarified and stabilized by written languages and machines, but in its depth nothing can be remembered except what comes from the heart. In the real Africa, time has no punctuation, and flows between misty green banks. There, the color and texture of the landscape, the grace of the animals, and the forbearance of man, are all linked in suffering, joy, and the comforting nonexistence of time.

Even on the northern margins raked by mechanized war, I felt the presence far south of Libreville, Mbeya, and Lourenço Marques, all places that I did not know but for their names, all under the same ocean of sky. And as I was walking on the Mediterranean littoral, other men were walking under the stars on longer coasts and in quieter hinterlands—on the Red Sea, the Indian Ocean, and the Atlantic.

What could be more poignant than a place where history has been lost, for there all value flows into the present. There, the present actually exists. We who have invented writing and planning have disinvented immediacy, but in Africa immediacy is everywhere. I had stepped into its realm when I left the coast and started walking in the direction of Senegal (never to reach it) and under the same blazing stars that lit warm and humid Brazzaville. Though I was in very poor physical condition, just thinking of what lay south made my heart full.

Then the sun came up, the orange clock of Africa, and lit the red desert before me. The way was flat now, with the rocks few and far between and most of them no bigger than grapefruit. The horizon at dawn jumped from an inexplicable union of black and gray inks to a sharply penned line, and as if to echo this newfound resolution, the road suddenly appeared before me. Had I been five minutes ahead of myself, I would never have seen it, because it consisted of two rows of rocks placed at intervals of about fifteen feet, with nothing in between the rows but a rutted track.

Had not the sun risen just then, I would have crossed the road in two strides and disappeared forever in the desert. By the time I was destined to meet Constance, my bones would have been bleached entirely white and half buried in sand. The only memory of me would have been in various registers here and there, culminating in a perfectly ironic listing in the Pentagon stating that I had been lost at sea.

Looking north, I saw something upright, and walked toward it, thinking that it might be a man, or, better yet, a woman. Had I met a woman, let us say Ingrid Bergman, in similar straits, I am sure that we would have achieved love and intimacy that would have made us happy for the rest of our lives.

It was not Ingrid Bergman but a pole supported by rocks, a signpost with two whitewashed boards across which were written in black paint the words *CANTIERE di BONIFICA, Azi SAFI EDDIN EL SENUSSI Ca, 148 KM,* and an arrow pointing south.

I waited by this sign for most of the day, and then, after I began to worry that I actually might die there, I saw a column of dust. It was moving toward me. After half an hour I could see that the dust had been kicked up by a group of British trucks.

When they reached me, they stopped, and fifty men jumped to the ground. I stared at them without speaking. A tall officer, a major as I recall, approached me and, when he realized that the creature before him was still alive, took off his hat. I have always loved British officers' caps, and even in the scarlet and green gardens of Niterói I remember their inimitable red.

Clutching a mahogany swagger stick capped at one end by a 50mm shell casing and at the other by an empty Enfield cartridge, he bent over and said, "Hello. Do you speak English?"

I looked at him for a moment, watching him await my answer. "From your point of view, probably not," I told him.

My sojourn in Northern Italy was my undoing as a flier, for it was there that a number of factors coalesced and deprived me of the edge I had had in the air over the Mediterranean.

The first was age. I was forty. I did not believe that I would live, as I have, to be eighty, for at the time people like me—which is to say unhappy, unmarried, mesomorphic investment bankers who felt that skimming millions off corporate and public bond issues was no more worthwhile than a fly shitting in the Gulf of Mexico—lived to about sixty-five. Many pressure-cooked and ate themselves to death—you would not believe the sauces available to a partner at Stillman and Chase—in their fifties, and some even in their forties. A few of my colleagues managed to achieve cardiac arrest in their middle thirties. One even checked out at twenty-seven, of apniated dyspnea, and with him went the economic future of the Sudan. These are the things about which historians seldom have the slightest hint. They look for structural causes and subject their readers to trans-actional analyses, when all they need to know is that Frederick Parts III had an overwhelming yen for lamb brains in double cream sauce. If you are five foot three, weigh 425 pounds, and your arteries are 85% sealed with lard, chicken fat, and marisco, it pays not to exert yourself in the Chutney School Alumni Squash Tournament. He died with his teeth clenched.

Being naturally pessimistic, I figured that (assuming I would get through the war) I had twenty years remaining, or perhaps only ten, and the forty years I had known had passed so quickly that they seemed misplaced. In memory, I groped for their meaning as if they were my glasses and I had lost them in the dark, and as I found no meaning I became intensely jealous of the years ahead, however many they might be. This made me sometimes unduly cautious, which greatly increased my chances of dying in the air.

I did not have the stamina of boys of twenty and even thirty, and unlike them I was unable to recover quickly as one mission bled into another. This was dangerous.

And, then, we sensed that the war was almost over. That we would win was a foregone conclusion. Every death past the point of that acknowledgment seemed not a sacrifice but a waste. Every action, even those in aerial combat, was laden with reluctance. Split seconds were lost, those marvelous, warriorlike split seconds that arise from desperation and anger and make the difference between living and dying.

The weather was terrible over Germany: many fighters collided with our own bombers or their own flights, and others, badly crippled, could not find their way home through the smothering clouds. I know the oppression they felt, tunneling into the gray without respite, because it almost happened to me once, when, instruments gone and surrounded by cloud, I flew in what I took to be a southerly direction, at an altitude I guessed would take me over the Alps, and suddenly I found myself over France, in an explosion of blue, in clear cold air, buffeting in a wind storm at the vanguard of a front that had come from the ocean or the Arctic, and was my salvation.

Lastly, I suppose, Italy itself offers such a beautiful alternative to war that you lose your taste for fighting, a taste always sharpened by the simple failures of civilization. In Italy I saw in the operations of daily life continual reference to greater themes and purposes, and there seemed no need to throw it all over, angrily, in a fireball, as I believe the Germans always want to do, vexed as they are by their painfully efficient darkness.

I used to walk along a river from the airfield to the town, on a path under rustling willows. The river was narrow, fresh, and clear. You could see brown-shadowed trout making the circles of their society in translucent pools covered with dancing rain. In places the water flowed over weirs or spillways, where it took on velocity and a coat of silver that cooled the air. The flawless tongues of water forced through the teeth of the weirs reminded me of piano keys, and by looking at them I could summon the memory of pieces written to honor the beauty of such things as dancing rivers and tempestuous rain.

In town I traded my coffee allotment for virgin olive oil, pasta, peppers, tomatoes, and tiny portions of long-cured prosciutto. It was remarkable to me that anyone would part with such things in return for a few handfuls of nauseating brown gravel. The other day, on the train to the naval academy, I saw a poster intended for Brazilian mothers. The gist of its message was that if their children poisoned themselves with various substances listed in the midst of the advice, they should make the children throw up. And how do you do this? You make them eat either a brown paper bag or coffee grounds.

I carried the coffee in a sealed pouch at the end of a pole. At the market, I would take the pole off my shoulder and maneuver the pouch onto a table for trade. The first time I did this they thought I had brought explosives, and everyone ran. Eventually they grew accustomed to my method of delivery, but they never understood it. I didn't want to demean my goods in trade, so I told them that in America coffee is carried at the end of a pole to assure that it does not reach the same temperature as the human body, which harms the flavor.

The food was, of course, better by far than Army Air Force rations. It was the only kind of meal I could eat if I knew that the next day I was going to escort a daylight raid on a heavily defended target. Even after the war, even now, when faced with something that I fear, I tend to eat spaghetti.

When I eat pasta primavera, or linguine with crushed tomatoes and hot pepper, I become tranquil and melancholy, and if I close my eyes I see dozens of planes, with propellers spinning like silver water thundering over a weir, waiting to get onto the runway and fly off to the battle across the Alps.

When the aircraft of three or four squadrons gather for a group assault, the air and the earth shake all around them. The planes crowd together at imprecise angles, and as those at the edges taxi away into the wind, the ones that remain are seized by the fear of inaction. The assemblage of camouflaged aircraft has appeared as if by magic from Quonset huts and revetments, from hangars and shops, and in the moments before takeoff, the airfield is the most exciting place in the world. But as soon as the last has ascended, all you can hear is the wind.

As the field was overcome by quiet I would be on my way north, seeking a great roll of air over the Alps that would lift me like a glider pilot to the top of an invisible platform from which I would descend an invisible ramp into battle over the ruins of Germany.

From the beginning our method of operation had been dispersal and convergence. It made tactical sense only when we did not have command of the air, but even after German fighters were as rare as jets—mainly because they were jets— the pilots we were aloft to protect were comforted by the perfection of our timing no less than by our particular method of appearance.

We would pick them up one by one, coming from the sun if it were available, or from above. We didn't like the idea of rising to meet another aircraft, and had been strongly habituated against it in all forms, so that we preferred not to rise even to meet our own bombers. The opposite of this was the approach of whatever was left of the Luftwaffe, which, at the end, always seemed to have been taken by surprise, perhaps because its communications net had been shattered, and which, at the end, always had to climb into a fight.

Holding back beyond the sight of the bomber wave, we would let it fly alone for a moment after our counterparts from British fields turned for home. In musical terms I suppose you could call it a rest; in gastronomy the water between courses; in poetry a caesura; in theology the test of remoteness, which is the great test of existence.

We knew that we overshadowed them in an immense hollow dome of light and air, that our eyes were upon them, that they feared, that in their huge planes they were silently looking for fighters either to rise from below to fight or descend on their wing to keep them safe. We knew that they were like us. I knew that any one of them could have been my son, that, indeed, they were sons, and that this was why we were above them in the air, holding back and ready to go forward.

I remember their faces peering from the glittering glass domes as we descended and came alongside. When they thought there was no one, that they were alone, that they had been abandoned, the first of us dropped from nowhere and quietly rode nearby. And then from another direction another of us would appear, and another, and another, until they were surrounded by more fighters than they could count, and every single fighter was willing to die for them.

Some were boys on their first or a very early mission. I would smile at them and give the thumbs up, just as our ground crews did with us, for this commonplace was purified, sanctified, by the circumstance that a certain number of us would within hours or minutes go to our deaths.

When they were fully surrounded by our shield, we would expand the envelope and keep watch from a greater distance. If, as we approached the target, we had no fighter challenge, we would speed ahead to join our elements already engaged in flak suppression.

As the bomber wave reached the target, we would rise. This was the moment when I felt the greatest blackness, when I prayed for a quick end to the war. Even thousands of feet above, in clear and insubstantial air, the concussions of the bombs made our planes vibrate like an old car speeding over a washboard road. Though fixed, the glass in the instrument panels somehow managed to rattle, and my goggles moved around my eyes like a piece on a Ouija board.

We knew that down below were armaments factories and railheads, but also children and their mothers, and how many of them we buried we did not know. At this moment, as the bombs found their marks or horribly strayed from them, we would have been easy prey for any fighter that rose to avenge its angels, but at this moment they never did rise, which is why we stayed alive.

We came together only as an accretion to the bomber wave, and we stayed together only until we passed the bombers back to their home escorts. Then we left as we had come, alone. The heart of what we did was that we were alone, our hallmark a single plane the master of a vast ocean of air.

At the very end, in the early spring of 1945, I was flying flak suppression on the outskirts of Berlin. I hated flak suppression, which was completely different from air-to-air combat and not what I was used to. I hated dive-bombing, which was one long note during which you had to overcome at least three very strong inclinations. It is not natural to align yourself along the path of fire and pursue it to its source, as if you wish to lodge yourself in the barrel of a gun. Nor is it natural to point your airplane toward the earth and keep it headed down at high speed. Nor is it natural not to evade enemy fire. That was what my wrists and reflexes had been for, what the musicality of my timing had allowed me to do in quick air battles that had moved like fast dances.

The only thing good about flak suppression was that after getting rid of the bombs loiter time was virtually zero, simply because the more bombs you carried, the less fuel you could take. With merely cannon, we jettisoned drop tanks and switched to internal supply immediately before we joined the bombers, but when carrying bombs for flak suppression we shed the smaller tanks before Nürnberg, and, though lightened for the trip back, would come in with only a teaspoon of gas.

It was very difficult to take out an ack-ack gun. Just because it stopped firing after you attacked it didn't mean that you had hit it. They were often arranged in groups in which one protected another, but they were spread out enough so that you had to hit them one by one. And although with the passage of time we destroyed more and more of them, as the Allied armies closed in, the Germans and their antiaircraft drew into a tighter and tighter circle, until it seemed that the more we hit them, the more there were.

As we watched the circle shrink, we knew that the war was nearly over—in Europe, anyway—and it was excruciatingly hard not to be cautious.

At the point where we were fighting something the size and strength of Rhode Island, a ruined city-state that we were turning to dust, I dropped my tanks one day as Nürnberg came up ahead, and went on to Berlin with a rack of 250-pound bombs.

The first flak I encountered was coming from a park, or what had been a park, in the city of Berlin itself. I could see the dust raised by distant columns of Russian tanks, and a circle on the ground in the center of the ack-ack guns, a circle that I judged once to have been a carousel.

The park was sufficiently isolated so that at least I would not have to risk loosing my bombs into a cellar full of children. I climbed to 15,000 feet and then dived at the puffs of smoke. This, I thought, was a unique opportunity, for the ack-ack constellations were always emplaced in fields or forests, maddeningly spread out. Here, they sat in a very tight ring around the carousel, simply because the park wasn't big enough for any other pattern. Undoubtedly, they had been ordered to set up in this park despite the fact that they would probably die in it, and that's what they did.

No way in the world existed to put all the bombs on one spot. The variables of inexact release, wind, mutual interference, and other high-school physics type of things meant that they would disperse. The later you pulled up from a dive, the less they dispersed; the earlier, the more.

I pointed my nose down, and, hardly breathing, aimed for the carousel. Were I lucky, when my bombs spread I would hit three or four of the five or six guns. I hated the g-force going down. It made my nose run afterward and gave me headaches. It was hard to operate the controls with several bodyweights' worth of me pinning my reflexes to the seat.

Diving at almost five hundred miles an hour toward the source of explosive shells aimed in my direction, I was trying to keep a tiny circle in my bomb sights, hardly able to breathe, with what felt like two huge wrestlers sitting on my chest. Eyes wide and teeth clenched, I emitted a steady stream of what newspapers call *expletives*. (You would think that, expletives themselves being so vivid, the word for them would have a little more punch, that it would sound like something other than part of a medieval windmill.)

Shaking, pressed, and hurting, I released the bombs, all of them, and pulled up. The g-force maximized in the trough, and then, I thought, I floated out of danger. I rolled upside down to check the damage, and, looking back, saw that though the park was all smoked-up and exploding, one gun still fired. Its crew was undoubtedly bloody and dirty, riding high on defiance. Undoubtedly their teeth were clenched and they were suffering the concussions of their gun.

They were persistent and lucky. Their shells were set for exactly the altitude of the target, and the target—me—was flying upside down, vulnerable parts exposed.

One shell burst so close that I thought it had actually hit the plane. Maybe it had. Every other bomber pilot had a story about a shell actually bouncing off his plane, or a plane he was watching, or a plane flown by someone he knew.

The first thing I felt was absolute surety that I was going down. Such a determination is not always easy to make, and can require half an hour of listening to dying airframe components and the implausibly complex engine. Much like medical diagnosis, the process depends not so much upon science and logic as upon experience that may not exist.

My plane, however, did not need four months in a sanitarium. No rare or elusive disease tantalized my sense of mystery. To use a medical analogy, the plane had had its head blown off.

The fuel line had been severed and was flaring like a gas plume atop an oil well. The engine, of course, had ceased to function. My canopy was blown away. The cockpit was full of vaporized fuel whistling through the shattered framework that had held the glass. I had a huge hole in one wing, and no doubt that the wing would fail. My body was stinging from shrapnel wounds. I prayed that nothing was deep, and I felt like a man undergoing an alcohol rub after running through a bramble patch.

Taking a chance that the wing would hold, I rolled back to level flight in one smooth movement. Though the wing bounced, it didn't separate. The propeller had already been feathered. "Who did that?" I asked the wind that flapped my lips as I spoke. I had probably done it myself without knowing it, for, after all, no one else was with me.

I wanted rather badly to glide over our lines, as I was fairly sure that if I parachuted into the German portion of the Götterdämmerung they would just shoot me. At the end, and this was the end, it gets incomprehensibly ferocious.

On the other hand, the plane was going to explode, I was already burned, and I didn't know exactly where the lines were. I held on for as long as I could, slowly climbing out of my seat, slowly hooking one leg over the bulkhead, checking the parachute to make sure it wasn't on fire, which would have presented additional difficulties, and trying hard to breathe.

I was dazed enough to have stayed with the plane until it exploded, but I realized that I was headed down, and, wanting to have enough air to fill my parachute, I stepped into the sky.

As I did, or an instant after I did, the plane blew up. I had gone out backwards, and was looking at it. An almost perfectly round orange-yellow fireball exploded in the ether—who knows how far from me—as I fell. It blinded me and then pushed me back, limbs trailing like a comet's tail, taking my breath away, punching my heart like a fist.

My parachute opened, but I hadn't pulled the ripcord: the force of the explosion had done that for me. The lightest, finest moment of my life, a moment of promise and elation, was, inexplicably, the instant when, falling through the air, I was blinded by unbearable light and hit by an almost unbearable shock. These traveled through the emptiness and came very close to killing me. My clothes were singed on their edges like the pages of a book that has come through fire.

All my life I have had a recurring dream from which I wake with gratitude. It is a bright June day on the beach at Amagansett, in the time of my youth, when nothing was there but the wild. I am weightless, held a few feet above the breaking waves and white froth. The wind is strong and, arms spread, I twirl in the sun, circling above a crucible of foam, bathed in gold.

Compared to what happened over Germany, at what I took to be the end, my fine companion dream is pedestrian. Had I not been in the frail and protective air, I surely would have died. And I am sure that, even were it only for an instant, I crossed into the world of light.

Across the Great Divide

*(If you have not done so already,
please return the previous pages to the antproof case.)*

I AWOKE IN utter moonlight this morning, at half past the terrible hour of four, fully awake and blinded by brilliance as if in the middle of the day, as if I were not old and the moon were not ghostly silver.

The Brazilians profess to know the seasons here, but not I. My lack of sensitivity to the particular waxiness or lack of waxiness in the evergreen leaves of the omnipotent brush that covers the hillsides, or to the impotent declinations of the sun as winter approaches, or to the appearance or disappearance of certain flowers, is evidence of my upbringing in a place of four explosive seasons, each of which sought you out like an expertly aimed shotgun blast, broke the world, and ushered you into a new life. Winter to me is a frozen landscape glazed in white under deathly blue winds, not the shift in back-coloration of a seasonally nauseated tree frog.

Here, I also have no sense of where the moon should be or

when it will appear. Even at home I found its motions confusing, but I was seldom taken aback by its presence as I am in Rio, where it seems to spring from nowhere, especially on nights that are inexplicably clear and temperate. When this morning I opened my eyes and it was shining in them through the upper window like a burglar's flashlight, I felt as if I were receiving a message.

Not from God or nature or anything like that, but from my own simple failures and regrets. Of course, I did feel the presence of God, as I often do and always have, but I believe that if He were there it was only because of the presence of truth. He cannot resist truth: it is what lures Him near.

The truth in this case was a simple and homely memory: my route to school. In my eightieth year, I awake in a blaze of cool silver, gravely going over the paths and roads that led to my school more than seven decades before. I do not remember each blade of grass, each rut, each smooth and dusty reach of white earth, but I do remember every alleyway, long prospect, and major turn.

But why? Why such a small thing? After all, I was captured by the retreating German armies as they compacted upon their center in Berlin. Each soldier was a Dürer, so firmly and savagely engraved, so tired, tragic, and clear, that I felt myself made ignorant by my own victory. I was taken to the courtyard of a ruined building and held in the open for two days and nights without protection from artillery or air bombardment. The score or so of Russians, Czechs, Khazars, and who knows what else said that as soon as the space filled up we would be shot. I believed them, and I am sure they were right.

But Berlin fell before the courtyard filled, and I was saved yet again by some unaccountable grace of timing. During the two days that I awaited execution the moon rose through the clear nights as if, with its brilliance, to escort us out. The moon appeared insistently and with unchallengeable beauty through rivers of smoke and dust that had risen with the day's bombardments and run silently on the still night air. This moon was a great comfort in what we took to be our last hours, the calming emissary of another world.

Why then, when I woke many years later, did the same light shine not upon the fall of Berlin but upon my walk to school? You would think that with so many memories of great events such a thing would long ago have been forgotten. The whole world watched Germany fall, but no one's eyes ever followed a lonely child to school, at least not this one.

I cannot explain it, but first memories, first sensations, first loves—when life was clear and unburdened—are what awaken you at night when you are old. Perhaps it is because now I am weak again as I was when I was a child, and without means.

Just as I had done almost three quarters of a century before, I awoke this morning in moonlight, dressed quickly, and, with paper and pens in a (now antproof) case that I carried at my side, went on dark paths through the woods, alone. At that time in the morning the birds have not yet begun to sing, but they are about to. I remember the moment. It was a very good time indeed, full of expectation. And, if I remember correctly, for a seven- or eight-year-old, walking on those dark paths took some courage.

Today I found myself in the garden so much earlier than usual that I had to wait for the light. While I was there the moon went very low and was quashed in the sea, and the stars pulsed lightly for a few minutes afterward.

Though I was happy to contemplate the stillness, I was there at that hour in service of a kind of spycraft. I was varying my route and time in response to a certain ineffable pressure, a tension unidentifiable to the senses. When assassins come, they are preceded by faint waves as delicate as starlight. Death comes lightly, but if you are listening, you can hear it even far away.

I had altered my route and arrived in the garden before the light so that if anyone came later I would see him first—unless I were bent over these pages. My eyes now take about a minute to change focus from small print to a freighter on the horizon or an assassin at the garden gate. I wish I knew how to speed the focus. There must be some kind of oil, or an exercise. Ah, but it's too late.

Soon after the light, just as the sun was getting hot, my heart jumped, I straightened in my seat, and I saw something that took sixty heavy years from my shoulders—a child running up the path, skipping like a ram, his little legs moving underneath him more rapidly than an eggbeater (do they make eggbeaters anymore? I haven't used one since the sinking of the *Lusitania*).

Upon seeing the child, I thought he was my own. And he was. Funio had been sent by Marlise to bring me a message on his way to school. No one could climb the mountain faster or more easily. When he reached me he was hardly out of breath even though he had run all the way.

His schoolbag was strapped to his shoulders and he was in his customary shorts and shirt. No longer is he in that state, as once he was as a baby, when he would suddenly forget everything in the world, drop what he was doing, and embrace me. Now embraces are only for arrival or departure, and his eyes get watery because he knows that, soon, he's going to lose me.

But he forgets that, and his eyes flash as he begins to chatter like a chipmunk, in English or in Portuguese, whatever you please.

Most children of his age would be given a written message to pass on, but not Funio, who remembers every detail, and conveys any length transmission either verbatim, in précis, or in code. If you gave him the American Constitution he could read it, run up the mountain, and deliver it word for word.

Once, Marlise had him carry a series of account numbers from her branch to another. He memorized them. To be sure that if he were captured by Indians and tortured he would not betray the depositors, he divided the numbers by 7.35 if they ended evenly, and by 11.14 if they ended oddly. With this store of information he sped through the streets, reprocessing the information at his destination.

"Mama says to tell you that the barber told her a man was looking for someone."

"In Niterói?"

"In Niterói. The barber followed him back to the city. He's staying in a hotel. He's very ugly and he has a pony tail, and lots of hair in his nose, and his nostrils are flat and he has an earring and big bones. Oh, he has a Turkish passport."

"Turkish passports can be bought in vending machines," I said.

Because he understood about assassins, little Funio began to cry.

"Funio, Funio," I said, putting him on my knee. "I have no fear. Look."

I held out my hand, and it was rock steady. Though I am eighty years of age, I have no tremor. "You just stay out of the way," I told him, "and I'll take care of everything."

He was not consoled.

I drew the Walther and put it in his hands. "Funio, I was in the war, and much more. I know how to use this. I'm not afraid. It even gives me a strange kind of happiness, because fighting has been so strongly intertwined with my life. . . ."

"Still," he whispered.

What could I say? I kissed him, and he ran off to school, skipping down the long path. I have never been able to tell him how much I love him, though that is perhaps the way it should be, because words could not express what I feel, and actions, too, would come up short. Someday, as sons do, he will come to understand me.

Meanwhile, I must be vigilant.

So I sit in this garden trying to be alert to the present as the comforting force of memory brings me back. I can relive a day in a moment or a year in a day, and for someone with not so much time remaining, this makes great sense. In revisiting what I have left behind I can sit on this bench and feel waves of affection, awe, and sadness, which in combination with the richness of the garden, the warmth of the sun, and the blue of the sea, makes my life full. Though I have no choice and I must write this down, I had no idea it would be so easy.

In middle age, I did not understand that I was still young. I was seasoned by loss, war, the simple passage of time, and the new and vexing qualities of a body grown imperfect. But I had never had terrible pains in my legs. I had never worn an appliance of any sort—I thought appliances were things such as dishwashers and refrigerators, and only later did I discover that these were *major* appliances. I had never collapsed in a public place. I had never had a catheterization, and, what is more to the point, I had never had a Brazilian catheterization. I had a wife with the grace and physique of a professional dancer, the perpetual youth of a koala bear, naturally blazing blond hair, a doctorate in economics, and the wonderfully entrancing qualities that flowed from having several billion dollars. Life had a gravityless air. I was able still to stay up all night in sexual enthusiasm and not pay for it with a visit to the Mayo Clinic. I had not experienced the period in my fifties when, despite all my efforts, I began to resemble Konrad Adenauer, and I did not yet envy things like bats, squirrels, and rabbits for their youth and physical vitality.

In the midst of what I did not realize was a hot hardwood blaze with nary a sign of white ash, Constance left me. She just walked away. That wasn't very constant, was it, but what's in a name?

Now I have Marlise. Marlise is beautiful, she always was. And as she has aged, her beauty has not fled: unlike so many women in her cohort, she doesn't look like a turtle or a lichee nut. Her way of speaking is ever fascinating, in English and even in Portuguese. Still, Constance left me, and there is a hole in the air where she once used to be. She's gone.

Miss Mayevska is also gone, but though I still grieve for her and for the children she must have loved beyond all measure, especially in the last moments when they were taken from her, she and they are either clasped passionately to the heart of God, or there is no God.

As my union with Constance was broken by mortal will, thinking about her is possible without tears or theology, two things that I'm often too weak to endure, and for which I am saving all my real strengths for the last, when I hope to exit like a fighter pilot.

In May of 1950, Constance and I flew to Denver and then to Jackson Hole. There we bought two quarter horses, two pack horses, saddlery, harnesses, camping equipment, down jackets, oilskin coats, and Stetsons that saved us in the days of rain. We had a compass, maps, two lever-action rifles and a few boxes of ammunition, some wire, and a fence tool.

On the route we followed, most of the range was open, which is not to say that we did not have to cross fences, for we certainly did. The horses we rode at home could have taken three-strand wire fences in their sleep, but even had we had them and they were able to survive the rough, the pack horses would never have been able to follow.

The way to cross fences was to cut the two upper wires and step the horses over the one that remained. Then you used six inches to a foot of the wire you carried (depending on the tension of the wire you cut) to mend the damage, and you went on. You did it as carefully as you could, out of respect and courtesy, and as the toll for crossing land not your own. We took a little lesson in how to do it properly, and the cuts we left behind were put back together with many more than the required twists, which is more or less what I wanted to do with my life and what I have not been able to do, but what I may do yet.

We followed the Continental Divide as much as we could, though it is often only a chain of impassable ridges and summits. Still, plateaux flank either side of it and run sometimes even at the crest, and along their many miles you can ride at the top of the world, just about as far from cities and settlements as you can get, your only encounter being a few sheepmen and their startled flocks.

From the shepherds, with whom we spoke—not knowing Basque—in a mixture of French, Spanish, and Italian, we bought mutton. I have always had a taste for mutton, preferring it to lamb for many reasons, and up there it was cooked until nearly all the fat was gone, and smoked very heavily to preserve it without refrigeration, which is just the way I like it. It was our staple protein, which we used sparingly with several kinds of lentils, and rice. Other than that, we had a few bags of dried fruit, flour, sugar, dried soups, and a bottle of lime juice from which, like British seamen, we took daily sips.

I didn't think at the beginning of the trip or in planning it that I would shoot game. I have killed men, but in almost every case they were heavily armed and about to kill me. And although to me it appears to be morally reprehensible, I bow to the necessity of eating animals. Nonetheless, I don't like killing them. The evisceration, skinning, and removal of head and extremities, all of which can leave you covered with blood in nightmarish fashion, is not my cup of, well, tea.

But the horses forced me into a different frame of mind. They were very stupid about snakes, of which, in the seven hundred miles on our twisting backtracking route from Jackson to Denver, we encountered many. We surprised them sunning themselves on the far sides of rolling hillocks or coiled like buffalo offal baking on flat rocks upon the snow.

The snakes, who had been sleeping at the switch, would make a big thing about being caught off guard—rattling, hissing, and posing like politicians. In a ceremony undoubtedly several million years old and inherited from their eohippine ancestors, the horses were never content with changing their path and leaving the danger behind. Instead, they went up on their hind legs, their flaming eyes riveted upon the disgusting adversary.

Physically, it made sense. A snake couldn't reach them if they were eight feet in the air, and dared not strike at their hind legs as long as the windmilling hooves and the head—shaking in negation, teeth exposed—remained cantilevered over the base. For the rider, however, it was hell.

I learned rather quickly to take my rifle from its scabbard, work the lever as I aimed, and blow the snake to oblivion. I could do this because the man at the store where we bought our equipment insisted that we take two boxes of bird shot. I had been fixed on long range, high velocity, Winchester loads, but he had directed my attention to snakes and birds.

The horses expected me to make the snakes as limp as an old

couch in a dump, and as I did this it put me in the habit of killing. When eventually we ran out of mutton, I felled game birds. During our six weeks en route we ate sparingly and lost weight, but we ate well. Our hunger, primed sometimes for twenty hours or more, never fully satisfied, and driven by days of hard riding, was a far greater chef than any that Paris has ever produced.

In all that time, we never surfaced. It was a matter of honor. Never once did we sleep indoors or seek either town or restaurant. For a month and a half we had no newspapers, and it was quite a shock when we rode into Denver on the 26th of June, which was, I believe, a Monday, and saw huge headlines proclaiming that North Korea had invaded the South. We knew that some of our relatives and friends would be going to war, and that I would sit it out, being finally too old and not wanting to push my geometrically extrapolated luck.

Depending upon trial and error as much as compass and map, heading for points that the eye found irresistibly beautiful rather than heeding the dangers and difficulties of rivers to be crossed and slopes too steep for horses, we went from Jackson through the Shoshone Forest and into the Wind Rivers, where we picked up the Continental Divide and tried to stay high in the cold. We left the Wind Rivers at South Pass and went into the Antelope Hills, which are not named that for nothing. Hundreds of racing antelope rocketed across the landscape like planes with wheels that barely touch the runway just before they are airborne.

We went shy of the Antelopes into the Red Desert, up to the Continental Divide again in the Sierra Madre Mountains, and then through an infinity of forests and meadows around Columbine, to the east of Steamboat Springs, through the Arapaho Forest, and down into Denver. Without knowing it, we had probably crossed and recrossed the Divide two dozen times.

We had become the readers of sun and shadow, content with watching the far-distant dappling of the plains below. With our sense of time elongated, our bodies hardened, our eyes sparkling, and our patience deepened, we lost ourselves and we were happy.

Constance said that the wind and sunburn were not good for her face, but never, never have I seen a woman as beautiful as she, with her hair sunbleached and disheveled, her cheeks reddened, and her eyes set from days of looking over great distances—to the horizon by day and the stars at night. This highlighted in her the quality that I love more than anything else in a woman: vision.

I have seen women play the role in films of the woman of the frontier, but although some with great gifts can do a passable job, none has ever held a candle to Constance after these weeks above ten thousand feet, in the sun and the wind, with not enough to eat. It was as if her womanhood had been polished by the sun.

Sometimes we rested for a few days by small lakes hidden in the mountains. Here, on the north side, in the middle of the day, on sun-warmed rocks sheltered from the wind, we made love in the open with no inhibition and the certainty that no one was within a hundred miles of us.

The weather was with us, clear skies and the stars unimpeded, an aerial traffic jam of pinwheels, flashes, and the apparent fluorescence of the Milky Way, perhaps the most mysterious and yet the most comforting thing that one can see. We became expert at navigation by the stars, at finding water by the complexion of the grasses, at sleeping on snowbanks, tending to injured horses, mending fences, and shooting birds as beautiful as startled angels.

I learned once again exactly what I loved, and I was happy. One night, in the south part of the Wind Rivers, on a rocky slab fifty times the size of Madison Square, when we were deep in the finest days of our lives, I proposed to Constance that we have a child, and she cried. That cold and hungry night of almost blinding stars, with the sound of white water never ceasing, was the highest that I had ever reached, and except for escaping my own death as my plane exploded, and except for the birth of Funio many years later, it was, I think, the moment for which I had been born.

Even though I did not know it at first, and suffered the illusion that all was perfect, from that night forward, I fell. Now, with some detachment, I do not regret it. One cannot stay very long in the holiest precincts, and should not expect to. And, upon reflection, my fall appears to me to have been not merely swift, but beautiful.

We left Denver for Chicago on the 28th of June at ten in the morning on one of the great transcontinental trains, which was full of children who had been born just before the war or during the fighting and were on their way to the summer camps of the East. The girls wore summer hats, dresses, and, sometimes, gloves. The boys were no less inconvenienced in dress shirts and, sometimes, ties, even though the air on the plains of Kansas was simple and hot. Despite their uncomfortable clothing and automatic politeness to adults (they treated anyone over five feet tall like a policeman), these children may have been the last generation with a life of its own—the last to know America as an infinity of regions and refuges hard to reach and safe to the touch, the last to understand the United States in the plural.

My heart swelled at the sight of these children, the girls in their white summer hats and the boys in bow-ties. It was an achingly pleasant feeling—paternal, maternal, parental—that I am afraid Constance did not share. I know this now, after having seen during the past thirty years various newspaper and magazine accounts of her marriages and misadventures, but I did not know it then, for I had read everything into her that I deeply wanted. Even she did not know at the time, enough to say or even to think privately, that she did not want children. She had yet to say to me, as she did in one of the last of her sentences that I was to hear, "The truth is, I prefer jazz to children," and she was not that fond of jazz.

All this began to find expression that morning when we boarded the train and I was still harvesting vast amounts of strength from the landscape. I was looking at the wheat, still green, outside the window, and at Constance. She was so lovely when her eyes fastened upon the horizon, and, having come down from the mountains and the thin air, we were elated by all the extra oxygen on the plain. I knew that this would carry us for a week, and that the month and a half in the saddle and in the wind could, if we let it, carry us for the rest of our lives.

It was the heart of the country, at the height of summer, in an age of innocence. I knew almost everything I know now, but it was pure and uncorrupted. If innocence sometimes has a bad name, it is only among those who do not or cannot remember purity.

I was deeply in love with Constance and taken up with the greater rhythms of life—the slow oscillations that make themselves felt through generations or longer and that you must have a span of some years even to comprehend. It was hot and bright, and the sound of wheels and rails stitched together the heat and the light. I was about to make love to Constance as I had never made love to anyone before, all the way from Kansas to Chicago and at the risk of twenty heart attacks.

Reaching across the gap of facing seats in our compartment, I took both her hands. She was surprised, but she lifted her arms. As she did so her neck and shoulders became irresistibly defined. I drew her to me and she made the beautiful adjustments that a woman makes, usually drawing in a breath, before you kiss her, speaking with her eyes and moving her lips almost as if to speak. Her hair was golden all about her neck. Her teeth were white as I have never seen since. She closed her eyes. I kissed her, and, as I began to go under, I thought that the next thing I would know as a mortal man would be the sudden change of sound as the train rolled into Union Station in Chicago and we rushed to pull on our dishevelled clothes.

Still, even in prolonged ecstasy, you have to breathe. And with her first breath after the first long kiss, Constance said, "There's nothing I'd like more now than a good cup of hot coffee."

When fish are pulled from the deep and find themselves in the greater light and substanceless air, they are stunned. Many fishermen, perhaps to spare them the heartbreak of having left a world of flowing emerald, strike the heads of their prey against the deck. Such fish then assume my expression after Constance's amazing declaration.

"I think they grind it freshly on the train. You know, they may even roast it on the train. I saw one of the kitchen boys pouring what looked like coffee beans into what could have been a roaster. Can you call the porter?"

I, who could not move, stared at her like a dinosaur in amber. She, as if suddenly possessed by the devil, chattered at the speed of a gunshot about what she called "varietals."

"I myself love the piquant, racy, wild aromas of Arabian Sanani," she said, "but Daddy's favorites were the Ethiopians. He had a man from Fortnum and Mason go twice a year to the

Abyssinian Highlands to bring back Sidamo, Yergacheffe, and Harrar. I'll have to look in Daddy's Rolodex to find the man's name. I'm going crazy with longing for Yergacheffe, but I'll take anything they've got. Call the porter, won't you? Call him now. I don't want to wait. I can't wait."

We rolled over much of Kansas before I was able to speak. "That's *funny*," I said.

"What's funny?"

"You know."

"No, I don't. What's funny?"

"What you said about coffee."

"What's funny about it?"

"You've never mentioned coffee. You don't drink coffee. And you know that I can't sit in the same room where coffee is served. You know that we go to restaurants only in summer, so we can sit outdoors."

She looked bemused. As she collected her thoughts, I began to panic. "I wasn't aware," she said in her mode of rational argumentation, "that your rejection of coffee was either categorical or ideological."

"It's not," I said. "I just think that coffee is a substitute for sex, exercise, a healthy diet, getting enough sleep, being happy in one's life, having a purpose, and having a brain." I took the bait. What a fool I am. Now, of course, I know. She simply did not want to have children.

"Well," she said, indignantly. "Most people haven't had the privilege of leading your freakish life. They suffer. Give them their daily caffeine."

"Freakish? Who's freakish? Wouldn't you call having a few billion dollars at least semifreakish? I started life as a messenger, a runner, a handcuffed and straitjacketed detainee in a Swiss mental asylum. I made my way through life with iron will. *My* father didn't have a big-game lodge in Africa. *I* didn't take wildebeest sandwiches to school, or dancing lessons with Nijinsky. Constance, I love you more than anything in the world," I said, and I did, "but you say things like, *Right now, I'd like nothing better than some giraffe top round,* and you think you're just being an all-American girl. You don't know what suffering is."

I thought that when I said "I love you more than anything in the world," and my voice cracked with emotion, she would throw herself into my arms. Instead, she got teary-eyed, held back, and sallied forth.

"I do so know what suffering is," she declared.

"Really."

"Yes."

"Tell me," I bid her.

She drew in her upper lip and furrowed her brows. After five minutes of silence, she said, "Grandfather Lloyd was on the *Titanic.*"

"You weren't even born then."

"I cried when they told me, and I feel his suffering deep in my heart when I look in his face."

"He survived?"

"Of course. They had lifeboats."

"Constance," I said, "I love you. Let me make love to you, now. I've never loved you more than in these past weeks, and in these weeks never more than at this moment. Come to me." I held out my hands. I could feel great force pushing us together, and the force that pulled us apart. The flux between the two was magnificent and terrifying.

She remained motionless. I stared at her face as the light of half a continent glinted from her sled-dog eyes and her silvery blond hair, and I felt the great weight of her soul drawing away from me the way an enormous ship slowly separates from a pier. The space between us was as tortured and perturbed as the aurora. To reach for her, I realized, I would have to cross nebulae, galaxies, and ethers.

"You can't tell me what to do," she said.

"I'm not telling you what to do."

"Good. I'm going to get a cup of coffee." She rose to her feet.

Perhaps she wanted me to spring to the door, block it with my body, and embrace her. Perhaps I should have, but she had set it up so that I could not. Her announcement about getting a cup of coffee broke my heart, and what argument is left with someone you love if she is willing to break your heart?

"You would think," she said, poised to exit, "that I was leaving you for a masseur. I'm just going to get a *cup of coffee.* I'll be back."

She was gone for twenty minutes, during which I felt the same torture and despair as I might have had she made love to every acrobat in South America. And when she returned, her drugged elation drove me down deep.

That satanic substance makes you smile at tragedy. It turns your inner self into a happy sparkling clockwork, hypnotizes you with artificial joy, and takes from you the sadness and deliberation that are the anchors of love.

She, however, was more than content. She was ecstatic, delighted, absolutely ready to forgive and forget, to let the whole thing pass. She wanted to have sex. I could see that she felt it down to her fingertips. She was exploding with sex. It would have shaken the train right off the rails, half the women in Africa would have refrained from pounding their manioc, clocks would have stopped from Newfoundland to Azerbaijan, Einstein's

General Theory would have been confirmed, and the Bank of England would have put donuts in the lobby.

"No," I said. "The sex that I see dancing through every atom of your body has been unleashed by a drug, a crystal, a substance."

"So?" she asked, aching for every part of me to run through every part of her. I, too, wanted to create a magnetic earthquake on the plains of Kansas that would make the Bank of England put donuts in the lobby, to stop clocks, to be a god, if only for a moment. But there is only one God, and for all other illusions and presumptions the price is steep.

Part of the near-invincibility of this drug is that it can switch sleds on the most precipitous slope of the mountain. Constance suddenly lost interest in having sex, and sought instead intellectual banter facile and quick enough to keep pace with her racing blood. The drug affects neither substance nor appreciation, but only pacing. I think she would have been just as satisfied in her caffeine cloud to have drummed her fingers or typed someone's term paper, as long as the timing was insistent and complex, as long as she had had the sense of rolling forward relentlessly. At that moment, however, her ecstasy masqueraded as tolerance for compulsive disputation. Without missing a beat, she began to talk like a lawyer's letter.

"Tell me, then," she commanded, "what it is, specifically, that underlies your objection to coffee. You do realize of course that in view of the habits and practices of the world, the burden of proof is on you. Most people drink coffee. Of those who don't you are perhaps the only one who objects." Again she looked at me as if she did not know me. "Or at least you are the only one who objects with such . . . with such . . ."

"Vehemence," I supplied.

"Yes. Vehemence. You stand alone."

"I know."

"So, tell me what you have discovered. Illuminate your feelings. What is their origin? I'll listen."

"Might you not," I asked, "knowing that this is the way I am, merely give me a gift?"

"Nothing inexplicable ever lasts."

"Nothing," I said, "except love and beauty, which are totally inexplicable and totally everlasting. Or were."

"But why?" she asked, truly puzzled. "Why coffee?"

I snorted, and sat back with a hurt look. With the patience of the destroyed, I said, "I hate coffee."

"I know you do."

"Coffee is bad."

"I know you think coffee is bad."

"Yes. It's very bad."

"Why?"

"I haven't prepared a diatribe," I said because at that time I hadn't. Since then I have developed a number of them. They run from thirty seconds to an hour and three quarters.

"Just tell me what comes to mind," she said.

"You think I'm crazy."

"No. I don't think you're crazy, but I love coffee and you act as if, if I drink a cup of coffee, I've betrayed you. What's going on?"

"You *love* coffee," I said. "Love should not be given to a substance."

"That's ridiculous. It's like saying, *I love roasted chicken.*"

"Would that it were, but when you said you loved coffee, your voice dropped an octave and a half, there was a caesura of numb passion after the very word, and you moved as if you had been caressed by a male succubus."

"You mean an incubus."

"Whatever kind of bus. But when you said that you loved roasted chicken, the love was a half-note expressed in the same range as the other words around it, with neither pause nor handsome incubus."

"The incubus is handsome?"

"Yes."

"You've seen him?"

"No, I've seen you as you see him."

She affectionately said my name. And then she said, "You're insane."

"On the contrary," I stated. "People who drink coffee are insane. Insane and possessed and, what is worse, willing to be possessed. Most people in asylums drink coffee. If you let them stop drinking it, they would regain enough equanimity to leave. But, no, they don't stop. In fact, they drink more and more, and they get crazier and crazier. They're dehumanized with every single goddamned drop, and although they sense it, they're like lemmings, or buffalo who jump off cliffs. People drink coffee and it makes them insane.

"Must you drink coffee? Why not cocoa, tea, cola tea, maté, yoco infusion, or guarana? Why caffeine? Why not theobromine or theophylline? I have had an occasional square of chocolate. It is the cause of uncontrolled ecstasy, but, afterward, you sink into Promethean despair.

"Note," I demanded, "that caffeine was introduced to Europe in the seventeenth century, *post*-Renaissance. Why is it, do you think, that the art of the Renaissance and the classical period has never been surpassed? The great heights were reached on angels' wings, not via a filthy corruption brewed from a bean that poisons its own tree.

"Yes, coffee plants are self-poisoning. The beans drop on the

ground and, after ten or twenty-five years . . . *sayonara!* Don't
tell me that flirtation with an addictive poison is salutary. I
suppose you haven't heard of the coffee adulteration scandals
of the early nineteenth century. You know what they put in
ground coffee to bulk it up?"

"What?" Constance asked, her eyes wide.

"Roots, nuts, acorns, rocks, baked horse liver, clays, ground
peanut shells, copra, sisal, feathers, and pig shit. And no one
knew. How would they have known? They were already Ho-
garthian zombies who professed allegiance to . . . to what? To
a king? To a messiah? To a belief? To what? To what? Not even
to a false messiah or to a usurping pretender, not even to a
wrong idea or a hypnotic creed. But to a bean, a bean, a bean,
bean, bean!"

"What would you do, outlaw it?"

"Why not? De Valera tried to ban tea in Ireland. Why did
he have to stop there?"

I went on, defending the light against the overwhelming darkness. "Caffeine, Constance, is similar to the genetic code."

"It is?"

"Yes, $C_8H_{10}N_4O_2$. 3,7-dihydro-1,3,7-trimethyl-1H-purine-
2,6-dione. As you know, DNA duplicates itself, but caffeine
interrupts this holy process like a typhoon blasting all the punts
on the River Isis, and explodes the genetic system. Caffeine
replaces adenosine at the receptor sites of the neurons, causing
the neurons themselves to fire at untenable rates. This usurpation
and its unbridled effects, its attack upon the balance of nature,
its liberation of the fire and light that serve as the battering ram
of the soul, is a sin of the highest order.

"It causes sterility in insects," I declared.

"What about humans?" Constance asked. "Humans are not
insects."

"That's correct," I told her. "In fact, to be honest, in making sperm more motile, it actually promotes human fertility. Is this fair?"

"Why not?"

"Only the dullard sperm, the caffeine-using sperm, the addiction-prone sperm, get to use outboard motors. The virtuous sperm that won't accept the outboard motors don't get to the egg, and since the outboard motors, so to speak, are left outside the wall of the egg, what is it that gets in? A weakling, a dullard, a dunce, a non-swimmer, a tailless basket case, a slovenly jerk that got upstream because it had an Evinrude strapped to its back. Spengler missed this point entirely in understanding what ails the West."

"My dear," she said, "my dearest one. . . ."

"The greatest per capita consumption of coffee in the world is in Finland. True, they held back the Russians, but they're the most nervous people on earth, no one understands their language, and they beat themselves with branches. The average American drinks seven hundred and twenty gallons of liquid a year, of which approximately half is coffee. That is, one gallon, or sixteen cups, per day. Three percent of the population drink fifty cups a day, and fifteen percent drink forty. Sixty-seven percent of American adults and twenty-three percent of children are dependent on caffeine or various coffee acids."

"Darling. . . ."

"Catherine the Great used one pound of coffee to four cups of water, which is, quite frankly, why she screwed horses, and, look, five thousand milligrams of caffeine by mouth is fatal. Someone once committed suicide by means of a coffee enema. Don't you see? What if you lost count of your cups of coffee? You could die. And all this has been known for ages, ever since its introduction. Way back then, William Corbett called caffeine 'a destroyer of health, an enfeebler of the frame, an engenderer of effeminacy and laziness, a debaucher of youth, and a maker of misery for old age.'

"Constance, listen to me. Trust me. I know whereof I speak and, in this, I assure you, I am totally unbiased."

Silence descended for the rest of the trip. Only in Chicago did I speak, when a derelict in Union Station politely asked me for a nickel so he could buy a cup of coffee. "Go fuck yourself!" I screamed, so powerfully that it echoed several times under the high ceiling and made flocks of illicit pigeons fly from their roosts.

Language like that was not tolerated in public then, and the Chicago police—who for some reason dress like taxi drivers— began to move in on me, but Constance turned them back with the disapproving scowl of a true billionairess.

The word *coffee* was written in a dozen places on our route from *The Chaparral* to *The Twentieth Century*. Little men in hats and seersucker suits stood at counters tipping back their heads as they drank it like patients in a mental hospital upending little white cups of Thorazine. In the winter, these same people would frequent the same counters and drink from the same cups, only their bulky coats and felt hats would give them the air of European police inspectors, and when it is very cold in Chicago light comes in the station windows in huge luminous beams that flash upon the pigeons as they fly through the dusty air as if through a raft of glittering stars.

I confess that I grew optimistic as we drew toward New York. After all, New York was my home. It still is, though I hear that it has changed immeasurably. But I have it in my memory as it was, and I love it as you love someone who has died—with gentle resignation, insistent faith, and absolute certainty. I see it in silence, but I know that if I were strong enough, if I could will it as you will flight in a dream, I would suddenly hear all the sounds from within and I would enter the enlarged image to begin my search for the people whose addresses I still carry in my heart. If I found them I don't know what I would do (or if they would recognize me) but I would be so happy just to see them. I would, for example, seek out my father in 1910, when he was still a young man and I was six. I would follow him on the El, and perhaps I would catch his eye. He might think the kindness he sensed coming from an old white-haired Civil War veteran was part of the wisdom and benevolence of age. Have you never seen old coots like me who smile at you and look as if they know what's coming and who you are, precisely? Maybe they're your son, who, because he loved you, was able to wish himself back through time.

New York gave me strength. The Hudson gave me strength, being, as it was, my garden of Eden. I decided that my love for Constance would enable me to change, and that, seeing that I had, she would change as well, and we would repair our failing relations. There was almost nothing I wanted more than to walk with her through shady, anonymous summer streets, lost in time, still in love.

As if I myself had had coffee, my optimism swelled out of all proportion, and after the taxi dropped us at the house I ran in like a general who has just won a war. Everything was going to be possible in the new age that I would will. First, I dashed to the bathroom and made the towels crooked. I de-alphabetized Constance's many bottles of perfume (it drove her crazy when I insisted upon putting *Ravishment* behind *Quantum Mechanique*, because *Ravishment* was her favorite and hard to reach), and then took the elevator to the kitchen, where I de-alphabetized the cheese and even took some of it out of the dairy section, placing it recklessly with the fruit. Surrendering entirely to depravity, I took a piece of Stilton and set it asymmetrically among bottles of newly disorganized beer.

I cannot assert that these slovenly actions made me feel good, that they were easy to accomplish, or that they made sense, but I thought to change all of what I was for the sake of my heart, and I pushed forward.

My study was next. I cried when I disordered it, for it seemed that in mixing up categories of stamps, de-parallelizing paper clips, and tipping lamp shades by three or four degrees I was abandoning all the efforts I had made in my life—symbolically at least—to bring order to a disordered world, to defend what was sensible and good against what was nonsensical and evil, to lay out a sort of aerodrome ready to receive in good order a flight of planes that had long been lost.

When they would break out of the clouds, I wanted them to have a clear field on which to land. I wanted them to know that the ground crew had never abandoned the hope for their return, that I was waiting, that I had not let down my guard, that I believed. Suddenly to accept the idea of disorder, to surrender to it, to cease caring for the beauty and balance of all things, *all* things, was going against every lesson of my life and every struggle that I had successfully struggled.

Neatness is so deeply ingrained in me that even the first dismantling threatened to push me over the edge. But I have believed from almost the beginning—perhaps unwittingly, perhaps instinctively—that life and love are inseparable, that to honor one you must honor the other, that love can be many things and the cause of many exceptions, and that, as the greatest matter of exceptions, love can be God's permission—indeed, His command—to war against His order to which one is sworn, to war against other men, against nature, against God Himself.

Only love can carry such a message, so strongly felt, so terribly laden, so right, so pure, and so perfect. Only love.

I decided to drink a cup of coffee, or at least to try.

Naturally, I couldn't just go out, walk into a restaurant or one of the many other disgusting dens where such things are accomplished, ask for a cup of coffee, and drink it. Constance saw my hesitancy as a license for debauchery, and during the six or seven weeks in which I put off my confrontation and conversion, she began to associate with obvious coffee users. And then, as she sank deeper into the corruption, she surrounded herself with coffee sympathizers, apologists, hacks, flacks, and drones. She would come home flushed, nervous, and arrhythmic. I smelled it on her breath from across the dining room table, and the dining room table was twenty feet wide.

At the end of July, several S. S. Pierce trucks arrived with supplies for a fiendish apparatus that had been delivered from Italy—a machine constructed to force live steam through ground-up coffee beans. I had seen these on the Continent and kept a healthy distance. Now one sat upon the main preparation table in the dessert kitchen. It had a bronze gargoyle at the peak of its bell-jar-shaped copper boiler. Clearly, the artisan who made it knew of what he made. I could not stare at the horrible visage: the bronze eyes seemed alive, the smile forced by the drug.

The director of one of the museums that Constance had endowed was talking with her in the reception room one Saturday morning when I came in from my run around the park. We always kept the reception room so full of flowers that one of the servants was employed as a full time bee guard, with a cheesecloth net that had been specially designed by Frank Buck.

This room was a paradise. Even in winter, with a hickory fire consuming itself amid cliffs of warm white marble, the flowers were full and fresh. As I was passing, I looked in. Everything seemed as it had been. Constance had had her teeth cleaned. Once more they were glacially white, free of the corrupt stains of the beverage that looks like the distillation of a cesspool. She was dressed in her tennis whites: she was irresistible in any kind of athletic clothing, even a catcher's outfit.

The museum director sat on the edge of his seat, bent forward, laughing too hard at the things she said that were just vaguely amusing. I heard Constance, her voice changed, earnestly, stupidly, saying, "On Saturdays I like to play tennis, wash my hair, and go to Jefferson Market to buy coffee."

When she said the part about buying coffee it was as if she were talking about a man with whom she was ecstatically in love. She filled with a softness and warmth I recalled from when first we met. And then there was a terrific crunch as I side-kicked the throat of her tennis racquet leaning against one of the Egyptian marble lions at the reception room door.

All right, I told myself as I ran upstairs (Constance didn't like anyone breaking her tennis racquets), if I'm going to do this, I have to do it.

First, I made a testament. As the joint owner of several billion dollars' worth of companies, real estate, art, and monetary instruments, I had, of course, a rather complicated will. It was in a Morocco leather folder that I used to smell for fun, and it had been drawn up by Grandfather Faber's old firm. The algorithm part took up the first twenty pages, and the inventory, duly updated every quarter, then ran to page 325.

But this will said nothing of emotions, regrets, and aspirations. Yes, aspirations even after the last aspiration.

My testament, which I drew up myself, without lawyers, had nothing in it about money. It was about how I knew I would be forced to leave this world and the people I loved, and it was a way to talk to them, even those who had gone before me.

In this document, I spoke to Constance. I spoke to her a lot. And I did not shy from addressing the subject that had caused our downfall. I did not shy from condemnation. I did not shy from a cautionary tale, illustrated by my own death. "I died because you allowed your woman's heart to fasten upon an object. I died because you were possessed by the bronze-colored gargoyle leering over the dessert table. I died because you allowed your beautiful soul to mechanize around a crystal of caffeine," I wrote. "Adieu."

Then I went to see a doctor. My regular physician was in the Hamptons, so I let the concierge find the best internist left on the island of Manhattan. This was a Doctor Xavier Gruffy of New York Hospital. I knew he had to be good, because he charged as much as a lawyer.

"Doctor Gruffy," I said. "I'm going to drink a cup of coffee."

"I beg your pardon?" Dr. Gruffy asked.

"What would you recommend in the way of preparation, stabilization, prophylaxis, and recovery?"

"From what condition do you suffer?"

"I beg your pardon?" I asked him, not having heard well, cupping my right hand to my right ear like a veteran of Antietam.

"What's your disease?" he shouted.

"I'm perfectly healthy."

"Then what do you mean?"

"I'm going to drink a cup of coffee."

"Oh," he said, thinking that perhaps he had been rude in not offering me some coffee. "Would you like some coffee?"

"No," I said, shaking my head and looking at the sky through the girders of the 59th Street Bridge. A long silence ensued.

"Well, what can I do for you?" he began, hopefully.

"Help me," I said.

"Of course, of course. Tell me what's wrong."

"I'm going to drink a cup of coffee."

"I'll have some sent in right away."

"Not now!" I said.

"All right. Anytime you'd like." He was polite and puzzled. "Are you well?" he asked.

"I'm fine," I said. "For a man my age, I'm athletic and trim, if I do say so myself. I was in the Army Air Force. I flew P-51's, and vowed never to lose air-crew fitness as long as I could help it."

"Then what's ailing you?"

"Nothing. I'm in excellent shape."

"Oh, I see," the doctor said. "You'd like an ounce of prevention."

"Prevention, stabilization, prophylaxis, and recovery."

He tossed his head like an owl, and then blinked like one, too.

"I'm going to drink a cup of coffee," I said.

"Now?" he asked.

"No, later."

"Fine. Anytime you'd like. Or would you like tea instead?"

"No."

"Then coffee it will be."

"Yes."

"I can have it brought in whenever you'd like."

"You mean here?" I asked.

"My secretary makes excellent coffee."

"You mean right now?"

"If you want."

"Do you have the proper equipment?" I inquired.

"I have a Melitta."

"What's that?"

"A filtration apparatus."

"Yes, and stomach pumps, atropine, antithyroidal prophylaxis, sea-salt enemas, cleaners, mints, and tooth polish."

"I really don't understand you," he said. "I really don't."

"Look," I told him. "I've come to you because you are a doctor."

"Yes, I am a doctor . . ."

"I want your advice in regard to prevention, stabilization, prophylaxis, and recovery."

"All right," he said. "You tell me the disease, the illness, the trauma, the congenital condition, and I'll recommend a course of prevention, stabilization, et cetera."

"I," I said, pointing at myself with my left index finger. "I am," I said, "going," I said, pausing, "to . . ."

"To?"

"To drink," I said, pretending to pour liquid down my throat from a bota, which I now realize he had never seen, "a cup." Here I made movements that pantomimed a potter at his wheel, "of *coffee*."

"Jeanie," he said to his intercom, "bring in some coffee, now."

"No!" I shouted, jumping to the bread-box-sized intercom and depressing the lever. "Don't bring in any coffee."

"Doctor Gruffy?" the intercom said. "Shall I bring in coffee?"

"No," Dr. Gruffy said. "Cancel that." He released the Bakelite lever. "I never wanted to be a physician anyway," he said. "I wanted to be a Rough Rider. Who knows? Maybe I'll be reincarnated."

I couldn't get any medical advice from *him*, so I was left to do the deed on my own. At home, I found no privacy. We had only three kitchens, and Constance or a servant might have wandered into any one of them, breaking my concentration. Can you imagine a maid or gardener coming into my presence at the moment the fetid cup was lifted to my lips? Despite their instructions not to make, drink, possess, import, or speak of coffee within the precincts of our house, they probably debauched themselves on the outside two or three times a day— in their tenements, in front of their own children—and would not even have noticed what I was about to accomplish. Perhaps just as I reached the midpoint of my tightrope over Niagara they would start some mindless chatter, or, worse, utter one of the satanic phrases, such as *Enjoy your coffee,* that occupy the hearts of the possessed like writhing worms. '*My* coffee,' indeed.

I thought to lock myself in, but what if, at the moment upon which all my life was about to divide, the door rattled because Maise wanted to extract her egg salad sandwich from the refrigerator?

Constance was taking an oxygen treatment for her hair, and the house smelled fresh and sweet. She had been told by Lawrence of Arabia—not T. E. Lawrence, but her hairdresser— that, to be beautiful, hair required oxygen and cold temperatures. Sparing no expense, Constance arranged for a box-car-sized installation to be placed in the garbage yard. At the end of a long pipe from this chemical works was something that looked remarkably like what we would know much later as an astronaut's helmet. Placing the helmet on her head and pushing a green button on what looked like an overhead winch director brought Constance's hair a stream of chilled high pressure oxygen. Stenciled in red letters on the front, sides, and top of the helmet were the words NO SMOKING, to which I had added, in black china marker, AND NO COFFEE DRINKING!

I left the house, and I wandered. It was August, so I went

toward the Bronx. I have heard that the Bronx is dangerous now, but at that time the most perilous thing about it was the Jewish grandmothers who zoomed up and down the Grand Concourse like bumper cars. These women had what we knew in the AAF as tricycle landing gear, and their tail wheels were shopping carts. My first sight of them after the war reminded me of hundreds of B-29's taxiing in a windstorm.

I didn't know where I was going. I could hardly see in a straight line. I walked to put off the moment, hoping that I could make the same sort of arrangement with the facts of life that a donkey has with the carrot suspended from the stick tied to his harness. I wanted my moment of reckoning to be bright, immediate, and always receding.

Though we had visited some of Constance's distant relatives in Riverdale and Fieldston, and I had worked one summer as an orderly in the fecal analysis hut of Montefiore Hospital, I did not really know the Bronx. Near Yankee Stadium, I hailed a taxi. "Take me to the interior," I commanded.

"The interior of what?" the driver asked.

"The Bronx. Deep inside the Bronx. Drop me into the dark well of infinity."

He drove for twenty minutes and let me off at the intersection of two lines of elevated track. In the summer shadows of steel platforms that held speeding trains were neon signs blazing at midday, phalanxes of jelly donuts on frosted glass, and lines of middle-aged women in beauty parlors having their hair lacquered lady-bug close to their skulls as if their dream were to return to the wombs of their husbands' bowling-ball bags. Then there was the meat delicatessen, where hot cuts of boiled beef sweated in a jungle of sauerkraut, and penile knockwursts revolved eternally on rollers of stainless steel. You could get coffee there, but I forswore it in such a circumstance. To drink the stuff was bad enough, but to do so surrounded by calves' feet, beef tongues, livers. . . .

Nor did I dare go into the bakery, fearing that the coffee would make me crazy and cause me to eat three dozen jelly donuts. Even without coffee I was good for at least a dozen, as they had been invented in my town. I used to try to bring a bag of them home from time to time, from the bakery where they had originated, but the walk was four miles and, especially when it was cold and the moon was full, I would arrive with an empty white bag, my loden coat dusted with powdered sugar. Even these days I can eat ten or twelve of those pastries that, at the bakery in Niterói, the children call *pusatas,* and that have a prune filling shaped to resemble the Crown of Thorns.

I walked for several hours on the residential streets, always returning to the shady nexus of subway platforms—only in New York does the 'subway' run mainly above ground. It grew darker and darker, hotter and hotter. Though it was only the middle of the afternoon, the world seemed black, and the red neon signs flashed like little wriggly eels at the bottom of the ocean. I was in the fog of combat that, in combat, my rage had always dispelled. I knew I could do it again, for just beyond the walls of fear is a blue sky where heart and mind are one.

"Take hold of yourself," I said gently. A few minutes later, I saw a pizza bakery tucked into a corner deep in the August shadows of the El. There was coffee there. Getting inside, closing in on the target, was like racing to Berlin through flak and wind. The closer you get to your objective, the more scared, the more focused, the more elated, and the less afraid you become. It's a paradox. As the world sharpens and gleams so intensely that even fighting at the greatest speed seems like slow motion, the growth of fear becomes the lessening of fear.

My courage firmed up as I entered, heart beating in the presence of a coffee maker. A number of silver ovens were on full blast, and inside the shop the temperature was no less than 160 degrees Fahrenheit, worse than Mexico in July. A girl emerged from the back, the sole employee. She was a blonde, almost my height. The great heat showed on her body, which glistened with water. To stay alive, she had to drink gallons and gallons throughout the day, which made her sexually insatiable, hair-triggered. But this was not apparent to me even as she devoured me with her blue eyes, for I was concentrating upon my mission. I stared at the coffee maker. It had come to this, finally. The trains thundered above. My heart was wild and I dripped with sweat. I was going to do it.

"Is it better when it's hot?" I asked, thinking that iced coffee might be less horrible.

The pizza girl breathed like an expiring animal. "Yes," she said, her eyes going slightly out of focus.

"I want it now," I said slowly and deliberately. "Let's do it."

"Oh!" she said. She came around the counter, rushed for the door, locked it, and turned the sign so that to the outside world it said CLOSED. "Let's go in the back. On the flour sacks."

"Right here is fine," I told her.

"The window," she said, motioning with her eyes to the glass store front. "People will see."

"You're right," I agreed. "I don't want people to see. Let's go in the back."

She led the way, and I said, "What about the coffee?"

"Coffee?"

"I'm going to drink a cup of coffee."

"You're not hot enough?" she asked, pushing her hair behind her neck and holding it, with both hands, like a rope. "I'll give you lots of hot coffee," she said as she led the way to the back.

They kept sacks of flour in a small room that had no windows but only a fluorescent light and a ventilating fan above the door. I saw no coffee there, and turned to look at the percolator behind me. When I looked in again toward the sacks of flour, the pizza girl was half kneeling, half sitting upon them, disrobing musically, rhythmically, swaying as she untied the white strings of her apron.

As evening fell, after having been forced to betray Constance for the first time in our marriage, I walked aimlessly into the deepest Bronx. It was still light, and people were eating dinner or mowing their lawns. The remarkable thing about the climate of the Bronx is that in January you can put a thick steak on your porch and it will be frozen in two minutes, and in August you can place it on a grill in the very same place, without a fire, and it will cook all by itself. And though spring lasts for only ten days, fall is a paradise that seems never to end.

Walking put me in mind of my youth, and I stayed hungry. I am almost sure that I did not, in two or three hours, pass a single investment banker or a single holder of a single seat on a single stock exchange. No Yale pennants, Duesenbergs, Jaguars, plaid pants, or perfect teeth. I did notice, however, that people seemed hostile. I took this to be the kind of resentment that I, as a graduate of Harvard, a partner at Stillman and Chase, and, now, a billionaire, would engender no matter what my real character, no matter that I was still the beleaguered runner from the branch office, no matter that I, like everyone else, had been fully set into my "class"—that is, my emotional home—before the age of ten, and we had been rather poor.

I imagined that it was the way I dressed, or perhaps my haircut, or perhaps, God help me, my bearing and expression.

When you are a member of the moneyed elite, you get used to a certain low-level hostility. But what I did not know was that children ran indoors as I passed, and women looked at me in fear, because my back, from heel to crown, was covered in flour, as were my hair, my face, and my neck. I looked like a mime, or the ghost of Christmas past.

As I was walking, I came up with a scheme. By luck and revulsion, I had never had a cup of coffee, and my recent efforts to accommodate to Constance, to surrender to what she referred to as normal life but which I feel is a serious addiction that wildly distorts the personality, had failed. Not only had I been unable to drink coffee, I had not been able to get within ten feet of it.

The only way for me to accomplish my normalization would be through force. Force is a remarkable instrument, and when it threatens survival it awakens capacities that have slept in the soul like giants. My idea was simple: I would bribe the police to force me to drink a cup of coffee. After all, they had guns and it was well known that they would do virtually anything for the right amount of money. The office manager at Stillman and Chase made monthly trips to see the captain at the precinct, and she always brought him several thousand dollars for the "fund."

"Why?" I asked her, and was told that it was to keep our runners safe and our operations smooth. The custom was for her to pay the captain a courtesy call, and give two hundred dollars to the benevolent fund. He would thank her, and leave the room to put the money in the precinct safe. Left alone at a little table with a single drawer, the office manager would stuff in thousands in tens and twenties, and slam it shut. At that sound, the captain would reappear, thank her for the contri bution he had just put in the safe, and shake her hand. That he kept on finding huge amounts of money in the drawer was something he explained as a kind of Miracle of the Loaves.

In New York, when a wealthy person dies with no relatives to take care of his affairs, the police seal the house, but only after they loot it. Sometimes they come back at night and break the seal to get something they forgot. They don't like to talk about things like this, though, because they feel that it is an insult to their dignity.

To my great surprise, a radio car came up even with me as I walked, and held itself to my pace.

"Are you going to get in the car, or do we have to chase you with a net?" I was asked from inside.

"I beg your pardon? Would you say that again?"

"Do you want the net and the straitjacket, or are you going to cooperate?"

"You read my mind," I said. "What I was thinking was so powerful that it brought you to me, but, before we've made the arrangement, don't get on your high horse. And, besides, I don't want to deal with anyone below the rank of captain."

I jumped into the car and laughed all the way to the precinct. There, as they handcuffed me, I asked that they leave my hands in front so I could drink the cup of coffee.

"*The* cup of coffee?"

"Yes."

"What do you mean, 'drink *the* cup of coffee?' Are you American?"

"Of course. Don't I look it?"

"No."

"What nationality do you take me for?"

The desk sergeant looked me over. "The moon," he said.

I was in trouble. They would not honor my request, and after

I was booked for disturbing the peace they threw me into a holding cell. Its one other occupant was a bearded ancient with a pink stump where his right hand should have been. He looked very much like Santa Claus, but his eyes were filled with terror. You could tell that he never stopped being afraid, that somehow the fear switch in his brain had been permanently welded shut, and that this simple problem had been the cause of his downfall.

"Are you afraid of elephants?" I asked.

He nodded, fearfully.

"Are you afraid of meteorites?"

He nodded again.

"Paper boxes?"

He shuddered with fear.

"You're afraid of me, aren't you?"

He shook his head purposefully, vehemently.

"It doesn't matter that I won't hurt you, does it. You're afraid of me because I'm here. You're afraid of everything. As long as you're awake, you fear."

He made no assent. Then I understood. "You don't sleep, do you?"

"No," he whispered. He was too afraid to sleep. He was like a fish. Perhaps fish do sleep, but he didn't.

"But why are you afraid of *me*?" I asked.

He threw himself back against the cage, which was as good an answer as any.

At four o'clock the next morning I was taken to a different floor, where, in the middle of a group of wooden desks, a detective sat near a pool of light.

"Don't people like you normally wear a dress?" he asked.

"What?"

"Where's your dress?"

Perhaps he was insane. "Why would I wear a dress?"

"Why would you make up?"

"Why would I make up?" I repeated.

"Yeah."

I held out my hands in the posture of universal puzzlement. "I wouldn't."

"You live downtown," he said, "not here."

"That's right."

"So what are you doing here? There are no transvestite bars here."

"Transvestite bars!"

"Did somebody steal your dress? Did they hurt you? What?"

I thought he was entirely mad, but what did that matter? He was a policeman. I leaned over and spoke like a conspirator. "Look," I said, "I'll pay you to shoot me if I don't drink the cup of coffee. Money is no object."

He was not exactly comprehending, but I had mentioned money. "*The* cup of coffee."

"*The* cup."

"What cup?"

"The first cup."

"What about the second cup?"

"Don't get greedy. If I drink the first cup I'll be able to handle the second cup on my own."

"Do you have a private doctor?"

"Yes."

"What's his name?"

"Dr. Gruffy."

"In Manhattan?"

"Of course."

"Is he a shrink?"

"No. He's an internist."

"Who's your shrink?"

"I don't have one. Why would I have one?"

"Oh, *I* don't know."

"I think Freud overdid it," I said, "in that virtually everything he maintained was either patently obvious or patently ridiculous."

At this moment Constance swept into the room flanked by several extremely expensive lawyers. I knew that I was saved, but I didn't know from what. The detective stood almost at attention when he saw these people, figuring that I was either a billionaire, Truman's mad twin, or a space alien who had escaped from an Air Force interrogation center.

"How did you get like that?" Constance asked, embarrassed to see me, made up like a New Guinea headhunter, in the presence of the senior partner of Happy, Tricky, Devious, and Rich.

"Like what?"

"Look at yourself."

I looked at my hands, my feet, my legs: they seemed totally Brooks Brothers.

She pulled a compact from her purse and snapped it open the way you snap open the barrel of a revolver if you have to reload to save your life. She shoved the mirror toward my face. "Like that."

"Oh," I said when I saw my face. Then I looked at each person in the room, shifting my eyes in silence.

"What happened to you?" she screamed. An aristocrat, an activist by nature, she was never content to let anything pass without intervention or explanation.

"This is flour," I announced in a tone of surprised self-satisfaction.

"Flour?"

"Baking flour."

"How did it get on you?"

"I had a pizza."

"That must have been some pizza," the detective said.

"It was the best pizza," I answered, with fanatic intensity, "that I ever had, in all my life."

I have never been divorced from anyone other than Constance, so I do not know if all divorces feel the same, but, when someone you love wants to leave you, God gives you no quarter. It's like ending a chess game with just a king facing your opponent's two queens, two rooks, and rogue judo-esque knight.

Whenever I slept I dreamed that the whole world had come to resemble Gary, Indiana, at night, but instead of producing steel and rubber, the great mills and factories were roasting, grinding, and brewing. Flour-covered women dressed by the tailors of the Third Reich inhabited this nightmare, drinking five and six cups of coffee a day. It completely crowded out my dream of the surf. Worst of all, it had as its background the totally insane, wild, caffeinated pounding of the harpsichord, an instrument that would have driven the world out of its mind had it not been for the invention—with not a moment to spare—of the piano.

I would wake in terror, dripping with sweat, and turn to Constance, who, even in sleep, would turn away. It was finished. Then I would telephone Holmes to tell them to turn off the alarms, and I would go downstairs to the music room to play the piano.

The music room was sixty feet long by thirty feet wide, with a twenty-foot ceiling and special acoustical flooring of Mozambique Jerko wood. Eight sets of French doors opened onto a marble terrace that gave out to the lawn. Over the tops of trees blackened by night you could see skyscrapers shining through the moist summer air. I would open the doors and let the breeze make ballerinas and swans of the white curtains while I played Mozart and Beethoven until morning—perfectly balanced pieces that were as beautiful and hopeful as a mother singing to her child. They put everything in perspective, even if sadly, and it is because of them that I was able to go on.

I had eventually begged Constance not to leave me, but only after I had long held my emotions in check, hoping that an appearance of imperturbability would create in her enough desire and respect to raise a doubt. But she had no doubts, for the naturally shady and cool places of her temperament were kept always light and hot by her regular imbibition of coffee, which she took from a cart wheeled-in the first thing in the morning, in the middle of the morning, at lunch, at 'tea,' and after dinner. Five cups a day. . . . She was gone. There was no way I could reach her.

It made her hard, cruel, and ambitious. She thought ruthlessly; she shone like metal. She would go out dancing with other coffee drinkers and for hours they would move in a trance. "What's it like?" I asked later, like a mouse.

"It's like riding a bicycle on the beach road in East Hampton on a sun-filled day, without the appearance of a single car, picking up speed until you feel that your lungs, heart, and muscles are a perfect machine and you can breathe the air like a jet engine. The best thing is the sense that you can dance forever, that you don't weaken, that the more you exert yourself, the stronger you get. Why don't you come with us?" she asked with the cordiality of a stainless steel scalpel.

"I don't think I should," I said. "I'm only your husband."

"You won't be for long," she told me. "I don't understand

you at all. You're a stronger and better dancer than any of the guys I go with."

"I couldn't drink the cup of coffee," I said.

"I know, but maybe it would work without coffee. Who knows. We could dance all night, and afterward. . . ."

"Constance?"

"Yes?"

"Do you sleep with those coffee-drinking guys you go dancing with?"

"Do you think I drink decaf?"

This broke my heart.

When I was a child I went with my uncle to the exposition of power machinery in Baltimore, where I saw a steam engine that ran magically and rhythmically, never failing of enchantment. Its colorful rods and polished arms danced through the day in hypnotic ecstasy. Bright lights shone upon the perfectly timed steps, rotations, and exhalations. Kept in water and coal, the engine could go on forever with nothing but a shot of oil now and then. It ran all day, and it ran all night. Its power never slackened, and though it was bolted down and seemed not to go anywhere, I felt that it was churning a path through the stars.

Constance had metamorphosed into such a machine. I respected her power, but I shied from it, for she had traded her womanhood for a gambit that was sure to fail. After we separated, though I missed her at times with a great longing of the heart, I began to think of her as a kind of locomotive, and I no longer envied the coffee-drinking guys with whom she danced.

The divorce itself was not simple, involving as it did several hundred companies, shell corporations in the Alps, and scores of lawyers who dressed a lot better than I did. When we had married, Constance, in a gesture of faith, tied me to all her great wealth. Now, unable to resist the panic of her legal advisers, she girded her loins to get it back.

For the divorce she put aside Happy, Tricky and turned to a firm that had started as Wagstaff, Leper, and Balloon, and had evolved into Leper, Colony, and Fike, known in the trade as Leper, Colony. Even this was not as bad as Crooked, Bienstock, Midring, and Swine, referred to as Crooked, Swine: as in "My lawyers are Crooked, Swine." The human dental drills of Leper, Colony offered me five hundred million in settlement. They were so frightened that I would accept, thereby depriving them of untold billable hours of litigation, that they almost had heart attacks as I sat mulling it over.

"No," I said.

You could hear lawyerly hearts springing ahead like a pack of greyhounds. As I looked into their eyes I saw new clay tennis courts, summer houses in Nova Scotia, Maseratis.

They had prepared their fallback positions as carefully as the defenses of Iwo Jima, and they asked me for my bid. They certainly weren't about to counteroffer before they heard my demands.

"What I want," I said, "is for Constance to love me."

"Oh Christ!" they said, to a man. I knew it sounded rather weak. The senior partner took the lead.

"You're an investment banker?" he asked incredulously. "We're talking about two billion dollars here, man. Get serious. Don't think that you can smokescreen us with this hearts-and-flowers crap. We've been through a thousand of these, and we know exactly how people think."

"But it's true," I insisted. "All I want is for Constance to love me."

I suppose she had had a cup (or more) of coffee. She was unmoved. Her eyes were no more wet or glistening than a piece of sandstone in the Sonoran Desert.

"What's your counter?"

"I don't have a counter. I don't want any money, or any thing."

"We'll offer you two hundred million, then, if we can close the matter right away."

"I don't want two hundred million."

"A hundred million?"

"I don't want money. I want my books and my clothes, the desk in my study, the Raphael that Constance gave me for my birthday, and a guarantee—in writing—that no one will ever kill Brownie."

"Who's Brownie?" Senior Partner asked.

"His pet pig," Constance told him, "in the country."

"Really?" said Senior Partner. "Is that all you want?"

I nodded.

"Why don't you take a hundred million just so I know that you can buy groceries?" Constance offered.

"I have a job, Constance."

"Jobs are nothing. You can lose them. Then what? You starve."

"I can get another job."

"As *what?*" she asked derisively. "You're an investment banker. That means you don't know how to do a goddamned thing but skim the top off money that real people make."

"Maybe I could get a job in a cheese factory," I said.

"Look," she declared, adjusting her new owllike hairdo. It was really sexy. It did something magnificent for her neck and shoulders, and it made her seem well considered, even-tempered, and wise. "I don't want to have to worry about running into you on the street begging for a nickel for a cup of coffee."

I raised my arms and smiled half-triumphantly.

"For vodka, then."

"I'd rather drink carbon tetrachloride."

"I worry. Do it for me."

"I can't."

"But I want you to. Everyone will know—*I'll* know—that you turned down half a billion dollars, that you could have fought for a full billion and more, and that I begged you to accept this pittance. No one will think that you're a kept man, or that you were. No one will ever think it, and no one ever did."

"I can't," I said, shaking my head. "The money's tainted."

"How so?" she asked pugnaciously, prepared to defend the legitimacy of her fortune against charges of slave-trading, bonded labor, monopolistic behavior, exploitation of unorganized workers, capital formation before the income tax, and half a hundred other accusations that attach to masses of money as naturally as moss to the dark side of a rain barrel.

"By coffee."

"You mean that, just because I drink coffee, my money's no good?"

"Correct," I said. "I don't want coffee dollars. I'd rather starve. One of the inalienable provisions of the Constitution of the United States is the right not to be forced to see other people drinking coffee. You can't buy that from me. No amount of money can draw from me the honor and freedom of my birthright. No bribe can deflect my resolution. No sinecure can lap at my purity."

This declaration did a great deal for the lawns of Westchester and Long Island, which would continue to soak up the sun undisturbed by bulldozers and fence builders, it helped keep the meadows of Nova Scotia in their windy and original isolation, and it humbled the luxury automobile industry in Italy.

The very last time I saw Constance, she was gliding over a marble floor on her way to a wood-paneled elevator. She didn't know I was watching, or perhaps she did. For about a minute she stared at the elevator indicator, a circle of white glass that glowed like the moon. I knew that if I had said, "I love you, Constance," all the lawyers around her in their expensive suits would have laughed. And, yet, it was true. It was the truest thing I knew. It should have had the power to reverse our late and sad history. I felt deeply that it could have, that it should have. But it didn't.

Sometimes love is taken away unjustly, but not until the very end do you stop believing, and then it is very bitter. It is bitter because somewhere within you the perfect standard still lives, the pure expectation against which failure and betrayal are contrasted like the dark shadows on a moonlit road.

The Second (Man I Killed)

(If you have not done so already,
please return the previous pages to the antproof case.)

I CANNOT TALK to my wife, because she is only fifty years of age and still imagines that the body can be the fortress of happiness. She exercises, she rubs expensive concoctions on her face, and uses the mirror like a detective peering at a suspect in an interrogation room. Her misconstruction of English, once so charming, has become (as she might say), a 'mushroom,' a 'night mail.' "Who you think I am? I old now, like you. Okay, I not menistruate, you not menistruate either. I automon in bank, but what you?" In answering her own question, something that she likes to do, she tried to demean my efficacity, and she called it 'efacity.' I shook my head, and she said, 'F-assity?' I shook my head again, and she said 'F-icassy?' I shook my head once more, and she said, 'F-ississy?' I had begun to lose hope, but when she said, 'F-ick-acky,' I despaired, having forgotten how to say the word myself.

Did you know that the president of the United States sits at the *Oval Desk?* Perhaps there he watches the *Annapolis 500,* while he worries about the *Ras Tufarians* in *Ha-Mocha,* whether American *aircat* carriers have enough *lifety* rafts, or if the *Plebs* at *Vest Pint* are reading *Ponmoy's Complaint,* sympathize with the *Dentistas* in Nicaragua, would rather have gone to *Bedouin* College in Maine, or will vacation in *Yoseminite* park—every other goddamned word.

I'm old enough to remember vaudeville but I never imagined that I would marry it. When I was young I assumed I would be coupled with a woman who spoke like a poet, but I will end my days with Marlise, a woman for whom it would be a great leap forward to talk like one of Xavier Cougat's girlfriends. Besides, she's having an affair with a German salesman. The whole country is sex-crazed—even middle-aged women, especially middle-aged women.

Marlise's Teuton bear sells jars of sea-green stuff that I believe is called *Zipfinster Mitgaloist Herbeschungen,* and is supposed to make you look ten years younger no matter what your age. I asked Marlise what would happen if an eight-year-old got at it, but she's not willing to consider cosmic questions. It looks exactly like the substance janitors use to keep down the dust when they sweep immense public floors. Perhaps it is. She mixes it with papaya juice, and when she drinks it Funio and I hold our breath.

Funio I love above all else. It doesn't matter that he's not biologically my son. He is my son. Though he understands the sense of everything, he cannot at his tender age understand the import. And if somehow I were able to convey to him the import of what I feel, I would be robbing him of his childhood. Above all, I want this time in his life to be unburdened, for I have never seen such a beautiful thing as childhood, and perhaps if he is not stripped of it early on, as I was, he will have the strength to live his life untormented.

So, I cannot talk to Funio, I cannot talk sanely to Marlise, and I cannot talk to anyone else. I sit in a place that has no seasons. I think about the cold air and the snow. For hours I am drawn back into a world that has vanished, that has the qualities and tenor of a dream, a world that I left behind. I watch the sun rise, I wonder when I will die, and I worry more now about things that are over than about what is yet to come.

A long time ago, in 1961 or 1962—before all that "Girl from Ipanema" crap—Marlise and I went on an excursion on the Rio Veloso. It's a very nice song, "The Girl from Ipanema," but I have heard it far too many times, and it's insufficient as an anthem, even for Brazil. I haven't been out of Brazil since the day I arrived like one of the rebellious angels in *Paradise Lost*, but sometimes I imagine that I can go home, and I see myself at a cocktail party in Southampton or on Beekman Place, facing an overweight woman with too much makeup, artificial birthmarks, and the idea that, even though she has not spoken one word to me, we are going to have an affair.

"Where are you from?" she asks.

"Brazil," I reply.

"Oh, 'The Girl from Ipanema!' " she exclaims.

"Only after years of surgery," I reply.

"I beg your pardon?"

"What did you do to your husband, madam? Boil him?"

"I beg your pardon?" she says for a second time.

"Aren't you a little old for infatuations, for all this boyfriend-girlfriend stuff? What I mean is, you presume quite a lot after having peeled the wrappers off ten thousand chocolate cakes, and I'll bet you drink coffee, too."

"Excuse me?" she says, and begins to sidle away, but she makes an insulting gesture by looking heavenward with her vacant black eyes, and I pursue her through the astonished guests, denouncing her for her ignorance, her sloth, and her addiction to coffee.

What do you know, her husband, who is still alive, gallantly places himself between me and that adulterous bitch, and I'm trapped. I have no option but to overturn the bar as I lunge for a garbage can lid to use as a shield. With this defense in place, I commence my offensive. Commandeering a cane from an old man who looks remarkably like me, I push them all back, and am left alone in an apartment that doesn't belong to me.

The Rio Veloso is very beautiful, but I hate pleasure excursions. I hate pleasure. I tried to enjoy the Rio Veloso as best I could, but at that time I was fighting interior battles at increasing velocity, and the river did not engage my heart. Nor did the sun-dappled green canopy, the ecstatic birds, or the twisted coils of white smoke from the steamer that had done nothing for half a century but cut through the sweet air of the jungle, swaying the orchid-laden vines.

The engine that powered the launch reminded me of an expresso machine. With each hiss and aspiration I saw in my mind's eye little cups of coffee descending in a heavenly arc into the waiting hands of coffee's self-condemned acolytes. I went to the foredeck, trying to drown the sound of the steam with the roll of black water from the bow. The river is warm, and the water is black. Despite its weakness and lack of clarity, in the tropics the breeze is something that can almost be embraced.

Then the animal—whatever it was—reared up in the middle of the river, angry because the boat had bumped one of its calves. It raged eight feet above the water, like a broken xylophone or a poor aquatic relative of the Liberty Bell, showing its horrendous dental work and shaking its fat like a crazed Philadelphia housewife.

Rather than bite the boat in half, it retreated to the bank and had a tantrum; screaming, weeping, its head resting sideways on a downed coconut log. I had never seen anything like it. Brazil is not supposed to have hippos, but sometimes animals escape from zoos, or children bring them home as pets and dump them in the sewers, where they grow to enormous size.

Marlise didn't see it. She was in the bathroom having a cup of coffee (she travels with powerful mints, and often disappears for five or ten minutes at a time). When I questioned the other passengers, hoping to share my astonishment, I discovered that very few were aware of it at all. It appears, in fact, that I may have been the only one who actually saw it.

At the navigable head of the Rio Veloso, within striking distance of the immense falls, is a little colonial town without a single slab of precast concrete, a single automobile, or one neon sign. On the night of our arrival we stayed in a small pension overlooking the river, exercising the springs on the bed until they turned red. Someone in the room below came up and banged on our door. "Turn off that goddamned machine!" he screamed. "I haven't been able to sleep for four hours! What do you have there, an air conditioner run by kangaroos on a treadmill?"

"It's a cement mixer."

"In a hotel room?"

"We're building an addition."

"At night?"

" 'Round the clock."

"Are you the foreman?"

"Yes."

"Open the door, I want to speak with you. Where are you from, anyway?" (He heard my accent.)

"I'm an Eskimo, and I can't open the door."

"Why not?"

"My wife is not dressed."

"Your wife? What's your wife doing there?"

"She's helping me."

"Without clothes?"

"It's for a nudist colony."

It went on like this for some time. He asked excited questions, and I supplied calm answers.

The next day, we made the hike up to the falls, arriving exhausted and dripping wet. From a platform just beyond the arc of the mist we looked over the pool where the water hesitated, came to a boil, settled down, and then began to flow downriver once again. The air was cool and fresh. If you bent your head you could see the river far above, hurtling into space in complete surprise, falling through the air in twisting sheets, unfurling like a stricken acrobat at his last, leaving a train of weightless drops, spreading a frigid white curtain in the air, and then crashing into the pool, where it died and was instantly reborn as aerated black water flowing to the sea.

I tried to explain to Marlise what it was like to fall, and she said, "How you know?" I told her about suspension at the top of a great arc, how the quick light of an explosion fills your eyes before the sound or shock, and how, in the interval, in an instant, you are paralyzed with love that seems like the opening of eternity.

She's a very practical person, one of those people for whom death means nothing except paperwork.

"How you know? You died once?"

"I was *killed*," I said.

"And you come back?"

"Yes. I came back, and I have been alive two hundred times ever since."

She thought I was crazy, but so do many people. They simply do not know what it is like to touch heaven and then to be thrown back. The world looks very different after such an encounter, and, to be frank, I know that many of the people who think I am crazy are, in fact, crazy themselves, and that I am not the least bit crazy.

I bent back and stared at the river standing in the air like the light-filled plume of a rocket. The sun filtered through the mist and touched our faces, rainbows crossed above us like vines, and the ground thundered under the onslaught of the water as it had for a million years.

That night, with the pleasurable exhaustion that follows physical exertion, Marlise and I wandered the few streets. In the plaza, she made me sit for a portrait. I was young enough then neither to have whitened nor to have compacted upon myself, and my eyes were not hollow.

I don't like sitting for portraits, and never did. Constance once commissioned a life-sized, dark, heroic, Sargentesque portrait by Buckman Wilgis, for which I dressed in a black suit and yellow tie. Even though she paid him half a million dollars, at the beginning of her coffee drinking she stuck pins into it.

The sketch done on the trip to the Rio Veloso is in charcoal, a singularly inappropriate medium for the Brazilian universe of pastel, but the artist rightly took me for an American and wanted to catch my sinew and my anger, which she did, although she did not understand for even the smallest part of a second even the smallest part of my joy.

Perhaps because of the Berlin Crisis, or the beginning of the buildup in Vietnam, she inquired of my military history. "Yes, I've been in the army," I told her.

"Oh," she said, as if I were a São Paulo Nazi.

"I fought the Germans," I said, with indignant pride, "for four very difficult years, in places that were sometimes colder and wetter than a Brazilian imagination can conjure."

"Oh," she said again.

"It was forty degrees below zero," I added, "a world of ice and light where you have never been and will never go." Marlise gave me a little kick, which only spurred me on. "While your father was fucking and dancing and eating fried shrimp and turning into such a soft bag of undifferentiated crap that his ethical sense became nothing more than crushed squash and coffee grounds."

Marlise tugged at my sleeve, and the artist, who by then had caught some of the flash in my eye—you can still see it, even in charcoal—was not, like her putative father's moral sense, crushed. I learned long ago never to underestimate the strength of the native vegetation. It springs to life, swaying in the breeze, even after the hand of man has struck it down. The jewel of Rio is not the turquoise sea, but the green fuse of life. She said, "When you were in the army . . ."

"The Army Air Force," I interrupted.

"Yes. Did you kill anyone?"

Suddenly, I was full of love for her. I wanted to embrace her, but, as is often the case, I was forced to continue the argument.

"Yes," I answered, furthering the distance between us. "At great remove, and they were always seeds in the heart of machines of aluminum and steel, tied to their killing engines as I was tied to mine. Everything that happened, happened on a scale that I have not known since, in miles risen in minutes and fallen in seconds, in thin air and brittle temperature, at speeds that threatened to tear apart victor and vanquished alike. And those on the ground that I killed were unseen, at the base of guns spitting fire as I dived at them as if seeking my death. We all were dressed like cockroaches—in goggles, armor, and pressure suits with bladders, masks, tubes, and laces up the sides."

She seemed relieved. "You didn't ever kill a man at close range, with your hands, did you?" she asked.

I didn't answer.

Everything starts so far back that to explain it you must begin with the beginning of the world, but the story of how I killed the second man I killed commences for all practical purposes with Eugene B. Edgar, the most senior of the senior partners of Stillman and Chase.

In 1934 he was already older than I am now. To him, everyone was always a kid. He had lived through everything, done everything, and seen everything, but none of that mattered. What mattered was that he owned everything. He had been born just in time to lie about his age and enlist in a New York volunteer regiment during the Civil War. He exited, at age eighteen, a captain in the cavalry, having fought as a mortality-blind adolescent in half the important engagements of the war. He then lived through the gilded age with the luck of the gods and the judgment to have backed Edison, Henry Ford, and half a dozen lesser but like individuals. By the depression of the Nineties he had turned Stillman and Chase into one of the major financial houses of the world.

Then he struck. He bought everything from everyone, putting the organization at such great risk that its stock plummeted, and he bought that, too. Another few months and he would have gone under, but he had timed it just right, and when the economic gloom lifted, Eugene B. Edgar was left in absolute control of Stillman and Chase, and Stillman and Chase was left in pivotal control of nearly everything else.

All his life he kept an eye out for the grand cycles to which most people are blind from lack not of wisdom but of courage, and in 1928 he sold out. Stillman and Chase had a rough year and a half until the stock market crashed, and there we were, sitting on a stupendous mountain of cash.

Perception swings as if in a breeze, and everyone came to value cash over equity, just as months before they had valued equity over cash. We waited, and waited, until, in 1934, Eugene B. Edgar started buying up the United States of America.

Slowly, he said. Carefully. By the time our liquidity had solidified into ownership of banks, corporations, works of art, energy rights, intellectual property, and real estate, and it appeared as if we had squandered our wealth, the wheel would turn. We would be in a position second to none.

When I pointed out to him that we had long been in a position second to none, he raised his old leathery turtle head from a starched white collar, rotated it a quarter turn both left and right, lowered it, and said, "Just multiply that by eight."

I was not a senior partner then, in fact not even a partner. I was peripheral to a cabal of sycophants that had won Eugene B. Edgar's favor and needed a person much lower than themselves to be kicked. When mules are slapped on the nose, they kick, and my job was to stand in back of them.

I was, even at the age of thirty, a glorified errand boy. This made sense, as I had started as a runner, whereas most of the important people at the firm had crossed over laterally from Harvard, Yale, or other firms, and had never done anything lowly in their lives.

But I, too, had gone to Harvard. I was a half-caste—harmless and embraceable, repulsive and eschewed. Further complicating my status was that I was not a veteran of the Great War, having been, unlike Eugene B. Edgar in the Civil War, just too young. And I had spent the most glorious part of my youth not at Groton but in a mental institution. This, however, I handled with such nervous brilliance that I shake to this day in remembering it.

I would be in the midst of a croquet match, or hiking out during a yacht race, when someone might say, "I know you went to Harvard, but where did you prep?"

Harvard was necessary, but still plebeian. The real qualification was St. Paul's, Groton, or five or six others, which established your caste. I prepped in a nut hatch, but I sailed over the trap every time. All I had to say was, "At Château Parfilage."

"Really!" they would say. "In Switzerland?"

"The Bernese Oberland. Great skiing, and Paris was only a hop away."

One day in the middle of May of 1934, I found myself with a group of sycophants and Mr. Edgar at a lunch in the executive dining room of Stillman and Chase. I could hardly hear him, especially as he spoke faintly and was used to people striving to pick up his every word.

The sun was streaming in through the windows, but coolly, as if the azure sky were ice. I felt as strong as a man of thirty will feel. I was not following the conversation, for my attention was lost upon the beams of light and the passing of the clouds. And then I heard my name.

"Yes sir?" I said. I had been called by the great man himself.

"You like to walk about, don't you."

"I do, sir. How did you know?"

"I see you walking now and then, and, each time, it is clear from the color of your face that you've been out in the air for many hours. I saw you in East Hampton, on the beach, at Thanksgiving. You didn't see me. I was inside the Maidstone Club, with a telescope. I saw you holding one of the ropes in the Macy's Parade (this was ridiculous: I never did any such thing), and I saw you striding down Madison Avenue at the little hill where we used to keep our milk cows."

He appeared to be amused, and we waited as an ancient recollection swelled up and died down. "I wish I had the body and the bones," he said, "to walk twenty miles, or run down a hillside, leaping fallen trees and sliding on the dirt. You turn from side to side, you know, like a skier."

We all smiled. Even the sycophants were genuinely pleased.

"Here's a question for you. What's the name of the bank in Brooklyn on the northeast corner of Montague and Clinton?"

"The Brooklyn Trust, sir," I answered. That was easy.

"Go there," I was told by Eugene B. Edgar. "In that building is a young man who works as a loan officer. I'm told that he knows every inch of commercial and industrial real estate in Brooklyn, and the ins and outs of every company or trust that owns anything. Hire that man. With him, we'll know exactly what to buy and exactly how much to bid for it."

"What's his name?" I asked.

"I once knew, but I forgot."

"Are you sure he can be trusted to stand by us?" someone asked.

"Of course I'm sure. He's my nephew," was the reply.

"And what shall I offer him?" was my next question.

"Go as far as to triple your salary, whatever that is."

I could see that Mr. Edgar wanted to cast bread upon the waters, so I took a chance and asked, "In the meantime, may I double my salary?"

"Yes, if you bring him in," pronounced the richest man in America. "If you don't, your salary will be cut in half."

The next day, I left for Brooklyn at ten in the morning. Most people are optimistic when they awake, and I have observed a noticeable spike in optimism after the executives and staff of an enterprise imbibe their coffee. Fifteen to twenty minutes after they lower themselves to this, they are euphoric. Even as they touch the cesspool cup to their lips, an angelic expression sweeps across their faces. 10:30 to 11:00 A.M. is the best time to float a proposition among addicts. I would strike then.

I took the wrong subway—I always take the wrong subway when I go to Brooklyn; everyone does, even people who live there—and found myself on the other side of downtown. Still, I thought, I can make it. In fact, it was possible that were I a little late the euphoria at the Brooklyn Trust would rise to an even higher pitch. I hurried along, bounding up the curbs and leaping from them.

Ahead I saw an uncharacteristic knot of people, a line blocking the street, and sidewalks that looked like what you see from the side streets of Manhattan when a parade is moving up an avenue. I'll have to go around, I thought, and made a detour. But at the next corner the crowd was just as thick, and people were straining against police lines. Beyond the barricade, the area around Borough Hall was closed off and full of police cars. Now and then I heard fusillades of shots as in a battle, and from a distance the wailing of sirens criss-crossed the city and sent confusing echoes from the walls of stone and glass.

Not twenty feet beyond the lines was a figure lying motionless on the ground, with a young girl crouched over it, sobbing. The man, who was dead, wore the blue smock of someone who worked in a shoeshine parlor or as a custodian in a hive of bureaucrats, and the child who would not let him go was a girl of seventeen or eighteen. A schoolbag was still hanging from her shoulder, although half the books had scattered out and were lying on the ground nearby, some open, their pages riffling in the breeze.

The man had woolly white hair, and even as she rocked slowly back and forth, he was still, having come to his final rest. A woman next to me cried, but no one went into the plaza, as the girl was a colored girl and her father a colored man. It was not so unforgivable that no one had moved to bring the girl from the plaza. Who would pull her away from her father? Not I.

My heart went out to that girl, for I knew that in these moments her life would be cast into a hopeless story of stubborn devotion, an exhausting argument with God, an existence apart from all others, a long and sad meditation on fate, and purpose, and love.

The sound of the guns brought up my strength, as it always has. Their cracks and booms banish from me every fear and care, and each time I hear them I feel an ancestral soldier stir from within, ready to march as required.

An ambulance broke the ranks in which I was standing, the barricades fanned out, and I walked through with the mien of a police inspector: that is, with quick and bothered steps and a troubled, angry expression. Only one uniformed officer sought to question me, and I turned to him with immeasurable impatience and said, "Houlihan, Manhattan South." Maybe there was a Houlihan from Manhattan South.

The police were crouched like idiots behind cars that, except with the engine or the wheels, would never stop a rifle bullet. I remained standing as I surveyed the open plaza ahead, in which lay three bodies—two women and a man—untended.

"Houlihan," I said, "Manhattan South. Someone tell me about this, quick."

And someone did. A sniper had barricaded himself on the top floor of a building across the plaza. He had killed at least seven people, and, as anyone could hear, he was firing like mad into the interior of Brooklyn, where sound trucks had begun cruising the streets but where—New Yorkers being New Yorkers—everyone was still very much in evidence and exposed.

"If he's shooting out at the Brooklyn roads," I asked, "why are all of you hiding behind tin down here?"

"He shoots at us, too," a cop said. It was clear that as long as I was the most exposed participant, they would doubt that I was an official. Officials are supposed to stand in the line of fire, but it isn't actually a requirement. It's more of an option.

Although they didn't know it, I was no more exposed than were they, and it wasn't really that dangerous anyway. The sniper was now agitated and aimless. Were he to fire at me he would undoubtedly miss, and at that moment he was shooting only in the direction of the Spanish Monument, hundreds of feet over my head. Also, I was driven to meet his bullets, and had one smashed into me it would have been the fulfillment of my destiny. Destiny breaks the surface near crime. Those who spend their lives in slippers ridicule the idea of destiny, but in a rain of bullets, or even just a shower, destiny is everything: it becomes palpable, you feel it the way you feel the hot sun or a hurricane wind. Had I died that day I would have been content. Had I sunk onto a pavement covered with my own blood, I would have felt as comforted as a child finally taken into its mother's arms.

"Who's in there?" I asked, speeding up because the sergeant in charge was looking at me the way a bulldog looks at a man who is doing a bulldog imitation.

"And who are you?" he said, breaking my thin ice.

"Houlihan, Manhattan South."

"I don't know you," he said. "And why is that?"

I shrugged my shoulders.

"Where's your badge?" he challenged, still propped up against the wheel of a car like a drunk trying to kiss a wall. I knew that with the bullets whistling by, even so far overhead, he would dare not move.

"I don't wear jewelry," I said.

"Christ Almighty," he declared, "we've got one more lunatic."

"I'm not a lunatic," I told him. "I'm an *investment banker.*"

"You're under arrest!" he screamed, floridly.

I stepped into the open, where I was born to be. The sniper saw me and began to direct a methodical stream of bullets in my direction. They ricocheted off the pavement, smashing the glass in the police cars. The cars were square then, with big windows.

I kept moving, so that the sniper could not correct his fire. He was off by several feet with each shot, laterally, and by almost that in range.

"Get in here you stupid son of a bitch!" the sergeant shouted. He tried to sound very authoritative, but in the bullet shower he was a gerbil.

"Make me," I said.

He closed his eyes and moaned.

"Give me a gun," I commanded.

"You'd need explosives," the sergeant said, trying to reason with me. "He's got the fire doors bolted and barred."

"I'll go up the fire escape," I said.

"You're crazy."

"Look, he's killed seven people already," I told the sergeant, rather full of rage for someone who was so calm. "What do you want to do, wait for a tank that climbs up the side of buildings?"

"You leave that to us!" he bellowed.

"No. I can't."

I ran across the plaza, jumping over benches, dodging left or right depending only upon the way my heart told me to turn, and as I ran the shots got closer and I could see the rifle barrel, the flashes. The police opened up. It sounded like a city trying to throw back planes—although, at the time, I had never heard that sound. Just before I reached the safety of an overhanging ledge, I realized that I might not get to the Brooklyn Trust before the end of banking hours.

Well, so what, I thought. I felt alive and angry in that wonderful taxing way in which you feel alive and angry when someone is firing a gun at you. I suppose that, early on, the wires in my brain were crossed, because when someone shoots at me I tend not to run away from the gun but toward it. I feel then, and only then, peace and joy. Even when I flew, when the world seemed full of light and all its edges were so well defined that they glowed like silver, I myself did not come afire until the sound of the cannon, and then it was as if a switch had been thrown and the lights of a great city had all come on at once.

After a moment of brief reflection and prayer, I ran to the side of the building and leapt up to the fire escape ladder. I thought my tremendous jump was, somehow, funny, and I weakened with laughter as I hung from the last rung of the ladder until I almost lost my grip. Then I scolded myself and began to climb. I think that if the sniper had been aware of my chortlings and ya-hoos he might have surrendered, but he was too far above me and probably too crazed to hear.

The fire escape dripped with chunks of masonry, iron, and lead, like a shot tower, or a waterfall breaking through a tangle of fallen trees. Each spent bullet, chip of stone, or piece of iron rail jingled not once or twice but a hundred times as it fell, striking different surfaces at different angles and velocities in a great concert of chimes and clinks. I myself was the only upward-moving pachinko ball pushing against this fragmented tide, rising story by story. It was perfectly safe. Because of the kindly suppressive fire of the police, the sniper was unable to shoot downward.

He was on the tenth floor, and when I got to the ninth, I stopped. Even I will not go straight at a gun at close range in a narrow field. There's no joy in that. I followed the fire escape as it wrapped around the building. Only then did I go up to the tenth floor. But you couldn't just round the corner, for the tenth-floor catwalk stopped abruptly at a turret window. I might have tiptoed across the ledge, but the sniper would have seen me in the window, shot through the glass, and I would have died like a bird in flight.

I climbed the roof until I sat at the very top, at the peak of a wedge of slate shingles, with my feet hanging out over the slope. To get to the ledge above the fire escape where the sniper had positioned his rifle, I would have to slide about twelve feet down the slate. I couldn't see beyond the end of the slide except to the plaza a hundred feet below.

My problem was how to get there without being launched into space in the last and most spectacular toboggan ride of my life. I had come to a dead end. I was on a narrow windblown projection 110 feet above the street, and a hundred guns were firing with astonishing imprecision at a target just a few feet below me. Every now and then a slug would smash a shingle, and pieces of slate jingle over the ledge and through the fire escape.

I didn't know what to do, so I waited, and as I waited my former happiness and ferocity boiled down into fear. I began to experience what Marlise calls *Impetigo,* by which she means an overpowering fear of heights, so I clung to a lightning rod, staring at my distorted reflection in the glass ball, hoping that something would happen and that the weather would not change. The firing intensified as reinforcements from other boroughs began to use tommy guns. These are short-range weapons of dubious accuracy. Lines of slugs whistled through the air and to the sides, shattering the slate. I thought that the ribs of the roof might be exposed by this excavating fire, which would allow me to climb down to the ledge. But for that to happen, I, too, would have to be excavated.

Then I heard a voice say, "Don't do it."

I looked around, still grasping the lightning rod. Hanging on to the wedge of the roof on the lee side of the firing was a stocky, bespectacled, sandy-haired man of approximately my age. I was, of course, preoccupied, and the last thing on my mind was the size of his ears. He had larger than normal ears, although I did not notice them until, many years afterward, he pointed to them and told me that they had been the coffee of his life, and that he was convinced that everyone on the street, especially beautiful women, saw them as clearly as if they were the Rock of Gibraltar. Apart from the ears, he looked like a young version of Father Flanagan. Of course, at the time, Father Flanagan was a young version (and, one hopes, a young virgin), and no one knew what he looked like, except those around him and possibly Spencer Tracy by instinct alone.

Though I thought he meant for me not to go after the sniper, he was under the impression that I was about to kill myself. "I have my reasons," I said.

"They're never good enough."

"How do you know?"

"I work for the Transit Authority."

"I understand," I said. "That makes you as infallible as the Pope."

"No. I'm in Maintenance of Way. My job includes talking down the suicides. I've never heard a good enough reason (from someone healthy enough to climb a hundred feet up a suspension cable) for ending one's life."

"I'm not a jumper."

"I suppose you work up here," he said, looking at my Savile Row suit and Peale shoes.

"Of course I don't."

"So why are you here?"

"To get the son of a bitch below."

"The devil?"

"I don't know who he is. Why do you think the police are firing a hundred guns in our direction?"

"A hundred what?"

Because of the wind, he could hear nothing from my side of the roof. I will never forget his expression as he looked over and saw the army below.

"What did you do," he asked, "double-park?"

I can think of no other explanation but that this man had been sent by an angel. He had seen me from a Transit Authority building and, assuming that I was about to take my life, had come to dissuade me. Having talked down many jumpers from bridges and elevated platforms, and persuaded others to remove their necks from the rails forward of onrushing trains, he was unafraid of heights and accustomed to great danger. Half the subway in New York runs on trestles and over bridges, and he spent his days deep in tunnels and high in the air.

"How do we get down to that ledge without flying off into space?" I asked.

He peered intently over the ridge of the roof. "It's simple," he said. "I'll hang on to the lightning rod, and you climb down me like a ladder. Then, when you're safe, I'll slide, you catch my feet, and lower me as if you were taking in a pole."

"You're Polish?" I asked.

"Swedish," he said, moving decisively to anchor himself on the lightning rod.

I climbed down him and, after holding his ankles for several minutes while he kicked my face and implied that I was a chicken, straightened out and let go. I slid for a few long seconds until the soles of my feet connected with the ledge.

Then he let go as if he were only a few feet above the ground, and I brought him in like a pole.

"Now what?" he asked, not quite sure of our mission.

"We turn around." We turned around. Though the fire escape was just six feet below, it was only two and a half feet wide, and unless we leaned out dangerously, we couldn't see it. I felt as if an unseen force were pushing me off the ledge and into the void. Though of course I had to resist it, I also tried not to offend it.

"What's next?" I was asked.

I improvised. "We drop to the fire escape and rush him."

"He has a gun. You go first."

"If he hits you, you won't necessarily die," I stated.

"Still, you go first."

"No no," I said. "It's safer for the one who goes first. It will shock him, and he'll aim for the second guy."

"Even so, you go first."

"All right, if you insist," I said.

"Good. I'll follow soon after. When I drop, he'll turn from you. Then you rush him."

I agreed to this. At that point I suppose I would have agreed to anything.

I waved my arms for the police to stop firing, and when they did, I dropped. Because I thought I would miss the fire escape and fall to my death, going off the edge was much harder even than my first parachute jump, when at least I had a parachute. But I was lucky. I landed not only on the fire escape but on the rifle, pivoting it like a lever resting upon the fulcrum of the windowsill. It struck the sniper in the jaw with a blow that knocked him back into the room.

The next thing I knew, the Swede landed next to me, full force, on his behind. He seemed unhurt, though slightly stunned.

I took the rifle and tossed it gallantly over my head. Seconds later I heard it clatter on the pavement.

"Why did you do that, you idiot!" the Swede screamed.

"He's unconscious," I said confidently. A second passed.

"No he's not," the Swede announced, dodging to the side as the sniper tried to impale him with a bayonet.

"Cut it out!" I shouted. Then the sniper lunged at me. I backed up and felt the rail slam against my shoulders. "Cut it out!"

This had an effect, and he froze. I saw him for the first time. I must say that I was surprised, and that he didn't fit my pre-conception of a sniper. He was about 5'3" tall, with thinning red hair and red beard, and his eyes, which were the most unusual pop eyes I've ever seen, made him look like a man who was being strangled.

"Pressure on your neck!" I yelled as I dived through the window, to my regret. I found myself in his apartment, or office—whatever it was—and this was not where I wanted to be. The floor was two feet deep with the decomposed remnants of food and coffee grounds. A pot of coffee bubbled on the stove, and paper plates of roast fowl were scattered around, some perhaps a day old, some perhaps as old as a year. It was like being in a three-dimensional time lapse film of a decomposing chicken.

Rising from the floor in disgust, I tried not to vomit. No good vomiting when someone is about to rush you with a bayonet. I could see that the bathtub was half-full of some kind of green slime, and that above the toilet was a picture of Al Jolson, with a throwing knife stuck in the throat.

Near the stove was domelike birdcage in which lay the bones of a dead parrot, and on the front door was a calendar from January, 1922, that said, "To do. . . ."

My friend jumped in the window, and his first words were, "This is disgusting. This guy is disgusting."

The sniper started to move his feet underneath him, which propelled him toward me. I dodged out of the way as if I were evading a punch, and he ran into the wall, but he turned in a flash. He was extremely agitated.

"Don't you ever clean up?" I asked.

"Don't tell *me* to clean up!" he shouted, in the only words I would ever hear him say.

"I'm not telling you to clean up, I'm asking if you ever do."

This drove him crazy. "Don't tell *me* to clean up!" he screamed, flailing at me, samurai-style, with the bayonet. He was quick, he was fast, and he was going to kill me.

As it churned the air, the blade made a wonderful sound, and no wonder. It was the only clean thing in the apartment. I backed up, mesmerized. Then the Swede charged from the side, but the horrible messy guy made a move as quick as a trout taking a fly, and cut the Swede's face, from which blood shot as if it were being pumped. He collapsed into the filth.

Then the sniper turned to me again, and I watched the windmill advance. I could not go around it, I could not fly above it, and I could not dive below it. I was very frightened at first. I thought I was going to die just like one of the chickens rotting on the floor.

As he moved close enough so that I was breathing the air pushed by the blade, I understood that the only thing I could do was to absorb the thrust of the bayonet, remain on my feet, and grab that son of a bitch's throat. His pop eyes were his destiny, and I would fulfill it for him even as I bled.

The bayonet struck me in the side. The cut was deep, but I did not feel it at first. Then he thrust it into my shoulder. I prayed in a flash that no arteries were severed, and I grasped his neck. He tried to withdraw the bayonet, but, for him, the distance between us would be fixed forever.

Never had I been so determined. But what choice did I have? All my strength flowed into my hands. Then I heard the pitter patter of little feet on the fire escape. It didn't matter. It was the police. That didn't matter either. By the time they arrived inside, grimacing at what they beheld, the filthy little pop-eyed sniper was hanging from my hands, his eyes bulging, his flesh as white as a cloud.

I failed to get to the Brooklyn Trust that day, and Eugene B. Edgar, the richest man in America, cut my salary in half. But it didn't matter, for in the Depression even half my salary was a princely sum.

The Spark of Transgression

*(If you have not done so already,
please return the previous pages to the antproof case.)*

WHEN I RETURNED to my rooms on the top floor of the
Hassler I held yet another bottle of ice-cold mineral water by
the neck: first in my right hand, and then in the left as I opened
the door. A woman had stayed in the suite before I took it, and
the scent of a high quality perfume clung to unexpected places
—I found it on my hands after I cranked up the awning, and I
spent a highly charged minute sniffing the base of the telephone.

It was not a perfume that Constance used, but of a rank
elevated enough to bring home to me that she was gone. I went
onto the terrace, put my feet up, and began to drink the water.
Called *Aqua Impala*, it was sharp and sweet. Late at night Rome
was silent but for the sound of wind moving through the trees
in the Villa Borghese. Fountains splashing coldly in the summer
air echoed off buildings that still held the day's heat in their
ocher-colored walls.

On my small terrace were planters filled with black earth and blooming flowers, and the stars that blazed over the Tyrrhenian lent to the night a soft mysterious light full of excitement and promise. Many a time I have contented myself for more hours than I dare admit, sinking into the slow but perfect rhythms of sunlight or stars, watching birds, or the plume of a fountain, or stalks of corn swaying in the golden air of a silent August afternoon.

It reminded me that, in the late Twenties and throughout the Thirties, I had to stay in New York during most of the summer, and on weekends I would walk the abandoned streets of lower Manhattan, where you could hear a pigeon from five blocks away as it rose into the stifling air. It was on benches in parks that had no name, alone on vacant Sundays, that I found my resolution.

And why not? I grew up on a farm, where I stayed until I was ten years of age, and there I took directly from nature and without difficulty what whole populations, lacking such privilege, decry as having vanished, what philosophers struggle to find in a lifetime of labor, and what I could see, knowing nothing, with one glance into a sunlit stream.

I have done well at times (and very badly at others) in society and at games of worth and dominance. But in the world of tilled landscapes run like lace with tracts of forest and rebellious creeks, in the world of broad fields and bright uninhabited bays, I invariably find solace and strength. It is where I have always wanted to be, even if I am seldom there, and it is where I will only chance to die on some windy perfect day like those I loved as a child.

For a brief hour on my terrace at the Hassler I was my own man again, or, rather, a boy, able to plot my course with the kind of dead certainty common to those who know exactly who they are, what they love, where they have been, and where they are going.

I knew what I had to do, though I was still puzzled as to why, and in the sad and tranquil Roman night I was left alone with the bottle of mineral water to translate my natural understanding into terms I could comprehend when strength and serenity were gone.

Unless you count as felonies innocuous actions such as overturning coffee urns, putting mice in the bins of coffee beans at the A&P, and the reflexive punching of waiters and waitresses who put coffee next to me *while I'm eating*, I had never committed a crime.

The murder for which I had been convicted was strictly self-defense, and in that I was given no choice. Had my attacker been anything but a Belgian, and were the Huns not to have chosen Belgium to trample first, I would have been acquitted. Should not a perpetually inebriated judge be grounds for a determination of mistrial? It was the system of justice that was at fault, not I. I was merely a child attacked without reason by a large coffee-drinking adult.

And the pop-eyed guy? That was violent, but hardly a crime. The police arrested me and the Swede, held us for a time, and then released us in the middle of the night with neither charge nor comment. A number of officers were awarded commendations for heroically suppressing a threat to public safety, and they did not have to explain why the sniper had died by asphyxiation, because when they arrived upon the scene they shot at the body for a full minute, driving bullets into the carcass in the same way that an explorer plants a flag at the top of a peak or on a palm-fringed beach.

The character of the police department of the City of New York was an important factor in my calculations, for the looting of Stillman and Chase would take place, of course, in New York. Which was encouraging, for most of the department had no connection with crime except on a random basis. They were a costumed career bureaucracy that, with the exception of some saints and heroes, did the minimum required to make it look as if they were doing what they were supposed to have been doing.

Whether they learned this from the other city bureaucracies, whether they exported it, or whether at some dim time in history—perhaps in the age of the dinosaurs—everyone learned it simultaneously, was immaterial: they were corrupt, they were ineffective, they did not come when called, they were incompetent, they were unconscious, they were asleep, and they were New York's finest.

These defamations were valid for street crime, crimes of passion, parking offenses, and armed assault, but they were especially valid for the kind of high-level financial crime I contemplated, for of the vast armies of blue-coated soldiers, only a few (and perhaps none) were not astonishingly deferential to the Wasp mores and institutions that made up the Wall Street overworld that was clearly beyond their ken.

How would a New York detective in the early 1950's react to a crime of arbitrage and straddling other than to think it was a violent sex perversion? Even were the violation more straightforward, the received wisdom was that the elite would take care of it among themselves. So, as far as police interference was concerned, I concluded that even if not completely in the clear, I had a gargantuan head start.

As for the moral justification, really, one need not strain to find justification for robbing an investment bank, at least as they were when I knew them. They were caste-restricted highly efficient cartels that escaped competition and maintained their position by relying upon reams of regulations and unfathomable established customs. The regulations were written by appointed and elected politicians either in the pay of these firms or soon to join them. The customs were protected by networks of cronies and middle-level clerks on the take.

In the Treasury markets the Fed gave Stillman and Chase a license to steal. It was a closed system that took money from the many and returned it to only a few, without affording to the many either choice or benefit. As a boy runner, I marveled at the way securities were traded. A broker would take an order from a school teacher or a milkman—a hundred shares of International Pickle at $5 apiece. The broker would say, 'I'll let you know by the close of the market if I can get that price.' He might then wait for the stock to drop to four dollars, buy it, and sell it to the milkman for five. Or he might buy the stock at five, watch it go up, sell it at six, and tell the milkman he had been unable to obtain it for five. In both cases the client was providing a guarantee for the broker's trading. I saw it happen a million times. Stillman and Chase did exactly this, and not only with money from the milkman but with pension funds, endowments, and municipal treasuries.

Within the organization itself, reward had less to do with performance than position. Clerks and runners lived on a pittance and sometimes risked their lives, while the top echelon prided themselves on how a word here or a word there could churn a billion dollars and create a fortune in commissions. Though it was not the same thing, it reminded me of the way thieves pride themselves in appropriating at one fell swoop what it may have taken a man all his life to earn. For those who would condemn the partners of Stillman and Chase more than common thieves, I say, judge them not by their take but by their dishonesty. Whereas the value of material things fluctuates, disappears, the constancy of honesty is well known, and cannot be made to vary.

Stillman and Chase had a particularly filthy habit, though not as refined as that of its Swiss counterparts, of husbanding the blood money of tyrants and sheiks. It was the vault of slave kingdoms on the Arabian Sea and Latin American dictatorships enamored of boots, belts, and bandoliers.

I neither needed money nor wanted it. I had had an ocean of it and it had hardly mattered to me. All I ever wanted, really, was to build a barrier between myself and coffee. And I was not obsessed with striking at Stillman and Chase. They were indefensible, but if I robbed them I would not be making the world either a better or a worse place. I decided then, on the terrace of my room at the Hassler, as Roman owls hooted at the shooting stars, that I was going to rob Stillman and Chase because it was there, because this was the right thing to do, because it would bring a ray of sunshine into my life, because virtue was its own reward, because of *ars gratia artis,* and because *excelsior timidus protectat.*

During the war the Swiss foreign minister protested to the American ambassador that an American warplane had violated Swiss neutrality by entering the country from the northeast, following the valley of the Rhine, and circling the Matterhorn at close proximity not once, twice, or three times, but *six* times—in figure eights, loops, and barrel rolls. The entire population of Zermatt had been transfixed, and several herds of goats stopped giving milk for days.

Who do you think it was that upset the goats? I did. I did it because I thought I was going to die. Having done it, however, I knew somehow that I was going to live. In breaking the rules,

I broke other things too, including the veils of falsehood that cover the truth like thunderclouds.

Were the world perfect it would always be wrong to trespass, but as the world is not perfect, sometimes one must. And when you do, you live, you break free, you fly. But you must do it responsibly, you must not injure the innocent. Then, at least before they catch you, it works.

I know that this is true, and the reason it is true, I believe, is that the spark of transgression comes directly from the heart of God.

The next morning, though I had stayed up most of the night and I was half a century old, I was full of energy. I strode to the front desk with the assurance and bravado I had had ten years earlier as an airman in the very same city. Although my plans had not solidified, my intentions were set. All that remained was to find a way, to hatch a plot, and I imagined that this would be quite enjoyable. Perhaps I would chance upon a brilliant scheme as I walked about the city that day. After all, I had been directed to the idea itself by my accidental encounter with the singers.

My luggage was sent through directly to the Georges V in Paris, and I was free until the train left. I had routed myself through Frankfurt rather than San Remo, for I knew that I would sleep well in the cool air of the Alps. It always was the same: leave Rome at 5:00 P.M., dinner in Milan, snowfields before darkness, a sound and perfect sleep under the virgin wool blankets of *Wagons Lits* as glacial air poured through the open window.

I would arrive in Paris by afternoon, shower, and walk the city until dark, sitting on a bench in Passy as I read *Le Monde,* observing with paternal joy the ranks of school children in blue uniforms, and then buying a tie at Hermès to go with the suits I would pick up at my tailor in London. Perhaps in Paris I would meet a woman with whom I might fall in love, although I considered myself too old in many respects for that kind of thing, and would feel this way until I was reborn with the shock of plummeting into Brazil.

All this while I drew my salary and qualified for the bonus. The work itself, when I did it, consisted of meeting with political egomaniacs who spoke not one un-self-serving word, and had less an idea of the state of their country's polity and economy than might a blind chicken on a provincial farm. Resident Stillman and Chase money people were there with the figures and proposals: I was the exposure guru. They used me to figure out the risk and, therefore, the charges, in floating a loan. I had a sterling record, and had never been wrong. My technique was simple. I looked at the fundamentals, I read everything I could, I paid great heed to history, and I talked to the people that investment bankers seldom talk to—small farmers, masons, students, policemen, factory workers, engineers, fishermen, dentists, and women hanging out the wash. From them I gauged the hope and corruption that determine a country's momentum, or lack of it.

I liked my work, and I had intended to take my time in coming up with a way to ruin Stillman and Chase. Being human, I probably would have taken fifteen or twenty years, by which time I would have retired to East Hampton and Palm Beach, with a large belly, horn-rimmed glasses, a lemon-yellow blazer, and fifty cases of Laphroaig sitting in the cool of each basement. I can see myself waddling into the Maidstone Club on astonishingly skinny legs, a monogrammed sterling silver cigar tool hanging from my waist, a mashie niblick in one hand and a copy of *The Singapore Business Digest* in the other.

The clerk at the Hassler saved me from this, or, rather, he was the instrument of my salvation. He handed me a bill. Of course, I gave it right back to him without even looking at it.

"That will be taken care of by Stillman and Chase, in New York," I said, with a sparkle in my voice that came from knowing what I was going to do to them. "We have an account here." I resisted the temptation to add, "and the economic health of your nation depends upon us."

I knew something was wrong when a look of tremendous pain crossed his face. It was generated by the conflict between his obligation to be obsequious and his duty to collect the money.

"Absolutely, sir," he said. "The room charges will be paid directly from New York, but the additionals are now on your account."

"My account?"

"Yes sir."

"My personal account?"

"Yes sir."

"I don't have a personal account."

"We opened one for you, sir, when the letter of instruction came from Signor Piehand."

"Signor Piehand? In New York?"

"Yes sir."

He was referring to Dickey Piehand, the managing partner, a malicious, alcoholic, glorified concierge who had married a suppository heiress from a rotted branch of the Edgar family.

"What did it say?"

"It said, sir, that you would take care of the additionals."

"That prick," I said. "He's just a Scarsdale maggot who married a suppository heiress."

"Yes sir."

The clerk was Italian, and did not understand idiomatic English. I decided to get on with it.

"What are the additionals?" I asked.

"I can read them for you, sir." He read in a magnificent Northern Italian accent, pronouncing each and every syllable gloriously and incorrectly. "Din-ner in the café. Min-er-al water. Min-er-al wa-ter. Breakfast. Telephone Call. Telephone Call. Telephone Call. Min-er-al wa-ter. Min-er-al wa-ter. Pistachios. Telephone Call. Laundry. Min-er-al wa-ter. Telephone Call. Telephone Call. Breakfast. Telephone Call. Pistachios. Min-er-al wa-ter. Min-er-al wa-ter. Pistachios. . . ."

Never had I had so objective a view of my habits, and I meekly paid the additionals, which, for a five-day stay, came to more than $800. At first it seemed like one of Dickey Piehand's moronic inefficiencies, or perhaps one of the Edgar practical jokes.

How could Stillman and Chase, I thought, be so formidable as to have known my decision of last night and closed me down today by means of a letter written a week ago? It was impossible, so it was either a mistake or a coincidence. A coincidence of what? On the one hand, I had my new resolution. On the other? Was it possible that, purely by accident, they had opened the battle just as it had occurred to me in my most private thoughts to do the same?

I finished my work in Europe, flew from London to New York, and went straight from Idlewild to the firm, where nothing seemed amiss until I reached my office. My secretary was gone and so was her desk. My reception room had no furniture whatsoever, not even a telephone. The only thing left was the rug.

"Where's Mrs. Ludwig?" I asked the fiendishly attractive Bryn Mawr girl who helped Byron Chatsworth track pork jowls, and who hated me because I had once told her point-blank that she was the most beautiful woman I had ever seen, but that she would never find love as long as she continued to drink coffee. She was offended because she thought that I was saying that only women should not drink coffee. No one should drink coffee. It makes both sexes equally disgusting.

"She moved to muni's," I was told.

I trod to muni's with indignant steps, and there was Mrs. Ludwig, lording it over the younger secretaries, her glasses hanging from a navy-blue cord that failed to match her sweater.

"Why are you in muni's?" I asked, like a husband who confronts his wife in the arms of another man.

"I was transferred," she replied. "I thought you knew." That . . . was a lie.

"Who transferred you?"

"Mr. Piehand."

"We'll see about Mr. Piehand." But I knew already that the cause was lost. No way exists for a rational human being (or even an irrational human being) to fight a bureaucracy. Even when the country of the bureaucrats is conquered, they flourish, effortlessly traversing from the arteries of war to the veins of peace. Huge bureaucracies are simply invincible. Nonetheless, I throttled Dickey Piehand and pushed him up against the paneling in his office. Red with rage, glottals pouring from my throat like a professional gargler, I shook his porcine body.

"You transferred Mrs. Ludwig without asking me!" I screamed. "I've been here since 1918, and you've been here since 1951, you filthy little suppository!"

"It was decided in the administrative committee," he said in a death squeak. "Talk to Mr. Edgar if you have a complaint!"

He knew that was impossible. Eugene B. Edgar was so ancient that he would no longer speak to anyone but his stunning 'nurses.' In fact, very few people could tell if he were alive or if he were dead. What a tragedy that this man, who once had known almost everything, had come so far that he had forgotten it. But he still owned. He owned so much that though he could not walk, refused to speak, and could hardly hear, he was still treated like a prince even by those who hated him. The hundred or two hundred other human beings in the world who were born in the same year and still had not died were wrapped in shawls and looked upon as hamsters. People walked past them as if they were pieces of decaying wood. But Mr. Edgar, who was as physically alluring as a June roadkill in the middle of October, commanded more attention than would have the Bryn Mawr girl had she come to work in a strapless dress and with a tiara in her hair.

Mrs. Ludwig's replacement, I was told, was not yet hired. As soon as the opportunity presented itself, she would be. Translated, this meant that as long as I remained at Stillman and Chase I would not have a secretary.

The administrative committee had also disallowed my expenses while traveling. They explained that though this reflected a general change in policy, it was confined to me. I felt, somehow, that my star was declining.

I went home. I was powerless and alone, and I slept for three days.

When I awoke I was no less powerless or alone, but I was well rested and hope had returned. It was a Friday evening in June, one of those evenings in New York when the air is sweet and the light is soft. In the sunset, all the glass turned gold. The breeze was as gentle as in a dream, and when the wind rose it was warm and reassuring. I knew I would be up all night and that I would watch the birds take to the air with the winds of sunrise, that I would see the change in the sky, the five o'clock powder blue.

I was finished at Stillman and Chase not because I could not do my job—I was really very good at my job—but rather because Constance had left me, and Constance had left me because of coffee.

My way had been clear as I had worked steadily and meritoriously, but then, after I met her, I rose like a rocket. As soon as I was associated with her immense wealth, success gravitated to me like cat hair. Investment bankers dream in billions, and everyone wanted to sit with me at lunch or in the boardroom. I was rapidly headed toward the inner circle that, more and more, did the thinking for Mr. Edgar and would emerge after the storm of his death with its hairy hands full of blood and money.

I took this for granted. I didn't need success at Stillman and Chase, as I was fully able to buy or begin my own investment bank. In those days I thought that no matter what I did my heels would click across polished marble for the rest of my life. But when Constance and I separated, I was culled from the herd.

After three days' sleep, I was hungry. I decided to take a long walk and have a good dinner. Having faced the reality of my situation, I was actually happy—in the way that you are happy when you pay a debt, even if it leaves you impoverished.

Dressed in khaki and white, I headed out into the perfect evening and walked diagonally through the park. I hoped I would not see Constance doing some sort of coffee dance in the sheep meadow, and I didn't. The air carried the scent of blossoms and billowed warmly over lakes and fields. By Columbus Circle I was walking fast, and by the time I arrived at the restaurant almost an hour later I was ready to confront my destiny.

And I did, although not right off. In those days no one except swamis and biochemists knew about the perils of fat, and I ate accordingly. At the Blue Mill you ordered from a chalkboard menu that the waiter placed near your table, and that evening the only thing on it was rack of lamb. I didn't protest. It was served with tiny, crisp, roasted potatoes, a salad with a (perhaps literally) heart-stopping Roquefort dressing, and a glass of Santa Maddalena. To be safe, I ordered two dinners, even though I knew that after the meal I would undoubtedly debauch myself on a tour of the bakeries.

Hudson Street was filled with courting couples—girls in their summer dresses and their beaus in whipcord suits and navy-blue ties. It was Friday evening, when Saturday and Sunday lay ahead for correcting the mistakes and addressing the sorrows of the week.

I saw a very beautiful woman at a near table. She must have come in from the Hamptons, for a new sunburn gave to her youthful face the color of life and strength. She wore a sundress that exposed her gorgeous shoulders and arms and the roseate plain between her throat and chest in a way that paralyzed every man around her. And I had the wonderfully disconcerting experience of discovering that, though she was with someone else, she was looking at me.

I was never much to look at, but for one reason or another I was always involved in love affairs, perhaps because I loved so strongly. Marlise has a different opinion. According to her, "Womens love you because womens loves crazy peoples." Anyway, I had become infatuated with the beauty from the Hamptons, and I found myself oblivious of everything around me except what I was eating.

This blimp ride came slowly to an end as I realized that the object of my infatuation had become distinctly uncomfortable. She had ceased staring at me, stopped talking to the jerky college boy who tried to be her dinner companion, and was shooting apprehensive glances over her shoulder as she nervously touched her exquisite auburn hair.

I became more alert watching her react to a disturbance unfolding at the far end of the dining room. I hadn't noticed it at first, but soon the sound of tense, adrenaline-boosted, breathless argumentation filled the restaurant. Everyone grew silent and stopped moving.

Three waiters had gathered around the table of a lone man who was making a lot of trouble. Just a drunk, I thought. But he didn't sound drunk. A young vagrant, I thought. But he was dressed much as I was, and he was about the same age. And, though he was heavier and a bit shorter, our coloring was the same and our voices similar, except that I could hear very distinctly that he had been educated by Jesuits. They have a characteristic pacing, rhythm, intonation, and tone that are as easy to spot as a style of dancing peculiar to a famous samba school.

This Jesuit was involved in hot dispute. A waitress charged out of the kitchen, followed by a man whose pencil mustache signified that he owned the restaurant. She was dressed like the waiters but wore a skirt rather than pants underneath her apron. A white napkin hung from her left arm, just as in Paris.

"He threw it at me!" she whined—hurt, amazed, and frightened—in a voice that was like a missile homing in on

Bensonhurst. "He took it from my hand, and he threw it at me. Call the police."

Her apron had a huge wet stain on it. What had he thrown? Wine? Coca-Cola?

"He could have scalded me to death!" she yelled, her anger building. "He could have scarred me!"

Even though my mouth was full, I stopped eating. My eyes went from side to side, although what I was looking at I do not know.

The Jesuit didn't just sit there. Jesuits never do. His left hand pointed at her, index finger extended, arm cocked close to the body in the manner of a warrior or a street fighter, a gesture that I have never seen in anyone of good upbringing and normal proclivities. "She," he said, accusingly, and his words carried Jesuitically throughout the room, "put a cup of live coffee right on this table, right in front of me, as I was eating."

I stood. My napkin fell to the floor.

"So what?" one of the waiters asked.

The Jesuit rose from his seat explosively. "So what?" he asked. "How would you like to have a river of sewage blown into *your* face?"

As they stepped back, I stepped forward.

"This satanic substance," the Jesuit boomed, "was the ruin of Adam, the ruin of Eve, and has always been neither more nor less than the devil's lubricant. If I don't ask for this filth," he bellowed, "then *by God*, don't set it down before me!"

"Let me pay for his dinner!" I said, approaching the Jesuit, but my mouth was full, and no one understood me. I swallowed, nearly choking, and repeated myself.

"Why?" the owner asked.

"Because," I said slowly, "he's my brother."

Of course, he was not really my brother. I never had a brother. I was an only child, but you can have a brother in more ways than one, the most important being perhaps the feeling of having been thrown down by the same omnipotent force after having failed at achieving the same noble aim. We walked out into the night, thinking about the fight against a common enemy.

Although I did not know why, he was strikingly familiar and I had the sense that I had met him before.

"She put a cup of live coffee right in front of me," he said, still amazed. "I didn't ask for it. She said, 'Here's your coffee.' "

"They do that," I told him.

"I didn't actually throw it at her, I just shooed it off the table, like a snake, and she was standing in the way. I might have thrown it at her. The smell makes me violent.

"The whole world has been overtaken by that disgusting stuff," he continued. "It's like a virus from outer space, sent to enslave humanity not in chains but by beans. Did you know that at the zoo when they want hippos to vomit they stuff a handful of coffee grounds into their garage-mouths, and the hippos retch so hard they practically turn inside-out?"

"Yes, I know that," I answered. "Everyone knows that, but people forget."

"Coffee makes them think alike. They find it hard to imagine that someone actually might have the courage to say that it's immoral.

"You know," he offered, as we sat down on a concrete slab next to a loading platform, "there's nothing you can do about it, so you might as well just kill yourself. The power of coffee is far too strong." He squinted at me. "Haven't we met?"

"I was thinking the same thing. Were you in the army?" I asked.

"Yeah."

"Air Corps?"

"Railroad troops."

"Italy?"

"Northern France and Germany."

"Where did you do your officer's training?"

"In sergeant's school."

"Did you go to Harvard?" (He looked so very familiar.)

An expression of uncontrollable disgust seized his features. "Did you?"

"Yes. Class of Twenty-Six."

"Twenty-six what? Assholes?"

"I beg your pardon?"

"I haven't met very many people from Harvard," he said, "but every single one that I have met is distinguished by one very brilliant thing."

"Brilliance is a prerequisite for admission," I mouthed.

"I didn't mean it that way."

"What, then, is the one brilliant thing that you think distinguishes them?"

"They think they're better than everyone else. And do you know what? They're barely distinguishable. And if they are, it's because they're actually worse. Early on they get coated with a kind of intellectual gel, and, as they go through life, it turns to glass.

"Then their buck-toothed children go to Harvard, and they really think they're something special, but the cycles of breeding and posturing have emptied them into nothing. I hate people who went to Harvard even more than I hate other arrogant sons of bitches like fighter pilots and investment bankers."

"How do you do," I said, and introduced myself.

"How do you do, I'm Paolo Massina," he said. "It was nice

to know you. I hope you keep up the good work with the coffee, but we were never meant to march side by side." He began to walk away from where we had been sitting.

I followed, speaking to him in Italian, but it was clear that he understood not a word of what I was saying. "You don't speak Italian," I said, suspiciously.

"So what?"

"Paolo Massina?"

"I changed my name because of my wife's parents. It was bad enough that I wasn't from Brooklyn. They would have died had their daughter become Angelica Smedjebakken."

He disappeared around a corner. I knew him. I knew that I knew him, but I just couldn't place him.

Slow defeat in seemingly inconsequential affairs is more painful than may at first be apparent, because nature does not compensate for a bank clerk's sneer as it does for, let us say, being hurled over Niagara Falls. No adrenaline comes to the fore when you place last in the office popularity polls (as I had begun to do, consistently), and mysticism cannot comfort you when your stocks go down steadily in a booming market or when you are bitten by a dog whose owner then reviles you and carries it off to get a tetanus shot. Day after day, like someone with a vicious skin disease, I sank lower and lower in the esteem of my fellow men—every single one of whom, I might add, was a coffee drinker.

I had expected to be lionized at the Stillman and Chase summer banquet, because I had really outdone myself just days before with a call that would be worth billions to Stillman and Chase in the years ahead.

Although the world did not learn of the Soviet-Egyptian arms deal until much later, my analysis of radio traffic and diplomatic comings and goings indicated to me that the alliance had been formed sometime in May. The CIA hadn't a clue, or, if they did, it was lost in the bureaucratic Parcheesi, and from those quarters emerged nothing, not even a peep.

Meanwhile, in early June, just after I had returned to work and even though I was being pressured and nitpicked, I was attentive to the right signs and I came to the right conclusions. For this, I might add, I owe a great deal to my tutors in Arabic at the institution about which I had recently begun to entertain serious misgivings, and to Sir Hamilton A. R. Gibb of Oxford.

That may sound impressive, but all it means is that for years I studied like a donkey, a ninny, and an ass, and when I emerged from my academic costume of black robe with white trees, scarlet-lined hood, and red fox-fur pompons, I was able to listen to the radio in Arabic. Then, instead of spending six more years in an institution of higher learning, I had hired a Russian émigré to monitor the Soviet broadcasts.

We had had signs of something in the wind, and were concerned about the emergence of Nasir, so while I was away my staff—except for Mrs. Ludwig—collected broadcast tapes, transcripts, notes, and data from the Egyptian airports.

To wit: many official Soviet visits, civilian traffic but mostly via military airfields, with that information supplied to us by M.I.5. I spent three psychotic days listening to the May Egyptian broadcasts. There, and in the Soviet programs, we found a pronounced shift. Most of all, the Egyptians were suddenly relaxed and triumphant, as if they had swallowed a canary and were secretly enjoying the aftertaste.

I went directly to the barely living body of Mr. Edgar with my judgment that Egypt had made a démarche directly into the Soviet camp. Perhaps because I had not previously been wrong about such things, or because he was a gambler by nature (but an *informed* gambler), he took me at my word and ordered a massive divestiture.

We decided that the Suez Canal Company, all Anglo-Egyptian and Egyptian-American joint ventures, and certain categories of investment in the Middle East as a whole, especially in the less stable countries, would go negative. We slowly began to slough off everything we held in the Middle East, and to short the stocks and bonds of companies that depended upon the region's stability. At the same time, we moved funds into other areas that we thought would strengthen as a result: for example, to the conservative Gulf sheikdoms to which, I guessed, much flight capital would find its way. As a result of the new policy we began to receive massive influxes of gold as loan collateral and to facilitate cross-investment among the Gulf kingdoms' swelling treasuries.

Admittedly, the results would not be known for several years. Still, it seemed a good bet, and it did eventually turn out exactly as I surmised. My discovery and analysis looked good even before the fact, and was at that moment the principal force driving the firm.

The summer banquet was at the Sleepy Hollow Country Club. It is hard to understand the glory of the world until you have stood upon the great lawns of this establishment and looked out at a view that comforts the heart as no other that I have seen in all my life. What I would give to be back on those hills prior to 1916, when, as a boy, I trespassed upon a grand estate, and my every step was the forging of my character, such as it is. My school was at the bottom of the hill, my house almost visible in the distance, in the hook of Croton Bay.

At sunset, we finished our scotches on the terrace and went in to dinner. I was particularly vulnerable that evening, for the events of long ago echoed from the past, and the lights in the near distance pulled me into the pleasant darkness of memory.

Inside, chandeliers sparkled and the table was set as if for a gathering of kings. I had kept to myself, coming up alone on the train and walking through the Italian gardens, the Vanderlip estate, and the school itself, where I saw a sandy-haired boy of about seven in the yard of what we used to call the Little School. He looked like me as a child, and, for reasons that I will never know, he seemed to carry the weight of the world on his shoulders. I winked at him, and smiled. He looked back. In his eyes I thought I saw the reflection of my own story. And then he went on his way.

At the head of the table, framed by the mantel behind him, was Mr. Edgar. Whatever painting had hung above the fireplace had been replaced by the full-sized Edgar portrait from the boardroom, the one with Mr. Edgar in the uniform—and hat —of a commodore. What a hat. Just looking at it always cheered me up.

Everyone else had come in limousines, and everyone else was drunk: I had the scent of the woods I had crossed still on me. I was content even if the others would not speak to or, in some cases, even look at me, for I knew that, in substance, I had triumphed. This would be my reward, my shield, and my staff. My inability to get along with the coffee-drinking majorities would be of no consequence. Inside, I felt equanimity. No matter how much they disliked me, they would have to acknowledge that I had hit the bull's-eye.

Dinner was served. I didn't participate in the banter, but, as no coffee was to be seen, I was willing to stay in the room, the black sheep. Every time I felt a stab of pain I remembered that at that very moment my strategy was driving the firm.

First we were served Beluga caviar in iced glass-and-silver bowls. Though it appeared to me that my portion was noticeably smaller than what had gone to the people around me, I did not object. And it hardly mattered that, while theirs was black, mine was red, because I think that in general caviar is vastly overrated. Then came the giant shrimp—eight inches long, a pound apiece, the prize of the Gulf fisheries, caught especially for the Stillman and Chase banquet and flown in by chartered plane. Mine, for some reason, were diminutive. They were also a different color, a dull pink instead of a briny paprika shade. I comforted myself with the thought that mine, being smaller, were likely to be more flavorful, but I began to feel rather uneasy. In fact, I felt incipient panic.

"I am happy to say," Mr. Edgar announced, with surprising alacrity for someone who hardly ever spoke, "that we are going to have steaks cooked exactly as they were recently cooked for me at the White House by my good friend, Dwight David Eisenhower."

Oohs and *aahs* filled the room. How delightful! Though we understand now that fat is naughty, one of the wonders of the Pax Americana was meat, the prize for conquering the world. It was well known, at least among the business elite, that the president, who was, after all, a Kansan, had a favorite way of cooking steak. He would take a huge slab of the very finest aged beef, a cut that Stillman and Chase chefs had come to call the Eisenhower round, and toss it directly on a bed of clean hot coals. All the stuff that we currently feel should be purged was sealed in, and the meat was cooked as much by internal boiling as by direct heat. Even though I was getting a little tubby, I anticipated this course with great pleasure.

One after another, dangerously hot gold-rimmed plates were carried out by waiters wearing asbestos gloves (uh oh) and set before the appreciative diners. On each plate was a great slab of aromatic beef that sounded as it sizzled like the static on a cheap shortwave set. I began to salivate as my turn came. The waiter, a Gypsy who could have been Gilbert Roland, set a rather plain piece of china, or maybe it was plastic, in front of me.

I blinked. I thought that perhaps I had drunk too much scotch. "Waiter," I asked, "what is this?"

"I believe it's a kosher turkey anus, sir," he said, almost fearfully, but at least he was telling the truth.

"It's not even cooked," I said.

"It's marinated, sir, in barbecue sauce."

"Wait a minute. I'm not kosher. I can eat the steak. Take it back and bring me the steak."

"I'm afraid all the steak is served, sir. Would you like me to bring you some American cheese? I can bring you the whole block."

"No! I want steak, just like everyone else has!"

I am afraid that, beneath my anger, my voice had a desperate, almost tearful quality. I looked over at Mr. Edgar, whose mouth was rolling around a giant hunk of meat. Once he had started, everyone else had begun to eat, and they all were humming with pleasure.

As I looked around, I saw that Dickey Piehand had his hand up the Bryn Mawr girl's dress, which was cut very low, and which made me reel with rejection and desire.

"Mr. Edgar," I said, laughing like an idiot. "Mr. Edgar. Look. They served me turkey anus in barbecue sauce!"

Mr. Edgar shrugged, as if to say, *So what?* Ever since my return from Rome, I had hated him more than anyone at the table could possibly have imagined, and I knew that, someday, I would kill him.

And then, as is often the case with those who suffer defeat, I participated in my own humiliation. In a wan, limp voice, I asked, "Would anyone like to trade some steak for a piece of kosher turkey anus?"

Of course, they all laughed. And that was just the beginning.

My demise was orchestrated with a brilliance that I recall with some fondness despite my distress at the time. I never discovered who was behind it, or if indeed it was a product of my own mental state and a series of harmless coincidences. But it couldn't have been. My devolution was too complex to have been coincidental.

I had had a Rembrandt in my office, on loan from the Edgar Wing of the Met. It was replaced, overnight, with a Dürer. That was all right: I think Dürer had, in many ways, a superior vision, though his craftsmanship, as great as it was, did not match that of the master. Within a week, however, it too was gone, replaced by a Monet. As far as I was concerned, if someone were trying to send a message to me, they were being incredibly subtle. In fact, they were. The next day, the Monet was gone and a Vuillard was in its place. Vuillard was not as well appreciated then as he has come to be, but I liked him very much. It was clear, however, that all was not well.

Soon the Vuillard was gone and in its place was a Bonnard. Then a Duffy (not a Dufy, a Duffy), then a Chamade, and, finally, after a few others that I could not recognize, a picture of the Brooklyn Bridge on a black velvet background. I demanded that this be removed from my office, and when I arrived the next day I found a cheap glass-and-fiberboard frame holding a black-and-white photograph of a dome-view railroad car clipped from an advertisement in *The Saturday Evening Post*. The edges were ragged.

Plants, too, headed down. I started with a fresh arrangement of my favorite flowers every day—at Stillman and Chase, each senior partner had to fill out a questionnaire regarding his taste in flowers, wine, hors d'oeuvres, and desserts—and was then shifted to a very lovely geranium plant with twenty blooms.

This was removed before it wilted, and in its place appeared a foil-wrapped pot of daisies. I don't like daisies, I never did, but I longed for them after I received my container of moss. Even moss, however, is nicely scented and wonderfully green. After the moss came liverwort, which you can hardly tell is a plant, because it looks like rotting crepe paper.

Still, it was a plant, and, because I had decided not to show my wounded thumb, I kept my lips sealed, put my toe in the water, and bit my tongue. But one morning soon after, I walked into my office and saw the Bryn Mawr girl—a nice surprise— bent over a brass-plated tub. "Aren't these lovely?" she asked as she stepped aside so I could see.

I recoiled in horror. Indian pipes.

"What are they?" she asked. "I've never seen anything quite like them. How can plants be white?"

"Get a digging implement," I commanded.

"What's a digging implement?"

"A shovel."

"I don't have a shovel."

"Find *something*," I told her.

She came back in a few minutes.

"What's that?"

"My coffee spoon."

"Boil it, please."

"Boil it?"

"Yes."

"It's clean."

"Please."

When she returned after boiling her spoon, I began to dig in the earth that filled the tub. "Indian pipes have no chlorophyll," I said numbly. "They draw their sustenance not from light but from death."

She made no reply except to scream and clutch her breast as I unearthed the head of a cat.

"What's that?!"

"It's a cat," I said, "after having been buried in moist earth for a month or two. Here's your spoon."

"I don't want it!"

"Why not?"

"How could I put that spoon in my coffee after it's touched the decomposing skull of a . . . ooh!"

"I should think," I said, "that your coffee would be flattered."

She did not understand what I meant, and, believing that I had insulted her, ran from the room.

It was only then, perhaps because of the stress, that I first noticed that my desk and chair were shrinking. Every other day they grew smaller, until after a few months I sat with my knees pushed up against an elementary school desk with a heart carved around the inscription "Jimmy & Buffy."

No one would sit with me at lunch, perhaps because they did not like the smell of the cheap mackerel I was served day after day directly from the same fifteen-pound can, and I was never able to find a squash partner. Squash, mercifully, can be played alone. After the game, however, as I showered in a room with ten stations, the water at my position would suddenly be choked off. I would move from one faucet to another, but it never mattered how much I moved or how quickly, which is why I got used to putting on my clothes while I was still covered with soap. It's not so bad at first, but after a few hours the cloth gets glued to your skin, and you squeak when you walk.

All of this I found rather depressing. Still, I hung on in a fog of misery and self-doubt, even when they told me my office was going to be redone, and I was moved to a tiny cubicle without a window. The janitor, who was a nice fellow, asked if he could leave his mops and pail-on-wheels there. When I asked him why, he said that he had always done so.

At least I was able to look out on the open floor where I could see flowers and beautifully lit portraits. But then the fire marshall came by and requested that I keep my door closed. "All right," I said in a barely audible voice, and closed it.

Hard. Very hard. Alone in a broom closet, with a bare bulb hanging over my head and a tiny school desk jammed around my knees. The bulb must have been on a hidden rheostat. Day by day, it grew dimmer and dimmer, and I spent hours in the twilight of the gods before it went out completely.

The work that I strained to see had become a set of dullard exercises. In normal circumstances I might have been desperately reading everything I could get about, for example, Bolivia, monitoring radio broadcasts, talking to experts in and out of government and the universities, and, then, when I had been saturated with all I could find out, hiking around Lake Titicaca with a pack mule.

It had been nothing for me to fly to Tokyo, walk the mountains of Argentina, or sit for a week in a cheap hotel in Algiers, soaking up the minor evidences that are just as valuable as the grosser measures for deciding the balance of power in a country about to explode. Sometimes it was very exciting, sometimes even dangerous. In hostile states I was often mistaken for an American intelligence agent (I was, after all, doing exactly the same thing), and in friendly countries it was sometimes thought that I was planning a crime.

Now, in my dim and finally dark closet, my job was to assemble a dictionary of Tagalog financial terms. Where they did not exist, I was to make them up. For this I thought it was incumbent upon me to know at least a little of the language, and so, for several months before it went dark I squinted at a book of exercises, repeating them in my airless cubicle until I did not know if I were sane or insane, if it were night or if it were day. Many times I pushed open the door only to discover that it was midnight, or two or three in the morning, and that everyone had left long before. I had simply been unable to keep track of the hours, lost as I was in learning phrases such as, *Nagkakaubo ako* (I am having a cough), *Ang aso at pusa ay mga hayop* (The dog and the cat are animals), *Magtakip ka ng panyo sa mukha* (Cover your face with a handkerchief), and politically useful tools of analysis such as the Tagalog version of "Happy Birthday to You":

> *Malagayang bati*
> *Sa inyong pagsilang*
> *Maligaya, Maligayang*
> *Maligayang bati!*

This little ditty would not leave me. I sang it for hours inside my closet until I imagined that I was one of J. Arthur Rank's great brass gongs, through which darkness and vibration pulsed as if at the heart of a very unkind and disappointing universe. I even sang it at home and on the subway, where I never had trouble getting a seat.

But, still, I did not leave the firm. I had resolved to hang on until they carried me out, and I held fast like a bulldog, breathing slowly through my crushed and humiliated nose.

———

They did carry me—not out, but down, deep down into the bowels of the earth, ten stories below the ground floor of our massive block-square building, where water ran in ancient underground rivers around a dry sarcophagus of reinforced concrete five feet thick.

When my appearance began to reflect my inner turmoil I was banished to the nearly silent and always stable underground, the place of death, the locus of safety and the absence of life. Still breathing slowly, I was moved to the stillest most passionless place on earth: the gold vaults.

"We're reassigning you to the custody section," I was told.

Of course, I was crestfallen. I did not dare ask if this meant that I had lost my partnership, though indeed I had, as the custody vice-presidency was, more or less, a junior position. The only reason the manager was called a vice-president was to reassure the potentates who left their gold in his care.

I suppose they thought it would be safe with a nasty, violent megalomaniac whose name was Wolf Brutus. I had hated it when he emerged from his caverns into the executive dining room, and was particularly happy when I was promoted to the inner circle and was able to take my meals in the smaller, far more splendid, Grotrian Room.

"I don't look forward to supervising Wolf," I said. "You know I can't stand him."

"You won't be supervising him."

"Who's going to take his place?"

"No one."

"He's left?"

"No. You'll be working for him, though not directly. You'll report to Sherman Oscovitz."

"Oh no, oh no, oh my God," I said, and that was when they carried me down, because I wasn't able to walk.

Sherman Oscovitz was the supervisor of the gold handlers. He was a very nice man, but he was a moron. He had been with the firm even longer than I had, and his job was to keep track of the gold and shift it from cage to cage with the flows between accounts. He always wore a blue lab jacket, and his yellowish red hair was confined to a ring around a domelike bald head as perfectly symmetrical as the Pantheon.

He and every one of his vault workers had once been in trouble with the law. When he worked for a big commercial bank, Oscovitz had been caught renting out the little rooms where safe-deposit customers went to clip coupons. The others had been apprehended while peeking in a customer's box, or giving a friend the master key to the boxes while talking on the phone, or placing bets from banking premises—small-time stuff that Mr. Edgar had had the brilliance to spot as an immunization.

Oscovitz and his entire crew had been burned trying to pick a few shrimp off the grill, and were now as reliable as eunuchs. And just as exotic. Oscovitz himself, whether as a result of disease, diet, or heredity, was flatulent in the manner of kings. In normal circumstances, this would have been hard to bear, but in a bank vault ten stories underground. . . . Yes, we had ventilation, but not nearly enough.

Sherman Oscovitz's "protégé" was a hulking acromegalic giant who looked like Marlene Dietrich enlarged sixteen times and baked in a kiln. It was he who intoned my lessons in handling gold bars, telling me never to drop them, never to scrape them with a fingernail, and always to wear my white cotton gloves.

"Why?"

"Human body grease rots the gold."

"That's ridiculous," I said. "Gold is inert. It won't rot—unless you sweat quicksilver."

"No, you're wrong. I've seen it get all rotten, and then we have to throw it away."

"You throw it away?"

"Yes."

"You throw it away."

"Uh huh, lots of it."

"Where do you throw it?"

"In the garbage can."

"Outside the vault?"

"Yes."

"What happens to it?"

"To what?"

"To the garbage."

"The garbage men take it."

"Do they know what's in it?"

"Yes, but they don't care about rotten gold. We explain to them that, because it's rotten, it's not worth anything. They complain because it's so heavy."

"How long have you been doing this?"

"Doing what?"

"Throwing away rotten gold."

"About three or four years. It never used to rot before then, but after the war a lot of bad-quality gold came in."

"How many bars a week do you throw away?"

"It depends. Sometimes six, sometimes two, sometimes ten."

"The next time you get some rotten gold," I told him, "give it to me. That way, the garbage men won't have to take it away."

"I can't do that."

"Why not?"

"Sherman says that rotten gold has to go into the garbage. If people get hold of it they might think it's valuable. You know how people are about gold. But not us!"

"No, not you!"

"You too!" he said, poking my chest and smiling. "Now you work here, too!"

The first time I was locked in a gold-cage—it was Argentina's—I felt very bad. Sherman had ordered me to rotate the Argentine gold and count it. I had to count and restack tens of thousands of gold bars.

We used scrap paper and a system of what Sherman called "variable check marks" to keep track. If, for example, you came up with thirty-five fewer bars than were supposed to be there, Sherman would pick up his pencil, add thirty-five check marks, and that was that. He never bothered to shuffle bars from one cage to another, because no one ever came to look. If anyone had, Sherman would have moved a few bars from here to there, and no one would have known the difference. The only danger lay in all the countries deciding to check their stocks simultaneously, and they had never even done so individually.

I was stunned not by the fact that close to a thousand twenty-seven-pound gold bars were missing, but that no one had stolen them: the simpletons had innocently thrown them away. At recent gold prices, they had disposed of almost $350 million.

I think, honestly, objectively, and without bias, that in that period I was actually insane. But I was supposed to have been insane, so I guess I was doing my job. After a few weeks of restacking bullion I was in extremely good condition, and the labor no longer tired me. I went to see Sherman Oscovitz mainly out of chagrin

"Sherman," I said. "I've come to talk to you about the rotten gold."

"Oh?" he asked. "Did you find a piece?"

"No, I came to tell you that gold doesn't rot. It doesn't."

"Of course it does," he said.

"No. It doesn't. It does not rot."

"That's not true, Dave," he said. (My name is not Dave.) "We find bad pieces all the time."

"No, Sherman. It can't rot. It can tarnish when exposed to certain reagents, but only on the surface. It wouldn't be rotten inside."

"No?"

"No. It doesn't rot."

"We think it does. That's why we throw it away."

"I know you think it does. I understand. Tell me, what do you define as rotten?"

"*We* don't make it rot," he said, shaking his dome. "If you get one bad apple in a pile, then the others tend to follow."

"I know you don't make it rot, Sherman. What I'm asking is, how do you know it's rotten?"

"We see it."

"What do you see, exactly?"

"Rotten gold."

"What is rotten gold?"

"Gold that's rotten."

"Uh," (I thought for a moment), "tell me what it looks like."

"It's not shiny."

I waited for more, but he said nothing. "That's it?"

"What's it?" he asked, looking around.

"It's not shiny?"

"What's not shiny?"

"Rotten gold."

"That's right, Dave. That's how you know it's rotten." His eyes turned to the ceiling, as if to say, *What an idiot!*

"So, you mean that gold is rotten when it's not shiny."

"Now you're catching on," he said, "but that's not what *makes* it rotten. We don't know what makes it rotten."

"Sherman?"

"Yes?"

"You have an awful lot of rotten gold around here, don't you?"

"Yes, we do."

"Why don't you stack the rotten gold in compartment forty-eight, which is empty, and maybe it'll get better."

"I would never do that," he said. "As soon as I see a rotten piece, I throw it out. I don't want it to spread."

"Put it in a bag."

"A garbage bag?"

"Yes, a garbage bag."

"Are you kidding? Do you know how expensive those are?"

I gave up. For a while I ran after garbage trucks, but then I stopped. Although I tried, it was physically impossible to go through a fully loaded garbage truck in the few minutes allotted before it reached its home base. They dumped their loads onto a barge in the Hudson, and the gold returned to the sea, whence it had come, and how could I object?

If I hate anything, I hate being inside when the weather is nice. Even in storms and when it's cold I always prefer to walk the hills and weave through a forest of sunny clearings where no one has ever been, or where, at least, no one has ever stayed for more than a few minutes. I have never been happier than by a clear lake or stream, or upon a New England summit, watching the sun glint off well kept fields and silent towns.

For this reason alone, never mind the tribulations of working for an idiot, I began to go mad. Whereas I had seldom been in my office, and when I was I could open the window, I was now surrounded entirely by rock. Thunderstorms, blizzards, hurricanes, and clear days came and went, and we did not know it. In winter, I never saw daylight: I went down in the dark, and came up in the dark. Above his desk Oscovitz had a calendar with a picture of a cow standing on a Swiss mountainside. The depth, distance, and color were so beautiful that every time I looked at it I asked myself, "Why am I alive? What am I doing here?"

As a child I liked playing with blocks, and this was now my job, underground, in light that neither flickered nor changed. We restacked the gold to keep it fresh. If a gold bar remained too long in an airless place at the bottom of the pile, it would decay.

In anticipation of dropping one of the twenty-seven-pound ingots, our shoes were housed in magnesium shells, and of course we wore white gloves to protect the gold from our corrosive body grease. The bars were seven inches long, about three and a half inches wide, and one and three quarters inches high. Those cast in America were rectangular, and, in Europe, trapezoidal. Some were 100% pure, the color of Goldilocks' hair, others reddish and tinged with copper, and others white, having been contaminated with platinum and silver. I did not mind stacking gold, and never ceased to be amazed by its density and integrity. Though the fact that it was worth immense amounts of money may have clouded my view, I was most affected by its purity, its rarity, its smoothness and incorruptibility. It was an element, a noble of the periodic chart, and I was surrounded by thousands of tons of it, in walls that looked like the brickwork of heaven.

I soon discovered that the most striking difference between me and the morons was that they did not ask questions. They were uninterested in how things work, how facts had come to be, and the relationship of one thing to another. Indeed, they treated my questioning with hostility, because they could not supply me with answers and because they took my curiosity for sedition. Each and every one of my questions, it is true, was canted toward obtaining the information necessary for a robbery, but who would not have had such thoughts in similar circumstances? What kind of dead-on-its-feet, pusillanimous drone would it take to be trapped within the world's greatest concentration of wealth—buried with it, breathing it—and not give some thought to stealing it? The look the morons reserved for me was one of offended innocence, as if my line of inquiry were immoral.

We were surrounded by ten thousand tons of gold, not a single ounce of which had been coaxed from the earth in conditions of morality. It had been neither mined nor bought nor sold nor accumulated nor accepted in conditions of morality. Sherman Oscovitz lived in a one-room apartment in Brooklyn Heights, with neither a toilet nor a refrigerator. He ate at Nedick's on his way to and from work, and though he spent no money on anything but hot dogs, sauerkraut, and buttermilk, and though he wore a suit that was so cheap I wanted to pull it off his body, shred it, burn it, and put the ashes in sulfuric acid, his accumulated savings were only enough to buy, for example, one water ski, or three nights in a cheap hotel in Antwerp.

His discipline and poverty were devoted to the service of gold that belonged to sheiks who had slaves, and Latin dictators with a fondness for leather. Of what use was his honesty? What did it accomplish?

I only wanted to know about the electrical system, the security procedures, the depth of the rock, the architecture of the vault, the methods of accounting, and other intellectual questions relating to my environment, but had I continued that line of questioning I would have been expelled, so I became a mute observer.

There was no chance of taking the gold up and out. You couldn't sneak it out, for each person who entered the vault was weighed on a scale that was accurate to 1/1000th of an ounce. The exact humidity of the vault was recorded on a Gretzel Pisogram. That and the weight, metabolic characteristics, and tissue data about each vault worker were fed into an algorithm in a little office just outside the vault door. They knew exactly how much you would lose in transpiration, you were forbidden to pick your nose or spit, and if you weighed more on your way out than on your way in, they peered at you through a fluoroscope and checked your bodily crevices.

You could, of course, leave parts of yourself behind, but had you done that these would have been discovered, and, after all, how many people would be willing to trade slices of their flesh for dinner at Mamma Leone's or a cashmere coat?

The Cerberus who weighed us had a separate entrance, a secret address, and when the vault was closed he was spirited home in a car with blacked-out windows. No one ever spoke to him, he was incorruptible, and you could see by his bleached expression of vicious and arrested development that he lived for the chance of catching a violator and was as loyal and devoted as a Dominican abbot. Who can blame him, though, for letting the morons take the rotten gold, walk it right past him, and toss it in the garbage. He, too, thought it was rotten. Wouldn't you? I thought of this as an option, but Sherman said that all the gold I chose as rotten was perfectly sound.

Storming the vault was possible, but out the question for me. It would require a disciplined army of 150 men, and I have never been able to get along with even one. The steel door weighed ninety tons and was set in a 140-ton frame. It was tapered and airtight, and once it was closed even an army would not have been able to open it.

Tunneling was out, too. Cutting ten storeys down through Manhattan schist would have taken years of a construction project so large that Stillman and Chase would have had to float a bond issue to pay for it.

They had thought of everything. I even suspected that Sherman and his helpers had been lobotomized. They were so nice! They were always so pleasant! But in New York no one was like that unless he had had frontal brain surgery or was on the verge of stealing everything you possessed.

In my days of stacking bullion I waited for a sign, but no sign was forthcoming. I was entombed in a limpid sparkling pool of riches, which was also a physical metaphor for impossibility. No planning seemed an adequate match for the infinite precautions of the vault planners. Not unless it were founded on the spark of transgression itself.

As I waited, it occurred to me that this spark might never be generated, and that I might eventually become a sub-Oscovitz. Several decades hence (i.e., now), I would get the thrill of my life on the boardwalk in Coney Island when a fat widow would sit next to me and talk about French fries. Flushed and hyperventilating, I would ride home on the subway, overcome with lust and awe, and the memory and feeling would have to last for the rest of my life.

Deep in the gold vaults I would reflect upon that partly cloudy day in July when we talked about French fries and I observed

her cleavage. I would remember as part of the legend the godlike
state I had achieved on my way home, when I glowed like the
filament in a lightbulb. And every time I heard the faint rumble
of the subway below the vault, I would . . . I would. . . .

That was it! I jumped into the air like an electrocuted cat. I
was sitting at the back of compartment 71, resting from a heavy
lift, when it came to me. Everything fell into place at once. The
Swede who was in maintenance of way with the Transit Authority, and the familiar-looking coffee-hater at the Blue Mill,
both Smedjebakken. And I, sitting deep under the ground surrounded by the gold of atrocious sheiks. My need to save myself
from becoming an Oscovitz. The vision of life ending in a small
lonely room in the infinity of Brooklyn. The courage of Smedjebakken on the roof. His hatred of coffee. And the rumble of
the subway beneath the vault.

Robbing an establishment such as Stillman and Chase was not
without its risks, but as I equated failure to rob Stillman and
Chase with death itself I did not have to fight for resolve. With
luck and divine guidance, which sometimes come by the buck-
etful when you really need them, Smedjebakken and I would
bankrupt those arrogant coffee-drinking bastards, and they
would not even know it until we were halfway around the world,
in a clean quiet country where coffee was all but unknown.

Poisoned by Champagne

*(If you have not done so already,
please return the previous pages to the antproof case.)*

I FOUND SMEDJEBAKKEN in Astoria, living under his
pseudonym, Massina. His wife was a career woman who would
brook no nonsense. When she met me at the door of their modest
row house she was turned out like a Wall Street lawyer—with
suit, scarf, and brooch, all of the highest quality. I assumed that
she had just come from Manhattan, with a Florentine-leather
briefcase full of legal documents. I was wrong, but I did not
discover this until later.

"What can I do for you?" she asked. She was severe in a way
that her husband never would be. He had been born to fight a
mythical battle that was denied to him, and he was saving his
strength and his power for a time that might never come, while
she seemed to have been suited to make efforts in a lesser world
that failed to interest him.

"I'm looking for Smedjebakken," I said.

Her expression changed immediately. When she heard her

husband's real name she assumed that I was someone from his past, who might, perhaps, excite his Viking sensibilities.

"He's in the back," she said, cooling to me. "Horowitz is buying a piano."

"I beg your pardon?"

"This evening, Vladimir Horowitz is buying a piano. He's picked two, and will play one, and then the other, until he decides. This happens several times a week, but it's not often that we get a Horowitz."

"Buying a piano from you?" I asked.

She looked at me as if I were an idiot. "From Steinway," she said. "The test studio faces our backyard. We look slightly down into it, and in all except the late fall and winter months they open the French doors."

"Ah," I said. "What a pity to miss it in the winter."

"We don't," she replied. I could see that she was beginning to form an extremely low opinion of me. "In winter, Paolo sits in the studio. They keep his lawn chair and table there. He drinks tea and eats rusks while he listens, just as he does in the summer."

"What a privilege to be allowed . . . what luck to live . . . how amazing . . ." I babbled on. It was my third strike with her.

"I suppose it is a privilege," she said coldly, "but they do pay him."

"Who pay him?" I asked. Strike four.

"*Who* pay him?"

"Pays, pays."

"Steinway."

"Why?"

"Over the years, the artists have come to rely upon his critique. They're superstitious about it, and won't buy a piano unless Paolo helps them choose. He has a fine ear. It all started with Toscanini, who, when he saw my husband sitting as if on a raised platform, assumed that he was some sort of judge."

"Toscanini?" I asked.

"Arturo Toscanini," she repeated, adding for my sake, "he's a music guy."

"Yes, of course, Toscanini, how extraordinary!"

"He thinks Paolo is an Italian who forgot how to talk. 'Every power of your mind,' he said, 'has fled to your ear, and it is the most beautiful ear. *Bellissimo!*' "

I heard strains of music coming from within the house. I pointed in their direction, and asked, "Mozart?"

Unfortunately, I was also pointing to a marble bust of Beethoven that stood in the hallway. Angelica was beginning to lose patience. "No," she said, "Beethoven," and led me toward the back.

"Don't talk until Mr. Horowitz is finished and has left," she commanded. "Unless, of course, you are asked a question."

I agreed. I was taken to a darkened terrace entirely overwhelmed by the enormous mass of the Steinway factory. The factory walls were of richly colored ancient brick, strewn with ivy and the old brown iron of fire escapes and shutter latches, old iron that, like old wood, was comforting not for what it looked like but for what it had seen. It had held its place serenely as all the things that now vexed me had long ago passed it by, not once, but a hundred times. It had been the patient platform for the thick ice of blizzards, the heat sump of the August sun, the gymnasium of ten thousand contemplative squirrels in gray flannel suits, the trellis of ivy and wisteria and blooms that had bloomed when my father was courting my mother.

The massive brick and solid iron was the frame of many score floating windows through which came sound and light. The factory was at work that night, for the war had destroyed many pianos, the piano factories of Europe were in ruins, and the children born to returning soldiers were now old enough to begin their lessons at the keyboard.

Never in my life had I heard so many tappings, so many tuning forks, and so many basso profundo woods knocked into place with mallets that even in themselves were works of art. And as for the pianos, well, it was not so much craftsmanship and its vagaries that made one different from another, but accidents of wood that may have occurred with great slowness as summers varied in distant forests, or differences in ores that were first apparent as rivers of molten metal cooled long before the appearance of the clouds or the birth of the seas.

And at the base of all this was a middle-aged Vladimir Horowitz playing like sixty and lost in music to the detriment of time, of which all of us became mercifully forgetful. What beautiful cadenzas. They exploded into the night like huge white waves jumping shoreward in a storm; they took all the darkness from the air on that late September evening, and filled very beautifully all the empty spaces that exist to test the soul with doubt.

Smedjebakken looked dead. Not only was he immobile, his mouth open, his eyes wide, and his body stiff, but it was clear that his soul had risen from him (tethered, of course) to occupy some ethereal space nearby, like a weather balloon. It seemed as if all his mental power had been put by the magic of the music into a purifying centrifuge. Despite its connection to dance, music is nonetheless the emblem of immobility, for when it is really great it seizes time and holds it still in an invisible grip. I had experienced this many times myself, and now I was watching a portly engineer behind the Steinway factory in Astoria get exactly the same religion.

I was shocked, however, to see that he was a drug addict. The paraphernalia were arrayed damningly on a table beside him—a plate of rusks (as a chaser); a cup with leaves settled disgustingly at the bottom; and, out in the open, unconcealed, absolutely brazen, a pot of tea.

In my younger days, when I didn't know any better and when the recklessness of youth made me sometimes dissolute, I myself had experimented with tea. One January night, in a Harvey's Restaurant on the Niagara Frontier, I was so chilled and exhausted that I dipped a tea bag in a cup of hot water at least six times, and drank.

What visions I had, what ecstasy, what equanimity! I was able to see the continual action of colors, which move like a fire, but more evenly. The bee sees this, it is said, and what the bee saw, so did I. I watched falling snow blind the lights of Buffalo, and all my memories came as if upon the flood of a deep unagitated river cutting through the countryside of the present to find the place whence it had come.

Powerful stuff, tea, but, like all drugs, false and dangerous. For two weeks I lay moaning in the cheapest hotel in Buffalo, wanting with all my soul to kill myself, but having neither the courage to do so nor even the ability to leave the room. This was payment for mechanical ecstasy, or, if not that, the price one pays for two weeks in Buffalo.

When the lights came up I realized that the music had stopped. Horowitz leaned his head against his left hand, and, with the gravest of expressions, he said, "For the life of me, Paolo, I cannot decide which has the better sound. The actions are equal."

Smedjebakken didn't move.

"Which one, Paolo? Help me."

"Uh," Smedjebakken said. "Uh, Vladimir . . . I think . . . I think . . . I think the one on the right. The one on the right has the contained magnificence of tone that you want."

"This one?"

"No, that's the one on the left. The one on my left is the one on your right. Artists," Smedjebakken said to me, acknowledging my presence for the first time, though he still did not know who I was. "The sonority of the one on the right," he continued, addressing himself entirely to Horowitz, "I would liken to claret as opposed to Beaujolais. Especially for Mozart, you want a bell-like sound muted by almost imperceptible mists of interference beginning at the strike of each note and following like a subtle echo thereafter."

"But what about for Beethoven?"

"Beethoven. Beethoven is . . . less pure, more rounded, not as metallic. This piano is perfect for the area where Mozart and Beethoven meet, and when you play either, that is the magic circle where you want to be. You must tug each slightly in the direction of the other. For they are like a bipolar star, and eliciting absolute perfection from either depends upon leaning away from their proclivities and toward the center."

"Bravo," said Horowitz, throwing a kiss, making a bow, and signaling to the Steinway people that he had chosen the one on *his* left.

Before he went into the glowing interior of the factory and then, presumably, to his limousine, he said, "Thank you, Paolo. See you next time."

A Steinway worker pulled the doors to him like a fat woman doing the breast stroke, and they clicked shut. He brought up a trolley and attached it to the triangular base upon which rested the piano that Horowitz had chosen, and pulled it out of the studio, switching off the lights as he left.

"That's the way it is with Horowitz every time," Smedjebakken said to me. "Cash and carry."

"How often do you do this?" I asked.

"A couple of times a week, on average. They pay me."

"I know. Your wife told me. Do they pay you well?"

"It matches my TA salary, and I'd do it for free."

"That's extraordinary."

"It's the only gift I can give to my child," he said.

"How do you mean?"

"Music."

"Yes, music," I repeated, having nothing but a vague and unsatisfactory idea of what he meant.

"Someday," he went on, "they'll have high fidelity that will be indistinguishable from the real thing—a technology we can hardly dream of now—and she'll be able to listen to anything she wants, at any time. I'm saving for that."

I dared not ask him to be specific, for, inexplicably, he was moved by his declaration to the point where his eyes had begun to sparkle in the light coming from the upper floors of the piano factory, and I thought it should rest, so I changed the subject.

"I play, you know," I said. "Not well, but well enough to appreciate someone who really knows what he is doing, and enough to understand that Mozart was a divine emissary. And I think he knew it from the time he was a baby. You know, you always hear about Freud, Marx, and Einstein. Of these I think only Einstein was truly great, but even he was far eclipsed by Mozart, who, in my opinion, was the greatest man ever to have lived."

"Yes," said Smedjebakken. "He wasn't like a baseball player or anything like that, was he, he was great beyond description."

After a few awkward moments when neither of us could say anything, because so much had to be said, Smedjebakken looked at me. "You're from the restaurant."

"And the roof," I added.

"Yes, the roof! And coffee."

"I hate it," I said, looking at the tea.

"Come inside," he told me. "It's getting cold out here. Let's go to the kitchen table."

"You drink tea?"

"If you come inside," he said, "I'll explain."

"I don't understand how a man sensible enough to figure out coffee could let himself get on the other side of tea," I said.

Smedjebakken was leaning over the kitchen table, his right hand on the throat of a lamp. After he pushed the switch, the room came up warm and his face glowed like a pumpkin. He looked at me, craftily. "I'm not perfect," he answered.

"But, to be a drug addict, in your own home, in front of your own family. . . ."

"They have forgiven me."

"Why do you continue?"

"As I grow older," he said, "I find that I can't spring back as easily as I could when I was young. Then, I could go for days without sleep, I could work until I dropped, and, after a nap, start right in again. There seemed no end to my power or energy. But I no longer have the stamina to contemplate sixteen orgasms a day, much less to achieve them. My present self, though wiser, is bodily of almost a different species. At one time, my excessive vitality distorted all my opinions.

"How could it not have? I thought everything was possible, and that time moved with compassionate slowness. Hard to believe, but I wanted it to pass more quickly. I used to listen to music all night and lay ties all the next day.

"Then, youth left, fleeing like a coward from the onslaught of responsibility. And now that I'm well along into middle age, I need more strength than I have.

"I was at a loss. I had no way, no clue. But I needed the energy of two lives."

"So you turned to artifice."

"Yes!" He leapt up and ran out of the room. I thought he was propelled by shame, but he was back in a minute, carrying a book that he slammed down so hard I started.

" '*Narcotic Plants,* by William Emboden!' " he read, quite excitedly. Then he flipped rapidly through the pages until he found the passage he was seeking.

" 'In Tibet,' " he began, " 'weary horses and mules are given large vessels of tea to increase their capacity to work. Mules are said to be gamboling like colts as a result of their tea rations. . . . The distance between villages is accounted for in terms of the number of cups of tea necessary to sustain the person traveling that route. It has been ascertained that three cups of tea is equal to eight kilometers.' " He banged the book shut. All that slamming and banging was undoubtedly the work of the tea.

"If this devilish substance," he said, "will work so charmingly upon completely innocent animals at terribly high altitudes, why should I abjure it? Tea, being translucent and light, does not, like coffee, offend due to lack of purity. The base issue of coffee is filth, is it not?"

"That and other horrors," I offered. "Conformity, sameness, compulsion, addiction, mental illness, et cetera."

"I agree, but there's something pure, angelic, and light about tea, isn't there? Admit it."

"I don't know. I had a cup of tea once in Buffalo, and it would have been the cause of my suicide had I been able to get hold of a barrel."

"I belong to the Church of Rome," Smedjebakken declared. "I don't commit suicide. What other drawbacks are there?"

"Weakness of character?"

"My character is weak," he said. "I've known this since I failed to become president of the United States. I'm sunk in my own depravity."

I looked at him and said, "I'm not sure if you're right for my project."

By the glint in his eye I could tell that he didn't want to be left out, so, to barb the hook, I rose from my chair.

"Still," he said, "I've never had a cup of coffee, and I've attacked a hundred urns, overthrowing them for the sake of everything that is just and good."

"That's admirable," I said, sitting down.

"How many people have you met who attack coffee urns?"

"Only me."

"Perhaps then, even if we differ, even if you are an upper-class asshole investment banker, we should work together."

"You misunderstand me," I said. "I started as a courier, a long time ago, and now I do manual labor in the vaults."

"Really."

"Yes. In some ways, I like it. It's simple. It keeps me strong, and I don't have to devote my attention to meaningless and ephemeral details. I can think all day, like a prisoner in solitary confinement."

"That's why I like maintenance of way," Smedjebakken said. "I get to make solitary patrols, like Lewis and Clark, in a world half underground and half flying above it."

"Lewis and Clark weren't solitary," I said. "There were at least two of them."

"Ah, but they were so lonely. Tell me what you have in mind."

At that very moment, Angelica Massina, the actual Mrs. Smedjebakken, came downstairs with a dinner tray.

"How's everything?" Smedjebakken asked.

"Fine," she said. "Sleeping."

After she washed the dishes, she left the room without looking our way.

"Is she a lawyer?" I asked.

"No. She was a typist for the Navy, but she quit when our daughter was born."

"Oh," I said. "I thought she had just come home from Manhattan: the suit and everything. She has the air of a career woman."

"She was in Manhattan," Smedjebakken said. "She was at the hospital. Look, I don't mean to pry, but what is it that you want to talk about?"

"Money."

"You go first." He insolently crunched a rusk, as if to suggest that he was not impressed by the fact that I was an investment banker.

"Do you need it?"

"Of course I need it. Everyone needs it."

"Yes," I replied, "but some people think they don't, or pretend they don't."

"Monks and stuff."

"Some monks and stuff," I agreed, "but even monks and stuff need money. They have to eat. They need a roof, clothes. They have to advertise their wine."

"Fine. Monks need money. Is that what you came to tell me?"

"No. How much money?"

"How much money do monks need?"

"No, you," I said.

"How much money do I need?"

"Yes."

"I never looked at it that way. That's like saying, how tall would you like to be? You're as tall as you are. You can't get taller."

"But?" I asked.

"But what?"

"But? Come on. Tell me the difference."

He crunched another rusk. "All right. You *can* get more money."

"That's right," I confirmed. "That's what all those upper-class assholes do, or what their forebears did. They say, *I think I'll get some more money.*"

"What do you want me to do, rob a bank?"

When I made no answer, and merely stared at him intently, he said, "You do. You want me to rob a bank."

I turned from him and walked to the window, where, to heighten the dramatic effect, I stood for the time it took to count to twenty-five.

"What are you counting, birds?" Smedjebakken yelled across the room, having heard me.

Then I came back to where I had been, and calmly said: "The biggest bank in the world. The greatest single concentration of wealth in the universe. We can do it slowly and methodically, and they may never know. If they do find out it could be many years from now, and no matter when they find out it's very likely that someone else will take the rap. We won't have to use weapons or resort to violence. We can split the proceeds equally. The only drawback is that you'll have to assume a new identity and live in a different place. You could be, for example, a Swedish count who has retired to a house in Geneva overlooking the lake. When you walk down the street in Switzerland you hear Mozart and Beethoven from within the houses, not boogie-woogie."

"I like boogie-woogie."

"So do I. But after five minutes. . . ."

"Look," said Smedjebakken, leaning slightly forward. "Honesty is more important than money."

"Of course it is."

"So, I can't rob a bank."

"What's dishonest about robbing a bank?" I asked, offended that he had questioned my integrity. "We'd be taking out gold bullion. Did you ever really think about gold? It's mined by slave labor. In Rome and medieval Europe the gold was mined by slaves and serfs. Today in South Africa and the Soviet Union the miners are slaves except in name. That means that whoever possesses the gold after it comes from the earth is tainted."

"What about gold mined in the United States or Canada?"

"Gold is fungible, and the greater part of it was extracted by slave labor. Every bar is corrupt. But eventually," I continued, "it passes into legitimacy. You can't expect a moral trail to last through many owners, because you can't expect people to know things they can't know. Still, much of the gold goes into the treasuries of criminals, dictators, drug traders . . . and to own it they have to put their mark on it, so to speak, so that you can know it's theirs and you can know you're taking it from someone who, on almost any scale of morality, has no right to it."

"Who do you want to take it from?"

"The gold I have in mind is kept in cages, and the most promising cage belongs to a sheik on the Arabian peninsula who has two hundred wives, several thousand slaves, and fifty Cadillacs. If he is criticized by his subjects and he can get to them, he will torture them until they die. I would say that, morally, he's compromised. Nothing you can do to a man like that is dishonest."

"What you propose is dishonest, whatever the circumstances," Smedjebakken said.

"No," I contradicted. "Actions are conditioned by contexts. As I see it, the longer this gold remains in its cage, the more evil will seep into the world. And if we lift the gold, we'll lighten the world."

Mrs. Smedjebakken reappeared. She looked drained and tired. I could tell that she hadn't yet had her dinner, and that my presence was blocking the way. I feared that even were her husband to decide upon my scheme, she would stop him. But it hardly mattered, as I had not yet succeeded in convincing Smedjebakken himself. This was due to either some fault of my own or some fault in him—excessive timidity, perhaps, or a badly formed sense of what was right and what was wrong. Or perhaps simple lack of imagination.

Picture my surprise, then, when he turned to me and said, "Yeah. The Yankees are playing Kansas City, and I've got two tickets. Here, you can take one of them, and I'll see you there tomorrow." He left the room, and as his footsteps pounded on the stairs, his wife, who seemed as if she were facing an unmitigated pain that never ceased, bravely smiled at me, and said, "Baseball fan?"

The image and the puzzle of Angelica Smedjebakken stayed with me. When she had asked me the awkward question, "Baseball fan?" across her kitchen table, she, though completely Italian, had seemed perfectly Japanese.

I had to clutch my stomach and moan to get excused from the vault early the next day. Oscovitz was not the paragon of subtlety, and telling him that you were ill meant nothing if it was not accompanied by something close to the last scene of *Madam Butterfly*. But it worked, and at noonday I rose through the rock and exited into the sunshine.

Though I had to go back underground, into the subway, in the subway were currents of air and huge spaces, and in the Bronx strong sunlight flooded through the open windows as we clicked along the elevated track. I believe that now the trains have plastic seats—I've seen them in movies—but in that era they were upholstered, wood, or wicker. To prevent the wicker from being snagged, it was covered with shellac. And overhead fans turned slowly in each car, as if tall people could be trusted not to decapitate themselves deliberately so they could sue the city, which is what they do now—and good luck to them.

In those days the Bronx had an awful lot of green in it and was mysteriously quiet. I believe that I'm being neither sentimental nor inexact when I say that things were slow because people had peace in their hearts, and people had peace in their hearts because things were slow. And, as I remember it, the dappled shade under the elevated tracks was as serene as the Amazon, neon signs in store windows glowed like jaguar eyes, and the traffic, which was quiet and even, flowed like black water under a bridge.

As I walked to Yankee Stadium I reflected upon the means that Smedjebakken had devised for our meeting. With seven pieces of information printed on a little piece of cardboard (Yankee Stadium, the gate, the section, the row, the seat, the date, and the time) you could, with machinelike certainty, bring two people from entirely disparate parts of the earth to positions side by side at a particular instant.

This, I thought, might be a way to salvage the potential of normally wasted encounters, such as sharing a train car on a late summer's afternoon with a woman as beautiful as summer itself. I sometimes think back to the earlier years of the century and women I saw then, to whom even now I would devote myself entirely if only I could see them again. I remember the glow of their faces and the color and sparkle of their eyes. They were in white dresses on the bluff at Long Beach, or in a Winabout at Three Mile Harbor, or on a train going up to Ossining at four in the afternoon.

If only I had seized those moments, but I was almost always too shy. A ticket, though, to some public event—a baseball game, a lecture, a concert—might allow the woman to whom you presented it to reflect at length upon her short memory of you on some public conveyance, and perhaps to be enchanted. And if she didn't show, you could at least enjoy a baseball game, a lecture, or a concert, sitting next to a mournfully empty seat.

Smedjebakken was no woman, and the sight of him sitting in Yankee Stadium, with a cardboard box of baseball food on his lap, jarred me from my revery.

"What's that?" I asked, pointing to the food in the box.

"This is food," he answered. "You've heard of it?"

"What kind of food?" After years of expense accounts I was unused to any but the most elegant restaurants, and at home I subsisted almost entirely on fish, rice, and vegetables.

"Beer," he said, handing me a paper cup. "My beer is Rheingold, the dry beer."

"It smells like a urine sample," I said, sniffing at it.

"Yes," he said. "One of them is a urine sample that I'm

supposed to deliver to my urologist. And one is beer. Who knows which is which?"

"What's *that* thing?"

"A kosher beef dog," he said, handing it to me.

"And what's this crap on it?"

"It's a yellow thing that most people in America call mustard."

"It doesn't look like mustard. It's too bright. It looks like paint." I tasted it. "And it tastes like shit."

"Blame it on the Bronx," Smedjebakken said.

"And what are those things?"

"These things are called French fried potatoes. How long have you lived in this country?"

"They're so little," I said. "I like potatoes either julienned or the size of a kosher beef dog."

The beer was a light pilsner, the kosher beef dog still hot fifteen minutes from the aluminum roller, and the French fries had flavor such as I had not experienced since my days at Monastir, when we used to fry potatoes in olive oil and season them with local herbs. It wasn't the Pavillon, but it wasn't bad!

The Yankees came out, followed by a huge cheer, and then their opponents jiggled sheepishly onto the field and stood like animals in the yard of a slaughterhouse. After the national anthem, the game started quickly and the radio announcers high in their booths spoke like mental patients into the void of empty space before them. At the first pitch the bat sang with the unique and perfect sound that is neither a crack nor a pop but somewhere in between. The ball had the faint, ghostly glow of an artillery shell that goes just slowly enough to be seen, and then it hit an apartment building beyond the elevated tracks.

"Goddamn!" Smedjebakken screamed, jumping to his feet,

punching the air, and casting the tray of food to the ground. "Did you see that! It'll never happen again!"

"Good shot!" I said, prompting everyone around me to turn.

Smedjebakken so enjoyed my comments, the food, and the game that I couldn't imagine he would reject the scheme, for what is more enjoyable than robbing a vault packed with the money of evil men? And, after all, it was he who had asked me to meet him at the baseball game.

At the top of the sixth inning, he said, "Angelica would never let me rob a bank." I hadn't brought up the subject, and he did so only when the Yankees had taken such a huge and demoralizing lead—rather like the United States vis-à-vis the rest of the world at the time—that the stadium had begun to empty.

"You need her permission?" I asked, considering the colorful tableau before us and the surflike noise of the remaining crowd.

"In regard to things like robbing a bank, enlisting in the Foreign Legion, or climbing Mount Everest, I would, yes, consult with her."

"So why are you here, or, rather, why am I here?"

"Put it this way: I don't think I can do it, but I can't stop thinking about it."

"Why?"

"My daughter, and the mechanical challenge."

"How old is your daughter?"

"Eleven."

"That's a lovely age for a girl."

"It would have been. Unfortunately, for her all ages are too much the same."

"Why?"

"The name of the affliction probably would mean nothing to you. But she can't walk, she can't control her arms, she writhes, and makes faces, and tosses her head involuntarily. She was never able to hold a doll."

What could I have said?

"At age eleven," Smedjebakken went on, "she has spent a lifetime of suffering, and she will suffer until she dies."

"But you love her. You love her."

"I want to die for her. I wish I could die for her, to make her whole."

"Your wife devotes herself to the child."

"When you saw Angelica, they had come home from therapy. For my little girl, water is the most merciful thing. They go to the pool three times a week. I wish it could be twice a day."

"I had thought that Angelica was pursuing a career."

"She dresses up when she takes Connie in. We've discovered that doctors are kinder and more attentive to people who appear to be wealthy, educated, and well connected."

"Connie?"

"Yes."

"Constance?"

"Yes. Why?"

"My former wife is named Constance."

"It's a nice name, and when she was born we thought that *Connie Massina* had a lovely ring to it. And *Constance* was elegant. Do you think I haven't thought of robbing a bank?"

"Everyone thinks of robbing a bank."

"Not as a daydream."

"For her care?"

Smedjebakken nodded.

"Does it take that much money?" I asked.

"It doesn't now," he said, "but what if I die tomorrow? How is Angelica going to work and take care of Connie? If we both die, Connie goes to Welfare Island. Have you been to Welfare Island? It's hell. And even if we both live 'til we're eighty, Constance would be fifty. What happens to her after that? Our savings would be used up in a few years."

"Then why didn't you rob a bank?"

"I don't want to take other people's money."

"Well," I said, "I've got news for you. If you rob a bank, you've got to take other people's money. That's the way it is."

"What if *I* get killed, or caught? Where are Connie and Angelica then?"

"What you need, obviously, is a bank that's filled with the money of despots, that you can rob surreptitiously without the risk of confrontation, and that you can knock over without the slightest chance of getting caught."

I was beginning to talk like a criminal, and I liked it.

"The first two, I grant you," he said, "but there's always a chance of getting caught, which is why I'll never do it."

"No. The reason you're still interested is that you think that. . . ." I interrupted myself to be more precise. "You're flirting with the idea of not getting caught. I don't think we will get caught, but it's true that you can't afford to take the chance. Even if we work on the plan until it's perfect, we still might be caught."

"Right."

"So what you need is not assurance of not getting caught—because it doesn't exist—but a very good chance of pulling it off, and insurance in case you don't."

"Yeah," Smedjebakken said, "bank robbers' insurance. I didn't know they had that. Do they have savings-bank bank robbers' insurance—SBBRI?"

"No bank robber meticulous enough to buy insurance would bother to rob a savings bank."

"Forget it," Smedjebakken said. "You made a good point. The way I am . . . because of my situation, I wouldn't even consider robbing a bank without first getting insurance."

"How much do you need?" I asked as the Yankees kept hitting home runs.

"Come off it," Smedjebakken ordered.

"How much?"

"How much? Enough to buy an apartment in an elevator building on the Upper East Side. Enough for a trust fund—managed by a bank that I couldn't rob—to support Angelica and Connie, and, eventually, just Connie: it would have to cover nursing care, hospital fees, and God knows what else. And I'd need a Steinway D in the apartment, and somebody to play it, because the one thing in the world that takes her from her lot is music, and what she requires is, more or less, the test studio. She's been listening since her birth. It would also be nice if, when they engineer them, and I'm sure they will someday, she could have a Victrola that played perfectly. And, oh yes, she'd have to be able to go to therapy twice a day, every day except Sunday, for the rest of her life. That's a lot of money, isn't it?"

"It is a lot of money, considering what you have to tip the doormen at Christmas," I said.

"We have a savings account in the Seaman's Bank," he said. "We've been saving all our lives."

"How much do you have?"

"Six thousand."

"Okay," I proposed, clearing my throat. "I own an apartment on Fifth Avenue overlooking Central Park. It's a quick ride to the hospital. There's an elevator, a doorman, the whole thing. It's got three bedrooms, a formal dining room, a big living room with a fireplace and French doors that open onto a sunny terrace.

It's on the sixteenth floor, very quiet. I'll give that apartment to you, with a Steinway D. I'll give you, in addition, half a million dollars in cash, and I'll establish a million-dollar trust. Everything can be in the name of your wife and daughter, the trust will be with Morgan or UST—which we won't rob—and I'll have it set up far enough in advance of even our very first steps that you'll be able to absorb the shock and believe in the reality of it."

"If you have money like that, why do you want to rob a bank?"

"That, plus the working capital to do the job (about six hundred thousand) is all I've got."

"You haven't answered the question."

"First of all," I said, "the money we've just been talking about is small change compared to what's at stake. It's my venture capital. Secondly, the bank has treated me very badly for absolutely no reason, and even if they hadn't I would have had to do it anyway. Suffice it to say that, despite the fact that I denounced them in full-page ads in *The New York Times* and *The Wall Street Journal*, they refused to ban coffee in the building. This went on for more than a month, day after day. It cost me a fortune, and they serve coffee all over the place even now. So there's that. And then there's Constance—my Constance. I hated living off her, and I'd rather like her to know that I'm financially independent. I'll never match her billions, but as she didn't earn a penny of them I figure that a couple of hundred million will do.

"And, then, there's your Constance. I haven't met her, but if I spend the next forty years in jail, what better way could there be to make use of the money that I now have than to give it to her? And if I don't go to jail, I won't need the money. The sums in question here are so enormous that I won't even ask for reimbursement of the seed capital or my grant to you. It all fits together very neatly."

By that time the game had ended and we were alone in the stadium except for the ground crew and the cleanup men. Neither of us had watched very carefully, but we assumed the Yankees had won. The Yankees always won.

"I like what you say," Smedjebakken said. "I think the benefits for Connie are worth the risk, but I'd die if I knew I couldn't see her for forty years. . . ."

"I'll take the fall," I said. "If we get caught, I'll tell them only name, rank, and serial number. You make a deal," I went on, unable to avert my eyes from the sides of his head, "and sing their ears off."

"What happens if we succeed, and I have to leave the country?"

"Then your daughter will have her own therapist, and her own pool, and you can build a piano factory on the grounds of your estate."

I was there when he asked Angelica. I had to be. I had to tell her the plan, and weather her hostile cross-examination. This woman should have been a customs inspector: absolutely nothing could get by her. She assigned probabilities to each action in the operation, dividing her fault analysis into several categories—an active mistake on our part, an omission, a deliberate discovery by bank security or others, an accidental discovery, the unplanned intercession of a third party, the possibility of machines not working, mismeasurement, illness at a crucial moment, and several other categories that, frankly, I do not remember.

Not being an engineer, I had failed to build redundancies into my plan. In fact, I had just the plan, and nothing to protect it —no precautions, alternative routes, or anything of that sort.

But there was the beauty of dialectics. I presented my raw thesis, Angelica countered with the brutal antithesis, and Smedjebakken—with his always constructive nature, woodchuck-like industriousness, and phenomenal engineering brilliance—the synthesis. For every task he had two machines, each tested beforehand and one merely waiting in pristine splendor. Where I had simply said, "Drill through the rock," he specified half a dozen types of bit and a dozen replacements for each. Where I had called for a landing field, he provided for two, and an alternate, and where I had envisioned drums of fuel at the side of the runway, he buried them.

His life, after all, had been devoted to maintaining the reliability of a highly complex mechanical system subject to more variables than anyone could imagine. In those days, the subway was efficient, and you could actually rely on it. After Smedjebakken left, it appears to have gone downhill.

Had I not happened upon a brilliant and experienced systems engineer and his critical, safety-conscious wife, I would have been caught at the very beginning. And even had I not been, I would not have been able to move what I had stolen. Gold is very heavy. That I knew, of course, but I was used to handling it one brick at a time. I hadn't considered adequately what it would be like to transport a thousand bars in one load.

We had stayed up all night, and the sun was beginning to rise. It was Indian summer. The night air was hot and dry. A stiff breeze blew from the north and brought an acrid, coffeelike smell from the Bronx, and on this ill wind crows were carried like the first and fastest troops of an army in panicked retreat. In such a high wind they had no choice but to be shot southward, and they cawed as if to announce an approaching megalossus.

When we had gone through all the planning and adjustment I said, "Well?" After which we sat in silence for ten minutes. So many emotions were welling up within Angelica Smedje-bakken that sitting across from her was like watching a teapot on a red-hot burner.

"You can get by as you are, or maybe not," I said. "With what I propose, you can lose everything, or gain everything. If you say yes, you may be casting yourselves into oblivion. If you say no, oblivion may catch up with you sooner than you imagine. Our parents or grandparents or those further back were faced with the same kind of decision before they left for this country. All the work you can do with your mind brings you nothing but perfectly balanced symmetry, with the reasons for one thing or the other equally convincing, equally forbidding. This is something that you must decide with your heart. Your families have made such decisions before, and you'll know what to do."

Angelica broke into tears. Despite the fact that I was deeply moved, I smiled, for I could see that to the central movement of her life, the part that had already been set down, she was going to add a cadenza, and if there is anything I love more I know not what it is—when the pianist becomes so enthralled with the piece that he is following that he begins to compose it himself. Cadenzas are full and fast and they come not as a matter of technique but from love, power, and elation. They are a great declaration. In their unfolding it is as if the pianist is saying to the composer: "Yes. I understand what you understand. I feel what you feel. I know you. Your hands are my hands, your eyes my eyes, your heart my heart." The cadenza Angelica was adding was not to a concerto but to her life, and she shuddered and wept because, in her resolution, she had glimpsed the whole of her existence as if through the composer's eyes.

I next returned to Astoria on one of those fall days when the sky is cerulean and the air like glass. These are the days when smoke rises in straight columns, and every detail of the landscape is as suddenly visible as if it had been emphasized by an engraver. The tugs were busy gliding downriver, green and black, coamings of white foam parting perpetually from their bows.

Smedjebakken himself was a handsome man, even if perhaps a wee bit too stolid, and his wife was the ideal model for an Italian painter of the Renaissance. And their daughter, despite her affliction, was more beautiful than even her mother. I met her that day, in the front parlor of her parents' house. From the back came a workshop of notes, as if from an orchestra tuning before a concert, but solely from pianos. And through the windows I could see the blue sky hanging weightlessly over the worn brick of Astoria.

Her mother and father were packing boxes in preparation for the move. Smedjebakken brought me to her room, introduced us, and went back to his work. Perhaps because of the child's incomparable beauty, I was almost unaffected by her involuntary movements. I didn't know it, but I began to move with her, to track steadily the slate-blue eyes that had to roam when she could not hold still.

She said, "It's okay to move with me a little: Mommy and Daddy do. It makes me feel that I'm not moving myself." She fought to get the words out, as if they were held by elastic bands that had to stretch with them as they were said, and that could stop them and pull them back.

"I didn't even know I was doing that."

"It's okay."

"I'm glad to meet you," I said. "I know how much your mother and father love you, and I understand why. You are a very lovely child. I've never seen a child with eyes like yours —or a grownup, for that matter."

"That's where my whole life is," she said, "in my eyes."

I nodded.

"I don't want to move to Manhattan."

"I know. Your father told me. When I was about your age, I had to move from the only house I had ever known. But the circumstances were much different."

"Why?" she asked, and though it sounded like *Wha-eee*, it was, somehow, perfectly natural.

"They were terrible," I said, "just terrible, but I got over them, and I got over the moving. And you will, too. I moved to a place where I had a rope that hung from a tree bent over a pool in a river. I flew off that rope ten thousand times, and each flight freed me a little bit from the unhappiness of having been forced from home. Now, I remember the tree leaning over the pool with the same affection and sadness that I had had for the place I left."

"I can't fly off the end of a swinging-rope," she said.

"But you can swim," I answered. "And in your new place you're going to swim twice a day."

She smiled.

"And, also," I told her, "because you'll be burning up so much food with all the exercise, I'll bet your mother will allow you to stop at the candy store every day you swim."

"She will?"

"I can't promise, but I'll suggest it. When *I* do a lot of exercise, I allow myself a treat. I just have to be careful not to eat more than one small bite, because if I do I tend to gain weight. But you're a kid, you won't have to be careful."

"I won't," she said. "I'm skinny."

"You're *svelte*," I told her.

"What does that mean?"

"It means just right, with a nod to the thin side. It's Swedish. You'll learn it when you learn Swedish." (Actually, as I found out years later at the Naval Academy, it's French. I had thought that it was one of those words, like *bistro*, that the French had borrowed whole from the barbarians.)

"Why would I learn Swedish?"

"Because you're a Smedjebakken."

"Because I'm a *what?*" she asked, amused. It was clear that her parents had not told her everything.

"Because all little girls with blue eyes are Smedjebakkens, and sooner or later they learn Swedish. Swedish is a language so wonderful that speaking it gives you the same feeling you get when you sing, play the piano, or paddle a canoe."

"Do you speak Swedish?"

"No."

"Then how do you know?"

"I speak fake Swedish," I said. And then I spoke to her for a few minutes in fake Swedish, which I can generate for hours on end, and with which I have truly stunned visiting Swedish businessmen and bankers, regaling them for the lengths of whole lunches with tales told in a language neither they nor I understood. When I was finished, I said to Constance, "Your father will teach you."

"How can *he* teach me?"

"He speaks it fluently."

"He does?"

"Yes."

She swelled with pride. "I do want to speak Swedish," she said. "I'm already learning Italian."

"Good. Italian is like talking to a bird. Swedish is like the bird talking."

She laughed.

"And here's another thing," I revealed. "Where you're moving, you'll be able to see Central Park, skyscrapers, a beautiful lake, and the sunset, all from very high up. You'll have a wonderful terrace with lots of plants and flowers—little dwarf pines in tubs, herbs, geraniums, roses, arugula. And guess what?"

"What?"

"The terrace has a drain and a hose. On hot summer days you can fill up a rubber pool and splash in the sun."

"That sounds good," she told me. She was beginning to change her mind about moving.

"You'll have your own room, on the same floor as everything else, so you'll be able to get around more easily than you can here. There's an elevator in the building, too. No bumping down the stoop. You'll be going to a new school, where you'll have many new and fascinating things to learn. And, finally, your father is going to buy you a Steinway D, which a Juilliard student will use for practice every day. You'll have what you love, because your father and your mother love you."

I embraced her. Her unstoppable motion felt much like that of an infant, and I realized that, in the transit of just a few minutes, I had come to love this child.

She was not likely to know love, marriage, and motherhood. The young, who court and breed, are ruthless. It is only natural. Think of the effects of, let us say, a large nose, or bad teeth. Then think of Connie Massina, of all the soulful beauty, of all the knowingness and deep feeling, of all the love, that would be wasted. It happens with elk and otters and hummingbirds, and it happens with us, as some of the finest of us, who are lame, are culled from the herd. The herd is the cruelest thing that ever was, and I have always hated it.

The idea was that Smedjebakken and I would isolate ourselves from Angelica and Connie. Because the greatest catastrophe would be if Angelica were stripped of what had been my wealth and sent to jail with us, she was not to know anything. None-theless, and I can certainly say this now, she extracted from Smedjebakken an astonishing promise, that he would never have revealed even to the Angel Gabriel, and this was that before we robbed the bank we rob something else. It made no sense to me, and probably not to Smedjebakken either. I didn't want to do it, but he was duty-bound.

"I'm an amateur," he said to me one afternoon as we labored to turn the house in Astoria (now mine) into sleeping quarters for me, and a machine shop in which to make the specialized equipment we would need for the operation.

"So am I," I answered.

"Don't you think it would be better if we had some experience prior to such a big job?"

"No."

"Why not?"

"Many reasons. For example, beginners' luck. The very first time I shot an arrow I hit the bull's-eye. In my first poker game I cleaned the table. The first time I kissed a girl, we rose into the air like two hydrogen-filled blimps."

"She was fat?"

"She was happy. As I said, beginners' luck."

"I'm an engineer by profession," Smedjebakken said. "I don't believe in luck."

"What about the engineering reasons?" We were standing in the upper hallway of the house (my only asset), with brooms.

"If we commit two crimes we're twice as likely to get caught. Even if we don't get caught the first time, we may leave clues that, in conjunction with those we leave the second time, will lead to our otherwise avoidable apprehension. I want to come onto the field clean. I want to come out of nowhere. One thing I learned in flying is that the second attack on a target is just like the hundredth."

"That makes sense, but I just can't do it unless we go through some sort of practice run."

"All right," I told him, "we'll steal the *Madonna del Lago* from the Metropolitan Museum of Art." I had intended this to be a joke.

"You decided just like that?"

"I thought you wanted to steal something?" I said, rising to defend my position.

"I do."

"Okay, let's steal the *Madonna del Lago*. I have a plan." At this point I was both fully committed, and, of course, fully committable.

"When did you make the plan?"

"Just now."

"In a second?"

"It needs some refinement, but the essence is there. The essence always comes in a second, always easily, as if from the blue."

I had had wonderful ideas all my life—the antigravity box, the camel ranch in Idaho, artillery mail—but I had never been able to translate them into reality. Smedjebakken, however, knew nothing other than the translation of ideas into reality.

I may have been inspired in the first place by the decided advantage that Constance's father had loved the *Madonna del*

Lago. It is a painting that, though much respected, is assigned
by the experts to the middle ground of the great works of art.
I think they are mistaken, or perhaps just timid. It is so strong
a painting that it cannot fail to alienate some of those whose job
is to appraise it. In recognition of its quality, they boost it to
the middle even though they hate it, while others, who love it
but know that it is despised, lower it for the sake of amity
between aficionados. This is what happens to strong things of
sharp and clear definition in a world of difficulties where com-
promise is necessary for survival.

The *Mona Lisa* I have always found to have too many browns.
She fills too much of the picture, and she looks unfortunately
like someone who could have been Burt Lancaster's sister. *La
Tempesta,* on the other hand, is one of those great paintings,
like the *Madonna del Lago,* that is too imaginative and bright,
too arresting, too colorful, too perplexing, for easy acceptance.

But the *Madonna del Lago* is a masterpiece of composition.
The Madonna stands with child in arms on a point of land
extending into the lake so that she is almost surrounded by blue,
and when apprehended from afar she appears to be enveloped
within a halo or an aurora. On her right side, a surflike wave
is rampant in the air, glistening in the sun, poised forever. The
water on the left is calm but shallow, its layers of shade and
color balancing the wave opposite. The form of the painting is
much like that of a Byzantine mosaic, with the waters taking
the place of orbital rings or bands.

It is a masterpiece of color. The sky is variously powder blue,
robin's egg, Wedgwood, gray-blue, and the gun-metal blue that
often accompanies atmospheric disturbances. The lake runs in
half a dozen colors, too, some nearly tropical, such as yellowish
turquoise, some otherworldly, some simple, and some cool. The
rocks are battle gray, the field a particular enameled green that

must have come from a magical pit known only in the Renaissance, for no green today looks so wet and so hard, so deep, light, and luminous.

And it is a masterpiece of expression. The Madonna is neither demure nor contemplative. Nor is she calm. She smiles gently, in triumph. This is the expression one would think she would have, is it not? The expression she deserved? Hers is not a mortal, invidious triumph but a look of angelic elation so lovely that I long for it even now, for never have I seen more beauty in a human face.

Constance's father felt much the same, and sent an agent to Paris to engage Hiro Matsuye. In the Twenties, Hiro Matsuye was the best copyist in the world. He was so good that he was watched, his output closely cataloged by museums in a constant state of terror. At the time, without electron microscopy and advanced spectrographic analysis, it was impossible to distinguish between an original and the homage done it by Matsuye, though he would change a key element in the composition for the sake of avoiding foul play. But Mr. Lloyd convinced him, just this once and who knows at what price, to make the copy truly exact.

In the basement of what used to be my house lay Matsuye's *Madonna del Lago,* perfectly aged, in precisely the same frame as the original. Constance never liked the painting, perhaps because she bore too close a resemblance to its subject, and as her father and Matsuye were no longer alive, she had crated it. It's a small painting. Even with the frame it isn't much bigger than a giant box of cereal.

Smedjebakken and I walked up Fifth Avenue until we reached the house. No one was home, and the street was deserted. We were able to climb the iron fence only because Constance had refused my suggestion of sharpening the spear blades. For reasons that remain incomprehensible to me to this day, very rich people with spear-blade fencing simply will not sharpen the points as required by logic and common sense. As we walked across the lawn without the slightest fear or hesitation (the house, after all, had been mine), Smedjebakken expressed his amazement that I had actually lived there. "The idea of living in such magnificence," I told him, "is better than the actuality."

We dropped into an immaculately clean limestone light well, where we sat with our backs against the wall and waited for Constance to come home for the evening. I knew that the window in this light well had a broken latch. You needed only to push, although someone had to be home so the alarm would be off.

"Don't you know how to work the alarm?" Smedjebakken asked.

"I'm absolutely sure," I said, "that the coffee has exacerbated Constance's paranoia, and that she's changed both the alarm authorizations and the locks. We've just got to wait."

Smedjebakken agreed and said that, indeed, if she were drinking as much coffee as I claimed, she would by now be a raving psychotic, and that the house was probably full of medieval instruments of torture and Doberman pinschers with teeth like those of an Oxford don.

"Don't gild the lily," I told him. "It takes years of coffee drinking to get that way. I'm not sure exactly how long she's been at it, but as I know she's a major user she's undoubtedly unapproachable, irrational, and maniacal, though not yet a total goner."

Then we heard the wonderful sound of a 1927 Nagy-Horvath, the one great Hungarian luxury automobile, of which only fifteen were built, all entirely by hand. The kerosene engine was a 750-horsepower masterpiece of stainless steel, nickel, and bronze. It looked (dare I say it?) like one of those gleaming expresso machines you see in fancy restaurants, and sounded like the quarter of the metal tinkerers in New Delhi. So many rods, arms, levers, valves, gears, and bushings would tap, turn, and click that when I used to drive the Horvath around town I saw shell-shocked veterans dive for the ground, convinced it was about to explode.

I will never understand how leather can smell so good twenty-five years after it has been installed, or why the interior refused to get dusty, or the metal to tarnish (though it may have had something to do with the man we hired to take care of the car). The engine stopped, and I waited for the distinctive paleolithic sound of the hand brake, a triceratops clearing his throat, which did not come. As the minutes passed I slowly lost my composure. I lay my head on my upraised knees and breathed like a dog standing on an examination table.

"What's the matter?" Smedjebakken asked.

"She's kissing someone," I said.

"How do you know?"

"She always sets the hand brake immediately, unless she's kissing someone. When Constance kisses, she throws her whole body into it. In a Nagy-Horvath, you can't do that over a raised hand brake."

"Oh."

"There!" I said. "Did you hear that stegosaurus-retch?"

"What stegosaurus?" Smedjebakken asked.

"Let's just get the painting and get out of here."

In a moment or two the lights went on inside. This we knew not because the basement ceased to be anything but dark, but because the waxen leaves of the Xyrothombus above us flashed yellow along their undersides as they reflected the light of the chandeliers in the ballroom.

"Why is she turning on the lights in the ballroom?" I asked. "But what do I care? She's called Holmes by now and the system is at rest."

I pushed at the window and it opened with just the sandy sound I had expected. "I'll go in first and get a stepladder," I told Smedjebakken. Jumping down from the window, I landed badly on my right ankle and fell against the wall. The blow knocked me out. Of this I am certain, because when I awoke I was choking on a bottle of 1933 Lafitte that Smedjebakken was pouring down my throat.

"What are you doing!" I screamed, unmindful of the fact that I was a burglar in my own house.

"You were unconscious. You were getting dehydrated. It was the only liquid I could find except for the champagne. I didn't want to open another bottle of champagne, because when the cork popped it made a huge sound."

I looked down and saw a magnum bottle of champagne at my feet, empty. "Where's the champagne?" I asked.

"In your stomach."

"No wonder I feel full."

"Yeah. I gave you a bottle of Château Haut Brion, too."

"Are you nuts?" I asked, my voice already starting to slur. "I hape wime. I'm going to spent next afternoon throweling up."

"Not if you don't eat."

I struggled to my feet and led Smedjebakken to the painting vaults. I don't remember much, but I do remember that as time passed and I became drunker and drunker I couldn't work the simple combination lock, so I lay there for four hours, declaiming the story of my life to Smedjebakken and listening to the player piano in the ballroom upstairs.

"What the hell is going on up there?" I asked.

"Someone's dancing, I think," Smedjebakken said, looking up.

"See what it is," I said, giving him the flashlight. "I'm too sick to move."

"Why should I risk it?"

"I have to know."

"Why do you have to know?"

"Because she's my wife! I fell in love with her once. I loved her, she loved me, and love stays. It's a fixed quantity, even if we're not."

Smedjebakken left, and more than half an hour later, when I was almost sober, he returned.

"What did you see?" I asked.

"Nothing."

"What do you mean, 'nothing'? Tell me what you saw."

"You want the truth?"

"I always want the truth," I said. "Don't you know that? Everyone always wants the truth."

"All right. After ten minutes I finally found the stairs: this basement is as big as Madison Square Garden. I was frightened that I might open the door in someone's face."

"It opens into the kitchen, not the ballroom."

"I know, but they were going in and out. Luckily, when I came up from the basement they were dancing in the ballroom. In the kitchen a ten-foot-high expresso machine was puffing away, and coffee cups were all over the place. I thought it was a party for fifty people, but there are only two, and they're drinking all that coffee. They use a clean cup each time."

"Who?" I asked, my heart between my toes.

"A beautiful, beautiful woman. . . ."

"That's Constance."

"And a tall, slinky, Brazilian-looking guy with stretched-back hair. He's wearing pointy shoes, black gaucho pants, and an embroidered shirt. He looks like a cross between a waiter and an acrobat, and he has really thin lips, like Rudolph Valentino."

"What was she wearing?"

"Nothing."

"Nothing?"

"There were panties and stuff scattered all over the place. She was totally nude, and she was dancing. Boy, was she dancing!"

"What kind of dances?" I asked, gritting my teeth.

"Snake dances."

"Snake dances," I repeated, my voice falling off.

"She has a way of moving that paralyzed me for half an hour."

"How could that be? For Christ's sake," I said, "they're dancing to a player piano!"

"Yes, but they dance in the coffee style, in a slow counterpoint."

"Do they kiss?"

"They kiss, they fondle, and they sip coffee. I'm sorry, but you wanted the truth."

"I always suspected," I said, "and now I know. It's better to know than to suspect. I still don't understand how it would be possible to kiss someone who drinks coffee, but it's finished, it's over. All I want to do now is rob banks."

After the great volume of alcohol Smedjebakken poured into me I was sick for almost a month, and I lay on the floor of one of the upstairs rooms in the Astoria house, watching all of Queens turn to winter. Smedjebakken was a first-class engineer, but he was no doctor: he tried to get me to drink a cup of tea. Why compound poisons when I was hardly alive as it was? I will make no metaphors to describe the pain in my head, because the brain, which makes metaphors, should not be forced to be clever at its own expense. My limbs ached like a kingdom that has lost a war, and my stomach swelled with the nausea of all the seas, but my head, well, it hurt. It really hurt.

Sometimes the soup of toxic residues circulating in my body gave horrible waking nightmares during which I would scream and pound the floor. Smedjebakken, who only several weeks before had poured a magnum of champagne down my throat, had the gall to suggest that my illness was psychosomatic. He said to take an aspirin.

"Are you insane?" I asked. "My uncle took an aspirin once and was sick for a year. The whole country is falling into the grip of drugs and will never recover."

"One aspirin?"

"One aspirin leads to two, two lead to four, four lead to eight, eight to sixteen, sixteen to thirty-two, and thirty-two to sixty-four. Before you knew it, I'd be seesawing on aspirin and coffee. Smedjebakken, the United States of America is becoming an opium den. Somebody, *somebody*, has to resist."

As I regained my strength, Smedjebakken worked tirelessly to equip the house. Because it was situated in an industrial neighborhood, no one took note of the things he trundled into it. When he was done, he was able to weld, cut, mill, grind, mold, tap, forge, plate, braze, drill, or extrude virtually any metal. He was expert in handling and processing, and had been building machines all his life. He told me that, given the time and materials, he could build, for example, a half-sized Rolls-Royce, or a power loom, or an antigravity box. And, because he was doing what he loved, it came easily and went fast.

He wanted to know how we were going to steal the *Madonna del Lago*. At first he thought that I intended merely to pass off

the replica to Angelica and cheat my way through her requirement, but I soon had him building a full-size powered wheelchair
that ran off D-cells stashed inside the metal tubing of the
frame.

"Why not just have a battery at the bottom, as with Connie's
wheelchair?"

"Because this is a wheelchair for stealing paintings, that's
why," I said, and fell back, too weak to talk.

Three days later he had the wheelchair. "Okay," I told him,
"make a box that looks just like a battery box, and mount it in
the normal place. Only give it a door that pops open at a touch,
and that you can't see—it has to look like the solid end of the
box. The button must be concealed, the door should open as
fast as a switchblade, and you have to be able to close it with
the foot. Inside . . . an extendible rail, set on ball bearings,
sprung so that it shoots out when the door opens. Between the
rails, a cradle that will hold the painting."

"I see," he said. "But what about the alarms? The guards?"

"Guards?" I asked. "Alarms? Oh."

The finished product arrived within forty-eight hours. The
battery box looked just like a battery box, but when he lifted
the cap on one of the grips and pushed the button underneath
it (just as, in a fighter plane, the cannon trigger is set in the
stick), the door lifted, and the painting, resting snugly in a felt-
covered cradle, suddenly appeared. He pressed the button again,
and the process reversed itself.

"It takes half a second to open or close," he said. "It uses
oil-filled cylinders, and I quieted the button, the springs, and
the latch. You may not have noticed, but you can't hear a thing."

"I noticed," I said.

Then I fell back, ill once more, and went through another
period of pain and sickness. Smedjebakken was beginning to

lose confidence in me. He was so disturbed that he came the next morning and said it right out.

"How can I trust you to do this thing and not ruin it?" he asked. "You're an invalid. The plan requires daring, strength, and stamina. You've been moaning and groaning for a month."

"I was poisoned!" I screamed.

"Poisoned by what?" Smedjebakken screamed back. "A bottle of the best champagne in the world?"

"Yes."

"Since when does drinking champagne make you sick for a month? What are you? I mean, how tough are you if your body thinks champagne is Drāno?"

"I'm as tough as anyone. Only I recoil from what is false or ugly or untrue (untrue being different from false). I can do extraordinary things at times, but I weaken in the presence of evil."

"Why?"

"Because, once, it beat me. I was completely vanquished, as powerless in its grip as someone paralyzed in a dream."

"And yet you're alive," Smedjebakken said, not to contradict me but to elicit from me the rest of the story, which was not mine to tell.

"Purely by chance."

"Well," said Smedjebakken, "you're not all that bad, but I do hope you get better. When will you get better?"

"Soon," I answered, "soon."

That night I dreamed that I lay in a summer forest, where the trees gave life and depth to air that otherwise would have been only an ether. The birds sang beautifully without knowing what they were saying or why, like a wave that rolls and breaks in the sun. The sea was close by, down a hill, vacant and blue. And the flowers seemed to have been lighted from within.

Though resting and at peace, I was not happy, for I knew that this was the last place, and that after it there would be no other.

When I awoke the next morning, the poison had left my system and my affliction had vanished. I was strong, energetic, and confident after the month of sleep.

"Let's go to the museum," I said to Smedjebakken, who was eating, or rather, was about to eat, a kosher turkey anus. (Since Sleepy Hollow, I had grown rather fond of them.)

"To scout it out?"

"No. To do the job."

"Don't be ridiculous," he said. "We're going to have to practice for a month. I've never seen the painting, I don't even know the plan."

"I have been practicing for a month," I said pompously. "And it will go just like that." I snapped my fingers.

"You've been in bed for a month, totally incapacitated, while I've been turning my house into a factory and making hollowed-out wheelchairs."

"Don't you understand?" I asked.

"Don't I understand what?"

"Where I get my capacities."

"No. I don't understand where you get your capacities. Where do you get your capacities?"

"From my *in*capacities."

"You get your capacities from your incapacities."

"Yes."

"Well, that's great. As for me, I get my capacities from my capacities."

"Then you've got a level road ahead of you. You're probably quite happy."

"As happy goes."

"The road for me has deep hollows," I told him, "and high hills. I can get to the top of the hills because I've been to the bottom of the hollows. By the way, do you have a wire-tool that produces a jagged cut?"

He looked at me without understanding. "Yes, though not deliberately: I've been too cheap to throw it away."

"Good. That's what we need. I'll explain the plan on the subway. Wear an overcoat that's very baggy."

"Okay. I have one left from my muffin craze. But why?"

"For the cat. Catch a cat."

"Catch a cat," he mumbled. There is no question in my mind that at that moment he was certain that we were both going to grow old in jail, but he stuck to my guns.

"Get the reproduction."

Smedjebakken brought up the chair, pushed the button, and lifted the painting from the cradle.

"Look at the back," I said.

Varnished to the back of the canvas was a row of parallel gold wires, all of which were connected in series to two copper wires about a foot and a half in length.

"I did it this morning before you got up," I said. "The wires still need to be snipped at the ends with your wire-tool."

"It looks professional."

"This is how the more valuable paintings at the Met are alarmed. I know because Constance is on the board, we went to many meetings, I asked, and they showed me."

"I see," Smedjebakken said, his confidence in me apparently beginning to return, "but did you say that we have to catch a cat?"

The cat, a huge gray and mother-of-pearl Manx that we scooped up from the back of a pizza place in Astoria, went into

Smedjebakken's coat at Madison and Eighty-sixth. For the few blocks to the museum and until I pushed the wheelchair into the Renaissance-Italian rooms, the cat fought like a Tasmanian devil, but Smedjebakken was so tough that he merely grimaced. Now and then a mother-of-pearl-colored paw would shoot from between Smedjebakken's lapels, he would cough and stuff it back in, and we would continue on our way. No one noticed, because people tend to avert their eyes from someone in a wheelchair, a fact of which Smedjebakken was well aware.

That was the hard part, the cat putting huge welts in Smedjebakken's torso, which bloodied him like a bird.

We came to the *Madonna* and waited until the room was empty. Smedjebakken gratefully opened his coat, and the cat leapt out and ran forward at about sixty miles an hour. We had aimed him at the adjacent room, where a guard was stationed: every three rooms had a sleepy old man in uniform, who was not allowed to sit down at any time, and to whom nothing ever happened.

"Get that cat!" I screamed at the top of my lungs. As the cat flew by, the guard instinctively gave chase. Smedjebakken rose from the chair, the pliers in his right hand, and I lifted the painting from the wall. I had opened the box already. As I removed the painting, Smedjebakken cut the wire, and every bell in the world began to ring.

He lifted the replica from the cradle and fell against the wall. I put the original in its place, closed the door with my foot, and toppled the wheelchair. In the last few seconds, I opened Smedjebakken's overcoat to reveal his blood-stained front. "Moan," I commanded.

"There's no one here yet," he whispered.

"*Ars gratia artis,*" I said.

He began to moan. It all had taken less than ten seconds. We waited and waited, until, finally, we heard the pounding of many feet. Just before a phalanx of guards arrived—two with shotguns—Smedjebakken interrupted his moaning to say, "We had so much time we could have done the crossword puzzle."

"Moan!" I said. "This is the moment of truth."

The first thing they did was lift the painting from Smedjebakken's hands, and as the bells rang and Smedjebakken (purely from excitement) began to scream, I too began to scream. "He was attacked by a cat! He was attacked by a cat!"

The cat, it seems, had gone straight out the main entrance and disappeared into the Upper East Side. Most of the guards had seen him, even if only as a blur, and Smedjebakken's wounds were nothing if not genuine: his blood made the floor around us as slick as ice.

The guards had absolutely no idea what to do. Having secured what they thought was their painting, they were faced with what they thought was the victim of a cat attack. One of them announced that he was going to call an ambulance, and ran off into an infinity of Flemish landscapes.

Then appeared a preppy in an expensive suit—the assistant director. (The director was, of course, in Florence.) "What happened?" he asked of the ranking guard. As he was briefed, I petrified. This was a classmate of mine from Harvard—Cuckoo Prescott, famous for having switched his major (we called it "concentration") from ornithology to fine arts in the last term of his senior year. His thesis was entitled "Evolutionary Raptor Flight Structures in the Paintings of Sir Thomas Boney." I recognized him, and he had just as good a chance of recognizing me, except that he was off balance.

I feared that his memory of me might be quite vivid, as I had punished him for drinking coffee, by reading him the Abbé Bobigny-Soissons-Lagare's *Les Mals du Café*, prior to which I had chloroformed him and wrapped him in real mummy tape that I obtained from the Department of Art & Archaeology.

What could I do? I messed up my hair, grimaced, and began to speak as if I were a Hollywood version of a Mexican bandit. (I'm afraid that Cuckoo Prescott was looking at me as I prepared for this role.)

"De cat almos keel my son!" I screamed. "We weel not forgeh dis!"

Cuckoo looked at us in astonishment. "Who are these people?" he asked.

"Visitors," was the reply.

All Cuckoo's flaccid genes strained to be responsible, worried, and polite. I could see that many whaling captains were spinning in the graveyards of Salem and Gloucester, sending out mystical transmissions about liability. It worked: his apologies were so profuse that they overwhelmed his suspicions. I tried not to look at him directly, and cursed myself when my Mexican bandit turned into a vaudeville Italian. I couldn't help it. One just slid into the other.

"Hey! Itsa no matta. We go to de hosp and itsa okay."

"Where are you from?" Cuckoo asked, his subconscious working meticulously.

To which Smedjebakken answered, "The District of *Colombia*."

What could Cuckoo say? The ambulance attendants arrived and put Smedjebakken back in the wheelchair. Then we received a royal escort through the museum, with offers of lifetime membership and huge discounts at the café and gift shop.

At Lenox Hill Hospital a doctor painted Smedjebakken's chest with Mercurochrome and gave him a tetanus shot. When he was discharged, we went straight to the apartment, showed the painting to Angelica, who was very impressed, and then wrapped it in tissue paper and green ribbon. When evening fell I went outside and walked through the clear dusk as orange and yellow lights blazed across Manhattan. I brought my package to the main desk of the museum just before closing time.

"This is a package for Mr. Prescott," I said to the receptionist, who was very gracious. "Would you take down a message for him?"

"Certainly," she said, seizing paper and pencil.

"One: It's always better for a museum to display originals, and this is the original.

"Two: He can keep the replica.

"Three: Coffee is bad."

After we stole—and returned, the *Madonna del Lago*—we were ready for the real thing.

On the day of the robbery, I was as excited as ever I have been in all my life. When I arose in newly greened Astoria on the fourth of June, I felt I would be leaving this academy of forfeiture and regret, and going on to another world at once more forgiving, more precise, and new. I imagine it is the feeling that one has when at age eighteen one is graduated from high school and all the world is ahead. I never was graduated from high school. My higher education was anxious and tumultuous, and when I finished I felt only that I had jumped from a merry-go-round.

This was all forgotten that sunny morning when I left the Astoria house and turned the key in the lock, knowing that I would never enter again. Inside, on a table in the hall, was a drugstore bequest leaving the tools to a vocational school and the house to the Campfire Girls. I had always liked the Campfire Girls, because when pitted against the Girl Scouts they were such underdogs.

It was so cool that the blues overhead were like flowing water. The shade was warmer than the shade of fall, but just as deep and just as tranquil. As the subway shuttled forth along the elevated tracks, I remembered my youth, when during the summer I would start my days on the train as the Hudson gleamed in a coat of sparkling mist. Then, I had the same sense of excitement and well being that I now possessed, but I had it every day, and I had it not because I was about to rob the biggest bank in the world but merely because I was going to work in it.

This would be my last subway ride. At its end I would take my last walk amid the canyons of Wall Street before the stone was heated by the summer sun, for when I emerged that evening the walls of granite would be returning the day's heat to the air.

It was my last elevator ride down to the vault, the last weigh-in, the last "Good morning, Sherman," to Oscovitz, and when I greeted him I did so with such sparkle that he shyly averted his eyes, for he was flustered by anything that varied from the routine to which he was permanently bonded.

"Good morning, Sherman! What a beautiful day! It's the day of days!" In a movie, this might have alerted him. In real life, nothing could alert him. He bent his head closer to his desk and pretended to read *The Daily News.*

"Sherman! Be it known to the stars and moon above, that Sherman Oscovitz is in love. And it was for her, the darling lass, that Cupid's arrow struck your ass! So, go with her to the South Pacific, where the girls are naked, and the sex terrific!"

Poor Sherman Oscovitz, who had never kissed a woman and never been held, and who had passed a million women who had never been kissed and never been held, who had not dared look at them long enough to make eye contact, and who had once said, "It snowed about an inch and a half in Brooklyn. That's what I call a *penis* snow," and blushed until he looked like a boiling jam pie.

"Sherman, Sherman," I said. "How many years do you have left? Why don't you cut the knots? Go waterskiing. Go to the state fair in Syracuse. They have kissing booths. Buy a kiss from a woman in a kissing booth: Sherman, before the grave."

About to flee, he said, "You're cracked!" He was quite agitated.

"Sherman!" I screamed. "For Christ's sake, get on the train to Syracuse! Do it today!"

"My job," he said.

"Fuck your job," I whispered.

"He said *fuck!*" he announced, as if to an invisible judge.

"Yes, I did."

"You said it. You said it. I'm going to tell Mr. Piehand. I'm going to tell him."

"Mr. Piehand is in Formosa," I stated, knowing, in fact, the whereabouts that day of every officer in the bank.

"I'll tell him when he gets back."

"Do that."

I left Sherman Oscovitz, now grape-colored, and went into Cage 47. One of Smedjebakken's chief worries was that after devoting our lives to tunneling into Cage 47 I would be shifted to another site. I assured him that this would not happen.

"How do you know?"

"I'm absolutely certain that I can stay in Cage 47, if need be, for eternity. Oscovitz doesn't understand time. Time requires at least two things—movement and variation. If everything were still, time could not pass, it would not exist. Without variation, movement would not exist, and, by extension, time. For Oscovitz, there is neither movement nor variation. He's a bureaucrat. If you dropped him in amber, and the amber was cracked after ten billion years, he wouldn't even blink. Believe me, if no one died and nothing happened for the next million years, he would show up every day except bank holidays and Yom Kippur, and he wouldn't even notice.

"I can take as long as I want in Cage Forty Seven, forever, if I choose, to finish restacking the gold, and Oscovitz will never give it a thought."

It was quite true. I stayed in 47 from the time we began to plan the robbery until the day of its execution—ten months—all to do a job that should have taken no more than a week.

Other problems were more serious and more vexing, but no matter, Smedjebakken's engineering genius solved each of them. He was a man of an era that has passed, and as with everyone in that position, his ill-fittedness sometimes became illumination.

He was made for the age of Edison, Brunel, and John Dee. I often confuse him with John Dee, for although they did not resemble one another they had been kissed by the same rebellious angel, and their enterprises, if not similar, were united by the verisimilitude of their approach. In mid-century the products of engineering that defined the mechanics of the time were not as cold, or as unfriendly, or as potent as they are now. They were still made of metal and wood. They still smelled of machine oil, cradled fires, spat-out steam, or were propelled by water or air or open magnets spinning on a gleaming shaft. They did not seem to contradict or evade natural law. They were quite different in spirit from those horrible dullard boxes called computers. They were crucibles of earth, water, wind, fire, gravity, and magnetism. You could smell them, hear them, feel their vibrations in the ground. They didn't just sit there like static dimwits until they exploded away a city. They didn't glow at you insolently in moronic green, overly patient, totally without voice or vulnerability.

The machines and processes that Smedjebakken loved so much were almost alive themselves, and had not crossed the sterile barrier of immortal precision that separates man and God. Nor had anyone crossed over with them in vain pursuit of perfection. So, you see, Smedjebakken was not arrogant. Even were he mistaken, the mistake had not yet made itself known, and all his accomplishments were concluded with a spiritual innocence that, dare I say it, does not anymore exist.

Our greatest problem was driving a shaft up through the bedrock so that it would exit exactly where we wanted it in Cage 47, not only in view of passing the gold through it without being observed from outside, but, far more critically, with the object of placing the opening between alarm wires cast into the concrete floor at one-foot intervals. This was an exceedingly difficult task, and in overcoming one difficulty, another, and yet another, were created, with seemingly no end. But that, Smedjebakken told me, is engineering. And the engineer's faith is not only that all difficulties can be overcome, but that they are finite in number.

First, we had to make a three-dimensional map of unprecedented accuracy. As our benchmarks were separated by half a mile and half a dozen turns—the benchmarks being one in the cornerstone of the Stillman and Chase building, and another (a surveyor's pin) in the street near the nearest subway entrance —and as the vertical distance was 250 feet, our diagram was a jagged, twisting path of approximately 5,780 feet. We had to start at a point that we could define only indirectly and surreptitiously, and, after 5,780 feet and more than a hundred angular measurements, return, blind, to that very same point. To accommodate the vinyl lining that would swallow the gold, and, more importantly, to accommodate the thickness of the telescoping bits for the long run we were obliged to drill, the shaft had to be eight inches in diameter.

This left two inches of clearance between the alarm wires in the floor. Just in linear measure, this was one part in 34,680, a rather exacting tolerance. But if you included the hundred angular measurements it was a task of such precision as to seem almost impossible.

Add to that the fact that we did not know where the alarm wires were embedded in the floor, and you may understand why, once apprised of these things by Smedjebakken, I wanted to give up.

"Don't," he said. "When you told me the plan I knew immediately the inherent difficulties. I knew as well that they would be surmountable. All we have to do is take it one step at a time."

"What's the first step?" I asked.

"Where do you get your shoes?"

"I *used to* buy them at Paul Stewart," I said, wistfully.

"Let's go get you a couple of pairs of new shoes in a very large size so I can fit them with magnetometers."

Smedjebakken had been working mysteriously in the well equipped machine shop that once had been his home, and, unbeknownst to me, had reconstructed five laboratory magnetometers so that they could be mounted within a pair of shoes, one at a time, and give their readings on a gauge disguised as a watch.

Why five magnetometers from three different manufacturers? It was simple, he told me, and then introduced me to a cardinal principle that I knew in my bones, and that is part of many techniques in engineering.

By their very nature as magnetometers, the magnetometers were accurate only to within twenty percent of their readings.

By my very nature as a human, I would be able to read the gauge and place the contact points with an accuracy of only about ten percent. We had to contend, therefore, with a 72% accuracy rate when every measurement had to be 99.99712% dead-on to meet the one part in 34,680 requirement.

What this demanded, Smedjebakken explained, was, though tedious, very simple. After taking a hundred readings apiece with each of the five magnetometers, we would have a scatter diagram that looked like Pinocchio's hat. The value on the horizontal axis at the apex of the hat would be the closest we could come to the exact measurement.

We would carry out the procedure five times, weighting the later attempts to reflect an assumed increase in competence on my part after so much practice.

I almost swooned at the prospect of taking 2,500 magnetometer readings, but was pulled into line when Smedjebakken reminded me that stealing an immense amount of money required an immense amount of work.

"All right," I said, "how do we map the location of the wires so we can record the measurements?"

"We calibrate the floor."

"How do you calibrate a floor?"

"With a rule and a five-point-diamond-tipped punch, both of which you'll carry in your shoes or in your pockets. They won't notice anything as long as you weigh out according to expectations. You'll also have to bring in a camera, a camera stand, and a micrometer gauge."

"Why?"

"You'll photograph each mark you make on the floor. If you use the camera stand, the scale will be uniform. When I blow up the points—if I lock the enlarger in place—I'll get good measurements that I can check against the gauge in the photograph.

Of course, we'll go through the process several times."

"I'll photograph each mark on the floor," I ventured, "so that you can measure it, so that when I measure the distance I can move from edge to edge, and you'll add in the width of the marks."

"Correct. You'll use a loupe when measuring."

"How many times do I have to measure?"

"Several hundred."

"Do you think we'll be able to get all of this done before we die?"

"We'll work hard," he said.

Before the weeks of calibration that then led to months of magnetometer readings I asked Smedjebakken why we could not assume that the alarm wires would have no current running through them when the vault was open. After all, we had only to punch through them once.

"What if that's true," he asked, "and we have to close up because the Transit Authority makes an unplanned inspection in the tunnel, or because Mr. Edgar brings John Foster Dulles to see the gold in the vault? Then what? They turn on the alarm at night, and we're through."

"You're right."

"Not only that, but who says that everything's on the same circuit? I imagine that many different circuits come into the alarm room, and that only those that must be broken are broken, with the rest kept closed."

The precision with which we approached the tunneling came not only from Smedjebakken's engineering background but also from my more mundane experience with navigation. By combining the techniques of surveying with those of solar and celestial navigation, we made our tolerances closer. After all, locating a point on the earth's surface to within five hundred feet of its actual position—which a good navigator can do with just a sextant and a chronometer—represents an accuracy of one part in seven billion: i.e., the ratio of the area of a circle with a 500-foot radius to the total area of the earth's surface, which, as any schoolchild knows, is 197 million square miles.

And this could be accomplished on a ship moving across the waves, shooting the sun with judgments dependent upon eye and nerve. Our measurements, with benchmarks etched into marble by diamond, were far more accurate. We had hope.

To do the surveying we started a subway project nearby. When I say we I mean mainly Smedjebakken, who was held in so much respect by the Transit Authority that when he told them he thought the bedrock under Wall Street was pressured by continental drift and might suddenly shift, causing an earthquake, they believed him. They funded his study of bedrock movement and gave him leave to enter under color of authority all areas of the Stillman and Chase megalith, including the basement, including the vault.

I was there, of course, when he came with his team. When they were in the vault itself half a dozen guards—armed with shotguns—shadowed them. Seeing the gold for the first time, in immense city-like piles, Smedjebakken wore an angelic smile. He had not understood emotionally when I told him that it was stacked in ramparts, walls, and cubes the size of small buildings.

The first time I stood in the presence of what today would be 150 billion dollars, I felt a rapacious electricity, and I thought to myself, this is here, I can touch it, I can pick it up . . . I can steal it. The sight of the gold made Smedjebakken work like Pushkin at Boldino or Handel in his great two weeks. Money means nothing and brings not happiness, but it can be translated so quickly into such interesting things—cashmere coats, Duesenbergs, levitation, perfectly white and straight teeth, English shotguns, ski chalets, flowers, clothes and contentment of sorts for needy orphans, chocolate bars, tutors in Japanese, surfing in Australia, string quartets, cedar groves, first editions, smoked salmon, single shells. I could go on and on, but these are just some of the things I like.

And for Smedjebakken it meant a crystal-clear swimming pool and a glass conservatory in a pine grove with a view of Lake Leman (which is not to say that he ended up there). It meant that his daughter might find companionship and command attention despite her affliction. It meant that she might even find love. And it meant that she would have the heartfelt pleasure of donating her vast wealth to those who shared the same fate, and perhaps seeing her own child, or children, float from the prison that had closed in on her from the moment of birth, and from which she herself could never escape.

Smedjebakken's surveyors came a dozen times and worked so carefully that, when it was done, it was done. Their great trouble in etching benchmarks and points, their repetitions, their heavy transits—five of them—all made perfect sense in the context of detecting a shift, in a large plane of rock, of only thousandths of a centimeter. No one suspected a thing, and yet when it was finished we had one of the most exact sets of measurements and one of the most perfect maps in the history of the world.

Three problems remained: mechanics, logistics, and timing.

We had to have the vinyl liner prefabricated in a swimming pool plant in New Jersey. They were intensely curious about us, wanting to know what we were going to do with a vinyl tube 6⁷⁄₁₆ inches in diameter and 128 feet long. We couldn't very well tell them that the distance from the floor of the Stillman and Chase vault to a point two feet above the platform of a gondola car in a siding below was 128 feet, and that by reconstructing a gold brick after a day of careful measurement, the purchase of a vast amount of gold jewelry (at that time, individuals were not allowed to hold gold except in jewelry, gold fillings, or antiques), fooling around with beeswax to make a mold, and burning ourselves in the refiner's fire, we had determined after many experiments that the lining had to be of precisely that diameter to rock the gold bar down 128 feet without either jamming it into the world's most expensive obstruction or delivering it with the speed of a gravity bomb.

When they asked us to explain the purpose of the thing in the blueprint—which, admittedly, looked exceedingly strange —we said, "We don't know."

Then we had to get an engine and 128 feet of bit into the subway, and position it in the right place. Fortunately, the siding from which we would drill was part of a 150-foot spur into which we could tuck everything we needed. Smedjebakken built a wall at the entrance and put a double iron door in it with a lightning-bolt encrusted DANGER: HIGH VOLTAGE sign. This immense compartment was for storing our equipment, and rock tailings from the bore hole. The doors were sealed with two Sheriff of Nottingham–style locks that were most forbidding.

The engine itself was a Swiss mining machine that made Smedjebakken flush with excitement. He had persuaded the Transit Authority to purchase it, and felt no guilt whatsoever about using taxpayers' money, because he told me that it would finally enable the city to take precision corings that would save immense amounts of engineering capital and, probably, lives. "Machines that do heavy work," he said, "are seldom precise, because they are put out of alignment upon initial contact with the medium for which they were designed. Also, the very mass of their components makes for extremely wide tolerances. If you want precision in a heavy machine you have two options—you can overengineer it, making it so huge and heavy that the medium doesn't knock it out of alignment, or you can design it to self-correct. That is, when it goes out of alignment, it readjusts.

"The former type of machine is too big for a subway tunnel. The latter is wickedly expensive, but that's what we've got. Because the components are not massive, they have to be un-usually strong. It's incredibly expensive just to make the alloys, and triply so for the casting and machinery. Once that's done, however, it's magnificent. The shaft on the Tinhoff engine is supported and directed by twelve cam assemblies—one every thirty degrees. Each cam has two teeth per minute of arc, both of which rest in a heavy molybdenum collar gear. When perfectly seated, they complete an electrical circuit. The contact is cali-brated to represent one-thirtieth of a minute of movement. If one of the cams rocks enough to break the circuit, the machine knows that it's going out of alignment, and pressure is exerted to reseat the cam tooth.

"It may be hard to visualize, but what it means is that the shaft is accurately supported to a second of arc, and that, when it goes out, it's immediately corrected. The Swiss invented this for drilling through mountain ranges in the construction of rail-way tunnels."

We started drilling early, before many other parts of the plan were in place. Smedjebakken hung a black velvet curtain under the rock before he aligned the shaft, explaining that he did not want to be subconsciously influenced by the angle of the ceiling. "You make allowances even without knowing it," he said, "Which is why justice must be blind."

As the drill bit pierced the black velvet and attacked the schist I thought of my former colleagues high above, smugly practicing their golf swings on antique carpets, yearning for the start of yachting season, and—if they ever thought of me—imagining that I was safely entombed hundreds of feet below them in the rock, laboring like a zombie.

At first we did five feet a day, but toward the end we slowed down to just a few inches. This was because we continually had to check and recheck the length and attitude of the shaft, and to do so we had to take down the drill and its many sections. In the very last days, we moved only an inch each session. When we were not working, late at night, on the actual drilling, we attended to many other tasks.

Smedjebakken constructed a number of specialized tools for the last section of the shaft. When he was sure that the hole was within one foot of the surface of the vault floor, he switched to a thin bit that ran on its own motor at the top of the extension rods. For ten days he lifted this into its tiny hole and pushed it ahead only a quarter of an inch from a spot he calculated to have been four inches below the surface. He was off only a little. On the ninth day, when I went into the cage in the morning, I saw a tiny black speck surrounded by a perfectly circular pile of marble dust no bigger than a polka dot.

It had come up almost precisely midway between the two alarm wires. I was so proud that I spent most of the morning singing and dancing behind my sheltering wall of gold, happy that we had taken the trouble to be exact. In all that suffering way, we were off by only ³⁄₁₆ths of an inch.

Smedjebakken had invented a circular milling apparatus that shaved the concrete and marble until it was the thickness of a pot cover. He had used the tiny drill hole as the center point for the milling, and I used it as my center point for a beveled compass cut in the marble. After five days of meticulous and quiet grinding, I freed the lid to discover that it lay on the shaft as tightly and evenly as a round in the chamber of a competition pistol.

I used a little bent prong to open this lid. When I peered inside, I couldn't see anything, but I could smell the air of the subway and hear distant trains rumbling across the underground prairies. The shaft led down at a slight angle all the way to the roof above the siding.

Next came the vinyl liner. Mounting took a week, with a full day just to glue the top to the sides of the shaft below the lid. At that point, we were ready to go, but we held back. We attended to our logistical arrangements and worried about the timing, for we wanted to get it just right.

From the time the shaft was in place, perfectly concealed, and ready to receive the gold bars, I was as dizzy as an upside-down baby. Although we hadn't planned to take all of it, at current prices the gold in Cage 47 was worth almost three billion dollars.

Immediately after the shaft was completed, something took hold of me that bridged the gulf between happiness and unhappiness. I thought at first that my sudden feelings of ebullience, optimism, and joy may have been due to my transit of the mid-century mark. But no one had ever said to me, 'When I passed fifty, I woke up and found that I was wonderfully happy.' Surely chronology was not the cause. Whatever happiness seized me far overshadowed revenge and easily eclipsed any thought of money. I don't care about money now.

The prospect of absconding with several billion dollars did, I confess, provide at least a little rapture, but no more than, say, getting back from escorting a bombing run. Perhaps that was it. I was young again, as if on the sea or in the air, made lively by having everything to lose and everything to gain, made content only by risk, for in the light of risk every earthly color catches heavenly fire. My woundedness after the divorce simply vanished, and instead of seeing women as part of a system of ropes and pulleys connected to Constance, they were reborn in my eyes with all the complex beauty and dignity I had understood before. After years in which I had forgotten love, I fell in love once again. It was, as usual, unrequited.

Two days after we completed the shaft, a group of Mexican bankers and treasury officials came to tour the vault. Previously, I would have received them upstairs and hosted a lunch in the small dining room. I would have taken them around to the various departments, and brought them down to the vault. Now Piehand, a fat preppy shitbird, did this.

As they passed my cage I hardly looked up, but then I smelled perfume and my head jerked like a whip. The instant I raised my eyes I saw a woman in profile. She was no older than twenty-six or twenty-seven, about half a foot taller than me, with a ramrod-straight back, wide soft shoulders, and the most regal bearing I had ever seen. Her long dark hair was tied behind her head, and, as she moved, it danced in a counterpoint that made me draw in my breath. I cannot describe the proportions of her face, the depth and joy in her eyes, the grace of her hands, the beauty of her walk. I guessed that though she might be easily hurt she was determined to see everything that she could see, and I felt that she wanted someone to be with her. She could hardly stand still: though she walked with natural dignity, it was clear that she wanted to dance.

I rose and pressed against the wire mesh. When she heard me, she turned. A woman like that would ordinarily have no truck with a man in a blue smock—a counter, a stacker, a returner to a one-room furnished flat—but I was so full of sudden love for her, so sure of myself, so risen from what I had been, that when I faced her through the wire she could not turn away.

For a moment I thought that I might be the man she wanted. I had magically blown away the barricades of class with my view into the future and my memory of the past, and with, dare I say it, love.

Her colleagues turned, and froze in puzzlement. I saw anger on the face of one, who, I imagine, was in the process of concluding that the only way I had kept her eyes and mine facing and flashing was by insulting her, and, being Latin, he may have been getting ready to spring to her defense.

I smiled and said, *"Buenos días,"* in an accent I had learned from Zorro. I was so cocksure that even my blue jacket felt like a swordsman's cape.

You should have seen her. She smiled, and her eyes came alight. I was separated from her by steel mesh, but I felt her in my arms. She stood too long and smiled too beautifully not to cause a stir. And then she turned away.

I could have sought her out that evening. Indeed I could have sought her out that afternoon, but, as I was fifty years of age, I thought about her father and her mother, and I saw it from their point of view: how terrible that their magnificent, world-conquering, heart-stopping daughter had run off with a North American bank robber. I neither found her nor grew less happy. Happiness was a flame that had come up within me, and though I could not explain it, I hoped that it would remain.

As gold is very heavy and rather conspicuous, and we had no assistance, we had given much thought to logistics. It was imperative that once the bullion was in our hands we could immediately lift it away to a safe place.

We bought an airplane, but, naturally, before we did that we bought a dairy farm in New Jersey. This may sound extravagant, but it wasn't. The land was a long rectangle of eighty acres, and had been worked only for a short time by a returning GI who had taken no account of the soil. Unfortunately for him, his cows produced milk with an onionlike taint, forcing him to sell it at a cut rate to a chemical factory that used it in making artists' colors.

As he slowly went under, the former soldier killed and butchered his herd. When he was left with only three or four animals, he tried to burn down his barn during a lightning storm, but the rain was so heavy that it put out the fire in such a way that the fire marshal was able to rule that lightning was not the cause. The insurance company paid him nothing, and he was left with a charred barn, three suspicious cows who gave onion milk, and eighty acres of land that had become a Van Gogh–like riot of dandelions.

He was asking $7,200, and we bought at $6,000, because his useless rectangle of dandelions was a serviceable airfield. After we had cleaned up the barn, repainted it, and put up a fence, we hung a sign that said RAMAPO MUSEUM OF FLIGHT.

I had stationery printed and opened a bank account in the name of Colonel Werner Guerney, USAAF Ret., and Smedjebakken became attaché Paul Coligny St. Maurice de Longpoint of the French Equatorial Africa Air Corps. It did not matter that he spoke not a word of French and could not pronounce his own name; we bought the airplane in Arizona, where they found his periodic exclamations in Swedish to be both very Gallic and very gallant. Whenever we encountered Air Force types in the course of tending the plane or the museum (which we neglected to open to the public) I was received very well as Colonel Guerney, for after my years as a fighter pilot I had an air of perfect authenticity. I never met anyone who knew me, perhaps because most of them were dead.

Drawing down my remaining financial reserves close to the point of freeing my spirit from my body, we bought a surplus C-54 that had been through the Second World War and Korea, but which, toward the end of the war in Korea, had been over-hauled in expectation of more years of fighting. It had four Pratt & Whitney R2000-11 engines, and could carry 30,000 pounds of cargo in 1,000-mile hops. This translated very neatly into 1,111 gold bars, which today would be worth about $325 million.

We bought landing strips in two directions from the Ramapo Museum of Flight, because we were going to take two loads to two different locations: one for Smedjebakken and one for me. We might have taken more than that, but we didn't want to be greedy. And I could remove 2,222 bars from the center of the pile, leaving what appeared to be a perfectly intact structure. The only way you could determine that it was hollow would be to look over the top, but because the cube went almost up to the ceiling of the vault, it was not possible for a human being to place his eyes high enough to see. The only way to realize that the core was empty was to unstack it. This was done every five or ten years, and I would have just finished that task prior to my departure.

I was surprised by how easy it was to buy landing strips. I think people in rural and desolate areas must regard the notion of someone buying their almost worthless land for a landing strip in the same way that the city people who sit on Coca-Cola cases in candy stores think of the Irish Sweepstakes. You say, "I'd like to buy your farm," and they immediately ask, "For a landing strip?" It may have had something to do with the way I dressed. As the proprietor of the Ramapo Museum of Flight I had to look authentic, so I sometimes wore a bomber jacket, flight cap and goggles, white scarf, and wrist chronometer (which, until I went into the Air Force, I used to call a *watch*).

I may still own some of the land I bought. The farm in the Ramapos was held under the name of Colonel Werner Guerney, as was the strip in Florida, on a snake-encrusted salt flat near Fort Myers that scared us to death because whenever the sea surged the runway was submerged.

The land I bought in Colombia, on the Península de la Guajira, is probably used by drug runners now. The owners, two bandits in a little town called Inusu, didn't even want to know my name. Besides, Smedjebakken was exceedingly uncomfortable in the outback of South America and we left before we had anything in writing, so it seems that what we paid was only key money.

The next stop, in a microscopic settlement called Boa Esperança, on the savannah near the Rio Branco, was actually in Brazil. There we bought a hundred acres for $45. A thousand miles further on, in the town of Alto Parnaíba, we bought another hundred acres for another $45, more or less, and so it went. The only person who knows the last stop is Funio, who doesn't know that he knows. Marlise might know, but I doubt it. At one very crucial point in our family history, she was probably thinking about some French or Rumanian acrobat, while Funio and I were fixed on something quite different. I promised Marlise not to tell Funio about the gold, but I didn't promise not to refer to fond memories that Funio and I share, did I?

Never have I seen a bird more completely out of water than Smedjebakken pretending to be a French Equatorial air attaché traveling in the forgotten interior of Brazil. His Swedish face was always so florid that I had to check periodically to make sure he was not being squeezed to death by a boa constrictor. Once, as we were being paddled up a cool tributary of the Amazon by two male Indians who looked exactly like my Aunt Louise and smelled like fried chicken, Smedjebakken's straw hat was lifted by a gust of unexpected wind and propelled through brilliant blue air until it fell onto the mirrorlike surface of the river. "Goddamit!" Smedjebakken screamed. The sun in his hair made him look like a medieval painting of an apostle with an electrified halo. "I'll die without my hat." He turned to the Indians: "Hatto! Hatto! Get hatto!"

They were perplexed, but by resorting to a combination of pantomime and bastardized Portuguese I conveyed the message. The problem was that the hatto was headed for a fork in the river that the Indians called "The Clouds of No Return." I pointed this out to Smedjebakken, and his response, which I remember vividly, was, "I don't give a fuck!"

The Indians observed his gesticulations and angry commands, and were perplexed. In their culture anger and urgency did not exist. Even conflict did not exist. They were in complete and hypnotic harmony with nature, and there is much we can learn from their gentle ways. For example, if they felt the need, they would calmly and gently shoot you with a poison arrow, butcher you, eat you, and shrink your head. They knew neither anxiety nor angst, and you simply could not get them riled up. Even as Smedjebakken was venting his hysteria they stood back in a kindly, curious fashion, like matrons looking into a meat case.

Nor did they seem to fear death, taking the canoe perilously close to a point in the river where we could feel invisible rubber bands pulling us downstream with the same attractive force that greets you beyond the rail of a bridge over black water. Perhaps they were unafraid because they lived with the knowledge that at any moment they might meet the basting brush, but whatever the source of their fatalism they kept paddling with such precision and verve that their muscles swelled and the air was just like the air in front of Nathan's at Coney Island. Even without speaking, they seemed to say that the choice was ours, but as Smedjebakken watched his hat bump and twist over increasingly

Homeric waters, he lost his enthusiasm for the chase. "Let's just go on," he said quietly. "I don't need it."

"*Avanti!*" I commanded, as if I were in an Italian hotel room and a messenger had arrived with my newly shined shoes. Luckily for us, in their language this did not mean, "Let's do it," and we soon found our way back to the sunny drudgery of rhythmic paddling in a green infinity.

Smedjebakken didn't like the food in the hardscrabble settlements because it was so difficult and dangerous, but I loved it. We would sit in the glow of a brazier just after sunset, sipping warm beer from brown bottles with no labels, as a man who had not shaved since the Battle of Hastings grilled what he claimed were tapir kabobs. These we had sizzling hot, drowned in a red pepper sauce that the devil had used to paint his Bentley.

With our eyes opened wide as if by laboratory grapples, sweat pouring from our bodies, and our stomachs screaming in despair, we would eat this personification of fire, guzzle warm beer, and try to deal with a bean dish for which the recipe began, "Take one bean and a thousand pounds of garlic. . . ."

Swaying and moaning, we would almost inevitably fall off our rickety wood chairs and collapse the tables upon which lay the food with which we did battle. But I loved this, I loved it even when we spent the night screaming in agony as tiny German scientists in our stomachs repeatedly built and blew up the Hindenburg. I loved it because it was so difficult, and because things that are difficult are good.

Smedjebakken looked at it differently. After all, he was used to eating golden rusks, cloud-white milk, and perfectly sugary lingonberries. He said, "I think, I think you like this, and I think you're crazy. I think *I'm* crazy for letting you pick the restaurants. Every time we eat, it's the Second Battle of the Marne."

"There's only one restaurant in this town," I told him, happily hallucinating with stomach pain. "There's only one building."

Every night, I "chose" the restaurant, and every night it was the same. Our stomachs were like soldiers in a winter battle, and to this day I remember the struggle so clearly that it is as if time had stopped still. Even the lizards would line up just beyond the light of the fire, watching to see how we would fare. Olé!

In Rio we took stomach drugs. I opened a bank account, found an apartment, and set things up so carefully that I began to get nervous. The apartment was small and elegant, its living room giving out onto a terrace that was expertly planted with miniature citrus trees, coastal pines, and geraniums. Their scent was enough to make anyone crazy with happiness, and I was equally pleased to be able to hear the waves rolling gently against the beach. After I had had bookshelves built in the living room, I went on a spree at the English bookstore. I still have today everything I bought then—the pocket version (you'd have to have clown-sized pockets) of the *Britannica*'s Eleventh Edition, the complete *O.E.D.*, sacred texts, Greek tragedy, Homer, Dante, Shakespeare, dictionaries, foreign encyclopedias, the great works of history, Clausewitz, *The Collected Poems of W.B. Yeats*, the 'Old Testament' in Hebrew, the *Commedia* of Dante in Italian, the works of Pagnol, which I value over those of Colette or Proust, and 495 other books.

If at the stone balcony rail you were not overcome by upwelling scent, you could see the surf, the white sand, and hundreds of half-nude recumbent women lying in the sun. On clear nights the stars came up in quiet brilliance, and when the moon was full it made a mother-of-pearl highway across the bay, lighting the waters to either side with a glow that revealed swells driven shoreward by warm wind.

My kitchen was well stocked and deliberately primitive: it was open to the courtyard in the back, like a balcony, and the drain was in the floor. I had a desk, a lamp, a filing cabinet, and a shelf with stationery, but no telephone.

"What are you going to do here?" Smedjebakken asked as we sat in the light of a fading afternoon.

"Why do you ask?"

"It's too good. You'll die. You know, the way they do in Florida."

"I'll figure out a challenge."

"Like what?"

"Like eradicating all the coffee plants in Brazil."

"You can't do that, and you know it."

"You're right."

"Then what will you do?"

"Just live."

"No such thing," Smedjebakken said. "You have to have something from which you can plan to escape."

"Memories."

"You can't escape them."

"Maybe I'll get married and have children, and I can start over. Meanwhile I'll read, go to the beach, and try to keep thin."

"You're as thin as a thread."

"After two weeks of tapir kabobs, anyone would be as thin as a thread. But that can't last forever, and we are of an age where we tend to get chubby."

"I don't care," Smedjebakken said. "I'm a family man. I don't have to worry about twenty-year-old girls who want me to look like a galley slave."

"What are you going to do?"

"You know what I'm going to do. You were with me."

"Only as far as Scotland."

"We go in a boat from Glen Larne. Then we disappear."

On the morning of the day it was done, I awoke in the house in Astoria knowing I would never see New York again. In some ways this was a blessing, and in some ways not. I have heard —and seen in photographs and films—that the city has lost its civility. It was always a difficult place, but its inhabitants knew to compensate for that with a rough sincerity and warmth that I left in full bloom, never imagining for a second that it would or could vanish.

On my last ride on the RR train I looked almost as lovingly at the faces and expressions of my fellow passengers as if I were staring at a photograph of times long past. They did not know that they made a photograph. They did not understand the vanishing background of their lives: the breeze that rustles the leaves in Union Square and Central Park, and the sunshine reflecting hotly from a meadow of golden windows; the valleys of rooftop water tanks; the spiderwork fire escapes; the vanishing wakes of ferries and tugs that churn across the harbor and leave drift lines of the whitest snow even in the hottest summer. They seemed so completely unaware of these monuments, markers, and memorials.

I loved the city. My blood was there, my family. I had left it and come back so many times that what I felt for it must have been love. I had seen it in wartime, I had seen it rich and kinetic and enraptured, I had seen it in gun-metal gray after a blizzard, and I had seen it in the Depression, when the streets were filled with wood fires like the roads leading from medieval cities—all quiet, expectant, waiting for a ray of light, as humble and perfect as a young child.

I had seen all this and loved it, and now I was on my way. I was saddened as I took in thousands of scenes that I would leave behind, but I knew the value of a final moment that comes like a sword-cut across the fibers of time. Though alarmingly quick, it gives eternal life to all that seems abruptly lost. And it makes for devotion, something that simply does not exist in busy undamaged lives that are allowed to play out according to plan.

When I went into the bank the electricity I felt crackling around in me was like a thunderstorm viewed from 40,000 feet, in which the lightning never ceases and its flashes dance like raindrops on a sun-saturated pond. I was afraid I would set off the alarms.

It was not enough merely to have engaged Oscovitz on the subjects of kissing and existentialism. I left the cage and went back out to him. When he saw me coming, he cringed.

"Sherman," I said, "Gorilla Boy sends his regards."

"Who?" Oscovitz asked.

"Gorilla Boy."

"Gorilla Boy who?"

"Gorilla Boy, O.B.E."

"I don't know what you're talking about," said Oscovitz, beginning to go into the mode of retreat to which he resorted when I was seized by moods he could not fathom.

"Gorilla Boy says: L, put suntan lotion on your head; B, open your heart to the love of a woman who loves you; F, learn to gallop a horse and cut pumpkins in half with a samurai sword; and, E, when you're happy, throw a kiss to the suckling pig in the meat case at Aiello's."

"Who *is* Gorilla Boy?" he demanded with unusual firmness.

With my thumb, I pointed to my chest. "*I* am, Sherman, *I* am. I'm Gorilla Boy. I work for you. Gorilla Boy . . . works for you. And today, Gorilla Boy is going to finish stacking Cage Forty Seven."

"Good, good," he said. "Tomorrow you can start stacking Cage Forty Eight."

This, for him, was a fairly big moment, and I believe he believed I believed it was a fairly big moment. I smiled like a Cheshire cat and danced back into Cage 47, and when the gate clicked shut behind me I heard the great sound of the shotgun starters on my four holy engines and I saw the sky stretching away in a lovely round carpet of baby blue and cotton balls.

I had planned the exact procedure for shifting the walls, emptying the center, dropping the bars, and rebuilding the outer perimeter. When the process was completed, the almost invisible shaft cap that I had cut into the marble floor would be covered by tons of gold, and Cage 47 probably would not be revisited for years.

Never have I enjoyed physical labor more than when I spent eight seamless hours feeding gold bars into the modest but voracious mouth of the shaft Smedjebakken had built. After a few hundred bars I was sure that Smedjebakken was down on the siding, receiving them. If he hadn't been, they would have backed up.

Four hundred more and I began to feel the strain, but the more strain I felt the more I caught fire. I felt waves of delight generated by the great exercise. My muscles tightened and burned like those of a moving man on overtime, and I wondered if the next day I would be able to fly the C-54 to Newfoundland as we had planned.

"Cage Forty Seven is finished," I told Oscovitz.

"Oh, good, uh . . . Gorilla Boy," Oscovitz said. "Tomorrow, you start on Forty Eight."

"No, Sherman," I said, soberly, seriously, quietly. My words felt to me like machetes cutting through a choking jungle beyond which lay the open sea.

"No?"

"No, Sherman."

"Why not?"

I hesitated. And then I said, gently, "Sherman, you'll never see me again." I smiled, turned, and walked to the elevator.

It was hurricane season. Baseball games were rained out, beach houses boarded up, and bobbing boats tethered in vain to docks that would flip in the wind. I had tried to convince Smedjebakken to delay the flights out, but he had to meet a schedule.

Whereas I had gone into the details of resettlement myself, he, being more adept at dealing with people, more trusting, and better reconciled to working within an organization, had delegated the tasks upon which I broke my teeth trying to fill out forms in Portuguese and waiting for an hour and a half in the post office line with office boys who read dime novels, talked about baseball, and ate shrimp candy. I have always hated Brazilian sugared shrimp: they smell almost as bad as coffee. But the worst candy is Chinese pigeon cakes. I took a bite of one once in Singapore and was hospitalized for a week.

Smedjebakken traveled to a European city and found a leading citizen to whom he offered this proposition. He wanted citizenship and new identities for himself, his wife, and his daughter. He wanted a château near the capital city, privately situated in its own huge park. He wanted extensive modifications made to the house, including an indoor swimming pool. He wanted a capable and trustworthy staff, a summer house by the seacoast, several automobiles registered in his new name, and a modest but elegant pied-à-terre in a pleasant neighborhood of the capital. And he wanted the protection of the government, were he to require it, indefinitely.

"Are you a dictator? I don't know you," was the response.

This question was easily answered, but the next, which made Smedjebakken hesitate, was, "Are you a criminal?"

"This country, the name of which I cannot divulge," Smedjebakken told me, "is a land of moral *philosophes*. Schoolchildren there learn categories of morality the way schoolchildren in America learn about Indians. So I said to him, 'Morally, I am not a criminal, for I have appropriated a vast amount of wealth from an *immoraliste*. I am as innocent as Saint Francis of Assisi.'

" 'Saint Francis of Assisi?' was the reply. It was, after all, a strange comparison.

" 'And anyone who aids me is a *moraliste* of the highest order. Those who aid me will receive not only just compensation, but a certain measure of glory, too.' "

Smedjebakken said that the man to whom he spoke inhaled until his chest swelled like a squab. He was quick to agree, and he was ruthless in setting a fee.

At today's gold price Smedjebakken's new start cost him $35 million, of which $10 million went to the squab, but it was well worth it. Assuming he held onto the gold, he now has at least $250 million for groceries, so he needn't have sought a bargain for refuge.

I'm somewhat different. I have to do everything myself, and I'm a big saver, which is why I have about $324 million left, even if it is hidden in a difficult place. I wanted to do what Smedjebakken did, but I was too well known in European circles and was forced to flee to the Antipodes, where no one knew me and everything was confusingly upside down.

As payments had to be made, officials bribed, a château made ready, and a swimming pool built, Smedjebakken needed to get the gold across the Atlantic during hurricane season. But September is the best time to cross the North Atlantic, where hurricanes appear only in such a deracinated form that they seem to be nothing more than an apparatus for keeping dwindling icebergs moist with dew.

For me, the season was somewhat more perilous. Immediately after I returned from Glen Larne I would have to load the plane and get to Fort Myers, across the Caribbean, to the Amazon, and beyond. The plane would be carrying its maximum load and no reserves of fuel, which meant no going around storms, no vaulting above them, and a hell of a time punching through them.

In the evening I met Smedjebakken for a strengthening dinner before loading the bullion from a Transit Authority maintenance train onto a flatbed truck at the end of an unused subway spur in Washington Heights. We had always eaten well at the air museum—venison, fresh corn, tomatoes, spinach, basil, clam broth—but on this occasion decided to have egg creams and boiled beef sandwiches.

We sat at the counter of a delicatessen on 100th Street and Broadway, a neighborhood I knew well from my days as a runner. The owner, a lifelike copy of Otto Preminger, never ventured more than four feet from us, so we had to speak in code.

"Did you get the brassieres?" I asked Smedjebakken.

"Yeah," he said. "Every single one of them."

"Did anyone see?"

"Not a soul. I thought I would die taking them out of the tube. My muscles are cramped. What about you?"

"I'm okay, but, don't forget, I was just dropping them down the hole."

I could see that Otto Preminger was drawn to what we were

saying by an increasingly powerful force. He was trying to conceal his interest by polishing a glass and staring off into space, ears cocked. Hardly a worry, as there was no way he could have known what we were talking about.

"Where are the brassieres now?" I asked Smedjebakken.

"Safe in the tunnel."

"We'll move them after dark."

"Why not just go whenever we get there?" Smedjebakken asked.

"New Jersey state troopers are notoriously suspicious, and they saturate the roads. In the daytime, especially in the light of sunset, the brassieres will shine with a diffuse glow. Better to move them at night."

"I sure as hell hope we don't have a flat tire," Smedjebakken said. "I don't think there's a jack alive that could lift the truck. We'd have to unload every single brassiere and pile it by the side of the highway."

"Don't worry," I told him. "By this time tomorrow evening, you'll be deep in the forests of Newfoundland."

I was not very good at flying multiengine planes. In fact, before the C-54, I had never flown one. I read a few manuals and thought about it a lot before we flew back to New Jersey, but you really have to learn this kind of thing incrementally, practicing the maneuvers at the behest of an experienced instructor. Unfortunately, I had to do everything at once and for the first time.

We were certain that we were going to die on takeoff when the plane stupidly battered the runway with its left wing tip. By that time, I was so out of practice flying even single-engine planes that I thought wing tips were shoes.

Landing wasn't so great, either. Never have I bounced as I

did on the dandelion-strewn airstrip of the Ramapo Museum of Flight, and I dreaded putting the plane down when it was fully loaded. Nonetheless, at risk of our lives, Smedjebakken and I refused to leave behind even one brick. We had set ourselves a task, and the money was not the issue but rather a sense of completeness. Most thieves would probably have found our attitude incomprehensible.

All our numbers had to be remarkable or round, all our times exact. Perhaps people who have never stolen anything think that you steal because you want something. That isn't so. You steal for the same reason that you would otherwise work or dare— and, trust me, stealing is work. You steal for the same reason that an ice-skater practices for the Olympics, a composer composes, or a truck driver strives to cut his time.

It is exactly the same spark that keeps factories running around the clock, that moved John Henry to take on a steam hammer, that makes a sled dog run happily for ten hours in cold that freezes smoke. It's what makes machines sing and your blood flow.

I refer not to taking someone's wallet or breaking into a house and pulling out all the drawers to find S&H Green Stamps. Nor to selling Bensonhurst retirees Florida land covered by water in which alligators swarm like maggots. Nor to endangering perfectly innocent people by walking into a bank with a necklace of dynamite. My definition of stealing is knocking over the Louvre, Fort Knox, the Tower of London, or the Antwerp Central Diamond Vaults.

All the rest is for termites. And, I ask you, what did you expect? Was I supposed to forget what I had seen and what I had done? I attacked Berlin when Hitler was still in it. I fled from a Swiss mental institution to run away with a woman I still love even though she is dead, and we went to the Arctic

Circle and stood at the foot of the aurora. I was once one of the richest men in the world, and once a kid who worked hard and saved his money for a sugared donut and some sheet music. I fought alongside the angels high above the earth where the air is as thin as helium and defeat is an exploding sun. I have tightened my grip and narrowed my eyes, rushing toward gunfire like gravity. I have been in a great army that took years to conquer half the world. I have sailed across the ocean, rocketed into the clouds, skimmed the Hudson and cut apart its lily pads with my propeller, and I have seen the demise of nations, and new nations arise.

Why not the Louvre, then? All it is is a big building full of the most brilliant reflections of what we know day by day, the great and the small. Had this been a quiet century and had my country been a backwater, perhaps I would have been more easily contented, but the world was swept by great and terrible things, and I was at the heart of them.

They were like the force that lights the aurora, stiffening and firing a host of insignificant particles into a fiery curtain. In times of greatness, every man becomes a king, which is the price paid by kings when they cannot stay the energies that keep them on their thrones.

So, we carried all of the bullion, even at risk to our lives, because it was important not to leave anything scattered behind. What we did cannot be justified except to say that it was much like music, where no theory can explain pleasure or depth, where mathematics cannot elucidate intractable beauty, but where, when things come together, they make a perfection understood by all.

And so it was that when I took off one humid unsettled morning when tall fat clouds drifted on winds that polished great patches of moist blue, I was happy. For me, and for Smedjebakken, what we had done meant not riches and not revenge, but daring and faith. And as we rose into the turbulent air, we were inexplicably moved.

I set a northeast course, and we flew on alone toward the blue-green forests of Newfoundland. Soon the Hudson narrowed to a small silver cord, and the broad lands through which it flowed, where I had grown up, were covered with cloud.

1914

(If you have not done so already,
please return the previous pages to the antproof case.)

THE NAVAL ACADEMY has released me from its employment. While I was in the hospital, Watoon took over my classes. With more than double the teaching load he was used to, and no one to whom he could turn for help in the language, he suffered a kind of nervous breakdown. Unable to carry on, he turned to his holy book, the Watoon English phraseology, and forced his students to drill from it directly.

During this time, the English ambassador, a dignified and imposing figure, toured the academy. When he was ushered into Watoon's class, he signaled that it should continue as if he were not there—and it did, for a while. Though it must have been peculiar, ambassadors are used to such things. Then Watoon pushed his luck.

"Phrase to greet English person from England!" he shouted at his charges.

"Blow me!" they chanted in unison.

"Blow me, what?" he asked, turning his head and cupping his hand to his ear.

"Blow me, English shitbird," they shouted, without the slightest idea of what they were saying.

"Say again to our guest. Stand up to show."

They all stood up, faced the stunned ambassador, and shouted, "Blow me, English shitbird!"

The ambassador turned to the commandante, who was smiling placidly, and, realizing that he was on his own, shot a fierce glance at Watoon.

To which Watoon responded, with an expression of absolute innocence and a huge grin, "Suck my ass."

That, of course, was the end of Watoon. And it was also the end of me. Trying to save himself, Watoon told the commandante that I had taught him everything in the holy book, and because the commandante had known for years that Watoon ran to me for help at every opportunity, I was fired, too.

Even had I the energy to contest this in the Brazilian naval courts it would have been immaterial. The academy has replaced us with two Englishmen who, I am told, speak beautifully and are expert at teaching English as a second language. Quite frankly, I think the cadets will have a great deal of difficulty trying to say words like *air*, which they will now have to pronounce "A, ah," but their problems are minor compared to mine.

I was pensioned off with a weekly stipend sufficient to buy a mango, two aspirins, and a postage stamp. I have the gold, but am physically unable to get it, and, quite apart from that, I have always believed that immense wealth would change Marlise for the worse. Great riches are like a tiger—beautiful, captivating, and, once you find them, they eat you. They even ate Constance, and Marlise at her best is less alert than Constance after a magnum or two of champagne.

Funio, for all his brilliance, wouldn't be able to retrieve a single bar or even reach the place where it rests. He will have to be a lot older and a lot bigger, and I gave my word of honor to Marlise that I would tell him neither where the gold lies nor even that we have it. Marlise knows about the tiger, and she doesn't want it to eat her child.

I myself am no longer strong enough, and I trust no one, because I know no one to trust. And what would I do with riches except to prolong a life that is saying to me more and more every day that it has reached its natural end? If I die I'll cheat the assassins of their chance to kill me. But should they manage to find me before I die, their bullets will bring me sublime satisfaction.

I'm in the garden in Niterói. Once again, it is early morning. It has just rained. The blue waves beneath me, silent at this height, are once again drawing me in. The flower beds are steaming, and I am the only one here. Sometimes I wonder what the purpose has been of all the years since 1914. I should have died then. I wanted to. I was nine years old when my time came, and I have lived ever since with immense sorrow. Death, for me, will be like the most comforting sleep.

I used to have a picture of my father as an army officer in the Philippines during the Spanish-American War. He was kneeling on one knee, flanked by two Filipino soldiers. The three of them were looking at a sand map on the ground, and though the Filipinos steadied themselves with rifles, my father didn't. He was wearing wire spectacles, and clenching a pipe in his teeth. Someone must have said something amusing, because the three of them were laughing. It was neither a polite, nervous laugh nor the kind that is so strong it makes you close your eyes and change your position, but, still, it was happy, fully realized. In fact, they looked just about as happy and healthy as anyone can. In all my eighty years I have never seen anyone quite so relaxed, so strong, and so content. As a child I used to stare at this photograph and dream that I would grow up to know the same feelings as these men crouching in the dirt, and at times, I suppose, I have, but never so well as had my father, before I was born, and this I could tell by the marvelous expression on his face.

The picture of my mother was much different, although it was taken at approximately the same time. Looking at the camera from a gazebo near the pier of a resort island in Lake Erie, she was standing tall and straight in a white Victorian dress and straw boater with ribbons, her dark hair cascading about her sunburnt face. She never would have been considered pretty, because she was too tall and her features were unusual, but her face had so much in it and her expression was so complex and full of life that she was, in fact, a great beauty. The ideal woman at the time was chubby, weak, and round, and she was angular, thin, and strong. She would do better today, but even so she would not meet the thoughtless standards that in matters of beauty so often prevail.

As a child I would consider these photographs, convinced that I would have neither the strength and vitality of my father nor the luck of meeting a woman like my mother. . . . And then a bolt of wonderful lightning would strike me and pleasantly ricochet as I realized that, because I was my father's and mother's son, I did have a chance, after all, of growing into their strengths and graces.

The photographs became icons. One glance was enough to suffuse me with memory and love, a careful study made me forget the present, and a profound meditation transported me in time until I did not know if, in fact, I had ever left them.

I treasured the images beyond all measure. I had wanted them with me when I was buried or burned, so that they and I would go together, whether by slow oxidation or quick fire. But I lost them when I landed in Brazil. They were taken by the rushing water, the water dissolving, the water flowing and full of oxygen.

I was born haplessly at the end of December, 1904. I have always believed, though perhaps illogically, that children born at the height of summer, when light floods the world, prefer summer and all that is bright, and that children born in the darkest days merely dread the cold and dark. Though at times I have loved winter when it is dry and the sun and the moon shine across broad snowfields, in the main I shrink from it. In winter I was never warm enough. Our house did not have central heating, and not only did I dislike servicing the wood stove, I resented that when a passage in a book or a problem in a text seized my attention it meant that one half of me would roast and the other half freeze. Winter with a wood stove was like being on the moon: there was fire and there was ice, and there was nothing in between.

My birthday and Christmas were Siamese twins. Faced with this coincidence, my parents would simply invest as much in a single present as they might otherwise have spent on two. But this was no consolation for me. I was a child, and I innocently wanted everything.

Of course, I never got everything, but my greatest present came in January, when the light began to strengthen and each day was longer, when Christmas and birthday presents were forgotten in favor of the signs of the whole world brightening. Even in February, the month of despair, when increasing light is hidden by increasing cloud, a month that, in my experience, has never been as crystalline as the one that precedes it; and even in March, the month of betrayal, when storms and wind fight the coming of the light; and even in April, with its well known cruelties and too much rain—even in the winter that remained, playing itself out slowly, the light grew stronger in a brilliant crescendo.

Long before June my broken heart had healed and the world seemed buoyant. We lived on the Hudson, and to reach the river (as I could do at incredible speed), you had to cross two very beautiful sun-drenched fields and go down a steep path through an oak wood, pass over a stone dam and leap across the gap that made the spillway, descend another small hill, and weave through a grove of tall reeds out onto the track bed of the New York Central Railroad. Only beyond the rails did the beach open to a vast bowl of water and distant mountains. The river's main channel, through which plied sailing ships and steamboats in all but the darkest winter months, ran in the distance over miles of water or ice.

My speed increased as I grew older and stronger and years of practice taught me every angle, every foothold, every slope. I could launch myself over trees that had fallen across the path, either the right or left leg extended, depending upon where in my stride I took off, without sight of the other side, for after thousands of runs I knew it exactly. This gave to my transit from house to river an appearance of recklessness. As I became more and more capable I ran faster, I took longer strides, and I sailed higher and higher over the obstructions in my way.

Sometimes I frightened myself when my limbs, knowing better than I both the path and what they could do, stretched longer and pushed harder than my intent. Sometimes, it seemed, I was suspended in the air for so long that I flew.

I would dream at night of leaving the path and never alighting.

This dream seemed more real than life itself, so I directed my efforts at learning how to fly—not by gliding or being lifted by a balloon, but as a kind of human projectile, an arrow loosed from rails of grace and strength. I was nine and a half years old. It was the summer of 1914.

Though many now believe that this was the last innocent summer the world would ever experience, theirs is the view of a younger generation that did not have the opportunity to know, as I did, the soldiers of the Civil War. How innocent were the men of Gettysburg or Chancellorsville? The only innocence the world has ever known has been the innocence of Eden, of Woodrow Wilson's understanding of foreign affairs, and in the hearts of each new wave of children. In 1914, not everyone lived as buoyantly as I did, and I knew it.

By the fourth of June, 1914, a Thursday, I was no longer bound in winter clothes that were not warm enough anyway, no longer a prisoner of mud and slush on my five-mile walk to school, too young for finals, and, with the summer ahead, unusually happy. Because the teachers were needed to proctor exams for the older grades, academic classes were over, and the younger children spent most of the day outside. That was fine with me.

My regal afternoon of damming up the brook—it was my generation that went on to flood half of Tennessee—came to an abrupt end when we were called inside for shop. Our teacher was a retired Marine major who had been at the Battle of Mobile Bay. He was a master mechanic and a natural archivist, and hanging from the rafters or on the walls of the huge loft where he taught were a Wright-Brothers-type flying machine, an Eskimo kayak, a used stuffed tiger, and hundreds of lesser things such as boomerangs, Gatling guns, Egyptian cutlery, Japanese kitchen utensils, masks, swords, paintings of whales hauled onto the beach, and an immensely heavy pendulum that defied the expediencies of the earth's rotation and held its place faithfully with reference only to the infinite.

The Major was a good and irascible man who made us pray before operating our machines. In the mechanics loft the whole class would clasp its hands and bow heads in silence as shafts of sunlit dust worked slowly to divide the room into perfect sections, and lost bees dashed through the light like drops of melting gold. Our prayer was simple: we asked that, in making something, we would not become enamored of our own powers, and we prayed that we would not cut off our fingers.

The machines were dangerous: band saws, circular saws fit for the Perils of Pauline, presses and cutters that could relieve a child of his extremities as quickly as a frog's tongue summoning a mosquito and with no more remorse. Today, children would not be allowed close to such hazards, but at the time machines like these were the promise of the future, their powers still not cloaked in shadows of malevolence. And, then, a notable local problem was that many hands had more fingers than they were supposed to have had, anyway.

The Major didn't want the children in his charge to have their hands chopped off, so in addition to prayers he had a strategy. He used coffee, or, more specifically, coffee beans, which he kept in a white paper cup upon which were drawn a skull and crossbones. Because he was accustomed to scanning the vast prairies of the sea from the bridges of naval vessels, and to sighting enemies on land as they peeped at him from deep thickets, not much escaped his attention.

He would watch the whole class at once as he stood smoking a Cuban cigar, and if he saw a child with his hands in the wrong position, or another about to whisk an obstruction from under a seething blade, he would haul back on a huge lever to disengage the overhead shafts from which leather belts descended to clasp flywheels attached to the drives of each machine.

Having saved the violator's fingers, he would then proceed to save his soul, which is how, on the fourth of June, 1914, I was commanded to approach the skull-and-crossbones cup.

The Major addressed me with the special formality he reserved for young children: he would call us "Miss Adams," or "Mr. Bernstein," and, if he wanted to point to an element in our character, "Dr. Smith," "Professor Alford," "General Osborne," or "Reverend Antrobus." He mocked us, but gently, and his tone was always that of encouragement and respect, as if he could see into the future.

I knew I was in trouble when he addressed me as "Inmate," and summarized my transgression, at first, in a Southern African language he had learned as an observer with the British Army, and into which he would lapse only when he was annoyed. I don't even know what language it was, much less what he said, but it came fast and furiously and it sounded like: "*Satto cooca satibelay, amandooka helelay pata pata. Desanday nooca, gezingay po walela. Soocowelay demandica coomanda. Ma me rotsuna contaga tu ay vaca doganda.*" It was like Italian with a lot of clicks, and it mesmerized us.

As I stood before the skull-and-crossbones cup, the other children gathered in silence as if to witness my execution. At the end of my indictment in the African language that—as far as I know—the Major may have made up, I was jolted by the question, in English, "Well, what do you have to say for yourself?"

"What did I do?" I asked.

"You tell us," he commanded.

"I don't know."

"Didn't I just tell you?"

"When?"

"Just now."

"Yes."

"So, tell us."

"Okay," I said, twisting up my face to free my memory. *"Satto cooca?"*

"Yes, go on."

"Satto cooca satibelay, amandooka helelay pata pata. Desanday nooca, gezingay po walela. Soocowelay demandica coomanda. Ma me rotsuna contaga tu ay vaca doganda."

"Fine," said the Major, "but *I* didn't do it, so don't accuse *me*."

"I'm sorry."

"Brown, green, brown," he announced, passing sentence.

From having witnessed other executions, I knew what to do. I reached into the paper cup and pulled out a brown coffee bean. These, I had heard, were somewhat more tolerable than the green.

There it was, between my fingers, a partly cloven bean of an earth-brown color, obviously very tough and dry. This was the stuff that grownups drank when they got up in the morning and so they could digest their meals. Even if it were not yet processed into the popular drink, I imagined that it might not be that bad. At the grocery store I had seen a glass jar filled with coffee beans coated with chocolate. If they were actually candy, how dreadful could they be? Perhaps my classmates who in this same situation had retched and bent double were simply oversuggestible. I wasn't worried at all. I had always been able to do things that other children could not. My father had taught me some sort of Hindu technique for shunting pain to a siding, where, although I felt it, it seemed to have little to do with me but was rather like a phenomenon I was observing in someone else.

Because of this and other predilections I knew how to weather assaults and had unusual self-discipline. My perfect self-control led the dentist to think that I was a midget. I lived in a converted stable, a wonderful place that was, however, infested with very large rats that we called "beef rats." Early on, I learned to kill them with a hoe or a poker, which was neither easy nor without risk, as they fought back. These weren't little chicken croquettes with legs, but the size of guinea pigs and small cats. Combat with them taught me fortitude, as did the lack of central heating in our house, the ten miles I walked every day to and from school, and the regular beatings I received when I passed through the tough parts of town.

What did I have to fear from a little bean, I, who could be silent while a dentist used his hand drill—on me—without anesthesia, I, who had been ripped to pieces in a mill accident and was sewn back together with hundreds of deeply driven stitches, again, without anesthesia? This bean was treasured around the world. It was eaten as candy.

I put it into my mouth and began to chew slowly, like a cow. In the first seconds I tasted nothing, and an expression of pompous mastery crept across my face. But as soon as the bean began to take possession of my mouth, my eyes widened and I breathed through my nose the way you do when you are just about to crash into something. I thought instantaneously of my parents' occasional disparaging remarks about coffee, and I wondered why they, tea drinkers, had not been more emphatic.

A bitter rivulet grew into a net of streams that crossed my tongue like a river fractionating across a delta or lightning cracking the blue-black glass of the sky. I was too shy to retch or bend double, so I simply let myself suffer, accepting the hideous internal contamination with each gasping swallow.

Then came the green, which was many times more powerful than the brown. I had known pain, but I had never known bitterness. Bitterness, it seemed to me, as much as I could feel or think at the time, was like the body and soul turning upon themselves, and I had never experienced that. Though tears poured from my eyes, I stood straight and proud, in absolute silence. I fought the bitterness by not bending, and in not bending I thought I had won. But I hadn't, because I had failed to understand that this was just a sign, a precursor.

It has been a long time since I have had a conversation with anyone who knows cold weather, the change of seasons, the coming of spring, the glory of summer, the dark of Christmas, and landscapes of blue and white. A city of the tropics with 200,000 people per square mile is somewhat different from a place where it is commonly ten below zero and there are fewer than twenty people per square mile. If I could import the silence, cold, and tranquility of my youth to Rio I would be the richest man in Brazil. Of course, I may already be the richest man in Brazil.

Over the years I've spoken to many Americans who come here and I sometimes mention that my father was a farmer. I've noticed that the more that time passes the more they stare at me like deer paralyzed by an arc light. They don't yet ask, "What's a farmer," but most of them have never met one.

To me, farming is more important than the simple sum of its parts. In some ways, it's like raising a child. You must work, and plan, and suffer the chances of what comes. You sow, you reap, and you keep a palm on the earth and an eye to the weather. Intellectuals tell me right off that my recollections of early life have been romanticized by time, but I remember many things that they could not possibly know, and I have full confidence in these things, because I have lived them.

Eventually, we were driven from our farm, and though times became increasingly difficult while we were there, it was the best life I can imagine. The closest I have seen to what I knew then is the existence of the coastal fishermen here. They go out on the sea day after day to pull in magnificent fighting fish that they sell or eat. Though they will never be rich, they will never be separated from the beauty of the sea. They practice an intricate craft in which reside secrets and lessons as old as the world. And the world can twist and turn as it wishes, while what they do remains.

We had seventy acres on a plateau above the Hudson north of Ossining. Flat land so close to the river was rare, and this was especially pretty land, with huge oaks standing in ravines between the fields, and views of the mountains and river. We grew corn, apples, vegetables, and hay for our twenty dairy cows. As a small child I rode with my father in his wagon to take our crops to the pier at Sparta, where we loaded them on sailing ships and side-wheelers. As I grew older we began to ship more and more by train, and then by motorized truck, but the city of New York, with its insatiable millions, was always our market.

We had been able to compete with the vastly more efficient farms of the Midwest and even California because our produce was fresh. But as shipping improved and the advent of more and more machinery changed the nature of agriculture, the huge farms in other parts of the country were able to offer food that was more attractive, and to drive down their marginal costs just as ours were going up.

From the time I was born, I watched my father fail. At first he didn't even know it, or would not admit to it. Then he allowed that he was having some bad years. When the bad years would not relent, he blamed himself and worked almost harder than was humanly possible. When that did not arrest our declining fortunes—I remember my lust for boiled potatoes and my sense of infinite well-being after consuming a small piece of meat—he tried new strategies. Suddenly we were growing all kinds of strange and delicate things, or trying to grow them: raspberries, endive, outlandish melons. His idea was to capitalize on the carriage trade. But these crops were fragile and you had to have harvest labor on the instant or they would spoil. We soon went back to the familiar, and then came the schemes—a resort, a clock factory, cutting ice, boarding horses. Perhaps some might have worked, but none was tried: he didn't think he had enough time left to start over, and anyway he wasn't the kind of man to do so. Like me, he understood the futility of success, and he had no heart for playing games.

So he failed, and the more he failed the more I loved him and the more I understood. At the age of nine and a half all I knew was love and shame, and as I myself had no powers, not yet even dormant powers, I did not even think of avenging him. I knew only the unparalleled affection one has for those who are loved and faltering.

Still, when I was eight I learned to guide a horse in front of a plow, and this I did with hidden joy and for long hard days, because my father needed me. The ground gives back more or less what you put into it. It was not the ground that had changed, or the substance of what we did, or the virtues, but everything else in the world. We understood that. Even I did. Even then.

The grand schemes were never tried, and my father continued to work the land. In winter he plowed snow, delivered for the druggist, painted interiors, and split wood. My mother took in sewing, and she would begin to stitch shirtwaists even before dawn, in the bitter cold, by lamplight.

My father and I also arose before the light. It takes a while to milk twenty cows if you have no milking machine, and then you have to feed them, clean their stalls, and turn them out on days when it isn't too cold.

After breakfast my father and I left—he to sell the milk and go to whatever work he had, and I to school. Other than walking two miles to shop in town, and walking back with the groceries, my mother labored at home all day, at cooking, housekeeping, and her piecework.

Except for study halls, the short time before dinner was all the time I had to learn what I had to learn. Dinner came at five and was over at five-thirty. While my mother did the dishes my father and I would attend to the cows. Then we would put more wood on the fire and turn up the kerosene lamp on the kitchen table.

Bent over a huge board covered with green felt, my father repaired clocks. He could fix any machine, and had been known for this since childhood. At first he had done it for free, but it soon became a business. He used two trays of tools and three trays of parts, and the lamp had to be burning bright.

My mother sewed, stacking her finished shirtwaists in a thin wood box with a red exterior, though, depending upon the store, sometimes the boxes were blue cardboard with gold lettering. Even in the early Fifties I could not pass the older department stores in New York and not feel love and sadness. As I looked in the lighted windows, my glimpse of warm interiors and golden logos would take me back to the time and people to which and to whom I was to become more and more loyal as years and miles came between us. For my mother, as well, the light had to be strong, for she did fine work and her stitches had to be perfectly spaced and absolutely straight.

In these hours I did piecework, too. With my mother's help I had bid for and won a contract, at the age of seven, to provide sealing-wax medallions for an elegant men's haberdashery that has long since vanished from Union Square. Above their mahogany doors was a gold-plated cameo of two lithe dolphins. This was most pleasing to look at, and always caught the attention of passersby. I think the beautiful carved form of the two dolphins, bulging with smooth and perfect gold, actually made people want to go into the store and come out with something in a deep blue box.

Over a covering of glossy blue paper, gold ribbons intersected beneath a thick sealing-wax medallion of the dolphins. For many years I was the exclusive purveyor of these oval sculptures the size of large cookies, and I worked every day, year-round, to make the minimum order of five thousand. In a good season I would double it.

I started off in primitive fashion, but by the time I was nine my production techniques were extremely efficient. Our stove had four rounds, upon which I set four cast-iron pots with long straight handles shielded in ebony. These were not cooking implements but a metallurgist's vessels. As each round was a different temperature, I kept the wax at various levels of liquification. The process demanded that the fire remain at a steady temper, and to achieve this I tended it continually and fed it wood that I had precut. I had three sizes of log (I actually measured with a rule when I cut and split), all of the same density, age, and moisture content. With the help of an accurate clock, and thermometers in the wax pots, I could keep the wax in any stage to within two degrees Fahrenheit of the perfect temperature—something that had taken months of experimentation to determine. When a vessel was empty, I filled it with gold-colored wax bricks and rotated the pots. After I tended the fire and cleaned my tools and surfaces, a supply of hot wax would be ready for another round.

I would sprinkle talc from a fine sifter onto a highly polished piece of slate the size of an open newspaper, turning it white as if by magic. On one section of the coated slate I set down a row of five stainless steel oval bands—each half an inch high and each with a line engraved two-thirds of the way up the inner wall. Then I used a ladle to pour the wax into the ovals. To flatten out and rise exactly to the line, the wax had to be molten, though if it were too hot it would stick to the metal. By the time I returned the pot to the stove, the first oval would almost be ready for stamping.

If you used any kind of oil or powder on the stamp itself it would change the surface characteristics and, sometimes, the color of the medallion. The only effective lubricant that left no trace was the sweat of the palm, and this I would produce by heating the stamp to a fairly high temperature and placing it against my hand, but not too high a temperature, because that would ruin the surface completely, and spoil the fine engraving.

Absent a thermometer embedded in the wax, the only way you could tell it was ready to receive the impression was to judge the quality of the surface. Were it too hot, pieces of wax would stick to the stamp. Picking them off after hardening them by immersion in cold water was difficult and time consuming. Meanwhile, you would have to yank the ovals lest the wax stick to them, too. If, on the other hand, you waited too long, the stamp would stick to the seal or the wax would not even take an impression. Ridding the stamp of wax was always a nightmare, because you could not simply melt it off, for fear of carbonizing it.

When all went smoothly, as it did when I had the hang of it, I would make my impressions, remove the ovals, and there before me would rest five golden medallions with dolphins leaping gracefully, faint smiles upon their faces, the curve of their backs clashing only slightly with the curve of the oval seals.

I was happier working at a hard, even pace for relatively little money, than I was later, hardly working at all for so much money that money lost its meaning. And it was there, in the warmth of the fire that heated my pots of wax and in the light of the lamp turned up full, that I came to know my mother and father—their histories, together and alone, their beliefs, and their dreams. Although most children who lived on farms had chores, I had become a pieceworker, and I knew my parents' gratitude for my industry, their sorrow that I had to work as I did, and that the source and union of these two emotions were nothing more or less than their love for me.

I sit in the garden in Niterói, looking down upon the sea, reconstructing my memories. The satisfaction I feel in recalling them is like that of a kiss. Except in those kisses freighted with sex you tend to close your eyes, as if you want it to last forever. When you kiss someone with real love it is as if this is the last thing you will ever do, after which you will disappear into infinite darkness. So that may be why you hold your breath imperceptibly, or perhaps even longer, and it is why when I remember simple things from my childhood I inhale slightly with satisfaction, close my eyes for an instant, and feel a smile so subtle it probably cannot be seen.

And then I open my eyes and they are filled by the sea, and I remember that in summer and on weekends throughout the year, I, too, was a fisherman. It was not sport, and I didn't have equipment worth a hundred times what I might have realized in a day had I sold my catch, which sometimes I did when the fish were running strongly or the crabs attending a convention in my traps. Usually, though, I stopped when we had a full meal.

I spent many hours on the small beaches of Croton Bay. If I wanted to fish in the channel, where the water was deeper and the fish had their main highway, I walked five miles to the tip of Teller's Point. In those days, the world was my fish store, and I brought home bass, shad, salmon, crab, oysters, and clams. From freshwater ponds I took catfish, perch, sunnies, and craw-fish. And there were seasons for blackberries, raspberries, wild strawberries, and mulberries. I wouldn't touch a mushroom, and my father did the hunting, something for which, as a child who loved animals, I had no stomach, and then, later, as an older boy whose parents had been murdered, I could not even bear to contemplate.

For a child whose parents are taken from him in this way, the world becomes, if not permanently broken, then at least permanently bent. If, as in my case, the actual murderers are never brought to justice, then one is condemned to live one's life with the knowledge that they are out there; that they've ruined, bested, and beaten you; that they might come for you; that any man with whom you deal, anyone you meet, no matter how smiling or how likeable or how good, as long as he is of a certain age, may be the devil incarnate, and that therefore you cannot trust, or believe, or confide in anyone; that your life must become a contest of endurance so that you can live to a hundred, so that you can be sure the murderers will be dead before you, something that you imagine would be your parents' fondest wish and deepest need; and that when your parents died they did so in terror, fearing that their assailants would turn on you, the child for whom they would gladly die, but for whom at the very last they could do absolutely nothing.

On Friday, the fifth of June, 1914, the day after I had been compelled to chew three coffee beans, we were released from school two hours early. Teachers, students, and even—or perhaps especially—the headmaster had had enough of sack races, picnics, and capture the flag. Finals had ended at noon with a whoop from scores of geometry students in suits and dresses far too hot for the stifling gymnasium in which they had spent three hours that seemed no longer than three minutes, manipulating compasses and protractors with the desperate efficiency of a bomb squad. The desks upon which they worked were too small for what they had to do, so the hall had been filled with groans, sighs, and tense breathing.

Then, heads packed with theorems, they emptied the gym of furniture and waited for graduation a week later. I, being nine and a half, looked forward to my own graduation with the same awe I now feel for death.

Some of the seniors were going to be married within weeks, which meant that the boy and the girl were free to go into a room, lock the door, and take off their clothes. Even at nine and a half I thought this was reason enough to persevere through high school, and although I didn't know exactly what would happen after the door was locked, just the thought of it sent waves of slightly numb pleasure from tip to toe. A hundred years for each ankle and calf, two hundred for the lips, the shoulders. . . . And yet I knew nothing beyond that, no mechanics, no hydraulics, no biology, no geology, just love and adoration.

I made my way home through town, staring at razor blades

and mustard plasters in the drugstore window and at cranks, jacks, and lanterns in the window of the hardware store. I ignored the clothing shops and groceries, glanced at the carved wood monkeys the barber had had on display forever (during which eternity they had not been dusted), and took the aqueduct bridge on my route to Eagle Bay.

My father was cultivating a field, and when I ran up beside him he hardly looked at me as he kept the rows straight. His chambray shirt was wet and he breathed heavily, but he looked as if he were enjoying himself as he shifted the plow and held the reins in a perpetual struggle of balance and strength. I remember our short conversation, because it was our last.

"Back?" he asked.

"Yup."

"That's it," he said, meaning, *school's over.*

I echoed his words: "That's it."

"What're you going to do?" From the way he said it, I knew he meant not for the summer but for the remainder of the day.

"Fish."

"I'll be here 'til eight," my father told me. "Be back for dinner."

"Okay."

"Don't fish from the tower."

I was already on my way when he said those—his last—words to me. Because I wanted to fish from the tower, I didn't answer. At least, though I turned my back on him, I hadn't lied.

My mother was upstairs in the house. Inside, I sensed her presence, I may even have heard her, but I wanted only to get my fishing tackle and run to the river. As I buckled the strap that held the shoulder bag to my waist so it wouldn't bang against my side as I ran, I did so quietly. And then I left, happy but uneasy that I had evaded my mother, for she had probably heard me, and would have wanted to embrace me, as she always did when I returned from school, as if to contain my fleeting childhood, but I gave this no further thought, for as soon as I hit the path to the river I began to fly, the two halves of my fishing rod pointing forward from my outstretched arms like the wind-shattering spears on a fighter's wing tips.

My father wanted me to avoid the tower not because he was afraid I would take up bad ways—it is very hard for a boy of nine to sin even if he wants to—but because he wanted to keep me from familiarity with bad ways. What is necessary is not so much that parents set a good example for their children but that they fail to set a bad example. The important thing is not that you see your father, to consider the case of the town barber, industriously carving wooden monkeys, but rather that you do not see him smoking opium or kicking small animals. If, for example, parents did not familiarize their children with the drinking of coffee, the children would no sooner drink coffee than they would spend all their money on tattoos.

The town of Ossining in those days was publicly sinless, all vices and most virtues being learned and practiced, if at all, at home. Thus, by following the Ten Commandments and then some, my parents were getting me off to a good start. The tower, however, was the seat of dangers and petty sins of all descriptions.

The underlying condition there, something not a vice itself but in its way an anteroom to the world of vice, was that this place was open all night. As a switching station on the Hudson Line of the New York Central Railroad, it had to be. The lights were always on, the little bulbs on the trackboard flashed as trains drew close or moved away, the telephone rang at all hours, and, often, a Victrola would play long past the time that almost everyone else in town was asleep, its horn pointed out the window at the river, because the music was too loud when it echoed from the windows that overlooked the tracks.

Though they were not supposed to have it, the switchmen kept a bottle of scotch in a compartment of the wainscotting. Had they abused this bottle, it might have been quite tricky for them to read all the lights that jumped around the trackboard like fireflies and glowworms, or to pull the proper lever in the long black line of switches that looked like rifles stacked in an arsenal. So they had a rule, which was that neither of them could take a drink without the other also taking a drink, and that only one bottle was allowed in the tower at any one time. Thus, they were automatically restricted to half a bottle per shift, which, I suppose, was lucky for the crowded passenger trains and heavily laden freights shuttling in opposite directions at seventy miles per hour each.

The practice of hiding a bottle in the wainscotting first introduced me to one of the rare beauties in the American system of justice. I was in the tower one day, in a snowstorm, excitedly awaiting the passage of the plow train, when a freight approached from the south. Because they anxiously awaited the plow, which was to appear from the north at any minute, the switchmen neglected to throw one of their switches, and the northbound freight derailed and flew into the swamp, leaving two engines, a coal car, and three others semisubmerged, while the forty or fifty freight cars behind them simply sat at the edge of the track.

It felt as if the waters of a flood had risen in the room up to our necks. The two switchmen knew instantly that they had lost their jobs, that their families were imperiled, and that, if anyone had died, they themselves would live the rest of their lives only half alive or less. And all because they had been as excited as I was about seeing a plow train.

And then the plow train came through even before we knew

if anyone had been hurt. It blazed down the track, its bright light making hash of the blizzard, and left a clear path behind it.

Before they or I began to run on the cleared track toward the swamp, we had an instantaneous trial in which the switchmen, who were the defendants, represented themselves, and I was prosecutor, investigator, judge, and jury. This trial took about ten seconds, but it was as fine an example of justice as any I've seen. One of the men quickly lifted the board in the wainscotting and pointed to the bottle. "Look, kid," he said. "The seal isn't even broken." It was not broken. The bottle was full. As seconds went by I realized my role in all this, and I nodded, saving them from an unnecessary crucifixion, for I knew exactly why they had been remiss, and I agreed not to complicate things by bringing up the existence of the bottle.

While one put in the derailment call, the other sped up the track. A few minutes later he came back with some wet and muddy trainmen who refused even to look at us. When the two switchmen left that evening they took their things, and they never returned. All night long the derailment crews worked through the blizzard to get the freight back on the track, and we could see the glow of their floodlights from the windows of our house. The officially stated reason for the accident was that it had occurred in blizzard conditions—something that was true at its very heart, although the railroad did not know it.

The next day came as if nothing had happened. The freight was gone, the track repaired, the depressions in the soil and splintered railroad ties covered with drifted snow, and a new crew installed in the tower. They didn't loosen up until spring, when they finally realized whose tower it really was and allowed me to fish from the iron fire escape above the Hudson. I never told anyone about the scotch, and if despite the advent of automatic equipment the tower is still there (in the early Fifties I used to see it from the Twentieth Century Limited on my way to and from Chicago), a bottle of seventy-year-old Glenlivet still sits behind the third board from the right in the wainscotting on the river side.

The new men in the tower were not too much different from their predecessors. They, too, brought magazines that by the standards of the day were brazenly pornographic.

"Kid, did you ever see bosoms?"

"No."

"Wanna see some?"

"Don't show him that, Newton, he's too young."

"I am not."

"The hell he's not. He wouldn't know what he was looking at."

"That's why I want to show him, so he will know."

"It's not right. You don't corrupt kids."

"I wanna see some b—" I said, and was cut off.

"You shut up. If you see bosoms, you'll tell your mama and she'll come down here and flatten us. I brought some pie. Go out on the fire escape and eat it."

As I ate blueberry pie on the fire escape I watched them, their eyes going in and out of focus as they studied every page of a magazine called *Firemen's Beauties*. I never saw it myself. They kept it in the center drawer of the desk, and to get to this drawer you would have had to move the huge girth of one of the switch-men as he sealed it shut by leaning against it while shouting into the two-piece telephone. They never sat back when talking on this instrument, but always strained forward, levitated over a green desk blotter like a hippopotamus floating above Ebbets Field.

As the night trains passed in early evening, bound for Montreal, Chicago, and points west, we looked with longing into the lighted windows where, we thought, we might see real life. The tower was consigned to perpetual dimness—only the burning embers in the trackboard and two fifteen-watt bulbs above the North and South schedules brought light to the room, so when the great trains flashed by, their compartments and dining cars bathed in a color that was a cross between buttercup and white, it was like watching a film with randomly arranged frames.

The things I saw in those snake-shaped magic lantern shows that moved sometimes at speeds of seventy-five miles an hour gave me my first really distorted view of the world, which is not to say in the least that what I perceived was not accurate, or that I have capitulated, for I have not. I persist, like almost everyone else, in trying to straighten things out, but I believe that the world is somewhat like a piece of paper: it can be folded only a fixed number of times, and then it refuses further adjustment. Cycles of history, in my view, consist of just this folding and unfolding, but with a kind of dance rhythm.

Before I knew the great city to the south, before I knew crime, or suffering, or death, thousands of brightly lit tableaux were pulled past my astonished eyes. I learned that many of these scenes would include a man and a woman in various states of undress grasping one another like wrestlers. This meant little to me, as the sequence was presented out of order, with the full set exemplified over a period of about two years, and with totally random stress on, say, ear kissing. More treasured was full frontal feminine nudity, something that occurred more often than one might initially expect, because at night the train windows became mirrors to those inside the fully lit compartments. But, still, it happened rarely. I would say . . . about four times in all—once at 75, once at 60, once at 45, and once at, bless the engineer, 5 miles an hour, and it was then that I learned not only what magnificent beauty the requirements of modesty had kept from my eyes, but also that even 5 miles an hour can be too fast.

Though forever reaching for pearls, many an irascible octopus flashed by me. Among the thousands of scenes that passed and vanished, I remember a tiny goatlike man with pince-nez looking over a pile of precious stones that had been emptied from a violin case onto a card table. He must have been some sort of jewel thief, but his technique is anyone's guess. I saw fat men in bowler hats doing victory dances. I saw an appendix being removed, I think. I saw a girl, creeping by at less than a mile an hour, stuck in the sweater she was trying to pull over her head. I had no idea at first what I was watching. She looked like a miniature elephant or rhinoceros bumping against the panels of the sleeping compartment. Then I realized what it was, and I wondered why her mother, who was reading a newspaper on the seat facing forward, didn't come to her aid, something immediately explained when a turn on the wheel of the binoculars brought the mother's neck brace into focus. What a family.

Although the dining cars were often full and bustling, a lot of people ate in their rooms. People are shy, and some, apparently, could afford to pay for a sleeping compartment but not the Pullman food, so they brought picnics. I used to play a game in which I would read salamis like the hands of a clock. "It's twenty of . . ." I would say, as a salami went by pointing to West Virginia, and, then, perhaps several trains later, "*three*," when a salami went by pointing to New Haven.

Sometimes we saw fights, or men beating women, though we also saw women beating men. Once, on a southbound from Chicago to New York, we saw two apes (I'm fairly sure they were apes) gazing at each other as if they were in love.

One summer evening we watched several cars pass slowly by, their windows partially open, with a musician in each compartment, each playing a different part of the same Beethoven piano concerto. It was either a symphony orchestra on tour or one of the greatest coincidences ever.

You can name almost anything in life—rabbis, acrobats, weeping women, greyhounds, accountants, bored children, loving apes, deathly ill Sicilians—and we saw it roll past. In this universe you could tell the time from the way salamis pointed, and sex was accomplished completely out of order, while the nude was still arrestingly beautiful, fully lit, at five or fifty miles per hour. Though I never could have known the exquisite 5 mph nude, and now she's either dead or a hundred and one, I saw her in all her grace for ten seconds, and have adored her ever since.

The real prizes, however, were the private cars. Some had grand pianos, marble kitchens, and bathtubs large enough to bathe an elephant. When these moving dachas appeared several times each day, you could see dinners served, meetings held, and tycoons working at huge desks and in burgundy-colored leather chairs the size of Italian automobiles.

The richness of interiors lit by electric lights or the glow of a fire was wonderful to behold not because of the decoration or pure color but because of what it suggested. It made me think of and long for real life, though real life was precisely what I had, even if I did not know that. I made a boy's mistake, common enough, of thinking that real life was knowing many things and many people, living dangerously in faraway places, crossing the sea, or starting a power company on the Columbia River, a steamship line in Bolivia. I used to wonder who were the tall and elegant women in the private cars, in magnificent attire that made them look like the heroic women on coins. Who were they that knew so many sins and sat so quietly drinking wine the color of rubies? I knew they had once been little girls, like my classmates, as shy as fauns, beloved, in gondolier hats with long ribbons. What had happened to them in the private cars, and would it happen to me, or was it something that simply occurred as one grew gigantic like the tycoons who were so big that they had to ride around in their own railroad cars?

I knew enough when I was nine years old to apprehend merely from glancing in the windows of trains that, as a group, tycoons were devastatingly unhappy. This unhappiness radiated from their magnificent and expensive nests like the odor of cattle in stock cars. If the wind were blowing in the right direction and at the right speed you could smell a cattle train half an hour before it came through and long after it left. So with the tycoons, whose unhappiness advertised their presence almost as if by magic.

There were at least four hundred families of tycoon, perhaps many thousands, but we knew of only the very famous ones or those with a local connection. We knew their names the way children today know the names of film stars and baseball players, and therein lay the puzzle that confronted the one detective on the police force of the Town of Ossining, for the records of the evening trains had somehow disappeared from the stationmaster's office in Grand Central, from the dispatcher's headquarters, from Harmon, even from Chicago. For the evening of June 5th, 1914, the history of trains was a blank.

At about twenty of eight the two switchmen and I sat up straight. A single engine and one car came from the south along the freight tracks, unscheduled and unannounced except for the automatic lights on the train board. As it passed illicitly, the switchmen struggled to read the serial number on the locomotive, and were incensed that it seemed not to exist. I was free, however, to look at the car in tow, a private car with darkened windows and no lights. It seemed as if it were heading for the Harmon Yards for maintenance or a refit, but it wasn't at Harmon the next day and it could have gone all the way west, never stopping until it came to rest on a siding in the middle of nowhere in Montana, or in an orange grove in San Diego. Who knows?

It stopped briefly about a hundred and fifty yards north of us, and in the failing light we thought we saw two figures jump from the viewing platform. Why wasn't the locomotive numbered? The switchmen were of the opinion that it had been, but that they'd missed it through some combination of ineptitude, accident, or a trick of the light.

"But I saw the initials on the side of the private car," I said proudly.

"You did?"

"Yes."

"What were they?"

Though I was not tall enough to stand behind the desk and see completely over the windowsill, I had seen, in strange, modernistic lettering, the initials F.P.F.

Only later did the chief of Ossining's detectives (of which, as I have said, he was the only one) go through the social registers looking for F.P.F.s, and he came out with quite a few—Franklin P. Fellows, F. Paterson Ford, Farley Peter Fainsod, and others, all of whom could account not only for their whereabouts that evening, but, more importantly, for the whereabouts of their railroad cars, if, indeed, they owned railroad cars.

It was not the detective but the reporter from the local newspaper who shed the most early light on the crime. The detective took plaster casts of footprints (he was very thorough, but even I knew that my parents had not been murdered by a deer), queried railroad workers about the trains that went through that evening (ten days later, they had no recollection, as most people would not), and analyzed the characteristics of the bullets, the method of execution, etc. I speak of all this in worldly terms and as if I were a stranger, but as I do I feel the deepest longing for my parents, whom I see in memory as I last saw them, silenced and still.

Unlike the detective, the newspaper reporter was interested in motive. Did my father owe a debt? Neither my uncle nor I were aware of one. Was it something that had arisen from the past? From the war? We did not know. The reporter, however, had a theory—a theory that could be neither proved nor disproved. He was a man who looked much like Theodore Roosevelt, only he hadn't come very far along and he was accustomed to being deferential, as he was often sent to ask questions of people who had just had great success, or who were long accustomed to having their way.

I was hardly one of those people, but he was interested in my story because I was just old enough to keep everything in memory so vividly for the rest of my life that my life would never be my own, no matter how hard I struggled, no matter what I did.

So, at one point—I don't remember when—he took me in his arms when I was crying and could not be consoled, and after a minute or two he put me up on the window ledge and looked at me with astonishing urgency.

"Stop your crying for just a minute and listen," he said gently. "We may never find the murderers of your parents. If the two men who did it, did, in fact, jump from the private car, they were just henchmen, and the question is, who sent them? To know who, we need to know why, and no one can come up with anything. But I have a theory. Though it has no basis in fact, I can't stop thinking about it. I turn it over in my mind again and again. Only God knows if it's true, and He can keep people in the dark forever if He wants. For the past year I've been hearing a rumor that someone—a syndicate, perhaps— wants to build a bridge across the Hudson somewhere around here, and that the value of the land between the road and the river will go up.

"Not all the land . . . only where the bridge would come in. Do you have any memory of anyone asking your father if he would sell his farm?"

I had no such memory. If it had happened, I had not known of it. Perhaps, if it had happened, my father and mother had talked of it privately for months, not wanting to upset me. Children don't like to move. Or perhaps my father had kept it to himself.

"You should ask my uncle," I said.

"I've already asked him and everyone else. Think hard."

"No," I said. "He never said that anyone wanted to buy our land."

"We'll have to wait, then. We'll see if someone approaches the estate."

I didn't know what he meant by estate, but he explained.

A year after the estate was dissolved into a trust that had been established for my benefit, my uncle, who was the trustee and who had leased our fields to several neighboring farmers, was approached by a man who said he represented a party interested in purchasing the property. My uncle broached this at one of the near-silent, sad dinners we had after I came to live with him and his wife. I was not a normal child, and no one expected me to be. I spent most of my time alone, and for a long period I said almost nothing: I hurt too much. And when everyone had forgotten what had happened to me, they resented my demeanor and my silence, and then they hated me for it, which hurt even more, but what could I do? I had a lifelong task, next to which the idea of being liked seemed completely unimportant.

At that particular dinner I had been drinking from a lead-crystal glass, and we were having roast chicken. Used to my alternating outbursts and silences, my uncle, who loved me in his way, nervously, optimistically, and completely innocently announced that a man had inquired if the land were for sale.

All at once I slammed down the glass, tensed my muscles, clenched my fists, and felt my hair stand on end. "Who?!" I shouted, tears coming to my eyes.

"I don't know," my uncle said, startled.

"Who!" I screamed. This was the first time I overturned a table. I loved my uncle: I didn't mean to overturn the table.

I went nearly mad for days, until we knew. I had plans for having every policeman in the state of New York skulk behind the staircase when this gentleman came to call. I tried to build a prison in the root cellar, there to hold and torture him until he revealed the name of his employer. Although I realized that if I killed him I would never know who had sent him, I polished up my single-barrel 20-gauge shotgun until it shone like a piece of Homeric armor. I even polished the shells, and spent hours in mock loading, pointing, and threatening, all in front of an oval mirror in which my mother had once checked her hat and the fall of her cape or coat.

When my uncle found two flat chunks of wood nailed with bent penny spikes into the posts of the root cellar, he called me to explain what they were. A clothesline that had been tied weakly around the bent penny spikes had been intended as manacles. "Why don't we just wait to see what he says?" my uncle asked.

The man whom I was going to put in my dungeon was a miniature old white-haired fellow named Smith. Apart from being as dapper as an ant, he was not distinguished in any way. He had no accent and spoke in no dialect. He did not speak with his hands, or express emotion or enthusiasm. I was sure that behind him stood the murderers of my parents.

He was inquiring, he said, in behalf of the Dominican Sisters of the Sick and Poor. At every stage, I expected that this would be exposed for the mere cover story that I assumed it had to be. When the mother superior came to discuss with my uncle the provision that allowed us to retain farming rights to the land until 1930, I pegged her for an actress and a con woman. When the papers were finally signed, I thought they were a fraud. When the abbey began to rise, I waited for it to become a toll booth. And when the nuns moved in, I assumed that it was all a trick, that they would soon turn around and sell to the tycoon who wanted to build a bridge. But the Dominican Sisters of the Sick and Poor stayed and stayed, and even as I flew on my Newfoundland run, I passed over the abbey, surrounded by fields that were still beautiful and of which I knew every contour, and there, in a ragged glen, I saw my house. It looked like a brick sugar cube, a model that would come with a Swiss train set. In all those years, the trees had grown, but the slate and brick had remained unchanged. Though I could not see the inevitable alteration of detail that, were I ever to go back, would break my heart yet again, it was easy to imagine.

When the two figures jumped from the railroad car it wasn't dark, but the sun was low in the sky, its weakening glare filtered through the trees of Teller's Point. The result was a broken pattern that with fading daylight and the background of trees near the rail bed made whatever happened pure shadow.

We had never seen anyone leave a train along this stretch of track, other than train crew hopping on and off. It was exciting and mysterious to see the shapes drawn into the summer shadows like barely perceptible puffs of smoke. No doubt the birds up the track had been silenced, but we still heard the din of a golden summer evening.

I left at a few minutes before eight and started to make my way home. By the time I approached our field nearest the river I had forgotten the mystery and begun to think about dinner.

But as soon as I burst from the woods I stopped dead. Just at the edge of the field, twenty yards to my left, two men were standing, looking at the house.

I walked toward them, and when I was close I said, too proudly, "This is private property."

"We're sorry," said one. "We're just trying to get to the road. We're tired and hungry."

"Oh," I said.

"I hope we don't have to go back to the tracks. Can we just go through to the road?"

They were dressed for the city—suits, vests, hats, watch chains. It would have been cruel, I thought, to make them march around in the swamp, so I said it was okay for them to pass through to the road.

They were the kind of men who are in terrible health but who by size and weight alone are ten times more powerful than they look, and, perhaps because they were so big, their exaggerated gratitude seemed fitting and, somehow, sincere.

"That's very kind of you," one of them said. "You know the area, don't you? And you're fast: you're a kid. Would you mind running into town to get us something to eat? We've been traveling since yesterday, all the way from Indiana, and we're very hungry."

"I can't do that," I said. "I have to have dinner." I thought it strange that they had been traveling from Indiana, because they had New York accents, they were dressed like Chelsea saloon rats, and their train had come from the direction of the city.

"It would take only a few minutes, and it would really help us."

I shook my head. I was getting uncomfortable, even frightened. I wanted just to run toward the house.

"I'll tell you what," said the one who was doing the talking. "All we need is something to get us going. Is there a place nearby where you can get coffee?"

"Yah," I told him, although it wasn't really nearby.

"Well here then," the talker said, pulling something out of his pocket. "Take this."

He held out a twenty-dollar gold piece. My father tried to save these, and hardly ever could. I understood what it was worth, how hard it was to get, and how harder still it was to hold. I took it.

"And here's two bits," he added, "so's you don't have to break the coin when you get the coffee."

Over the years, many people have told me that I was blameless. I was not even ten years of age. How could I have known what was to happen? But as I ran to buy the coffee, I felt guilt and sorrow. I was hoping that I could do everything quickly enough to freeze the danger in place. If I could do it in a dash, duck out, and hurry back, everything would be all right.

I ran so fast to the Highland Café that when I arrived I was too winded to speak. And yet I couldn't wait to catch my breath, so I slapped the silver down on the counter, pointed to the coffee urn, held up the index and middle fingers of my right hand, and then upended them and walked them across the counter. Soon I had two coffees to go, having dismissed with a wave the usual queries about cream and sugar.

In those days, most restaurants had nesting containers for

outservice. These were made of tin and stacked under a handle, like something you might see in a Chinese dairy. I carried two of these containers, one atop the other, but I had no handle and they burned my hands. Every few strides I would have to stop to put them down and blow on my palms. After a while, when the whole thing was not quite as hot, I held it and ran.

I wanted to get back to the field so I could see the two men. I would slow down only after I had confirmed that they were still there. As I ran, the coffee sloshed out of the containers and scalded my hands. It flowed down my arms and wet my sleeves. My shirt front was soaked with it, and my pants had an oval stain centered on my fly.

Though only half the coffee remained, the gold piece was safely in my pocket and I thought that if the two men didn't like the service I could always give back the money. But before I came to the edge of the field I saw through the trees that they were not there.

As I froze in place, my hands carefully cradling the tin containers of coffee, I feared above all that my parents would think I had betrayed them. My thoughts were half shadow: I knew what was coming, and yet I did not. My father had seen everything. He would be self-contained no matter what his fate. He had once told me that every day of his life made him less afraid of death, and that, at the end, no shock or surprise would be too much to bear. But my mother was different. She always went into everything with a full heart that could be broken.

I threw down the tin containers and started to run. As I neared the house I saw one of the front shutters moving slowly in the breeze. My father would not have tolerated that. He would have fastened it.

I was queasy with fear. At the same time, I was sure that I would be scolded for being more than half an hour late and for having stained my clothes with coffee. I was afraid that my father would be severe with me for accepting money from strangers and leaving the property without reporting their presence, and even for throwing down the coffee before I brought it to them. How embarrassing it would be, I thought, if the two men were sitting in the parlor, waiting for the coffee that had soaked into the ground.

But I was also aware that something totally unknown and far worse might enable me to avoid these lesser catastrophes. The most terrible thing I could imagine, therefore, had its attractions, and even though I sensed that its promise of freedom was entirely false, I was drawn to it. As I ran toward the house I tried to banish my thoughts, but what good is trying to forget thoughts that have already occurred?

Despite all this I was sure that everything would be all right, that my childhood was not suddenly about to end, and by the time I opened our front door my agonies had begun to subside. Apart from clothes soaked with coffee, I was at least half presentable. If the men were there, I would give them back their money and apologize for the rest. Such things happen. They would think I was an honest boy who had tried hard and met with a painful accident.

But they were not in the parlor, and the house was still. I called out. "Mama?" I asked, and no one answered. "Mama?" I said again, my voice shaking.

The whole world changed for me when I saw that the dining room table had been overturned, and that everything that had been on it—food, dishes, cutlery, water, candles, bread—lay on the floor.

I went into the kitchen, where my mother and father lay a few feet from one another in death.

I called to them quietly, but they did not move. Their eyes

were open. My father held a kitchen knife that was stained with blood. He had fought. And yet his expression was one of contentment. And my mother's, as I might have predicted, was one of anguish.

She had a small bullet hole in the back of her head. She had been executed. My father, too, had a small-caliber bullet hole, at the temple, but he had also been shot in several places with a .45, and the blood on the floor was his. It must have been his assailants', too, for the knife blade had not a spot of silver upon it.

All I said was, "Oh oh oh," over and over again. Then I stopped. Tears poured from my eyes, but I remained perfectly silent. I lay down between them, in my father's blood. I put my hands on their bodies, and felt with my fingertips that at least they were there, that I could still touch them. And then I closed my eyes. As I fell asleep, I was certain that I would join them, and of course some day I will.

The Glacis at São Conrado

(If you have not done so already,
please return the previous pages to the antproof case.)

AS A CHILD I often heard the expression "the resilience of the human spirit," and it was my luck to understand it as the *Brazilians* of the human spirit. This misconception instilled in me an almost theological awe for a people that I might otherwise perceive as hopeless and dissolute. Though they are prodigal, undisciplined, and morally blowzy, because of an accident at an early age and because I heed those voices that I first heard, I cannot help but see their redemptive side.

While the snow fell and the fire burned, my mother spoke from the semidarkness, commanding me never to underestimate the Brazilians of the human spirit. "When you are a man," she said, "you'll face many tests that now you cannot even imagine, and you will pass each one if you have faith at the outset in the magnificent Brazilians of the human spirit."

Who choreographs these Brazilians that swarm and strive in their millions, sexualizing the esplanades like grunion, obsessed with vanity and passion, swirling through the days and nights like so many Paolos and Francescas, driven as obviously as puppets. You see them on land, in the water, and in the air, twisting in lazy switchbacks in the blue after sailing off the Gavea under hang gliders.

The reckless among the hang glider pilots wear neither clothes nor helmets, just the sock that passes for a loincloth on the South Atlantic beaches, and to see them flying naked and by the score in the sunlit sky is to see an invasion of angels, for to glide properly they must stretch and extend their limbs like figures in Renaissance paintings—dancers, angels, recumbent gods. Who has choreographed this extraordinary flight? Chance? It would seem to me that in this world the virtuoso mixing of the colors alone would tend to rule out bangs and booms and other 'singularities,' although I know that, these days, if people believe in something, just as often as not they believe in a boom. "The boom is my shepherd, I shall not want. . . ."

I was raised on a bay of the Hudson that by historical and natural accident was a refuge for eagles. As the nation lamented that they were lost, I used to see them many times a day, and I thought they were as common as gulls. Inter alia, I learned to sense the presence of an eagle when I could not see him, in the broken patterns of common birds that flew in groups. Sometimes extremely subtle variations served to announce that presence. Their unity and surety would shatter and their wings would tense, ready to be pulled tight to the body for rolling and diving in evasion. Sometimes they passed over the trees in an even pattern against the clouds, like the spots of an ermine coat or the fleurs-de-lys of wallpaper, and then their ordered formation would explode into chaos, a sorrowful sight and a fine lesson.

The gliders of São Conrado swarm in chaotic splendor. I come here to watch them against the blue sky because I have discovered that toward the end of one's life one begins to understand the idea of angels. I have for many years seen angels in the faces of children, in the lovely drawn-out cries of singers, in painting, and in poetry. But only recently have I learned that they can appear apart from perfection, that it is their fate to be scattered across the sky, their formations exploded, their hearts stopped in shock.

I station myself on the huge glacis at São Conrado, a hillside of gray rock that projects into the sea, and spend the day looking up at the hang gliders. For this I also have a practical motivation. The beach where they land is white and wide, but (even if not by Brazilian standards) it is by my standards quite crowded, and the smell of expresso wafts from the coffee carts on the esplanade.

So I have found a ledge on the hillside of rock, where I come to sit during the afternoons with a newspaper, a water bottle, and the antproof case. Although the beach nearby is covered with people like a cake sprinkled with confectioners' sugar, never have I seen a single soul on these rocks. I have only a little tree to keep me company.

Its smooth trunk is curved and weathered, hammer-forged by wind and sea. It is harder and at the same time more supple than its cousins, and is the last tree out, rooted indelibly in the rock through which, when it was very young, it was obliged to burst.

I left the garden in Niterói, for a while, at least, because I sense danger there. After weaving through the confusion of Rio, I can come here, sure that I am and will remain alone. Though I'm high in the air, the sea is so close that sometimes the wind will carry a small particle of spray and wet my face or my page, so close that I've seen fins break the emerald surface. When I inhale I taste the minerals of the Atlantic.

I enjoy the full beating sun as never before. I don't eat when I'm here, though I do occasionally imagine dinners in intricate detail, but I need to drink, so I have a water bottle that I fill with the water I used to drink in Rome. The night that I met the great singers, I had thirsted for it on my walk from the Villa Doria to the Hassler, and had gone to the bar to get it, which is why I met them. I had drunk it during our talk, and then, the next day, I was drinking it when I saw the streetcar.

I am hesitant even to mention streetcars, having covered your eyes whenever one passed with boys surfing on top (now you know that I know who you are). I have tried to instill in you from an early age a natural revulsion for this practice, as it has caused the senseless death of so many children. Though I have always believed in your intelligence, adolescent boys have no probity. If you are anything like me, you will survive, but only by a hair, and, quite frankly, that makes me nervous.

You may think that shielding your eyes from boys surfing atop streetcars was manipulative. It was, and I have manipulated you in other ways, too. Perhaps by now you will have discovered that not all small boys are required to read through the Encyclopaedia Britannica volume by volume. In fact, in all of Brazil, you may have been the only boy of any size to fulfill such a requirement. Nor must other children commit to memory logarithmic tables, but I believe that someday, when others express awe at your mental agility you'll thank me.

I apologize, though not abjectly, for manipulating you, the last instance of which is your discovery of this memoir. For years I would put chocolates in the hidden drawer in the left-hand cabinet of the partner's desk. You are unable to come into my study without looking in that cabinet. As that is where I will place the antproof case when I have finished my account, I trust that you will have found it.

I know to do this because when I was three or four I discovered candied fruit slices in a drawer of our china cabinet. To this day I cannot refrain from looking in drawers, even in someone else's house. I have often been embarrassed by people who put me on the spot when they see me obsessively looking in their desks.

"Excuse me," they say. "*What* (the emphasis is always on the *what*) are you doing?" They breathe lightly at the end of this question.

"Do you have any candied fruit slices?" I ask.

"No. I *don't* (emphasis always on the *don't*) have any candied fruit slices." More indignant and amazed light breathing.

"That's all right," I say, "I don't even *like* (emphasis always on the *like*) candied fruit slices." And I don't.

I've never had many friends, and this is but one reason why. Opening drawers isn't so bad, really, and, besides, I can't help it: I open my own drawers incessantly, sometimes just seconds after I've looked in them. During my years as an undergraduate I once (emphasis on the *once*) went to Thanksgiving dinner at the home of a classmate who lived in Beverly Farms. Perhaps because his father had been a member of the cabinet, there were cabinets and drawers all over the house.

We went upstairs to tell his father,-who was sitting on his bed trying to pull off riding boots, that a snake was in the coal bin. Wouldn't you know, I went over and yanked open a dresser drawer, and it was just my luck to discover an inflatable sex doll. Of course, I didn't know what it was, so I pulled it out and asked, "What is this?"

My friend came over to examine it. "It's an inflatable sex doll, Dad. Whose is it?"

"I don't think it's your mother's," I said.

"No, you little son of a bitch," I was told. "It's not my wife's, but since you made it your business perhaps you ought to know that she has one, too, and that mine and hers are having an affair."

"Oh," I said.

"Why don't you keep it?" he asked bitterly.

"She's not my type."

Our Thanksgiving dinner was rather awkward.

Streetcars. If it hadn't been for a streetcar I wouldn't be here and you would probably be living in a *favela*.

Which might not be so bad. It all depends on how you take it. The truth is that the most wonderful times of my life have been when I was utterly impoverished, at least when I was young. Young people of character have no need for money. It's only when age knocks the joy from you that you need cash and coin to prop up your failing ability to thrive. When I think back to the times I have most loved, I realize that it was always when I was whittled down to nothing that the world seemed most colorful and full. At the field in Monastir I owned a few uniforms, two books, and a pistol. Every day I risked my life and every day I returned to a meal and a tent. But I lived in the clouds. Use riches only to increase vitality, for the moment you lean back on them you are lost.

Streetcars. I see men in suits, riding to work in air-conditioned limousines. There they sit, bound by ties, belts, and their own constrictive dignity. I also see people riding the Santa Teresa trolley as it crosses the Lapa Aqueduct. You've seen it, too. There they are, seventy feet in the air, hanging off the side of a creaking, dilapidated, saffron-colored claptrap as it hurtles across the void to the beat of African music.

The Santa Teresa trolley is life in the sun, it is motion, music, risk, and color. And the air-conditioned black cars are nothing more than coffins. Is that what people strive for? Is that their dream? To take themselves from a windy trolley flying above Santa Teresa in the sun and air and put themselves in a black casket stalled in a traffic jam on the Assembléia?

I have everlasting affection for streetcars, not least because the sight of one awakened me from my long dream. It was in Rome, the day of the evening train to Paris, the day the desk clerk said, "Min-er-al wa-ter, min-er-al wa-ter, pistachios, min-er-al wa-ter, min-er-al wa-ter. . . ."

By some miracle, I had already decided to rob Stillman and Chase. The three singers had been the agents of my resolution, and the desk clerk's min-er-al wa-ter aria had been the beginning of its confirmation.

Dazed by my own decision, I began my walk through Rome. Knowing that I would have dinner at my favorite restaurant in a quarter south of the station, and that I would then make my way through a mild evening to the absolute privacy of my compartment, where I would sleep under a lustrous Scotch-plaid blanket as Alpine air chilled the room and the train pushed through the night over rivers that were explosively fresh and cool, I refrained from eating during the day. The Trattoria Minerva was so good that I didn't want to burden it with frivolous competition. It was a neighborhood restaurant unmentioned in the tourism guides. The windows and doors had white curtains stretched over them, cold dishes were laid out on a table near a fireplace, and the food was inimitable. I, who for years had an investment banker's expense account, have never had better.

I wonder if it's still there. I can't direct you to it—I'd have to walk there to find it—and I can't go there myself. First there is a matter of the law, and second there is a matter far more serious than the law. If you are reading this, I'm dead. Dead people don't go to restaurants (except in New York).

I walked all day through Rome, twenty miles through museums, churches, palaces, and piazzas upon which hundreds of the world's greatest artists and tens of thousands of its greatest artisans had worked for thousands of years. Every now and then, Brazil goes through a science-fiction mania, and during the last decade or so many of the movies that fuel the craze have had an obligatory three or four minutes of breaking through the time warp and exiting the universe. In the canon of these movies, the tunnel that leads to the other side of everything is a lava lamp gone berserk, and in these scenes, which are about as theological as Hollywood can get, I always feel as if I've been sucked into a tornado along with ten million bowls of lobster Cantonese.

But the long tunnels of art through which I walked in Rome that day had no ragged edges, cowardly colors, or shades of pastel that didn't know what to do with themselves. The wisdom, perfection, and beauty of the colors and forms I passed were more than enough, in their collectivity, to hint at the principles that govern the hereafter, whatever that may be. Indeed, even a detail of one painting can offer solid direction in this regard if one knows how to look.

I was in an elevated state, as one might expect after a twenty-mile walk through such extraordinary beauty, after months and years of loneliness, after not having eaten that day and perhaps the day before—except for celery, pistachios, and min-er-al water. But though I was in an elevated state, the discovery I made, that brought me from my long dream, was purely an accident.

Granted, it was strangely coincident with encountering the singers, but it was an accident independent of my state of mind.

Crossing the Tiber from Trastevere, I followed the Aurelian Wall until I approached the southerly *borgo* where the restaurant was located. Save the approaches to the Via Appia, nothing in this place appeals to tourists. Nothing here, at least on the surface, is very old. Here is where families live and grow, where children are loved, where marriages play themselves out leading either to wise contentedness or persistent horror. Like Brooklyn Heights or Beacon Hill, it is a retreat, and one cannot enter it without a drop in pressure and pulse.

Not far from my restaurant I found a little park with a fountain at its center. I bought a large bottle of min-er-al wa-ter, went over to the fountain, and sat down, as those who have walked twenty miles will do, with great relief.

For half an hour I listened to the sound of falling water and felt my blood coursing through my body in alert exhaustion. I breathed slowly. My pulse dropped to forty-five or fifty, which is what it does even now when I feel tranquil and strong. I thought neither of Stillman and Chase nor of Constance, nor of anything, least of all disappointments. In my exhaustion I felt only a fine surge of equanimity. I closed my eyes.

I don't know how long I kept them closed—it wasn't long —or even if I slept for a moment, but I opened them when I heard the sound of a spark. Nothing in this world sounds exactly like a high-voltage spark.

Almost silently, an orange-colored streetcar glided from the right into my field of view, motors disengaged and pantograph dropped. It proceeded quietly but for an undying sound of metal rolling upon metal, until it reached the little bay in which it would wait for a northerly departure. As it rolled to a halt, I smelled ozone and burnt oil.

I thought nothing of this, and closed my eyes once more. Then I opened them. The streetcar (in northern countries, streetcars tend to be green; in southern, orange, yellow, or saffron) stood half hidden by a low stone wall. Had I stood up, I would have been able to see the undercarriage and the wheels, but as it was I could see only the top half of the carriage. Despite the import of what was before me, it took a second or two for me to come awake.

Mounted on the side of the carriage was an advertising sign about ten feet long and three feet high, but I could see only the top of it. There, in capital letters, were the initials—or what I took to be the initials—F.P.F. They were spaced very far apart, which suggested that they were capital letters, and that the whole words would be intelligible were I only to rise.

The last time I had seen the initials F.P.F. was also on the side of a rail car, and, then, too, I realized only now, I had been able to see just the top of the letters, because I was too short to look over the obstructions in front of me. Never would I have believed that this sequence of letters would appear before me on rolling stock twice in a lifetime.

I thought against all reason that, if I were to stand up, the name of the murderer would be there for me to see. Of course, this made no sense. Why would it be written on the side of a Roman streetcar four decades after the fact? It made no sense whatsoever, but, still, I stood up, as if I were about to face my executioner. I didn't breathe, and the electricity within me was ricocheting about like a lightning storm in a bell jar.

What disappointment I felt when I saw, alongside the picture of a coffee bean, the words, EXPRESSO BRIGANTE ECCELLÉNTE.

I sat down. It wasn't the name of the murderer, of course, but only an advertisement for—what else—a brand of coffee.

In fact, it hadn't even read F.P.F. It was, rather, E.B.E., but the lower part had been obscured.

"My God," I said. "My dear God." For there I had my revelation.

As a child, I had not seen F.P.F., I had seen E.B.E., and though the years had passed and the snow had fallen a hundred times on my parents' graves, I had not known until now. The F.P.F.'s were innocent. Most of them hadn't even had rail cars. We had foolishly pursued the F.P.F.'s, and all the while . . . it was E.B.E. who had killed my parents.

And who was E.B.E. if not Eugene B. Edgar?

I thought, wait, wait! What if it were someone else? And then I thought how strange it was and perhaps how just, that I would be able to examine the long-forgotten documents of Stillman and Chase, and that I had been trained to make estimations and deductions, and to follow a clue to its unimpeachable source.

I did not eat in my restaurant; I was too agitated. And I did not sleep on the train. I stood at the window all night long, even when we raced through hellish tunnels, and I drank mineral water and threw the bottles into the forest. They sparkled and they tumbled in the moonlight as we climbed into Switzerland, crossing the great white torrents that from ancient glaciers had recently been unfrozen and now danced with the delight of waking from a sleep of ten thousand years. I was alive as I had never been since 1914.

I had assumed that I would return to New York with Tarquin's ravishing strides, rape the Stillman and Chase archives, and, proof in hand, lift Eugene B. Edgar from his gold-and-mahogany wheelchair and kill him by snapping his disgusting little chicken neck. But it was not so easy.

Though I had long before passed the tests of manhood and was well into middle age, the knowledge the streetcar brought propelled me backward in time until I was a quaking ten-year-old, as if the previous four decades of my life had not existed. I felt every fear and vulnerability of a child, and found it hard to believe that I knew what I knew. The contradiction and strain of living simultaneously in two states of mind catapulted me into a slight nervous breakdown.

I know this because, among other things, I saw a new color. Eye doctors always think I'm a little funny. Apparently they are unfamiliar with what I see when I close my eyes, because when I describe it to them they ask if I use drugs. I may be the most drug-free person in existence, but when I close my eyes I see the Battle of Baltimore, the Star-Spangled Banner, bombs bursting in air, star shells, fireworks, the Chinese New Year, undulating dragons of fire. The panorama of flashing lights is so wide and so detailed, so surprising, intricately patterned, and unpredictable, that if I could bring back only half a second of it, it would take an hour to describe. It has always been that way, but after I returned from Rome the flashes disappeared and in their place flowed a deep, bright, most unusual color that I had never seen and have not seen since, but for months it replaced the battles in darkness. It was very much like a blinding magenta—though not magenta—a color that was unsettling, persistent, and unexplained.

Then there was also the question of my relations with the opposite sex. I was totally unsure of what to do or say, and the prospect of making love to a woman was too astounding for words. I called up one of Constance's friends, whom I hadn't seen since the separation. Like Constance herself, this woman was extraordinarily athletic and devastatingly beautiful. When she and I had played doubles tennis against Constance, who was so good that she always played doubles without a partner, I would get that tossed-out-of-an-airplane feeling of weightless ecstasy as she stretched for the ball, and by the time she was sweating with exertion I was virtually good for nothing.

So I called her up, and I said, "Sydney, I don't know how to tell you this except bluntly."

"What?" she asked, nervously.

"Something has happened. My abacus has been snapped back to the time that I was ten."

"Your abacus?"

"Yes. I'm a grown man, but I'm ten."

"Mentally?"

"No."

"Physically?"

"No."

"Emotionally?"

"Perhaps."

"Oh," she said. "I don't know what to say. It's unusual, isn't it?"

"Yes," I said.

"Is there anything I can do to help?"

"Oh yes. There is, there is."

"Uh, would you like to talk? Would you like me to read you a story?"

"Not really, Sydney. It requires much more than that."

"Just tell me."

"Sydney," I said—that such an exquisite woman had such a name was really a crime. "If I can . . . and I'm not sure that I can . . . I need to make love to you for about four days on end, without stopping, in a ceaseless trance."

Despite silence on the line, I continued. "You'd have to tell your friends that you were going away, you'd have to stop the mail and newspapers, cancel your engagements, turn off the telephone, and stock up on food—lots of creamy cold things, chilled fruit, oysters, champagne, and chocolate." I didn't add, "and big bloody steaks," because I didn't want to upset her and I didn't want her to think I was a dog.

"Are you all right?" she asked.

"No. I'm ten. I've never been with a woman before. I want to devote myself to the discovery and worship of every part of you. That's why I need at least four days."

The line went dead for so long that I thought she had hung up. Then she said, "You get over here as fast as you can, and by the time you come I will have returned from Gristedes with the strawberries and clotted cream."

And then there were other things—other women, other colors, visits to Palisades Park and F.A.O. Schwarz—but I finally faced my fear of looking upon the documents that might confirm that for almost four decades I had been serving the man who killed my mother and father.

I began to get (relatively) well. I no longer saw otherworldly colors when I closed my eyes, or needed to make love to Sydney for a week at a time, or spend vast amounts of money on roller coasters, cotton candy, and toy guns. During that strange interlude, Piehand had sensed my vulnerability and had accelerated the chain of events that were eventually to put me in the broom closet.

But my inner machinery began to revive, and one day I was a man again. Though when I went down to the archives I was as nervous as a child before a piano recital, I was a child no longer, and my experience had come into play. I stepped from the elevator my old self had returned just in time to be defeated by practical difficulties.

I had never been in the archives. These were separate from the library, where for years I had done research, and were of no use to anyone except economic historians, though neither economic historians nor anyone else was allowed to see them. My intention was to use the dregs of my fast-disappearing rank to buffalo my way in.

It was easy enough to enter the paneled anteroom of the vault of ancient Edgar memorabilia, where I stood upon an Oriental carpet so thick that I found it difficult to keep my balance, and asked the custodian if I could see the records of the years 1913 and 1914.

This woman was a cross between the archetypal librarian and Sophia Loren. I found it as difficult to talk to her as it would have been to address a pushmepullyou. "Of course you can't," she said. "The archives are closed."

"I'm the executive vice-president for research and investment policy," I told her, "*and* a full partner."

"That doesn't mean a goddamned thing," she said, and she was quite right.

"What good are archives if no one can use them?"

"They can be used," she stated.

"By whom?"

"By Mr. Edgar."

"He can hardly move and he can't read. He couldn't bear the weight of a drawer," I said, pointing to the interior of the vault, where the information was kept in giant safe-deposit boxes, each of which—I noticed—had three locks.

"Mr. Piehand and I are supposed to accompany Mr. Edgar to help him with the materials."

"So you see them."

"No, I don't. I can't read through folders."

"But you and Mr. Piehand have access to them."

"No. Mr. Piehand has a key, I have a key, and Mr. Edgar has a key. I know that only Mr. Edgar may see the documents, and Mr. Piehand knows that only Mr. Edgar may see the documents, and Mr. Edgar knows that only Mr. Edgar may see the documents. Believe me, only Mr. Edgar sees the documents."

"Why? What's so secret about them?"

"I have no idea. They belong to Mr. Edgar."

"How often does Mr. Edgar come to look?"

"If Mr. Edgar came to look, I would tell you to ask *him* that question. But the fact is, he doesn't come to look."

"Ever?"

"Not in the fifteen years I've been here."

"You said you can't read through folders."

"I stand by my statement."

"Why did you say it, if you've never seen them?"

"It's the procedure, in case he wants to look."

"He's probably forgotten that this archive exists," I told her, my irritation mixing with amazement. "He's as senile as a baseball bat, you know."

She turned her palms up, as if to say, *So what?*

"So you sit here, in an office fit for the president of France, and once a year you receive a set of new materials."

She shook her head slowly from side to side. "This archive spans only the time from the founding of the firm to the creation of the Securities and Exchange Commission in 1934."

"What do you do all day? Why are you here?" I demanded, as if an investment bank had any reason to worry about efficiency and expenditures.

"I'm here in case Mr. Edgar wants to use the archives. What I do all day is my business."

"But what *do* you do?" I asked, purely out of curiosity.

"You could come down sometime and find out," she said, with a piercing look that took my breath away. "This place is *very* quiet."

I staggered away. Yes, she was pneumatic, and were she to have taken off her spectacles—black plastic frames that weighed almost as much as she did, and lenses that reduced her eyes to the size of sequins—she would have been devastatingly attractive. But you can't have affairs at the office no matter how much you might want to, and not only that, but given that I so badly needed her key, whatever I would have done would have been certain to have made me a gigolo.

This was long before my reunion with Smedjebakken, and this vault was high above the street. That was when I began to think about vaults, but none of the means I considered would have kept me dissociated from the murder of Mr. Edgar, or allowed me to continue at Stillman and Chase.

I was at a standstill.

I imagined everything from having the affair with Miss Dickstein, the archivist, which I would not do on principle, to having an affair with Dickey Piehand's secretary, which I would not do on principle, to having an affair with one of Mr. Edgar's 'nurses,' which I would not have done on principle but which I might have done anyway, not being able to resist. His nurses were the most beautiful women in the world. I don't think a single one of them was less than six feet tall, and they all were, literally, stunning. I couldn't take my eyes from them. No one could. Though Mr. Edgar had the world's greatest physicians, it was the presence of these women that kept him alive so far beyond his time—an old trick known mainly to kings.

Their relations were, of course, purely platonic; his body was long gone. What kept him going was a series of wonderful ideas reverberating in his half-dead heart. But even had I been able to subvert a nurse or two the chances of being able to subvert Miss Dickstein were almost nil, and as for Piehand's secretary, I didn't even know if she had access to his keys. Despite its allure, the sexual approach was out for many reasons, including one that I've neglected to mention, which is that though I have always been in love and almost always have had someone to love, it has been one blind encounter after another, the play of perpetual accident. Whenever I've set my mind to winning over a particular woman, only disaster has followed. And then, finally, I was actually afraid that Miss Dickstein would be so intense in her amours that after our first encounter I would be reduced to the mysterious residue that announces where a bird has done battle with a cat. And so much for that.

Then came the next set of possibilities—the violent penetrations and commando operations that depended upon quick insertion, ruthless execution, a stick of plastic explosive to blow away the door of the lockbox, and fast escape. Unfortunately, these required the murder of Miss Dickstein or the erasure of her memory. As I would not have murdered an innocent person to discover who had murdered my parents, and as erasing Miss Dickstein's memory would undoubtedly have proved more difficult than having an affair with her, I realized that I could not reinvent the S.A.S. I would have to employ stealth alone. No one could know that I had been in and out. I needed the keys, for without them I would have to damage the locks, after which Miss Dickstein, who was on to me in more ways than one, would need only tell the police my address.

Hence the next avenue—chloroform. I would simply put all three people in a trance for long enough to press their keys onto a duplication tablet. I could have done it with Miss Dickstein, but the others were too risky. I'd either never get them alone or it would take a million years, and Mr. Edgar didn't have a million years. In fact, my major problem was that I had to race against time so I could kill him before he died.

I had killed only people who were in the midst of trying to kill me or someone else, and I had left a way out for all of them. Had they merely broken off their attacks, I would not have harmed them. This was different. It was vengeance and it was premeditated and the man was totally helpless.

Would the proof be sufficient, and was I able to judge? I thought about this for some time, and concluded that my reluctance to do the deed would ensure that the proof be really unambiguous. And if it were, I would not shrink from what I had to do. Nor would I worry about abandoning traditional forms of jurisprudence, or taking the law in my own hands. I knew that, even were he charged before he died, Mr. Edgar would spend five hundred million on lawyers and that no matter how guilty he was they would delay the disposition of his case until he was comfortably within his fully staffed mausoleum. (His favorite cooks, maids, and gardeners, but mainly maids, were to attend to him for the rest of his death. Those who were alive would dust the mausoleum and take telephone calls, those who were dead were buried standing up next to the parthenon in which he would lie.) I also knew that, even were he convicted he would get some sort of community-service rehabilitation sentence—which is another way of saying that for having my parents shot through the head and left to die on the floor, he would be forced to spend three months playing Ping-Pong with disadvantaged children, or explain to a group of failing dry cleaners how to maximize cash flow and cut expenses. But the son of a bitch couldn't even play Ping-Pong and he refused to talk, so his sentence would be just to continue staring at his Scandinavian nurses.

I wondered if I would be able to do it, and I didn't know. Meanwhile, I had no idea how to get into the 1913 and 1914 lockboxes.

That is, until Smedjebakken and I were well on our way to robbing the gold vault. Then it came to me, and it was easy, though he was entirely against prejudicing or risking our main operation with yet another subsidiary action such as stealing a painting. He refused to do it, until I told him of how, on a day early in June, I had lain between my mother and father, wanting to sleep with them forever, and then how I had awakened in the cold night when nothing had changed except the constitution of their flesh.

"All right," he said, "I'll help you do it. What do you have in mind?"

"I have to get the keys."

"How?"

"That's where you come in."

"Don't forget," he pointed out, "I can't enter the building. I've already been there as a surveyor. And even if I could, how would I get the keys? I'm not a pickpocket."

"Don't you think I have a plan?" I asked.

First, we bought a van. These days, vans are common, sleek, and carlike. Then, they were huge, they had rounded backs, and they looked like hearses. We cut a window into the side and put some machinery on a rolling table in the cargo space. A sign painter lettered the panels of the truck, and we were in business.

Considering that we already had the machinery and that the truck was used, the start-up cost was minimal.

The signs on the panels informed passersby that this was the place to have their keys "buffed, polished, deburred, and permanently glycerine-waxed." Were they to do so, they were told, they would "Never have trouble opening a lock again! Save precious time! End the fear of breaking a key in a lock! Preserve your precious keys! Give your keys a pleasant new odor and jingle!" Best of all, it was, "Only 5 Cents!" and it was, "Fast Fast Fast!"

It caught on like wildfire. Poor Smedjebakken spent days and nights in the van, polishing, deburring, and waxing the keys of Wall Street office workers. At lunch hour the line was ten deep. Every other customer asked him how he could make a living at only five cents a shot, and he told them that he was thinking of doubling the price.

Over a period of weeks we had him stationed at all points of the compass around Stillman and Chase. His starting place four blocks out became three, then two, then one, until, finally, he stayed right in front of the Stillman and Chase main entrance.

We were hoping, of course, that Miss Dickstein, Piehand's secretary, and, somehow, even Mr. Edgar, would have their keys polished on the street. In fact, Piehand's secretary did, but she wasn't carrying the key to the lockboxes. Piehand himself must have carried it, and he always walked by in a hurry.

We were going to have to go in. It wasn't very difficult. Everyone at Stillman and Chase was used to the presence of the key-polishing service, and I put up leaflets announcing that Stillman and Chase had arranged for everyone's keys to be polished at their desks, free of charge.

On the appointed day, Smedjebakken rolled the cart with the deburrers, polishers, and wax right into Stillman and Chase, and started off on the many keys of the security staff at the front desk. They didn't recognize the surveyor they had not too long before accompanied over a period of many hours, because . . . well, this was the part Smedjebakken didn't like.

The service was called Mr. Tubby's Key to Perfection, and Smedjebakken was Mr. Tubby. We bought him a pair of fat-men's pants, the kind that look like the funnel on a rock crusher or an air vent on the *Queen Mary,* and strapped two down pillows to his waist. With a fake mustache and a fedora, he became Mr. Tubby.

Mr. Tubby worked the Stillman and Chase building for almost a week, polishing everyone's keys, even Mr. Edgar's. Because he was providing this very valuable service to them for free, saving them an entire nickel per key, everyone at Stillman and Chase from the janitors (who, granted, had a lot of keys) to Mr. Edgar himself, was overcome with joy. For weeks thereafter you could hear comments—no, whole conversations—about a key's new jingle; or how easy it had suddenly become to open locks; or about the wonders and delights of glycerine-waxing; how good the keys felt; how pleasant they smelled; how they glittered.

Amid the clutter of machinery and wax pots on his roller cart Smedjebakken kept waxen blocks that looked not at all incongruous and against which he skillfully pressed the lockbox keys and the big key to the bars that blocked the entrance to the vault in the daytime. He knew which they were because he made a point of doing Miss Dickstein before he got to the executive floor, where he knocked off Piehand's and Edgar's in a single half hour. After one more day at Stillman and Chase, Mr. Tubby vanished from the face of the earth. No one gave it a thought. No one in New York ever does.

I clocked Miss Dickstein's lunches. Because she had nothing to do all day, lunch must have loomed very large. As she was not only sensual but precise, she left always at 11:50 A.M. I used to follow her through the very bright sunshine of the financial district, where, when people come out of their offices, they shield their eyes from the light of morning and the sparkling flashes of sidewalks embedded with crushed glass.

Every day without fail this crazy woman walked twelve blocks to a café near City Hall, and every day she had the same lunch: a bowl of smoked oysters and watercress, a gin and tonic, and a banana split. After her meal she lingered over a cup of tea while finishing a chapter in *The Economic History of Liberia*. With her glasses removed as she read, I saw that she was rather beautiful, and that despite her daily banana splits she was rather trim. She always took an hour and a half for lunch, and even if she finished early she would walk around the block until she had to come in.

At 11:51 one day I got off the elevator on the archives floor and walked through Miss Dickstein's magnificent office. I could still smell her perfume. At the þars I used a waxed, polished, deburred, fragrant copy of the key to let myself into the vault. The 1913 lockbox was to my left. As soon as I stepped in front of it I could be seen neither from the office nor the hall.

Though I shuddered when I looked one box over to the right and saw the numbers *1914*, I used my glittering keys on 1913, swung open the door, and pulled out the box. It weighed about fifty pounds. I carried it to a leather-topped table in the corner, where when I turned on a reading lamp that hadn't been lit in many years the filament oscillated in shock.

The records themselves smelled like New York in the Teens. Perhaps it was the way they made paper then, or the effect of age on leather, but if I closed my eyes I could imagine that I was a boy again, and that on any block you could see horses, hear their exhalations, and smell their bridles. I listened to the crackle of fires and watched many lines of wood and coal smoke ascend into what were clear blue skies nonetheless. I felt entirely at home and in my element. This was *my* time, I had known it, I had been born in the previous decade, and I would be familiar with any truth that I might find.

My fear that the papers would be unorganized was groundless. They were foldered and tabbed, and I merely shuffled through them. It had been a rough year for Mr. Edgar. The tabs read: *16th Amendment* (the income tax), *Pujo Report* (the House Banking Committee findings of monopoly concentration), *Federal Reserve, Owen-Glass, Panama Bankruptcy, Mexican Revolution*. Those were the obvious. Then there were others: *Knox vs. Nichols, Failed Debentures, Pacific Palisades, Sharpton Steel*. And others, too, but by 12:40 nothing had even hinted at what I was looking for. With half an hour remaining, I grew very nervous. I was more than nervous. Suddenly, I was terrified.

Breathing fast, I put back 1913 and opened 1914. Moving the drawer to the desk seemed to take hours; raising the lid, minutes.

The tabs told of the *Clayton Antitrust Act*, the *Federal Trade Commission*, and, now, of not just the advent but the consequences of the *Income Tax*. I read on: *Vera, S&O, Dutch Steel Contract, Exchange Profits*, and, then . . . and then, I was blinded. I could hardly breathe. I had found a folder that was labeled *Hudson River Bridge*.

With only ten minutes left I dared not try to read it. Besides, I was not in full possession of myself. I put back the 1914 box, locked it up, turned off the light above the desk (sentencing it to sleep for perhaps another several decades), and left with the folder held casually in my hands.

When the elevator door opened on the archives floor, Miss Dickstein got out and I got in. She smiled at me, and I smiled at her. Even had she noticed what I was carrying, which I think she did not, she might not have recognized it. She may never have actually seen any of the records she guarded. And even had she suspected that I had removed something from her domain, she probably would have dismissed her concerns when she returned to her station and saw that the locks were solidly in place.

This was a Friday. When I told the moron Sherman Oscovitz that I was leaving early, he tried to play medical detective.

"Oh?" he said. "Why?"

"I don't feel well."

"Where?"

"In my mongus," I said.

"Is it a dull ache or a sharp pain?"

"It's an enthralling torture."

"Do you have a fever?"

"I don't know," I told him. "Feel my brow."

"What's a brow?"

"Up here." I pointed.

In the moment that Sherman Oscovitz stepped closer, raised his right hand, and slowly brought it to my face, I closed my eyes and thought of the things that Sydney wanted me to do, things I had never heard of, things *she* had never heard of, and my temperature went up to about 105 degrees. Oscovitz recoiled in alarm.

"You're burning up!"

"Associative caffeine thrombolysis," I said, and left for the weekend.

By this time my own apartment had been taken over by Angelica and Constance Smedjebakken, and I didn't want to go to Astoria or to Sydney's, the former because I found it depressing when Smedjebakken was absent, and the latter because I needed to retain my ability to walk.

Instead, I went up the Hudson to Athens, the quietest most forgotten town in the world, and stayed in the hotel there. On the train, I touched my briefcase again and again, but rather than open it I read the *Wall Street Journal* and the *New York Herald Tribune*. I no longer had any need of newspapers, either professionally or personally, but they were a habit and I was glad that they kept me from my task.

Once in the hotel, I stationed myself by the window, and, for two days, I starved. The management thought that I had come to commit suicide, and sent the chambermaid into the room every few hours to check on me. Finally I said, "Don't come in here again, and tell the proprietor not to worry that I'm going to commit suicide. I'm a physicist, and I need absolute tranquility to reconcile Newtonian Mechanics with the Theory of Relativity."

I don't think she caught my drift, because the next thing I knew the kitchen delivered a plate of Fig Newtons, but then, perhaps happy that I was eating, they left me alone.

I stared at the Hudson for two days without seeing a single boat, and for two days I gazed upon the railroad tracks and did not see a train. I love forgotten towns, for it is in forgotten towns that you can appreciate the curtains moving inward with the breeze, and in forgotten towns that you can breathe easy, and listen to the ticking of a clock, and see the light come up.

In forsaken towns the world is not a symphony of distractions, it is the lovely sound of wind blowing across the water, or an old tree bending under the burden of its half a million young and impatient leaves. I sat by the window in the hotel in Athens, the green file on the table next to me, and was still for two days as I fell back into the reverence of childhood. I knew God when I was a child, seeing His presence at every turn. It was easy— saints, and lambs, and an eye that had just awakened and was keen for detail. And, most of all, I was happy in the absolute love and devotion of my father and mother, and free, therefore, to see beyond the pain of the world.

The wind quietly moved the white curtains, made ripples on the bend in the river, and swayed the trees just enough for me to hear. The radiator hissed and knocked. Once in a while I would hear a door close, a car go by, or footsteps on the stairs. I could not open the folder.

I stared at the rug, which was green with pale roses woven in a garland of dusty red. I slept and dreamed. I looked at the river. It was not that I was afraid. I was not afraid. And it was not that I thought for even an instant that I would fail to open the folder. I knew that I would not fail.

It was that I was mourning what I assumed would be the imminent destruction of the previous forty years, and preparing myself for a great change. As long as my mother and father had died in mystery, and were unavenged, my heart had been open to them. Now I was preparing to close the chapter, and, I feared, close my heart.

I could hardly take my eyes from the river and the waters I once had known so well. I watched the wind move the diaphanous curtains. I suppose you might say that I was crazy, but love moved me. In that long abandoned long lost town, on the shore of the Hudson, I spent two sleepless days loving the quiet things that were left to me, preparing myself, saying goodbye.

When, on the train to New York on Sunday evening, I finally opened the folder, my eyes were as cold as steel. It was dark outside, and as all the Vassar girls were riding in the opposite direction, the train was nearly empty. In yellow light reflected mercilessly from blackened windows I was incapacitated by tenderness no longer, which was good, for although tenderness has its place, life is driven not by tenderness but by vigor.

Though the folder was an inch thick, I knew within a minute or two that the mystery would be solved. In ten minutes I had skimmed the documents and tied together an indictment, and by the time I reached Grand Central I had read the entire account and knew it indelibly.

It was all fairly simple. The first entry was a letter dated 27 August, 1909, when I was not quite five. In it, a Mr. Schellenberger pointed out to one of Mr. Edgar's lieutenants that it was physically possible to bridge the Hudson. He had in mind a suspended span from the Palisades to the heights of Kingsbridge in the Bronx.

Such a bridge would have been spectacular, especially since, to match the altitude of the Palisades, a great ramp would have had to have been constructed on the New York side. The bridge would be visible, Schellenberger claimed, from the Catskills, Long Island Sound, the Ramapos, and New York's seaward approaches. The key to its placement was simply that the river at the point he proposed is relatively narrow.

Mr. Schellenberger disappeared, but in the year of Wilson's election came a flood of memoranda, notes, and letters in which the focus shifted northward. The City of New York was unreceptive to a public bridge built for private gain. As the wood there was too hard, Mr. Edgar's chisel would have to be directed elsewhere, but the Yonkers politicians, as happy as they would have been to accept a bribe, were beholden to the bosses in the great city upon which Yonkers was fated to sit forever like a cat on a Percheron.

North of Yonkers the river widened and the rock gave way to marsh. According to consultants hired by Stillman and Chase, it was not technically feasible to bridge the Tappan Zee—too much shifting of the river floor, and too wide. The nearest available site was Teller's Point, where the distance to both sides of the river was a mile and the geology favorable.

Advice to Mr. Edgar was that if a bridge and its associated approaches were built on this spot, a vast city would spring up on both banks of the Hudson. With the automobile's conquest of distance, no one would think twice about approaching New York from the rest of the continent via a bridge only thirty miles to the north.

"Why not just take over the ferry traffic?" Mr. Edgar had scrawled in the margin. The answer must have come verbally, because it was nowhere in the folder, but it was undoubtedly that no ferry has ever been able to compete with a bridge.

In January of 1914, Mr. Edgar wrote instructions to his lieutenants. The project was to go ahead. Everything had to be done in the greatest secrecy. If not, the price of surrounding lands would rise, defeating the rationale for the scheme in the first place, by unacceptably raising the cost of construction in relation to the probable returns. The most important parcels were obviously those directly in the path of the crossing and nearby, and no effort should be spared in securing them. The farmers were not likely to want to sell their land at prices low enough to allay suspicion of development. "In this case," he wrote, "do what is necessary to secure the properties, dealing as harshly as may be required with the first people with whom you deal, so that the others will understand and fall into line."

When I read that, I thought of Mr. Edgar, and, even though he wasn't there I said to him, "It may have taken forty years, but you blew it, and you're going to die." I was hardened by those lines to the point where my moral qualms about killing a helpless man receded so far that I could no longer sense them.

In the middle of the dossier was a foldout map of both banks of the Hudson and Teller's Point in between. My father's farm was clearly delineated and identified. Across the property, in engineer's or draftsman's style, were drawn the main approach ramp for the bridge, and the easternmost pier and anchors. The roadway went right through our house.

I suppose Mr. Edgar was right. My father never would have sold out, because what was at stake here was not money but love. Without killing my father, Mr. Edgar never would have been able to put his bridge in place.

But even though he did kill my father (and, for good measure, my mother, too) he did not put up his bridge. He would have, but that summer the war came. He would build ships instead, and direct his capital to the expansion of steel and rubber production. My parents were killed not even for a bridge. They were killed for nothing, like birds that hunters shoot and leave behind in the field.

The evidence at that point was enough, though it may not have been sufficient in a court of law, but any lingering uncertainties vanished when I came upon two receipts bound into the pages of the folder. Both were dated June 8th, 1914, and each was for $1,000. One was signed by a Mr. Curtin, and the other by a Joseph Nevel. In a businesslike hand that matched neither signature, someone had written, "For services rendered, June 5th, 1914."

Never have I been quite as relaxed about anything as I was initially about the murder of Eugene B. Edgar. I realize that this might seem a trifle coldhearted, but look, you know, he killed my mother and father. I realize that the impulse of many people would be to help him, to *rehabilitate* him. I can only say, let them help and rehabilitate the murderers of their families, I will deal with the murderers of mine somewhat differently. I was neither proud of what I was going to do, nor ashamed. I would take no pleasure in it, but I knew what was required of me, and that I simply could not shirk.

I brought no tools or weapons, and was outfitted only in a pair of Florentine driving gloves, a navy-blue polo shirt, a pair of khaki pants, and rubber-soled shoes. This is what I normally would have worn, except for the gloves, which I kept in my pocket until I needed them. They were fashioned of very strong and supple leather, they were extremely thin, and in my pocket they looked like a folded handkerchief. I took some cash, in $20 bills, for train fare, gasoline, and tolls, and I carried a newspaper. I have always loved to travel light.

The gold was already loaded on the plane, along with some photographs, letters, and a few mementos: my father's pocketknife, his gold-rimmed spectacles, my mother's wedding ring, a locket of her hair, my pistol from the war, and a beautiful little Sargent that Constance had given me, in which a woman in a white dress is walking down a garden path, holding the hand of a young child.

The Smedjebakkens were gone; all my possessions sold, donated, or burned. The remnants of my bank accounts had been converted to Swiss francs and were in my flight bag with the pistol. The landing strips were prepared, the apartment in Brazil waiting. Most reassuring was that the Smedjebakkens had arrived safely at their destination, and this I knew because I had received a telegram that read: GREAT HAPPINESS MOZART SNOW COVERED MOUNTAINS MAGNIFICENT CITIES MARBLE HALLS CRYSTAL POOLS AND CHOCOLATE CAKES STOP PAOLO.

No one knew that the gold was missing. No one knew that the plane was gassed, loaded, and waiting in the barn. No one knew that I had liquidated everything I had and that the Smedjebakkens had started a new life. No one knew what I was going to do, or where to find me. Even Sydney had broken off our affair, saying that such a thing was acceptable only once in a lifetime, and not for too long, which I thought was both sensible and a great relief. I was free. I had no friends or family and I would never be missed, but I was free. I walked through the streets of New York like a visitor from another world, and yet this was my city, that I knew and loved so well. But, still, I had the lightness of being that you feel when you are graduated from an institution that you intend to put behind you forever.

It was early September, and still hot. The humid storms had been replaced by summer heat in declining light, the prelude to golden autumn. I took the train out to Greenwich at commuter time, sitting in the rear car with the conductors on their last run. I knew that investment bankers habituated the forward cars, so I had boarded the train early and was the last to get off. No one saw me in the Greenwich twilight as hundreds of engines started in the parking lots amid the scramble to get in position for the race home on horribly winding roads. In the dusk I walked briskly onto Fishcake Lane, and as darkness fell I found myself at the edge of the Sound, looking across a beautiful rolling moor at the light from Dickey Piehand's estate in Mianus.

It was as immense as an ocean liner bobbing and twinkling on the brine off East Hampton. All the lights were on, and from the darkness in the still fragrant vegetation it looked as bright as if someone inside were filming a movie. I wondered if Ed Murrow were visiting Dickey Piehand, but not a truck was in sight.

I walked across the moor in the dark, smelling the sand, the heather, and many plants that I couldn't identify, having been terribly ill in the weeks in which I was supposed to have studied botany. I love plants, but have always hated it when people go from one to another saying their names. Quite often, people, especially very rich people, are overcome with joyful contempt when I don't know the name of some lousy fucking plant. "You mean, you don't know that this is a palustral he-lichrysum?" I always reply that these plants about which they are so irritatingly reverent don't know what they are, either. And just because, two hundred years ago, a clerk in a Danish arboretum called the vegetable we are discussing a palustral helichrysum doesn't mean that it really is a palustral helichry-sum. The plant is what it is, and palustral helichrysum be damned.

Shielded by darkness and nearly overcome by the scent of the sea, I approached the house, and the closer I got the better I heard the sound of a hi-fi. It was a recording of a woman singing a ballad from a Broadway musical. Perfect.

The garage was located at a civilized remove from the house. As I knew from having been at several Piehand soirées and picnics and having had to eat there because of the coffee, it was far enough away for the sound of starting an engine not to carry. With a record going inside the house, I could have laid down an artillery barrage and no one would have been the wiser. Perhaps because it was such a benevolent evening that even

Dickey Piehand was not afraid the night air might hurt his automobiles, the doors were open.

The top was down on the little MG, and a cat was sitting on the canvas cover that snapped across the gap in back of the seat. "Go away!" I said. It didn't move, so I picked it up, but, before I could throw it, it jumped from my hands and settled on the passenger seat. "All right," I said. "If you want to come with me, you can." The cat blinked, as they do, like a king.

I jumped into the MG, inserted the key provided by Mr. Tubby, and drove slowly down the driveway, with the lights off. When I got to Fishcake Lane I turned on the headlamps and picked up speed. Though driving on winding roads in a sports car on a moonlit summer night, I was subdued. I was thinking about things that were sad and true, and before I knew it the cat and I were flying high over the Sound on the steel deck of the Throgs Neck Bridge.

I had been to the Edgar place on Biscuit Neck a dozen times, for parties, small dinners with ministers of finance, and, most recently, to brief Mr. Edgar as he lay on his sickbed. I knew the inside of the house, the outside, the grounds, the paths through the woods, the exercise pavilions, tennis courts, and pools.

He owned all of Biscuit Neck, even the village. The Biscuit Neck police force was a public institution, he was the one taxpayer, and their primary function was to guard his two-thousand-acre estate. Needless to say, the town was rich, even if it was not heavily populated. As Mr. Edgar had begat no one to beget anyone else, there were no schools. Because his estate had its own sewage, water, and electrical systems, there was no maintenance to speak of: if a pothole had to be fixed on the main street, the gardeners would do it, and they knew how, because they were always repaving the forty-five miles of roads up at the house. The shops in the village were the tiny offspring of Tiffany, Dunhill, Mark Cross, S. S. Pierce, etc., and they were not really shops but offices from which to service the estate.

I parked in the shadows between the village and the heavy spear-point fence that went for many miles around the Edgar compound. That the police would carefully inspect the car and record the license number was a mathematical certainty.

Whereas the cat fit right through the bars and waited passively on the other side, I had to climb over. I listened carefully for the sound of approaching police cruisers, and when I heard nothing but existential silence I went up and over the fence, balancing precariously on the rail beneath the spear points, and then dropping to the ground. Had the spears been sharpened, I would not have been able to do it. I frankly do not understand why Mr. Edgar spent six million dollars to build the fence and left the spears dull. For another half-million he could have affixed razor-sharp blades instead, and though he would not be alive today at least he might have lived to have seen color television.

With the cat purring in my arms, I walked for half an hour over small hills and through forested groves, across vast fields of hay that had just been harvested, and under the ponderous black moon-shade of English oaks on the hundred-acre lawn.

Mr. Edgar had dinner at four. That he was not exactly Italian in his eating habits was well known. I doubted, however, that he was asleep, because the lights in his bedroom were blazing. He was home, and not in any of his châteaux or town houses, or on any of the yachts, the three largest of which were called the *Interest*, the *Dividend*, and the *Capital Gain*.

Suddenly, blinding lights slewed in my direction and dogs began to howl. Had the dogs been loose, they would have done me in. You don't have much chance with bull mastiffs, as their passion for hunting people down is what ties them together and sets them apart.

Luckily for me, Mr. Edgar did not want his dogs to foul his footpaths, so their handlers trucked them about in golf carts, and golf carts move very slowly. The cat and I ran behind the hedges that screened the pool. The dogs' noses kept leading them to us, and they got so close you could hear the springs of the golf carts knocking as the dogs strained to jump out. They were fifteen feet away, and the headlights were blinding even through the hedge. Dog saliva flew in the air. The droplets sparkled in the intense light and then were vacuumed up by the night. It was like the Trevi fountain in a high wind.

The moment I heard the leashes unclipped and the rocking of the golf carts as the dogs left them, I pointed the cat through the hedge and pinched his flank. Off he shot, as straight as a rocket and as loud as an ambulance, and he led the dogs so deep into the darkness that in less than a minute I could barely hear the whine of golf carts chasing after them. Then, they, too, disappeared, and I was alone in the restored din of the crickets.

I sat on one of the chaises near the pool. The water was black, pure, and gurgling. One of the options of a man with as much money as Mr. Edgar is to have the filtering house a quarter of a mile away, so that one can sit by the pool without thinking of the West Side Highway. I lay back and looked up at the stars. Toward New York, the sky was bordered by a scalloped orange glow as the city's vast system of illumination backlit the tops of the oaks. Straight up, stars trembled and meteors flared in breathless white lines. The moon was somewhere, somehow whitening the black sky. I slept for at least an hour.

When I awakened I was calm and a little tired. I sat up and

swung my feet to the ground, reflecting on the means by which Mr. Edgar had accumulated his wealth. Undoubtedly he had done many fine things. They could not, however, serve as a balance for his depravities. What a mistake it is of juries and judges to consider a man's good deeds when weighing his sins. Such-and-such a fellow raped and murdered someone's daughter, but he gave to charity and he was always cheerful. In the final ledger, one entry can easily disqualify every other, for more important than doing good is to refrain from doing harm.

As I sat near the pool trying to come fully awake—something I can usually do rather quickly by wiggling my toes—I remembered a meeting that I attended with Mr. Edgar and half a dozen others at the River Club. I was there to give a country estimate, but I never got around to that: Mr. Edgar was in a fury, and he held to one subject like a bulldog.

"We have many billions on account from institutions, governments, and individual investors," he said.

"*Zillions,*" asserted a young Edgar grandnephew. That was the end of him.

Mr. Edgar pulled out a cigar knife and placed it on the table. "Put your pinkie in here, Selwyn," he commanded the nephew, who did. "Good. Now, you shut up. If you so much as open your mouth, we'll feed your finger to the fish."

With the nephew out of the way, he turned to the comptroller. "What is our current return?"

"Four and a half percent, net."

"Which comes mainly from loans and investment."

"Yes sir."

"How much, exactly?"

"Three points, more or less."

"And what is our net, currently, from participation?"

"About one and a quarter."

"So tell me where that other quarter point comes in," Mr. Edgar ordered.

"Asset rental and leasing, prepaid charges not accountable as reimbursements, and fees."

"Fees!" thundered Mr. Edgar. "Fees!"

"Yes sir."

"How many points?" he demanded.

"An eighth of a point, sir."

"Asses!" he said. "Fees! No one questions them. They take advantage of people's lifetimes of passivity, their years of education and molding. There are two kinds of creature in the jungle—the tiger and the iguana. The tiger sets the fees, and the iguana pays them. I want *more fees.*"

"Arbitrarily, sir?"

"What the hell do you think a fee is, Nichols?" he screamed at Nichols. "Do we have transaction fees?"

"On what?"

"On everything."

"No."

"Levy transaction fees. And maintenance fees. And fees for opening an account, closing an account, having less than three accounts, and having more than two accounts. I want to see late charges, early charges, and surcharges on other charges. I want a fee fo. foreign accounts, a fee for domestic accounts, and a fee for accounts subject to audits. You get the picture? Gradually double or triple these fees over a period of two or three years, and index them to inflation. Institute a contact fee, a telephone charge, a bookkeeping adjustment charge, a flotation fee, a sinking fee, and, you, Nichols, go to the New York Public Library and—I don't care how long it takes—find five fees that no one has ever heard of. Look especially hard into Babylonia, the

Sumerians, Byzantium, and the Holy Roman Empire. Those guys knew what they were doing, and they had balls."

"But Mr. Edgar, we'll drive away our customers."

"No we won't. Just be prepared to drop the fees of any customer who appears to be making good on a threat to leave, and increase those on the ones who stay put. It never fails."

"Yes sir."

When Mr. Edgar left the River Club that evening, he was—although not immediately—several hundred million dollars richer. He returned ten percent of that to charity, and for this he was universally acclaimed. As he said, there are two kinds of creature in the jungle: the tiger and the iguana. The tiger sets the fees, and the iguana pays them.

I rose to my feet, feeling quite unlike an iguana, and walked across the lawn. Outside Mr. Edgar's room was a huge rooftop terrace over the indoor swimming pool. Like a small park floating fourteen feet above the ground, it was two hundred feet long and a hundred feet wide, with perfect stone railings, a fountain in the center, crushed marble paths, dense and tiny lawns, and, of course, flowers. If your eye could bear to look beyond the shocks of red, white, and yellow, you would see the vast lawn with its watercourses and stands of spruce and pine, and then, beyond that, Biscuit Neck harbor, where half a dozen sailing yachts were moored in a pattern that had been designed by a maritime painter.

The stonework of the mansion was, of course, magnificent, but unfortunately for Mr. Edgar the precisely cut granite blocks at the corners, coming together like cabinet joints, made perfect ladders to every terrace and bedroom. I climbed up to the floating gardens quite easily.

I walked on the lawns rather than the paths, and jumped flower beds from one rectangle of grass to another, making no

more sound than a salamander. The French doors leading from
the bedroom to the terrace were open wide, with no screens.
Depending upon location, temperature, wind, time, and humidity, insect liberation day on Long Island can come in September.

Mr. Edgar was watching a ticker tape that was connected
perhaps to the Tokyo market or the New Delhi Menthol
Exchange—I never found out—and he played it through his
hands like a spinner making thread. On the desk next to him
was a cable switch with a number of buttons undoubtedly for
calling security, a nurse, a butler, or a secretary. I walked behind
him, found where it plugged into the wall, and unplugged it.
Then I came around the front of the desk and sat down. Leaning
forward, I switched off the ticker tape.

"It's still half an hour to close, you idiot," he said to me. Senile
or not, he was still Eugene B. Edgar, Conqueror of Worlds.

Though he knew me, I was so far out of context that he had
not recognized me. Still, he was not alarmed. I suppose he had
so many servants and aides that my sudden appearance in his
bedroom at night did not disturb him.

"No," I said. "It's just a few minutes to close, but no bell
will ring."

"What! Turn it back on!"

"Shut up," I said, "and listen."

At this point he began to press buttons in a way that I had
never seen and would not see until, many years later, video
games came to Brazil. He was going as fast as a court stenog-
rapher, but, hearing no bells or whistles, he looked at the wall
and saw that the cord had been pulled. As if to confirm this,
he reeled it in and held the plug in front of his face.

"That's right," I said. "It's not connected."

"Help! Help! Help!" he shouted in a voice so weak that I had trouble making out the words.

"Look," I told him, "if I can't hear you, no one else will. Do you realize that, through some freak of nature, you speak louder than you shout?"

"What do you want?"

"The Hudson River Bridge, nineteen-fourteen."

"What bridge?"

"You know what bridge."

"No no no no no!" he said. "No bridge."

"Try yes."

I could see the rapid movement of the great machinery behind his eyes that had, over the years, maneuvered his enfeebled body to commanding heights that now meant absolutely nothing. "What about it?" he asked.

"You decided to be severe with the first people to resist your offer for their land, so that others would cooperate."

"What if I did?" Then he recognized me. "I know you," he said.

"Of course you do. I've been at the firm, on and off, since that time."

"If this concerns something that happened then," he said with a fair amount of useless oil, "we can make adjustments. Bring it up in the next meeting. You haven't been to the meetings for quite some time. Where have you been?"

"I was demoted to the gold vault."

"If that's what it is. . . . Yes, I remember, the coffee ads. Why did you do that? It was uncalled for. But your lesson is learned. We can bring you back. With a bonus."

"I've already taken my bonus—an unusually big bonus, I might add."

"Urrgh, urragh!" he said, clearing his throat. "How big?"

"Probably the biggest in the history of the firm. You see, what I did was, I cleared out one of the larger cages in the vault. I dropped the bricks down a shaft into a subway tunnel below. The pile that's left is hollow. Half of what we took is already gone, in Europe. The other half is loaded into a waiting C-54, which I will pilot tomorrow morning to Brazil."

Mr. Edgar was a brilliant man, who understood immediately upon hearing this that I was going to kill him. And I regret to say that he was a courageous man, for from that moment on he was neither coy nor afraid.

"Who were those two people to you?" he asked. So, you see, he knew. He was the one.

"They were my parents," I said, moved at last, but only to sorrow.

"*I* killed your mother and father?"

"Yes."

"I'm sorry."

"I am, too."

"It took this long to find out?"

"It took this long."

"And now you've come to kill me."

"Yes."

He thought for a while, and I let him, perhaps because, somehow, I could see that he was not thinking of evasion. "Young man," he said, "it was the worst thing I have ever done. Unforgivable. In later years, but only in later years, it has caused me much grief. You don't have to believe that. Whatever I am, I know what's right, I know what's wrong, and I know what I've done." He laughed. "Go ahead," he said. "It will bring me peace. I hope it will comfort you, although, after what I did to you, so long ago, I doubt it."

After that, I didn't want to kill him. And killing a helpless person is the most horrible thing you can do. All my life I have believed that you defend the helpless, protect the innocent, love the child in the man.

And here before me sat an old man in a wheelchair, with a voice that could not call, and a body that could not move. I knew that if I killed him at least half of me would die, and that he might finally accomplish, as he had not in 1914, the murder of my entire family. And I thought to myself that my mother and father would not have wanted it that way. It was clear that all they would have wanted was to see me safe and happy, and that this would be their final embrace, their fondest desire, their last wish—as it would be mine with my child.

But then I thought of my mother and father lying in the pool of blood, with me between them trying to will them back to life. And I thought, to hell with me, I don't really much matter in this.

I then did the most difficult thing I have ever done. I killed him, and in so doing I killed the part of me that was best. But I was willing to sacrifice myself if only for love so strong that it may have turned out in the end to have been self-defeating. But it was love nonetheless, and I followed where it led.

"You'll hardly feel it," I said. I moved quickly and hit him at the base of the skull with a heavy pewter paperweight. He wasn't dead, he was merely unconscious. Then I pressed my left hand against his shoulder blades, cupped my right hand under his chin, and snapped his neck. My childhood was over, the circle was complete.

As I drove west toward the bridges I began to feel regret that my plan would incriminate Dickey Piehand, so instead of taking his car back over the Throgs Neck and quietly returning it to its garage, I kept on all the way to the city. I had thought at first that it would be good fun to watch Dickey trying to snob and grease his way out of a murder rap, but then I realized that, if he didn't, he would go to the chair. You don't electrocute someone just because he's an ass, just because he torments you, just because he tries to bury you alive with flatulent morons. You want to, but you don't. Because he was home that night without an alibi, I had to make sure that the authorities knew his MG had been stolen, and that the person who had stolen it was not just Dickey Piehand pretending to be someone else. What I did with his automobile was fairly dramatic and somewhat risky, but still a lot easier than finding a parking place on the Upper East Side.

I didn't want to hurt the policemen, and yet I knew I had to immobilize their car, so I followed until I could approach at the proper angle, though with an agile little sports car it was easy to maneuver quickly to strike position. The geometry of such an enterprise is much like that of a dogfight—but simpler because it's only two-dimensional.

After half an hour, they grew suspicious and pulled up next to a Department of Sanitation truck, motioning to me to come alongside. I could see that the right-hand doors of their cruiser were almost touching the garbage truck. All I had to do was make a loop and hit them directly from the left. I knew I had to do it quickly, so I gunned the engines, went up on the opposite sidewalk a little, smashed a few store windows, and came head-on at their left doors.

I didn't want to hurt them: I just wanted to stun them and trap them inside their vehicle. So, to decrease the tremendous speed that might otherwise have stove in their car and killed them, I slammed on the brakes and threw the MG into reverse.

What a noise! But the velocity at which I floated toward them as my rear wheels screeched and smoked was perfect, and I crunched their doors and windows tightly shut.

They were indeed stunned. I ran over to their car and pressed my face against the windshield, shouting, "Are you all right? Are you all right? What have you done to my car? Look what you did to my car!" What could they do? You can't shoot someone for being a bad driver, at least not right on the spot.

Their struggle to get out was just to save face, for they knew that they would have to wait for the fire department. Meanwhile, I knew that they would never forget what I looked like, which meant that they would know the difference between me and Dickey Piehand, who looked like, well, a suppository. I told them to stay put and that I would go for help. I said, "Wait here, I'll get the police!" I then calmly hailed a taxi and asked the driver to head uptown. After a few blocks I made him turn right and go over to Park, which he then drove down at lightning speed, dropping me at Grand Central, where I got on the shuttle, transferred at Times Square, and, eventually, took a bus to New Jersey.

The bus stopped in almost every town in New Jersey, I had to walk the last five miles, and I reached the airplane museum just before dawn. I knew I'd have to rest before my flight out, and checked my natural impulse to think of this as a delay. I had no schedule to meet, and was not running from anyone. In fact, time itself was suddenly as pleasant as June, when the scraggly bushes of winter surprise you not only with leaves but with flowers.

No one knew where I was or what I had done, and no one might ever know. Even had Stillman and Chase or the police tied it all together that very morning, it hardly would have mattered. I could probably have lived undisturbed at the airplane museum for a year.

The rising sun lit the plane, which had remained immobile and at the ready inside the barn during the mad motion of the preceding hours, the gasoline absolutely still in its tank and without a ripple, the engine oiled, the struts and ailerons as stiff as when I had last seen them.

I took a shower and shaved, icing my face with a foot and a half of mentholated foam: I brushed my teeth—like Lady Macbeth—for at least ten minutes, with five loads of extremely minty tooth powder. Rather than have breakfast, I drank a quart of ice water. Lean, cleansed, exhausted, and having neglected to put on my clothes, I took a new canvas tarpaulin and walked into the center of the airfield.

The gate was closed, no one ever came within half a mile of it anyway, and I was in the center of seventy acres of dense wildflowers illuminated by a full sun streaming through an ether-clear sky. I rolled out the tarpaulin and lay upon it. Never in my life had I lain in the sun without any clothing whatsoever, but now it was almost as if I were directed to do so, as if I had no choice.

The morning air was cool, and I pulled the canvas over me like a coverlet. Then, at midday, it grew so hot that I sweated for hours, the droplets on my skin shining in the sun as they transpired. By then I had slept enough. I put on my khaki shorts and went out the gate, down the road, and to the river. This was a weekday in September, in the most rural part of New Jersey. I didn't see a single soul, which gave me a marvelous feeling of peace.

I swam in the river, which was warm and fresh, and went back to the airplane museum, where I cooked a dinner of steamed vegetables, broth, and grilled salmon. After going through that crazy tooth brushing thing again, I went to bed and had the most tranquil, restful sleep I had had in forty years.

When morning came, I cooked myself some pancakes. I do not now and did not then eat pancakes—they're too fattening, and they're not very common in Brazil—but when I was a boy my father used to make them for me, so I pretended that I was he, and I served them to me, and for a fleeting second it was as if he were there.

Then I brushed my teeth again for twenty minutes or so, thinking to myself that if I kept this up I wouldn't have any enamel left. I determined to brush less, and it has been a struggle ever since. Even now I have to use an egg timer to stop myself at three minutes.

I wondered if I should visit my parents' graves one more time. I had spent a day there the week before, knowing that I would never go back, and I poured out my heart to them. When I was young, right after they died, I used to lie on the ground and rest my cheek against the gravestones. I had stopped doing that, but the last time I was there I did it once more, pretending, in case anyone had been watching, to be asleep.

When I came back from overseas I went there with tremendous excitement, as if my mother and father were still alive, to tell them that I had survived. And then, when I reached the headstones, I felt awkward, and I said, "But don't worry, it's only a matter of time. Soon."

It was better not to go back. Instead, I taxied the plane onto the field and sat near it, this time fully dressed, until about eight A.M., feeling the terror and regret of one who is about to leave forever all he has known. I did what I used to do when I was nervous about going on a mission. I stood up, brushed the dust from my hands, and said, "Fuck it."

The engines of the C-54 started slowly, but I brought them up to the point where the plane strained against its brakes and the propellers were making their magic silver circles. I don't know what it is about propellers whirling at such great speed —perhaps it's because you can't hear yourself, or because of the pounding in your chest, like an excited heart, or perhaps it's because of a disturbance of magnetic fields—but when propellers gather speed, they wake up the world.

Looking from left to right to check the engines by eye, I released the brakes and brought up full power. Ever so slowly, but then faster and faster, the plane rolled down the long strip of bright wildflowers. I couldn't smell the scent that must have arisen as they were crushed, because I was hurtling so rapidly forward.

And then I pulled back on the stick, and was airborne. It was a slow, heavy climb, and I worried as I approached the barrier of trees, but the airplane just cleared them, bending back the supple tips of half a dozen evergreens.

To my left I saw the Hudson and the wondrous gray mass of New York. Steam and smoke streamed from glittering backlit skyscrapers and long ramparts of stone. The river blazed with reflected morning sun, and ferries moved across it as if on a brass tray, churning the spangled water behind them. The bridges were loaded with slowly moving cars, the parks deserted, the offices still empty.

I thought of all the children awaking or on their way to school. I thought of their mothers and fathers, forever busy and forever taking them for granted. If they had known how distant and sad they looked in this last high view, they might have stopped what they were doing, summoned the children, and held them as if never to let go.

Rising to 20,000 feet, I slipped over the great sugarloaf of air that pours from west to east along the Appalachians. I had no crew, my plane was in suspect condition, I was heavily loaded, proceeding without a flight plan, and headed for landing strips that I had not checked for months. My cargo was more than a thousand gold bars and I was going to spend either the first night or part of the second day and then the second night on the Península de la Guajira, where there were three professions—farmer, priest, and bandit. I sensed an enlivening tension.

I didn't want to stay over at Fort Myers, because the tide would rise that night. I would have to wait until the water subsided, but if the wheels broke through the salt crust I would never get off. And spending the night at Fort Myers would mean a far longer wait at Inusu than otherwise, because I couldn't count on landing at (or even finding) Boa Esperança, the next stop, except in broad daylight.

Then there was the normal anxiety of flight. Passengers have their own anxieties, but those common to pilots are different. A pilot's profession is to hold impossibility at bay. His plane of many tons and tens of thousands of parts rises into the air to power its way through turbulence and thunderheads. If a nut comes loose, a hose falls off, a cable snaps, or a piston fouls, impossibility reasserts itself.

Things tend not to stay together or to be strong forever. Things have no courage but only endurance, which cannot be extended by a miracle of the heart as it can in a man. When their time comes, they snap without regret or apology. So your eyes are never still. They must hop from gauge to gauge as you recall the place of each measurement in the whole, and dart across rows of warning lights looking for frightful illuminations. You peer out in all directions, scanning the sky and guessing the weather ahead. For fighter pilots, this is a habit that takes a particularly heavy toll. No matter how long it has been since you knew combat, you do not ever take for granted that the sky is a place of peace. Your eyes do not accept the course of history but sweep the air instead, looking for an enraged black spot enlarging in your direction. You cannot keep yourself from this compulsive scanning, you cannot keep from listening to your engines for broken patterns of sound, and you cannot keep your hands from flying like little birds to touch for reassurance the important switches, the stick, and the levers you need to pop the canopy.

On the many commercial flights that for Stillman and Chase I took reluctantly after the war, I was able to spot Air Force veterans because their eyes never stopped moving. They, as I did, felt that the stillness of the passenger cabin was a bad omen. They didn't like to be flown, and neither did I. Civilians think you're crazy or afraid, but being flown and fed makes a military pilot feel that he has been remiss, that much has gone undone, that something is terribly wrong.

As I threaded through thunderheads and cut across immense columnar clouds, I worked without cease. Once in a great while I would think about the ground underneath or the blue of the sky, but then I was back to the quick eye movements and talking-to-yourself stuff that you do when you haven't flown for a long time and you're piloting an overloaded four-engine plane.

The mountains changed color and shape, the fields and rivers were transformed, and the land grew flatter and the air wetter. I landed at Fort Myers at two in the afternoon.

The salt and sand were blinding, the humidity almost unnatural as sea air flowed through my cockpit window like water pouring through a hole in a submarine. I taxied to the end of the field where the oil drums were, and swung my tail around. The sea nearby was so intensely blue that it retained light like a gel, and even though I had just come through a New York summer, when I jumped from the plane to the ground, the heat and the glare nearly made me pass out.

I ate a smoked chicken and watercress sandwich, drank two Coca-Colas, and walked across a strip of marsh to get to the sea. There, with the sun burning the back of my neck as I bent toward the lapping water, I brushed my teeth for about eight minutes, wondering why this obsession had taken hold of me (I am not, generally, an obsessive person), but the water smelled good, and I was happy to be alive.

I went back across the marsh to start refueling. I carried a fuel pump with me, and we had chosen to leave a hand truck with each set of oil drums. Unfortunately, someone had stolen the hand truck at Fort Myers. Rolling and upending the drums added to the strain of hand-cranking each ounce of fuel into the wings. After several hours every muscle in my body ached, I was flushed with sunburn, my hair completely matted with sweat, my hands blistered. I drank a gallon and a half of warm bad-tasting water and loved it. Then, throbbing and red, I secured the fuel tank caps, kicked away the empty oil drums, and climbed back into the plane. I had to fly across the Caribbean before dark, and I was pushing it.

As I closed the door, my eye caught sight of something. Against a background of reeds swaying to and fro in the hot wind off the sea, a little boy was standing stock-still at the edge of the field, watching me. No older than seven or eight, he still had a few gaps in his teeth, his hair was the color of platinum, and his skin dark from the sun.

Well, I thought, children love airplanes, and they make things up. No one will believe him when he tells them what he saw. On the other hand, what about the empty oil drums and the tracks in the sand? I sealed the door and went forward. The engines started with great eagerness, as if yearning to cut paths through the air. I kept the propellers just below the magical threshold beyond which the plane would begin to strain ahead, but then I dropped the rpm on each engine, unbuckled my belt, and ran to the back. When I opened the door, I waved to my audience to approach the plane, and I began to throw out gold bars. I don't know how many I jettisoned. I had to remove them in a symmetrical pattern so as not to affect the trim, and at the end I retied the load. I jumped to the ground and stood amid the several million dollars in bullion that I had just scattered.

The boy came forward cautiously. I put my arm on his shoulder and spoke in shouts so as to be heard above engines and propeller wash.

"I have to go," I shouted. "These are gold. I stole them. I'll never be back, and no one is following me. Take them. . . ." I looked around and saw nothing but marsh and sand. "Take them somewhere safe, and bury them. When you're older, if you want money, use them slowly, one at a time. You can't ever let anyone see the seals or numbers. Melt down the bars by putting them in a pot over a hot fire. Pour the molten ore into clay molds. It's easy. The gold is pure, and you can sell it for roughly the prices cited in the *Wall Street Journal*."

He looked at me blankly, never having heard of the *Wall Street Journal*.

"You can find out how much it will fetch by looking in the newspaper," I shouted. "Be careful."

He nodded. I straightened my shoulders and smiled at him.

"Who are you?" he shouted back at me, his high voice clearing the roar of the engines more easily than had my own.

I had to think before I was able to answer. "You see that?" I asked, pointing at the airplane, and still shouting above the roar. "It's a time machine. I came back here to help you. Do you understand?"

"Yes. But who are you?"

"Don't you know?" I asked, looking directly into his eyes. "I'm you."

As I flew across the Caribbean, the sun sliding down my right windshield, I grew careless but I got happy. I had many reasons for dropping my guard. I was pleasantly exhausted and I needed rest: to remain tense would only have exhausted me further. My hope was that as I flew in a semisomnolent state, luck would be with me, and that by the time I landed at Inusu I would have a combined second and third wind.

And, then, after I had flown over Cuba and held the eastern shore of Jamaica on my right, I was over water and could not turn back. Were I to go down, I would go down. My enterprise would fail and the gold would be lost at sea, not to mention me. Why, then, check oil pressures? Why scan the sky for nonexistent enemy fighters? Why suffer any torture of the soul when the only thing below was the sea, that quickly swallows planes and pilots into blue invisibility.

The world was changing beneath me, the islets, capes, and coasts were of an entirely different character than those in the north. Here, everything was green and sunny, and the sea blazed with color. The palm trees were as uniform and docile as well behaved lapdogs. They lined the beaches and grew in rows as if by command. The palm is a conformist, its trunk and fronds monotonously regularized, whereas the oak, for example, is as idiosyncratic as an English aristocrat, its hardwood bred to stand up to storms and hold its ground. And the oak is modest: it has acorns, not coconuts. As for the waves, they had a different curl and a languorous pace, and the color of the depths and shallows seemed rich and relaxed even from 10,000 feet.

I knew I was going to a place where nothing would be the same and where things did not move but drift. Though the greater part of those who lose themselves in these regions of the world, where fate is not an enemy but an ally, come back, some are lost forever. They die there in unconscious ecstasy, having been long forgotten in the clarity and cold of the cities of the north.

Because I could not return, it was as if I had come to the end of things, as if I had already died, which is why I was so relaxed. Sometimes I even closed my eyes and flew by feel. As I had no solution to the problems of landing on an unlighted airstrip after dark, or of defending myself and my cargo against bandits in whose code killing is a necessity of self-esteem, I refused to worry. Instead, I happily gathered strength for the improvisations to come.

Much light is lost in flying east, and I saw the peninsula looming ahead in midnight blue even though, to my right, I could still see the glow of the departing sun. It was only because I was so high that I could observe dusk and the deep night at the same time: at sea level not a trace of day would have been apparent.

How was I to find the landing strip in the dark? I didn't even care, and then as if by magic the moon came over the horizon in otherworldly saffron. I cut my airspeed and started to descend, knowing that by the time I reached the midpoint of the peninsula the moon would be as white as a house on a Greek island and low enough to cast sharp identifying shadows. It was, it did. With the lights of Inusu to the northeast, I found the stream, flashing like a white thread and blackening when my angle changed, and I found the cleft in the hills, and there was the landing strip, a black plinth that had been knocked over and now lay breathlessly on its back.

I had extinguished my running lights, but I went in with a roar of the engines I could not do without. When the ground was so close that the wings no longer glowed in the moonlight and were immersed in shadow, I switched on my landing lights. Their bright illumination after hours of darkness was almost like daylight. But as soon as I touched down on three points, I extinguished the lights. I would have cut the engines, too, but I had to taxi the final two hundred feet to the end of the runway, where, as at Fort Myers, I pivoted the tail and pointed the nose for takeoff.

After a day of flight, the silence was hard to bear. Blood pounded through my arteries so hard I could hear nothing else.

The night air was sweet. In Florida it had been fragrant, too, but the salt and iodine of the sea had been a counterpoint to the sweetness. Here, I felt as if I were inside a sugared pineapple.

Though I wanted to make a fire for cooking, I dared not. I had no idea who had heard my engines, how curious they might be, whether they could find me, how long it might take, and what they might want. For the moment, I felt quite safe, so I left the plane and went to the fuel. It hadn't been touched, and the hand truck was there. It was possible that no one had set foot on our airstrip since we had bought it.

I went back to the plane and ate a dinner of two cans of tuna fish, a bunch of celery, and a French bread that was as hard as a torpedo. And min-er-al wa-ter, something I associate with health even though it's only water. I brushed my teeth. Though I had intended to refuel in the darkness, my limbs grew numb and I knew that, no matter what, I had to sleep, so I climbed into the plane, closed the door, and slept in sweet air flowing gently through the cockpit windows. My sleep was so profound that even before I closed my eyes I forgot who I was or where I was, being aware of only the fragrant air. I slept not the fitful sleep of someone who wants to die, I slept, instead, like someone who no longer cares, and in this I found miraculous rest.

Awakening at dawn, I opened the door of the plane upon a carpet of golden grasses. The field was empty, with no sign of life. I couldn't imagine that anyone who might want to take advantage of me would be up at such an hour, for in my experience the rising sun is anathema to criminals. But something made me hurry, skip breakfast, and neglect to shave. Though it seemed like years, I had been gone from New York for not quite twenty-four hours, and I was already quite comfortable being uncomfortable. In fact, I looked upon comfort with disgust.

I rushed the oil drums as if my life depended on it, running with the hand truck in the hot sun. The more I pumped, the better I felt, even if my arms and abdomen were burning with the effort and my eyes stinging with sweat. And the more fuel I loaded, the later it got, which made me work harder. I was one man, in the open, with only a pistol.

When I had three drums left to load and had nearly killed myself transferring fifty-seven drums of fuel and running back and forth from wing to wing, ducking under the fuselage like Toulouse-Lautrec, I climbed up to set the cap. As I crouched on the wing, I looked to the end of the field, and I stopped breathing. Half a dozen men were coming toward me from about half a mile away. While I was working the pump, they hadn't been able to see me, but after I climbed on the wing they started running. Each one had a rifle slung across his back, and they moved with the age-old urgency of hunters closing for the kill.

Never in my life have I moved faster. I fixed the cap on the fuel inlet so fast I cut my hands. Then I jumped from the wing and grabbed the fuel pump with such force that the hoses snapped past me and sprayed the side of the plane with gasoline. Throwing the pump into the plane, I ran beneath it, without slowing, dwarf-style, and jumped onto the other wing. That cap was locked tight quicker than the first, and shortly thereafter I was inside the plane, breathing like an antelope.

I yanked the hoses in so I could close the door, and was sprayed with gasoline. No matter. The door was locked. With no time to have checked the progress of the six men, I had not known how close they were. Only from the cockpit window did I see that they had slowed. They weren't runners, it was hot and humid, and they were carrying a lot of weight. They looked miserable but they refused to quit, and they were near enough now for me to see them clearly.

To a man they were thin and dirty and they carried bandoliers of ammunition. Going through the order as rapidly as I could, I started my engines and they took fire quickly and eagerly, as engines often will in the heat. I brought them up to full throttle faster than I should have, and I felt a shudder in the metal.

The roar of more than five thousand horses was encouraging. I released the brakes and began to roll. The moment the plane moved, my friends began to wave their arms. Then, one by one, they dropped to a kneeling position and lifted their rifles.

The plane was heavily loaded and moving on a rough surface, so it was going very slowly. I was banging my right fist on the center console, screaming, "Go! Go! Go!" and even before they fired I had begun to squint ahead and keep low.

As the C-54 began to roll and pick up speed, moving straight at them, I saw muzzle flashes even in the morning sun. At first every shot missed, but then they started to bite. When they hit the body of the plane they sounded like plums thrown against a wall, and when they hit the propellers they sounded like the bells in a bingo hall. I hardly breathed.

The closer I came, the better their shooting. Every hair on my body stood at electrified attention as the windshields exploded with random holes that were immediately twinned on the bulkhead behind me. Thirty seconds and I would sail over the rifles, but the shots kept coming.

"Oh Christ," I said, clenching my teeth as I watched a hole open in the glass right in front of me, and then the left windshield turn red. I couldn't lift even one hand to my head because this had happened at the moment I pulled back on the stick and held. I was airborne over the men who had shot me, so low that I made them kiss the ground like shadows on the pavement. Blood is red, I thought to myself as it poured over me rhythmically with the beating of my heart, for the same reason that fire engines are red, so that you will be sure to notice.

As I ascended to the southeast and into the sun, I wrapped my shirt around my head, surprised that I was still alive. I knew that one does not feel true head wounds, and was grateful that this one had a terrible sting. The bullet had slid along the bone and cut a channel in my scalp, and to this day I have a long scar there. Is it not strange, I thought, that the men who shot me had no idea what was in the plane?

But no matter, I was in the air again, as if for many years I had been a bush pilot and this was the way things were. I was separated from my recent past as much as a man can be, flying over the Gulf of Venezuela and on toward an interior so vast that it broke the blade of time. The wind whistled through the perforated glass in the strangest harmony I have ever heard. It sounded like a cross between a glass harmonica, a tin whistle, and the chorus of La Scala.

Only ten years before, I had done this kind of thing every day, and although I had been luckier then, I was not unlucky now. I liked it, because, among other things, it was excellent confirmation that I was not just another Dickey Piehand.

Not long after I reached cruising altitude and crossed the gulf of Venezuela two fighters rose to greet me. I had the right to innocent passage even were I crossing their country without a flight plan.

"What is your destination?" queried the one to my left.

"Abadan."

"Where will you refuel?"

"Recife."

"Where did your flight originate?"

"Los Angeles."

"What is your cargo?"

"Flying empty," I lied. "I'll be bringing back an ape, two ostriches, and a boa constrictor."

Although this shut him up for a while, I noticed that he was staring at me. "What is on your head?" he asked.

"My shirt," I responded. "I have no shirt on my back, because it's on my head."

"Why?"

"The heating controls are broken. It's very hot in here. I soaked the shirt in water. Do you have any ice?"

Just before they swooped away, they told me they would go get some. They were two young men in jet fighters, and I was in deep middle age, with a shirt around my head, in a used C-54. They didn't want to bother with me. They were dismissive. I don't know if they did or did not go by the book, because

I don't know what their book required, but soon I was alone, out of all reach, above the Amazon.

The Amazon has many characteristics of the sea. It seems never to end, and the clouds above it, like the clouds above the sea, are free of human observation. I imagine that clouds above Chicago, the Mississippi delta, or Ulan Bator are on their best behavior and rather inhibited. That's how they look, anyway. But over the ocean and away from the sea lanes they congregate in vast columns that fill the sky for thousands of square miles, rising so high and with such stateliness and show that if I didn't know better I would think that this is where they mate and die. And the clouds above the Amazon are sea clouds, though their sea is green.

The rivers were clear at first, but then they turned the color of the Afrika Korps or café au lait. I found the almost equal elevation of land and water unsettling. Why did rivers carve channels if they could just run riot all over the green? If the Andes have more snow than usual, the vibrant green forests will be soaked in my least favorite drink. For that reason alone I would not live in the Amazon, and there are other reasons, such as bugs.

Looking down, I thought of all the animals in a timeless eternity among the trees, and of their unbreakable connection with everything that can be sensed and much that cannot. As a boy I had seen animals in the woods, breathing hard, listening, smelling the air, focusing their powerful eyes upon a thousand things without distinction until a threat or a lure leapt from the background. I envied the billions of unconscious creatures below me, except for the fact that they would have to drink from vast rivers of coffee.

Landing without incident at Boa Esperança, I spent the late afternoon and evening refueling, ate quickly, and then fell asleep

near the door to the cargo compartment. Though I slept on my pistol, I knew I didn't have to. I was entirely alone, with no company but trees: the savannah, with its little casuarina trees growing here and there, looked like a bankrupt golf course. The stars shone and the night was mute except for the wind, which blew like the steady wind over the ocean.

I had a headache, which may not have been unreasonable after having been shot in the head, but, still, I told myself to stop thinking about it, as I was unable to depart from the plan. The grasses smelled very sweet, the stars stretched from horizon to horizon, and the wind stayed gentle. I slept, knowing that when I awoke I would feel as if I had been away from New York for a million years.

And when I awoke, I did. My previous life had disappeared. If I would never again see a single person who might remember what I remembered, how could I know that I hadn't dreamt the whole thing? Pieces of paper, that's how. Contemporaneous records and accounts, the work of disinterested parties. But not only could these not draw a real picture, I would never have access to them.

I sat in the early morning light, my legs dangling from the door of the plane, completely and forever out of context. This wasn't so bad, and anyway there was no going back. I had arranged to live out my days in peaceful luxury, which seemed rather odd in that for most of my life I had detested luxury and never known peace, which is why the war, though insane, seemed to me to have been the true state of things, and the years in which war did not rage, a grand illusion.

I wondered if I might fall in love again. I was still moved by feminine beauty, although not so much as when I had been young. Unlike many men my age, however, I didn't desire women in their twenties, for they inspired in me a strong paternal

and protective feeling, and consorting with them would have been out of the question (except for Marlise). I thought that I might end up married to a dowager shaped like a 1927 Pierce-Arrow. After all, I was almost old enough to be a dowager myself, although I was physically intact, and as strong as an ape.

As I dangled my legs over the savannah, a strange and homely creature walked out from under the plane, stopped, turned to look at me, and froze in amazement. I think it was a kid anteater. About the size of a dog in a cartoon, it was buff-colored with traces of pink, and it had a huge proboscis. It had lumbered into sight like a tiny prehistoric mammoth, and it stood its ground, staring at me, with the air of something that could think. I was probably the first man it had ever seen, in the first C-54, and it was the first kid anteater I had ever seen.

"Hello," I said to him. Perhaps I was attributing to him my own emotions, but I sensed that he felt affection. I knew it was just a baby anteater that neither spoke nor understood English, but I felt much the same as when I had had dinner with the Pope. Just as the Pope had radiated benevolence, so did the anteater. It occurred to me that I might adopt this anteater, but I didn't know what to feed it. Of course, I *did* know what to feed it—that was easy. But I didn't know how I could get four pounds of ants into my apartment every day, or if I wanted to.

"Where are your parents?" I asked, as they were nowhere to be seen.

He turned his head and looked shy. I was moved by his modesty, his gentleness, his innocence, and his trust. It was plain that he had never met a jaguar, a hunter, or a hyena, and I hoped he never would. Meanwhile, one tear after another had been rolling steadily down my face. "Sorry," I said, wiping my cheeks with the sleeve of my bloody shirt. "Something has got-

ten hold of me." There I was, on an empty savannah, my head wrapped in a bloody shirt, apologizing to an anteater.

Just as the Pope had gone back to his work, this little creature left, too, turning away and loping over the grass. I started the engines and took off, rising into a clear blue sky.

The flight was uneventful but for a series of disturbing rattles. The landing strips had been rough on the wheels and struts, and raising and lowering the landing gear after Inusu was like listening to lake ice breaking in the spring. I had only three landings and two takeoffs left. Though the landing gear sounded bad, it sounded as if it had some life left in it.

At one in the afternoon I arrived at Alto Parnaíba, landed with a thump, and went into my routine of eating not nearly enough (for I had very little left), drinking lots of warm water, and working for hours to pump fuel into the wings.

When I finished I was the color of a glowing coal. Perhaps because I felt good after having worked hard, I decided that instead of sleeping at Alto Parnaíba I would push on to the next-to-last stop. Then, in the morning, I would fly to my destination, where a heavy truck was waiting, and my new life would begin in earnest.

So I took off at a quarter to four, and landed, hours later, just as it got dark. I was tired, and the landing was brutal. I finished the last of my rations and began to refuel. In a depleted, almost hallucinatory state, I turned the pump for six hours, sometimes as slowly as a drunk, and I kept on telling myself that this was the last time I would need to refuel.

Sometime around midnight, the wind picked up and I felt big drops of rain blown at me from the side. In the distance the black sky was occasionally lit by a quick flash that would spread laterally across a low combustion chamber with a roof of angry clouds. It's good, I thought, that I don't have to fly through that. The rain liberated the smells of the ground, and the wind brought them thick and fast from what seemed to be the heart of the storm.

Though the wind was not strong enough to necessitate tying down the plane, I had to remain awake in case the storm tracked in my direction. After so little sleep and so much exercise, this was very hard. I had to distract myself without dreaming, for a waking dream would have led quickly into sleep. And yet I had very few distractions. I had no lantern, and did not dare tap into the plane's electrical system to supply the cabin lights, because I needed all the power I could get for starting. I could not, therefore, attend to a stamp collection or read a magazine. And I knew that if I stared at the storm on the horizon I would be hypnotized as if by a swinging pocket watch.

I walked into the night until I bumped into one of the little trees that dot the grassland. This I climbed until it could no longer bear my weight and it broke. I then dragged it back to the plane and snapped it into many little pieces that I stacked under the wing.

Though jet fuel is relatively hard to ignite, the engines of the C-54 used high-octane gasoline, which isn't. Even so, I risked a fire underneath the part of the wing that had no tank in it. The distance between the wing and the top of the flame at its highest was three or four feet, the whole structure was clad in aluminum, and the heat that was unreflected was harmlessly dissipated by the conductive mass of the metal.

I filled a pot with water and set it on the coals amid still-flaming branches. I hadn't shaved or washed for days, and blood was matted in my hair and beard like mud. Soon I had a gallon of roiling hot water. I dipped a cup into this and let it sit for a while before I used it with a bottle of German shower gel that was made from chestnuts and foamed up as thick as whipped cream. I lathered this stuff into my hair and spread it over my face until I looked like someone dressed as a marshmallow. It was supermentholated, and the longer it stayed on the more it stung and the better it felt, so I made a little detour by brushing my teeth yet again, having done so many times that day and at least twice after my dinner of United States Army pork surprise with mummied vegetables and World War I brownie.

The toothpaste was as white as a swan, and the huge amount I had ladled onto my battered toothbrush cascaded from my mouth like fire-fighting foam. I must say I was having a whale of a time getting clean. Then I realized that someone was watching, and I turned around.

Behind me stood a wan, diminutive, shoeless peasant in the midst of what seemed like cardiac arrest. He wanted to run, but was paralyzed with fear. His chest moved visibly with his heartbeat. I assumed that he thought I was some sort of goblin.

"No no," I said. *"Ecce homo, ecce homo."* I didn't speak any Portuguese, and certainly not the incomprehensible dialects of the rural north. "Shaving," I said. *"Rasoio."* I picked up my razor and began to shave, holding out my signal mirror at arm's length. This calmed him. As everyone knows, devils don't shave.

"Hot water," I said as I finished shaving and began to rinse out my hair. It was wonderful, and when at last I was done I stood before him looking like one of those new investment bankers in New York with slicked-down hair, $5,000 suits, suspenders (which, if you are rich, you call *braces*), and glasses with hair-thin frames. Why do they do that? For decades investment bankers were physically indistinguishable from Harvard deans. Do these young people think that slicked-down hair and zoot suits were once acceptable on Wall Street? They dress now the way gigolos and gangsters used to.

The peasant pointed to my plane, spread his arms, and laughed in amazement. I took that to mean, 'What the hell are you doing here with that huge plane at one o'clock in the morning in the middle of nowhere?' so I said, *"Et tu Brute?"* but he didn't understand.

I tried to tell him, in Italian, some of my life story. The few cognates that he recognized probably made for an otherworldly tale, and he laughed at totally inappropriate moments. How could he have had the slightest idea of what I was talking about? I pantomimed the theft of Dickey Piehand's car, Constance's coffee dances, killing Mr. Edgar, and meeting the singers in Rome. Then he used the same method to tell me his story, which was, as far as I could ascertain, that he had been a clown in a provincial circus, who, after his wife had been gored by an ox, had left the circus to become an electrician. His dream was to go to Germany. He had a radio—or he wanted a radio. This I gathered as he turned the knobs on an imaginary box and lowered his head to place his ear next to it, smiling.

"Ten radios," I said. "Fifty radios, just for you." I climbed into the plane and retrieved two gold bars that I then presented to him. "Melt them," I ordered, in what was getting to be a habit. "Get rid of the numbers and the seals." He was stunned, I suppose, because when he understood that I was giving them to him, making him immediately the richest man he had ever met, he tried to kiss my hands, but I wouldn't let him. Finally, he hobbled off into the night, barely able to carry his new wealth.

Up ahead, lightning warred in the clouds as if the world were coming to an end, and daylight struggled in vain against the weight of darkness. Despite the stinging wind-driven droplets, the crack of not-so-distant thunder, and the lift and drop of the wings in the violent air, I reeled in my seat and had difficulty keeping my eyes open. At two o'clock in the morning the fire was pink, with white ash that the wind blew into the night, layer by layer, on its stronger gusts.

My sight well accustomed to darkness, I saw quite clearly an agitated glow crawling from the direction in which the peasant had disappeared. It was light from the headlamps of a line of twenty or thirty cars or trucks speeding in my direction. That idiot had undoubtedly made a spectacle of himself and the gold in front of his entire village. Though they might have been peaceable people, it didn't matter. They had probably been drinking coffee all night, and with the plane loaded as it was my life was worth nothing. I was exhausted, and the storm was furious, but I had to get into the air.

I closed the door behind me, ran forward, bumped my head, fell into the pilot's seat, and began to start the engines. If the trucks turned onto the landing strip I wouldn't be able to take off, or, worse, I wouldn't be able to stop, and as I incinerated myself and every vehicle in my path, the flames would light up the night for fifty miles. What would these people know? They were capable of turning onto the field even as I was hurtling toward them far past the point of no return.

I worked as fast as I could, but it takes time to start four engines, and in the terrible moments of waiting I watched the string of foreshortened lights approach in darkness and rain, bobbing up and down with the contours of the road.

Right inboard, running . . . left inboard, running . . . right outboard, running. The left outboard, however, refused to start. It spun around, it coughed, and it sputtered. I adjusted the fuel mixture. The engine spat out a huge cloud of white smoke. "Come on!" I shouted, giving it another try. "Come *on!*" It cycled with determination, it coughed again, it sputtered and sputtered, and then it took. Soon its many knife blades were twirling faster than human vision was made to see, and as I pushed against the throttle the noise and vibration lifted me in my seat.

Brakes released. The plane pitched forward and began to roll. Fully loaded with fuel and a cargo of metal, with engines hot at maximum rpm, it would have made a magnificent sight as it plowed into the trucks. And if there were thirty trucks and each one carried, who knows, ten people, or just half that number? I would kill or maim two-thirds of them—a hundred people.

In an instant I had to decide whether or not to put on my lights. If I put them on, the convoy would see that I was rolling at great speed. Presumably, this would stop it from turning onto the runway.

I threw the switch. Now, I knew, the people on the trucks could see two great blinding lights rushing toward them on a parallel but offset track. They would have to be insane to turn onto the runway.

They were. They did. Not the lead vehicle, but one from the middle, the others following instantly and without hesitation. I was going too fast to stop. Had I tried to stop I would have plowed into them too slowly even to skip over them, like a perfectly aimed, slow-motion bowling ball.

So I pounded the throttles forward and my eyes leapt from the lights ahead to my instruments. I wasn't going to make it. I blinked the lights. Those idiots blinked their lights back at me! What were they thinking?

Then, as if struck by lightning, I realized that with the winds of the storm coming from directly ahead, my airspeed was more than sufficient for takeoff. I pulled back the stick as fast as I could, and I rose.

But the plane was so heavily loaded that the angle of ascent was nearly flat. Only seconds remained before a collision. I started to pull in the landing gear. The landing gear was normally slow to retract, and it had been damaged. It made all kinds of new noises as it was pulled in. I was suddenly right on top of the first truck, which had turned left to avoid impact.

With a tremendous thud the left wheel hit the roof of the cab and my right wing rose. I compensated but the left wing rose too much, because the landing gear had been snapped off like a chicken leg. I lifted the right wing, which had come within a few feet of the ground, and then, having cleared the other trucks, I was level and rising.

Never had I flown directly into the heart of a storm, for the P-51 has the speed and agility to dodge just about anything, and neither bombing raids nor fighter patrols were run in impossible weather. The lightning-infested bales of black cotton that lay ahead were new to me. I was awake, but I had neither the confidence nor the anger that swells as combat approaches. I was, however, unafraid. The immensity of the storm was the antidote to fear, if only because it was impossible to be afraid of everything, and as it got closer, it expanded until it became everything.

All I could do was climb. No fuel was left at Alto Parnaíba, and my tanks had fuel enough only for a straight shot through the storm. I knew I was going to hit the wall, but hoped it would be above the lightning.

Water sprayed from the holes in the windshields and ran over the instrument panels. Eventually its weight could take down the C-54, and I could do nothing to stop it. I reentered the clouds at fourteen thousand feet. It had been turbulent outside, but once within the clouds the plane immediately dropped down four thousand feet, caught in a column of air pushing toward the ground like a piston. It felt like a dive even though the nose was angled up, and the only way out was to move slowly forward through the downdraft.

Finally, at 10,000 feet, the plane exited into relatively tranquil darkness that lit up like a flashbulb only several times a minute as lightning was diffused throughout the clouds. The wings were vibrating, the engines straining, and water sprayed through the windshields. When it had cracked the sky with lines like those in shattered glass, the lightning was less terrible than when it turned everything in the universe to the color of magnesium.

The plane was lifted, dropped, rolled, and pitched with such ferocity that I felt as if I were inside a bone in the jaws of an atropine-injected terrier. The cabin jingled like crazy. Straps and belts beat against the bulkheads like whips. I saw screws turning in their holes, and watched the needles on my many gauges snap back and forth in unison like the Rockettes. One second I had full tanks of gasoline, and not a tenth of a second later I was totally dry. One second I was at sea level, and another at 40,000 feet.

The vibration was so bad that my eyes started to dance in their sockets. I had no idea how much time had passed, or what altitude I had reached, or even if I were pointed up. I was freezing cold, with water spraying in my face, and my muscles were cramped from fighting the controls. But as the plane rattled and shook and I was about to lose my influence over it, perhaps to be turned upside down and slammed to the ground, I began, as always, to enjoy it.

I heard a note of music, a single note that rose as if from nowhere and was held impossibly long. I had heard it before, when I would dive after a plane evading me for its life, and shell casings flew from my cannons like tailings flying from a milling machine. There, in the storm, in ten-tenths cloud, once again, nothing of me was left as I rode on waves of pure force.

I had no objection to this. I felt neither pain nor fear. I sank from chamber to chamber deeper into the darkness of life and the light of the soul. All in all, it was a remarkably gentle thing, and the greater the force of everything flying apart, the stronger the presence of absolute tranquility. The feeling is like that of coming home. I wanted the plane to break apart, but at twenty-one thousand feet I broke through the surface of an endless mass of cloud and rode into a clear sky blazing not with the insanity of lightning but with the solidity of stars.

Dry air flooded the cabin, and, despite the roar of the engines, the world was silent. Below, the clouds flashed white in random syncopations that kept them continuously bright. I took my oxygen, found my course, and continued on with moonlit speed.

I came fully awake only at dawn. For hours I had been thinking and dreaming, shivering and faint. Though I would often fall asleep and then find myself jolted by the plane nosing up or down, I managed somehow to keep the compass dead on the right heading. When the sun finally lit the cabin and I came to my senses, I discovered that the source of this navigation miracle was that the water pouring over the instrument panel had shorted out half the electrical system. The compass had been faithful through the night to the magnetic field of the instrument panel. No matter which way I turned the plane, it always read the same.

I had absolutely no idea where I was. Though the sun had risen more or less where it should have, previous to that the sky had lightened far to my left and somewhat behind me. The land below looked like the interior rather than the coastal plain. All across the horizon fat clouds like the floats of jellyfish rode in the buoyant blue sky, trailing dark veils of rain. But everything was mostly sunny and depressingly green, with hardly a river in sight and not a single road that I could see. It wasn't the Amazon; it was far too hilly.

Though I had less than an hour of fuel I thought that perhaps everything would come out all right if I flew east, that I would sight the coast and then discover that I was within striking distance of my destination. So I flew on for half an hour, searching for the thin blue line that would mean my salvation, but it did not appear. With, at best, twenty minutes' fuel remaining, I realized that I had been defeated.

The country below me was an endless carpet of corrugated green hills and occasional rocky outcroppings. In the creases of the hills flowed streams or brooks, but nothing sufficiently flat or wide for an emergency landing. The best I might do would be to come in along the top of a ridge, but as the ridges were covered with tall trees, that held very little promise.

Even an airport might not have been enough, in that a large part of the landing gear was missing or stuck. During the war I had seen bombers trying to land on a wheel and a door, and more terrible a sight does not exist than that of a plane, full of wounded men, that slowly cartwheels and breaks into flame.

If I survived the crash, I might not survive the wilderness. And even if I did I might lose the gold either to the undergrowth or to someone who would find it before I could return. Now the best that might happen was that, unharmed, I would reach my apartment in Rio de Janeiro and have to start all over again in a strange country where I knew neither one word of the language nor a single person. Though this was defeat, I felt immediately younger.

When I had only ten minutes of fuel in my tanks, I saw a road, one of those newly cut orange ribbons stretching like a ray of light through endless green. The corrugated landscape stopped at the edge of a green sea. The clay was probably impassable in the rainy season, and the track was empty for as far as I could see.

I flew along its length, reconciled to the fact that when my fuel was exhausted I would land on it as best I could, hoping to settle the fuselage into a narrow slot after the trees had clipped off both wings. I was unable to see from the air that the road was following a grade, but this came clear when a river appeared two miles to the right, where an outcropping of rock stepped down in the gradual descent of the terrain. The river issued from a green berm and a tangle of trees, plunged in a dazzling white fall, and then turned forty-five degrees from the road.

Though this stream was no wider than the road, I thought it might be more forgiving of a landing, so I flew along its length for a few minutes looking for an opening, but the straightest and widest section was at the beginning, just after the fall.

Banking 180 degrees, I began my descent. I didn't think I was going to come out alive, but at least I knew that the river was white and fresh, and that it ran fast.

As I dropped lower I discovered that I had underestimated it. It was wider than it had appeared from altitude. Were I to risk crashing headlong into the fall, I might be able to take the plane in over the water and clear the obstructions on the banks. I decided to do this, though I hadn't much running space.

The left outboard engine began to skip, so I knew I was just about dry. I lowered the flaps, knowing that once they hit the water they would act as a break and throw me and everything else in the plane forward with a shock that would probably kill me. But I had no choice. If I raised the flaps even at the last moment, my speed would be too great and I would crash against the cliff behind the waterfall.

I was too busy to think. The foam at the base of the waterfall looked like snow, and when the plane hit, the impact was not as great as I had expected, because the water was so full of churning air. The plane slid faster than I thought it would, which was alarming. In an instant it went right through the fall and smashed against the rock wall behind it.

I was still conscious as the cockpit filled with water. The nose of the C-54 pointed slightly up because the waterfall pushed down the tail.

I unbuckled my seat belt and floated from it quite easily. The glass was still in all the windows, so I swam to the door in the fuselage, but it had been jammed shut. Sure that I was going to drown, I looked up in a gesture of pride and acceptance, and when I did I saw a rupture in the fuselage, and that right above me, in the ceiling of the plane, was a spacious opening.

I pushed hard with my legs and flew through this into a chamber of roiling water in which I had so little buoyancy that I could hardly float. I breathed in a few times even though I was not in air, and when I broke through to the surface I was choking and deafened by the thunder of falling water. The chamber behind the fall was like the surf on a brisk autumn day. It was only half light in there, and almost impossible to breathe.

I tried to swim out, but the force of the water pushed me down irresistibly, held me against the bottom, and then threw me backward. I knocked my head against part of the plane, and floated up again, just as slowly as the first time.

As water fell into the chamber the same amount of water had to be cast out. The exit wasn't on the floor, so it had to be along the sides. I dived down, hugging the wall, and halfway to the bottom I felt a strong current. The more I followed it the more I was accelerated, until I was no longer even swimming. Soon I was going so fast that I curled up and put my hands over my head for fear of being hurled against an obstruction. I was not hurled against something solid but, rather, thrown out of the water and into the air. I breathed during my moment of free flight, fell again into the foam, came to the surface, spread my limbs, and, as usual, found myself riding at great speed on the cool torrents of a river that had saved me.

The Finest School

(If you have not done so already,
please return the previous pages to the antproof case.)

AT SÃO CONRADO I discovered that what I had written
would not fit in the antproof case. Perched on the glacis, with
wind ruffling the pages, I had tried to stuff them back in, but I
was afraid that I might drop them into the sea, and my efforts
were half-hearted. With a blooming rose of pages clutched
against my chest, I teetered in the rock face, got to the road,
and made my way to a café on the beach, where I sat within
fifteen feet of an expresso machine, breathing hard and soaked
with sweat as I struggled to get the manuscript into the case. I
was so enraged by the odor of coffee that I was unable to do
anything. On the bus coming home I tried again, but was still
trembling because of the coffee, so I gave up.

I float on a raft of troubles that intensify day by day. Long
ago I would have thought that by ending my life an inconspicuous failure—a *poor* inconspicuous failure—I would at least
have been free. But problems are torturers: they are encouraged

by your defeat, like dogs that go wild as their quarry sinks to its knees.

The next day, after a long and fitful sleep, I put on my bathrobe, went to the desk, and, trembling with despair, tried to get the São Conrado pages into the antproof case. I summoned all my strength and could not do it. I might have done it were I to have wrinkled them, but I would rather die than wrinkle a clean sheet of paper.

"Well," I said, trying to comfort myself, "it's simple. I'll go to the store where I bought the antproof case, and buy a new one in a larger size." That would be much better than stuffing everything in anyway, because getting the pages out would be a nightmare, and if the contents were under as much pressure as I am the seams might start to open, which is dangerous because some ants are very small, and others, though they be not small, are tiny nonetheless as juveniles.

I allowed a full day for obtaining a new and larger case. For me, shopping is one of the most physically and emotionally exhausting things in the world. This is because I am somewhat inflexible and fairly exact. I'll decide, for example, that I want a tie of a certain pattern and color—neither of which has ever been heard of in the worldwide history of neckwear—and then spend the rest of my life looking for it. I will look at a million ties, and never will I find the one I want. I will then add to my burgeoning store of regrets and disappointments yet another, like a lost and unrequited love, that I carry with me. I cannot give up on things, I simply cannot. If they, like Constance, are animate and have wills of their own and they push me away, I have no choice. But I do not have the right to give up on those things that are silent and still and forever unobtainable . . . I do not have the right to let them drop.

God help me if I actually need something in a day. I'll walk from store to store, monopolize the phone system, and veer about the streets, totally devoid of blood sugar. And I knew that finding a good antproof case might not be so easy, as I had bought the original in 1955 or 1956.

Very early one morning, less than a quarter of an hour after the stores opened, I walked into the stationers where I had obtained the first case thirty years before. Nothing had changed in those thirty years. When I first settled in Rio I'd come to this place for my supply of stationery, but as in the case of many establishments that one patronizes in the beginning of one's residence in a strange city, after I had abandoned it I had come to associate it with the period of ignorance and naivete when I would pay double for almost everything.

In the early morning, merchants are somnambulant and subdued. They expect and want little. As the first customer, I was, therefore, semi-invisible. The fan was turning, moving air laden with the smell of printed paper and oiled leather. In the back, a mimeograph machine was spitting out flyers, and near the cash register a parrot slept on a wooden perch.

This was the emporium of a man who had been sewn into the sleeve of routine. Probably not a single thing had been changed since the moment when, for him, life had finally lost its sparkle. The shelves were half empty, the stock obsolete and covered with dust. Still, he carried certain items—lecterns, pointers, stamp-licking machines—that enabled him to survive at the edge of the business district. The faded colors that surrounded these things—green, brown, and beige—had evolved rather than been chosen, his decorators and designers being oxidation and the sun streaming through the front windows. Nothing had been placed where it lay, either deliberately or less than twenty years before.

A little old man with two-inch-thick glasses and salt-and-pepper hair slowly approached me. "May I help you?" he asked, as listless as a dog in a fish store.

"Yes," I replied, for even though I had slept little and arisen early, I was as eager as always when enraged. "I'm looking for a large antproof case."

"For a what?"

"An antproof case. A large one."

"What's an antproof case?"

"It's a case," I told him, "into which an ant cannot obtain entry."

"I never heard of such a thing."

"I have one," I said triumphantly, "and I bought it in this store."

"When?"

"In nineteen-fifty-five, or six."

"I'll ask my father," the man said as he turned.

After some muted mumbling from the far recesses of the back room, a sound that I imagine must be familiar to the halls of monasteries, a man far more ancient than I walked slowly toward me. His glasses, twice as thick as his son's, were so powerful that were he an astronomer he would not have needed a telescope.

"I used to sell dah hantproof case," he said, "in dah Tventies. Did you buy von den?"

"No, I bought one only recently, in the mid-Fifties."

He thought for a moment, sleeping with his eyes open. "It must have been von of dah last vons ve had out. Vhat color vas it?"

"Green canvas, rosewood, brass fittings, and a scarlet inlay."

"Oh yes," he said, in slow motion. "I tink dhat vas dah last von ve solt. Vhen people vent on hexpaditions to dah Hamazon, ve couldn't stock enough of dem. Ve had dem," he said, lifting an arm to indicate expanse, "stacked hup to dah sea-link. Ve had dem for men, for vimen, for children heven. Big vons, little vons. Heverytink!"

"And not one is left?" I inquired. "If you have one yourself, and it's the right size, I'd be happy to trade my smaller one for it, and pay the difference."

"None left. Such a tink vas for a different time. People cared about different tinks. Dah vorld vas different. Dey don't make dem anymore. No von vants dem."

"*I* do."

"Vhy do you bother? Now, if such ha tink vere made—hand people don't tink about hants hanymore—it vould be plostic."

"I think about ants."

"It vould be ha color new to dis hearth."

"Ants still exist, just as they used to."

"Hevrytink is different now."

"But not me. I'm not different. I haven't changed."

"No?" he asked.

"No."

"Vhy not?"

"I can't," I said. "I can't leave them."

"Who?"

"All those left behind."

"If hit's your pleasure," he told me. "But, deh fact remains, I have not ha sinkle hantproof case. Der is not ha store in hall dah vorld vere you vill find von."

I had managed to find a light in every dark chamber of the past eighty years. But suddenly hearing that no one made an antproof case, that no one cared, that they were forgotten and strange, suggested to me that this was the end.

How perfectly natural, expected, and perhaps in certain circumstances even admirable it had seemed, when I was young, to buy an antproof case. Now, if I am to believe the astronomer, no one thinks about ants. Is there one less ant in the world now than once there was? Probably the ant population has grown by quite a few trillion, and yet no one thinks to use an antproof case.

It is as if all the ants had somehow been eradicated, and, yet, they are everywhere. If the president of France dropped a brioche from his breakfast tray and it rolled unseen under his bed, the ants of the Élysées Palace would emerge en masse to claim it, streaming from hidden veins beneath the parquetry and damask.

This is not a condition peculiar to France, for if they so desired the ants could dance upon the desk in the Oval Office or take a nap in Queen Elizabeth's ermine robes. They can go everywhere because they are so little that hardly anyone bothers to kill them. I'm not obsessed with them (I'm not obsessed with anything). It's just that when you have something of any importance you put it in an antproof case, don't you?

Half the time that we imagine things are changing for the better they are actually changing for the worse. The glory of accomplishment is misunderstood by later generations merely because of the ugly progress of quantities. For example, Lindbergh's flight was truly great. One man, straightforward and unafraid, did what had never been done, where richly funded syndicates with multi-engined planes and much greater power had failed and prevaricated. With a single engine, a small but brilliantly conceived plane, and no fear, he did what they could only plan. It was not so much that he flew the Atlantic, but that he flew it alone.

And now he is nearly forgotten as, day after day, the Concorde makes the crossing in a few hours as its passengers sit in

silence facing their champagne and caviar. Is it not better to be
Lindbergh, suffering sleeplessly through dark nights over the
Atlantic, than a tycoon in a silk tie traveling faster than the speed
of sound and not giving it a thought?

The world leaves behind unseen that which is great and that
which it loves. New loves are born, and then they too are left
behind. In this oversped and cowardly rush, devotion has no
place, consistency no value, love no other reward than forget-
fulness. I don't like it. Apparently only one antproof case is left,
and I have it, but unfortunately it is not large enough to hold
everything in my heart.

So, as you can see, I'm doubling back now, writing on the
reverse of each page and heading toward the beginning. This
has made me somewhat giddy, because I feel as if I possess a
time machine. If only I did. I would pilot myself back to that
perfect evening in June, and wait for the two gentlemen from
Mr. Edgar's private car. As they came through the woods, I
would put a Winchester slug into each of their brains, and then
roll them down the hillside into the marsh. And then I would
go home for dinner, unable to tell the tale, too moved to speak.

The antproof case is truly beautiful. They don't make things
like it anymore, and even if they did they could not age them to
match the glow of its suffering, or condition them to know what
it has held and where it has been, or teach them sixty years of
absolute inanimate patience. True, it may have seen only the sky
as it sat upon the shelf near a window, but it may have sat upon
that shelf for twenty years, master of nuances among the clouds,
or of the silence and darkness of years in a drawer, or of breezes
that swept across the cool tiles as it spent nights on the floor.

You have been my little ally, always on the lookout, running
up the mountain to give me warnings from the barber, listening

for footsteps near the door. Though as I write this you are a child, your early understanding of such things will be perfected. You will never find a weapon to which you will not take quickly and easily. You already know how to walk quietly at night, how to arrive unexpectedly, how never to be caught unaware.

I cannot imagine not teaching a child these lessons, but I must beg your forgiveness not only because they are such early sorrow but because I brought you to what you know by bringing you to me. I hope that, if and when the time comes, the things you learned from me will save your life, and that you will embrace my memory as I embrace my imagination of you as a man.

The gold is in the water, which is where it should be: water flowing, water dissolving, an eternal collision of oxygen and spray, a cool cloud that scours the walls of rock and the notion of time.

It rests behind the turbulence, protected and safe. The sweep of the current and the power of the backwash cannot carry it away, and the river will never run dry, for the simple reason that the territory of its tributaries is vast and green. Many years ago, the parts of the plane that could be swept downstream were taken into the flow, never to reappear, or, if they did, only to puzzle whoever happened upon them.

I have returned to the site several times, and at night I slipped into the river. With a telescoping aluminum pole I probed close to the backwash and found the fuselage, what was left of the wings, and the tail. The weight of the gold and the engines has kept the plane in place, and there it lies.

If you want it, you may have it. Because I promised Marlise never to tell you, and because this memoir may fall into the hands of others, I can't say exactly where the gold is. I dare not break my promise. And, anyway, knowing that it lies at the base of a fall is not enough, for I have changed my description of things so as to keep the actual location a mystery. Is it in Brazil, or some other country? Is it really a waterfall? Keep your mind open, and think of my description as a construct, a code.

By the way, Funio, do you remember where we saw the ducks? We ate something that Mama did not allow us to have at home or in her presence, and it was our secret. We have discussed it on several occasions since. That day, I brought the air pistol, and I let you shoot it. The occasion and the location are engraved in your mind, and I have confirmed several times that you remember.

There. The transfer is complete. All of this is not so strange, really: wealthy people often give their children surprises like this, only instead of gold in the water the gift is usually a numbered account in a Zurich bank. If the revenue agents could have their way they would probably be flies on the walls of nurseries, or frogs hiding in the rocks of trout streams, as fathers tell their sons and daughters those numbers in rituals that, unbeknownst to the children, impress the code in their memories like a branding iron sinking into wax. Half the people I knew at Harvard had a number, but that was then, when it was different, when virtually everyone there—except me—was rich.

You may wonder why I chose not to retrieve that which I had rightfully stolen. One might even say that I had earned it —in the odd way in which I earn what I earn, do what I do, and come to know what I have come to know.

Which is exactly the point. These were wages that I did not want, and only by leaving them uncollected could I live with myself. I didn't take anything because I wanted it, I took it because I was driven to it, and had I been unable to refuse it I would have continued to suffer as before. As things unfolded, I took it and I left it, and in refusing it I suffered a little less. It's true that the moment I realized I had become too frail to get it myself I changed my mind, but had my strength been miraculously restored I am sure my mind would have changed back.

Whatever I do I've always done not because I want something but to compensate for a loss, to bring about a balance, to create amends, to make things right. I never cared about money, though it was at times exciting to have a great deal of it. And one of my strong beliefs is that there is something right and holy about gold lost in flowing water, as if this were one of the harmonies of nature, as if prospectors removing it from mountain streams create an imbalance that I was born to redress.

Be that as it may, your mother and I did well enough without it. In fact, she would have been unbearable with it. When first we met she actually took me by the hand and brought me to the window of a jewelry store, where she greedily and seductively pointed to a pair of gargantuan gold earrings. They were so big that they had a wire between them for passing through the hair and over the crown of the head, as no earlobes could support such weight unaided.

Had we had money, she would have had her face lifted a half a dozen times by now, wasting her life and mine on appearances. I experienced enough of that kind of thing at Stillman and Chase over the years, and when I was married to Constance I learned to keep away from it. Most fabulously rich people, Funio, become idiots.

Some are idiots to begin with, but, of those who are not, my guess is that seventy to eighty percent later succumb. They foolishly convince themselves that they are better than others, and holding yourself above others strips you of intelligence and vitality. I do not know exactly why this is, but I have seen it far too many times to believe otherwise.

We lived simply and happily on my small income as an

instructor at the naval academy and her salary as a bank teller. It was as good a life as I would permit myself to have. And perhaps because I never wanted Marlise to share my penance, I did my best to forgive her when I grew old and she was still so young.

Though I am your father, I am not your natural father. Your natural father was biologically an acrobat. But it doesn't matter. I have loved you like a son, and you have been devoted in a way that I admire beyond measure. Now you may claim your patrimony, or you may be like me, and quietly do without it.

I don't know when I'm going to die or how old you will be when I do, or how long it will take you to find this. Still, I'm close to the prospects that overlook the unending plains of death, and I must set some things straight while I'm still alive and can tell the truth.

Your mother was always impressed with her own beauty, and wanted to be attended by those who were her equals. That is why, in a biological sense, you are not my son. As hurt as I was by this, it was impossible not to love her—one more woman whom I loved and who did not love me. Ironically, I loved her for her beauty. And I also loved the way she speaked English.

It was difficult to defy the commands of blood, which made me want to make love with her as often as I could so that I might soften my own imperfections by mating them with her glories: her statuesque teeth whiter than an igloo, her flashing green eyes, her hair the color of blood and gold, her unceasing vitality. All nature drove me to her and her away from me. She would touch me, and her mind would wander. She would fly from me, like every woman I have ever loved, and drink coffee.

Coffee. When I look back I feel neither shame nor regret about my war against coffee, but sometimes I wonder why it had to be me, why I was the one who was chosen. I wasn't born to throw a man from a moving train and impale him upon a spike, or strangle a mass murderer above a bed of decaying take out chicken, or shoot German aviators out of the sky above the Mediterranean, or obliterate soldiers in trucks on the road to Berlin, or settle the fate of a nonagenarian in a wheelchair by snapping his neck like a biscuit. What led me to such things? Was it coffee alone? I hate it. It has conquered the world. I lost to it a long time ago. My only option was to harry it until I die, but I cannot ever conquer it. How many people in this world have even the vaguest idea that it is the handmaiden of evil? Only a few. The rest go blithely about their business, smiling and happy under its spell. At best, they feel that it is neutral, neither good nor evil, but only a hot drink. When I try to tell them, they're amused at my distress, which pierces me to the heart. Only Smedjebakken knew. The others don't understand. They can't understand. But whereas they have been captured, I remain free.

As I've said many times, in this matter I am unbiased. It is purely a question of fact, and my view is *trumpeted* by the facts. Why, might you think, is coffee officially considered a doping agent at the Olympic Games? Because of his asthma, Che Guevara was addicted to yerba maté, a caffeinate, and look what happened to him. There is no hope. Coffee is second only to petroleum as a commodity traded among nations. 750,000 tons of it are consumed every year in Brazil alone. In Rio and São Paulo coffee is served to clerical workers as they labor, which explains why our electricity bill sometimes amounts to a billion and a half dollars, and why I receive letters addressed to "Dear Mr. Deceased."

It isn't right to go on and on about coffee, and I never do, so I will end my discussion of it with the core of my case against it. Coffee is evil because it disrupts the internal rhythm that allows a man or a woman to understand beauty in all things. It speeds up the metronome that rests within the heart, until the heart pounds forward like a locomotive off the rails. It blinds the eye to that which is gentle, shuttering the soul like a breech lock in a machine gun.

We are all perfect clocks that the Divinity has set to ticking when, even before birth, the heart explodes into its lifelong dance. If you doubt this, then why is it that a Carioca at rest will start to drum his fingers, and why is it that a composition of notes and intervals can make us cry, and why is it that when men and women are drawn together in a fusing of spirit and body, they move, they dance, they come together rhythmically, as in the ebb, the flow, and the rocking of the sea?

This drive, this beat, this universal tempo, is the most powerful thing I know. It overrides all calculation and greed, it runs gracefully past almost every imaginable sorrow, and it imparts harmony and sense to many things that, absent its insistent and flawless syncopation, would seem to make no sense at all. But when the metronome of the heart is driven forward, and the gentle pulsing of the soul attacked with a whip, darkness and misery come like storm.

I know this, though I have never had coffee. I know it because I have not allowed the rhythm to be altered, and I never will.

On a windless morning early in June of 1914, the sun burned the mist off Croton Bay and turned the water from silver to blue as herons alighted upon the Hudson with the delicacy of angels, gliding above the surface for time unending before they touched. Huge trees like clouds or brush strokes rose in tumbled confusion on the banks, embracing within the curls of their greenery more black spaces than the heart could imagine, and yet the sun shone through from behind, from the east. The forest was thick with birds, and the flowers within it were blooming, for the destiny of June is to be perfect.

It was too early for trains, too late for fishermen, and not yet time for the wind to break the river's surface into spangles for the sun, but from the darkness in the trees emerged a child who quickly mounted the track bed, crossed the rails, and found his way to the water. His eyes were motionless and dull from lack of sleep, his face tense and almost without expression, and his clothes stained with blood. He walked over the sand to its westernmost point, and stood with his left foot braced against a rock just below the surface of the river.

For the whole length and breadth of the Tappan Zee and Croton Bay . . . not a sound, not a ripple, but only a dense tapestry of ferocious colors raked by the newly risen sun. With his right hand he reached into his pocket and withdrew a heavy gold coin. He looked at both its faces and at the edge, and then lifted his arm behind him, cocked it for a throw, and pitched that coin into the air as hard as he could. The sun never touched it as it flew, and when it fell into the dispassionate waters of the Hudson it was swallowed without a sound.

Have you ever wondered what kind of life someone would lead if, after wanting more than anything to die, he were to live for seventy or more years? Now you know. But that is not why I have written. The object of elegy is not to revive or review the past, the purpose of a confession not to right a wrong, the piecing together of a twisted childhood is not to heal the man who journeys through memory. No. The object is not remedial, but only a song to the truth. I have not recounted what I have recounted just so I may finally drink a cup of coffee. I have recounted it for the reason that a singer sings a song or a storyteller tells a story: once you have come to a place from which you cannot return, something there is that makes you look out and back, that makes you marvel at the strength of the smallest accidents to forge a life of sweetness, ferocity, and surprise. For the first songs are the gentlest and the most beautiful, they last forever, and they are the test of faith.

I was graduated from the finest school, which is that of the love between parent and child. Though the world is constructed to serve glory, success, and strength, one loves one's parents and one's children despite their failings and weaknesses—sometimes even more on account of them. In this school you learn the measure not of power, but of love; not of victory, but of grace; not of triumph, but of forgiveness. You learn as well, and sometimes, as I did, you learn early, that love can overcome death, and that what is required of you in this is memory and devotion. Memory and devotion. To keep your love alive you must be willing to be obstinate, and irrational, and true, to fashion your entire life as a construct, a metaphor, a fiction, a device for the exercise of faith. Without this, you will live like a beast and have nothing but an aching heart. With it, your heart, though broken, will be full, and you will stay in the fight unto the very last.

Though my life might have been more interesting and eventful, and I might have been a better man, after all these years I think I can say that I have kept faith.

All this time, my heart has told me nothing but to love and protect. The message has been strong through the twists and turns, and it has never varied. To protect, and to protect, and to protect. I was born to protect the ones I love. And may God continue to give me ways to protect and serve them, even though they are gone.